A MURDERED Peace

A Kate Clifford Mystery

CANDACE ROBB

PEGASUS CRIME

NEW YORK LONDON

A MURDERED PEACE

Pegasus Books Ltd.
148 W. 37th Street, 13th Floor
New York, NY 10018

Copyright © 2018 by Candace Robb

First Pegasus Books edition December 2018

Interior design by Maria Fernandez

Library of Congress Cataloging-in-Publication Data is available.

ISBN: 978-1-68177-862-4

10 9 8 7 6 5 4 3 2 1

Printed in the United States of America
Distributed by W. W. Norton & Company

for the flock of my heart, you wise & courageous women

GLOSSARY

BARS OF YORK: The four main gatehouses in the walls of York (Bootham, Monk, Micklegate, and Walmgate).

BEGUINES: A community of women leading lives of religious devotion who, unlike those who entered convents, were not bound by permanent vows; they dedicated themselves to chastity and charity and worked largely among the poor and the sick, usually in urban settings.

CANDLEMAS: February 2, the feast of the Purification.

DYMYSENT: A woman's girdle with ornamental work on the front half, often in gold or silver, and a silk back.

MARTINMAS: November 11, the feast of St. Martin.

MICHAELMAS: September 29, the feast of St. Michael.

STAITHE: A landing-stage, or wharf.

Kate Clifford's
York

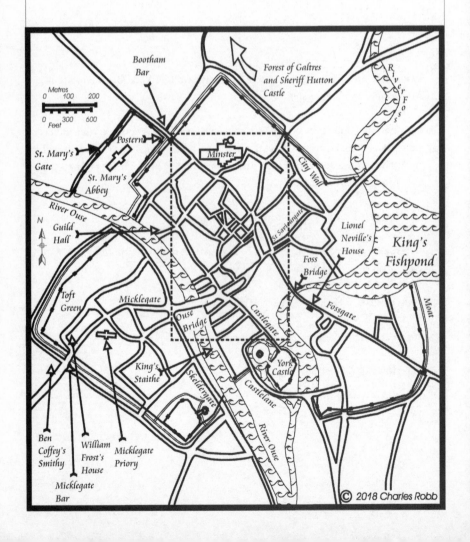

Bootham Bar

Forest of Galtres and Sheriff Hutton Castle

River Foss

Metres
0 100 200

0 300 600
Feet

Postern

St. Mary's Gate

St. Mary's Abbey

Minster

City Wall

River Ouse

N

Guild Hall

St Saviourgate

Lionel Neville's House

King's Fishpond

Foss Bridge

Toft Green

Micklegate

Ouse Bridge

Castlegate

Fossgate

Moat

King's Staithe

Skeldergate

York Castle

Castlelane

Ben Coffey's Smithy

William Frost's House

Micklegate Priory

River Ouse

Micklegate Bar

© 2018 Charles Robb

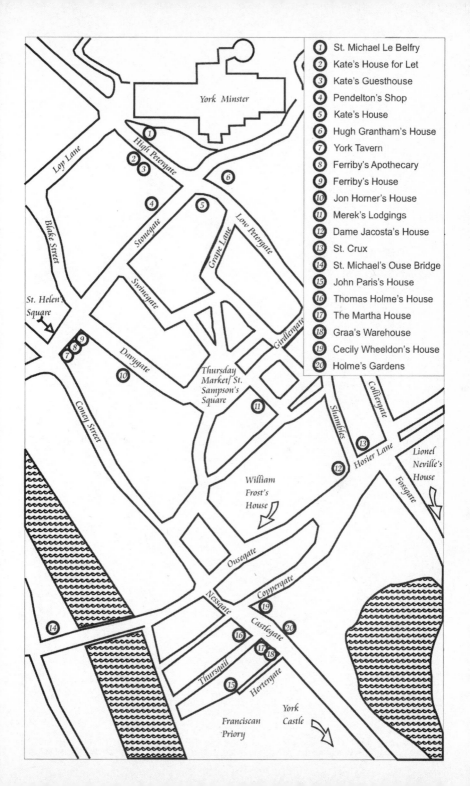

1. St. Michael Le Belfry
2. Kate's House for Let
3. Kate's Guesthouse
4. Pendelton's Shop
5. Kate's House
6. Hugh Grantham's House
7. York Tavern
8. Ferriby's Apothecary
9. Ferriby's House
10. Jon Horner's House
11. Merek's Lodgings
12. Dame Jacosta's House
13. St. Crux
14. St. Michael's Ouse Bridge
15. John Paris's House
16. Thomas Holme's House
17. The Martha House
18. Graa's Warehouse
19. Cecily Wheeldon's House
20. Holme's Gardens

York Minster

Loy Lane

High Petergate

Blake Street

Stonegate

Grape Lane

Low Petergate

Swinegate

Girdlergate

St. Helen's Square

Davygate

Coney Street

Thursday Market/ St. Sampson's Square

Shambles

Colliergate

St. Crux

Hosier Lane

Lionel Neville's House

Fossgate

William Frost's House

Ousegate

Coppergate

Nessgate

Castlegate

Thursgail

Thomas Holme's House

Hertergate

Franciscan Priory

York Castle

1

A PLEA AT TWILIGHT

York, late January 1400

It was deep winter in York, the ground frozen, the short days dimmed with the smoke from countless fires, the sun, when it shone, low in the sky. If it reached beneath the jettied second stories to the streets and alleys below, it created but a momentary brightening that made the ensuing shade seem all the darker. King Henry sat uneasy on the throne he had pulled out from under his cousin Richard. Emboldened in summer when a mighty army gathered round him as he rode west across the land to confront his cousin, Henry had wrested the crown from Richard. But not all the powerful nobles were comfortable with Henry's unseating a divinely anointed king and locking him away in Pontefract Castle, where he denied Richard the comforts traditionally offered royal captives, even those from foreign realms. It was said that the earls of Kent, Huntington, and Salisbury had plotted to right this wrong by ridding the realm of Henry and his sons, mere boys, and returning Richard to the throne. Forewarned, Henry and his family had escaped the danger. But now the usurper knew he could never rest easy until the former king was dead. And so, it was rumored, he had sent one of his most trusted retainers to Pontefract to see that the royal cousin would never inspire such an act of rebellion again.

In York, the soldiers who had crowded the walled city in summer were long gone, and the merchants prayed that King Henry would remember the financial aid they had rendered him in July. And just in case, they heeded the king's recommendation and elected William Frost mayor for the next year. They looked forward with happy anticipation to the day after Candlemas, when Frost would hold a great feast for the aldermen and freemen of York, an obligation every mayor-elect must fulfill in order to be officially recognized as mayor. They counted on William's wife, Isabella, to plan a feast even grander than those of her late father, John Gisburne, a legendary mayor of York.

At the moment, Kate Clifford was indifferent to her cousin William's new status. She had more important things on her mind. She had moved her household to the house on Low Petergate that her uncle had deeded her before leaving York, a change intended to improve life for her wards as well as herself. When she had considered swapping houses, she had thought of the financial benefit—the house on Castlegate, her former residence, was part of her widow's dower, so the money she would receive by renting it would benefit her little family. Her mother, who had arrived in York the previous spring to form a household of beguines, was quite able to pay the substantial rent. So it seemed a happy solution. Kate would have the added pleasure of being close to her ward Phillip as he began his apprenticeship in the nearby minster stoneyard, as well as the ease of being closer to her other two properties on Petergate, the guesthouse and the house next to it. But she was soon disabused of her rosy expectations. The children missed the gardens that ran down to the river. The city noises frightened Petra, giving her nightmares. Phillip still only joined them for dinner on Sundays, and Kate was so busy she found little time to run the dogs in the fields outside the gates—it had been so much easier to take a short time in the morning to cross the street to the gardens. The list went on and on, each individual item minor in itself but adding up to discontent where she had anticipated delight.

It did not help that rumors abounded of violence following the failed rebels as they scattered across the realm. Mobs set upon them, bludgeoning them to death. Indeed, it was said that King Henry had commanded the city's aldermen to elect her cousin William Frost as mayor because he expected him to take a firm hand in keeping the peace in York.

The King's Peace. What precisely did that mean? What was peace to Henry, who had usurped the throne of his divinely anointed cousin and now held him a prisoner in Pontefract Castle—and anxiously awaited news of Richard's death?

As Kate stepped out of the lamplit hall of her guesthouse into the colorless gray of twilight, the pair of wolfhounds flanking her growled a warning. She placed her hand on the small axe hidden in her skirts as she stepped to one side, allowing the light from the hall to illuminate the alleyway. A cloaked figure huddled beneath the eaves opposite.

"Who are you?"

"It is Carl, Mistress Clifford." The man stepped toward her, dropping his hood to his shoulders so that she could see the paleness of his bald pate. "Manservant to Lady Kirkby."

She remembered him. He had accompanied Lady Margery Kirkby the previous winter for a fortnight's stay in the guesthouse.

"You are in trouble?" she asked.

Carl eyed the hounds, clearly anxious not to alarm them. Kate signaled Lille and Ghent to stand down.

"It is my lady who is in mortal danger, Mistress Clifford. She needs a place for the night. Can you help?"

Mortal danger. *Deus juva me.* Is she with you?"

"Just outside the gates. I am to fetch her if you agree."

"Have her come here, to the guesthouse." Not her home. Kate would not bring danger to her wards. "Be quick about it, the gate will close at nightfall." No time to ask what trouble Margery was in. "Will she be recognized?"

"Pray God she will not. My lady has blackened her hair and taken on the guise of a lad."

For Margery to go to such lengths she must indeed be in fear for her life. Her husband's failed peace mission?

"Go. Fetch her here!"

Back in the hall, Griselde, who ran the guesthouse for Kate, was already ordering young Seth to put a fresh lamp in the second bedchamber.

Kate countermanded the order. "Prepare beds for Lady Margery and her manservant in the kitchen. You must not call attention to her by treating her as a guest."

"Is she to stay beyond tonight?" Griselde's broad brow creased with worry. "I have much yet to do for the celebration tomorrow evening."

3

"Until I speak with Lady Margery I cannot say how long she might be here. I am sorry to burden you with this, Griselde, I know you've much to do to prepare for Sir Elric and his men, and we must proceed as planned."

"I suppose we must confine the two of them to the kitchen."

"Yes. Both Lady Margery and Carl must be treated as servants. You are not to wait on her. She must see to herself, and assist you where she is able. A woman of her rank might have never seen to kitchen chores, but she can be taught simple tasks, eh?"

The thought brought a momentary smile, but worry won out. "And if she is seen?"

"I trust you and Seth to keep her hidden."

The nature of the establishment required that their guests be confident their patronage was kept secret. When not occupied by guests of the dean and chapter of York Minster, or noble visitors such as Lady Kirkby, the two bed-chambers above the hall were rented to the wealthy of the city for entertaining their mistresses or lovers in discreet luxury. Griselde had perfected the art of discretion, which included preventing guests from encountering one another.

At the moment, the elderly woman was shaking her head, but she did not waste her breath arguing. She called to Seth to assist her in preparing the pallets in the kitchen.

While they saw to that, Kate woke Griselde's husband, Clement, who had fallen asleep by the fire, and explained what was happening.

"You are a staunch ally to all in need," he said as Kate helped him rise and limp to the couple's bedchamber off the hall.

Kate had just turned away when the hounds alerted her to someone at the door. Outside, a lad stood hugging himself against the cold. Inviting him inside, Kate pointed to the fire.

"God in heaven, how do the poor bear it?" Lady Margery groaned, holding her delicate hands close to the heat.

Griselde bustled in with a blanket and a bowl of hot spiced wine. "My lady," she whispered.

"Griselde!" Kate said sharply. "Call her anything but that."

The woman crossed herself.

"I shall be Mary," their guest announced. "It is close enough to my name that I will answer to it. Call me Mary." It was only after she had draped herself in the blanket and taken several sips of the warm drink that she looked round in confusion. "Where is Carl?"

"Coming with your things?" said Kate.

"He should have preceded me. I sent him ahead to let you know I was on my way."

"Yes, we spoke. That is how I knew to expect you."

"No, the second time. A lad dressed as I am does not travel with a serving man. I sent him ahead with my pack."

"You saw him enter the city gate ahead of you?"

"I did. He should be here." Margery's voice broke.

Already the troubles multiplied. "I will leave you in Griselde's competent hands," said Kate. "You are safe here. Now I must see to finding Carl." She glanced at Seth as he set a bowl of stew on the table beside Lady Margery. "If someone comes to the door, you answer, Seth. Only you. Armed. If it is anyone but Carl, send them away. I will return in the morning."

He nodded.

Calling to the hounds, Kate hurried out.

2

EVERYTHING IS WRONG

At the top of the outer stairway Kate gazed up at the patch of sky between the houses where the stars still glimmered in the wakening dawn, obscured now and then by the smoke from her neighbors' morning fires and that from her own chimney. She'd paused to say a prayer for Carl's safe delivery. Last night she and the hounds had searched, but found no sign of him. Worry weighed her down.

Lady Margery had last come to York to raise money for her husband's efforts to bring the royal cousins Richard and Henry together so that they might discuss their differences and come to a peaceful resolution. At that time Margery's husband, Sir Thomas Kirkby, was in France trying to meet with Henry of Lancaster, now King Henry. Kate had thought it a fool's errand, however noble in spirit, and time had proved her right. A king come to rule in such a way would never be at peace. She guessed Sir Thomas had become a casualty of Henry's ambition. If this was so, danger must surely ride the wind at Margery's back. Pray God Carl was not the first casualty.

She had expected to feel a happy satisfaction this morning, for this was the day she would pay off the last of her late husband's accounts and be free of that burden. It felt as if she'd spent every waking hour since Simon's death almost four years earlier raising the money to pay off the enormous debt he'd managed to hide from his guild and his partners—and her. She'd hoped the sense of victory would buoy her spirits through tonight's celebration at the guesthouse, which would mark the departure of Kevin, the Earl of Westmoreland's retainer who had been convalescing in her home. He had become dear to all the household, his loss all the more difficult on the heels of another deeply felt absence among them. And now Lady Margery and her missing servant added to Kate's worries.

She and the hounds were not the only ones who had searched for Carl in the night. Her servant Jennet had rallied the street children she called her eyes and ears, but she'd had no news for Kate when she woke her.

Damn the royal cousins. Kate laid all blame at their feet.

Wrinkling her nose at all the smoke, she tucked one end of her mantle over her shoulder and descended the frost-slicked stairs with care, then hurried along beneath the eaves of the house to the kitchen behind it, the refrozen snow crunching underfoot. As she pushed open the door she reveled in the warmth . . . until Petra, her seven-year-old niece, yanked a bowl out of the hand of Kate's ward Marie and dashed the contents into the hearth fire as she shouted, "You slurp so loudly you make me sick to my stomach."

Older than her attacker by a few years, but smaller, more delicate, Marie shrank back, white-faced, tears brimming. "Why are you so mean to me?"

This was not the Petra that Kate and all the household had come to love; yet, of late, this darker aspect of the child surfaced more and more often. Marie and her brother Phillip had taken to avoiding the girl as much as possible. It was particularly difficult for Marie, who had grown so fond of Petra that the two girls did everything together. No longer.

Petra turned to rush from the room.

"Not so fast." Kate caught her up, pinning her arms and ignoring her kicks while quietly commanding Marie to leave, and to close the kitchen door behind her. "Wait for me in the hall."

The girl obeyed without argument.

"I hate you," Petra hissed as Kate maneuvered the child onto a chair and called to her wolfhounds Lille and Ghent. Already sitting up, alert, watchful, they trotted over and settled to either side of the struggling child.

"I do not believe that," Kate said.

"I will hurt them," Petra warned.

Resisting the urge to smile at the child's threat that she might injure the giants who each weighed more than she would until fully grown, if ever, Kate motioned to Ghent to lay his head in the child's lap. The struggling stopped. A sniff. Kate smoothed the child's hair, so wild, just like her own. They were much alike, often taken for mother and daughter.

"What troubles you, my love?" Kate asked as she knelt between the two great hounds.

Petra sat on her hands and stared down at Ghent.

"Is it the dreams?" Kate asked.

Silence.

"Did you dream of Berend again?" A few days before Christmas the child had dreamed that Kate's cook Berend had gone away, having said he was duty-bound to answer a summons, but refusing to tell them more, or whether he would return. Petra had been inconsolable, even after Marie had flopped down on the bed with the announcement that Berend was in the kitchen, going about his usual preparations for the day's meals. When Kate had told him of Petra's dream Berend had assured her that he was going nowhere. But he had not met her eyes. Less than a week later he was gone. Damn him. He knew how much her wards loved him. "Is it Berend?" she asked again. "Or is it the other nightmares?" A leper king haunted the child's dreams, his skin torn and hanging from his body, his hair a mass of squirming lice.

"I want to go back to Castlegate. I want to live with the sisters."

Her mother's poor sisters, or beguines, now living in Kate's former home. One of them, Sister Brigida, tutored the girls in French, and had become their confidante.

"Is that truly what you want, Petra?"

A tear rolled down the girl's cheek. "I want things to be how they were."

"Oh, my love." Kate leaned close to kiss her niece on the forehead and gently wiped the tear from her cheek. "I miss him too."

"Everything is wrong."

"Sometimes it feels that way."

"And now Kevin is leaving."

"I know," Kate whispered. "But I am here."

More tears. Suddenly Petra freed her hands, wrapping her arms round Kate's neck and sobbing. Ghent sighed and moved aside so that Petra could slip onto Kate's lap. For a long while they sat there, until Petra's grief was exhausted. By the time the child quieted and rose to go out to apologize to Marie, Kate's legs had gone numb on the cold stones of the kitchen floor, and her heart was heavy. *Everything is wrong.* Life *was* change, and it was not always comfortable. Her niece had perhaps believed that in Kate's welcoming household that would not be so.

Kate called out to Petra as she reached the door, "Kevin will be just round the corner in Stonegate with his comrades, watching over us. You will see him often, I'm sure of it."

A fleeting smile, a shrug, and the girl was gone.

Kate pulled herself up from the floor, shook out her legs, and took a few turns round the room to warm herself. Her hand brushed against the bowl Berend used every night for the next morning's bread, letting it rise in the warmth of the kitchen. She wanted to come out here in the evening to talk over the events of the day with Berend as he kneaded the bread, his sleeves rolled up, arms white with flour, his calm radiating through the room, more comforting to her than the warmth of the hearth fire. And, in the morning, as she and the children stumbled into the kitchen, she wanted him there, always up before them, tending the fire, humming as he stepped out to check the bread. Bald, one-eared Berend with his three-fingered hand and eyes that pierced to her soul, muscles straining the sleeves of his linen shirts—old shirts worn soft with many washings. He was her anchor, her confidant, her best friend, a man she trusted with her life, and those of Petra, Marie, and Phillip.

Honor-bound. He was honor-bound to stay. He had promised to be here for her always. He had promised. And now he was gone. Damn him.

⚬❦⚬

At the guesthouse, Griselde shook her head when Kate asked whether Carl had appeared. She had known it unlikely. If he was in the city, and in distress, or lost, Jennet would have heard. But she had held out a slim hope that he might have been trapped outside the gates, and would have appeared first thing.

"I must be off to the market. A few last things for the celebration this evening," Griselde said. "And Lady Margery is yet abed. I do not like to leave her." Kate promised she would return as soon as she had completed some business in Stonegate. Roland Pendleton, the silversmith, expected her.

"Ah, the last payment on the debt." Griselde patted Kate's hand. "That will take your mind off your troublesome guest for a while. Go now. I can wait."

Pendleton opened the door himself, greeting Kate with a smile. "Today is the day!" The silversmith had been most patient since Simon's death, assuring her month after month that he knew he would eventually see his money. Escorting her into the office behind the shop, he called to his servant for a flagon of fine claret he had set out the night before, and two cups.

"I know it is early, but this calls for a toast," he declared, motioning Kate to a seat by the table on which were strewn tally sticks and pieces of jewelry, some whole, some broken. He reached up and pulled down an old ledger in which to record her payment—Simon's debt had been first recorded years earlier.

Kate's eyes were drawn to a shiny object that had been tucked behind the old account book. It was a woman's girdle, the type called a dymysent, the front of the belt an elaborate ornamental silver clasp with silver wings radiating out from it, the back a simple gray silk. An exquisite piece, and one she recognized with puzzlement. It belonged to Lady Margery, a piece she recalled her wearing on several occasions the previous winter. Was it possible that Margery had taken it to the silversmith for repair on that earlier visit, then forgotten it? She had traveled with trunk loads of elegant clothing, so one item, no matter how valuable, might easily be missed. It would explain how it came to be shuffled to the back of the shelf, though she was surprised that Pendleton would be so careless with an object of such obvious value. Or had someone sold it to him? Recently, perhaps? Carl?

She was debating whether or not to comment on the fine workmanship when the servant returned with the wine. By the time she and Pendleton had toasted the settlement of the debt, Kate had decided that until she knew Lady Margery's reason for arriving on her doorstep in disguise it was best not to call attention to anything regarding her. As soon as the silversmith finished his cup of wine, Kate took her leave, anxious to ask her friend about the girdle.

—◦⊚◦—

By the time Kate returned to the guesthouse, Lady Margery had risen and now sat at the worktable in the kitchen staring at the opposite wall, ignoring the bread, cheese, and ale set before her. Her pale, freckled skin, so lovely with her natural red hair, looked ashen against the harsh black dye, and her pretty eyes were sunken in shadows.

"Margery?" Kate slipped onto the bench beside her and took one of her hands, noticing not only how cold it was, despite the warmth of the kitchen, but also how rough. The journey had certainly taken its toll.

But her eyes burned with anger as she turned to Kate.

"What is it?" Kate asked. "Has someone in the household upset you?"

The lady blinked and her gaze softened. "Katherine! No, everyone has been so kind. Bless them. Bless you. Have you news of Carl? I fear for him. We were followed, I am sure of it. But I thought, once I bought the clothes from the lad . . ." She stopped, staring down at the food.

"Who followed you?"

Margery shook her head.

"I must know how to protect you," said Kate, "and from whom. Why are you being followed? Where is Sir Thomas? Why are you not with him?"

"Thomas?" Margery crossed herself. "He has passed through fire into eternal grace."

"Dead?" Kate pressed her friend's hand. "Margery, what happened to him?"

"What happened to my beloved . . ." Margery shook her head. "One would not think such a thing could happen in a Christian realm. Thomas was a good man, the best of men. He was slain by a mob at Cirencester. They butchered him at Henry of Lancaster's pleasure." She spoke with a cold precision Kate had never heard from Margery.

Pleasure? Surely not, Geoff whispered in her mind. Her twin, dead now seven years, lived on in Kate, protecting her. Womb companions, nothing, not even death, could separate them.

"I will not rest until I have restored my husband's good name," said Margery. "Henry Bolingbroke will not ruin the Kirkby family." She withdrew her hands from Kate's grasp.

Henry of Lancaster is no king to her, Geoff whispered.

"Forgive me, but I must know what happened," said Kate, softly. "Tell me." Now Margery lifted the bowl of ale and drank a little. "It is an ugly tale," she said.

"I must hear it," said Kate.

"Of course." Margery crossed herself and bowed her head in silent prayer. Then, in a voice devoid of all emotion, she began, chronicling Thomas's return from France, where he had attempted to convince Henry of Lancaster to invite his cousin Richard, then King of England, to a meeting at which they might discuss their differences. If not a meeting of the two cousins, then their representatives. He had been granted a hearing, but the day before it was to take place Thomas learned that Henry had sailed for England. Her husband returned to England defeated, obsessively recounting to Margery each failed attempt to reason with Henry, agonizing over what he might have done instead. He could turn his mind to nothing else. It was madness. And then a guest mentioned that Henry had fallen ill during Christmas festivities at Windsor, and Thomas saw an opportunity. "I might go to him, offer him the leech my excellent physician recommends. Then, when he is on the mend, I might broach the subject of his cousin, how he deserved better treatment, some of his family with him, visits from friends."

He presumed much, Geoff noted.

From the first Margery feared the plan, but Thomas would not be dissuaded. First, he went to Pontefract, gathering information about Richard's circumstances, whether the rumors were correct that he was cut off from all friendly companionship, solitary, in a steward's chamber, hardly appropriate for a former king, with poor rations and no physician to see to his health. Richard saw only his prison guards, men of noble family who had every cause to hate him.

"Thomas was incensed. Richard might have lacked much as king, but he had been anointed with holy oil. He was the son of a prince and the grandson of a king and this was no way to treat him," said Margery. "The letter I received at this point chilled my heart. Thomas spoke out to Richard's jailers, chiding them on their treatment of an anointed king, and asked to visit him and reassure him, permit his leech to examine him and ensure that he was receiving at least his basic needs."

Kate could see why the king might think him Richard's man.

"He himself planted the seed of King Henry's distrust," said Margery, still in the flat tone. "I already feared for him, but this—for a grown man to act out of such innocence. It is not credited. Of course his behavior would be suspect. He would be seen as cunning, manipulating his adversaries. And what could I do? Even had I been able to reach him before he approached the king, he would not have heeded my warning. He did not believe that we are born already marked by sin, you see. He was certain that to be made in God's image meant that we are all good, that we err because of circumstances, but that such error is not inevitable. He believed that King Henry, to have gained the throne, must live in God's grace."

So would say many churchmen. Kate's own uncle took part in Henry's crowning. But she wondered at the naïveté of Thomas Kirkby. To succeed he would have needed to match cunning with cunning. How had Margery not seen that? It was not like her to be so blind to others' follies.

Her love was so strong she did what he asked, simply for love of him? Geoff proposed.

Kate had not thought Margery a woman to act simply on ideals. Was such a love possible? If so, how immense her loss.

She poured more ale and offered the bowl to Margery, who took it with thanks, but let it rest in her hands.

"Thomas reached Windsor before the king had word of his visit to Pontefract. He was warmly received, and the following day his leech received permission to examine Henry. While the leech was consulting with the king's physician, Thomas enjoyed the pleasures of the season with the king's family and friends."

The leech diagnosed the king with humors too heated and dry, a common result of the spicy foods and abundant wine served during Christmas festivities. With the blessing of the king's physician, the leech prepared a tonic for Henry that would ease the cramping and cool his system. Though still the king did not sleep well, the physician assured Thomas that was a chronic problem having nothing to do with the stomach ailment.

But Lord Kirkby had by then realized the state of King Henry's mind, how he saw enmity in the mildest disagreement, a threat to his hold on the crown in every raised brow. As soon as Thomas understood that his leech's remedy could do little more than calm the king's indigestion, he took his leave, fearing that his attempts at reconciliation would be seen as threats.

Too late, Geoff whispered.

Sometime after Thomas departed, one of the royal retainers arrived at the castle to warn the king of the plot against him and his sons. He implied that Thomas's visit to Pontefract was a key part of the plan.

"If I ever learn who condemned my husband, accusing him of an act so vile—Another man, a better man than Henry, would have dismissed the accusation. But he is so poisoned by his own ambition he cannot trust that anyone would approach him without guile. He sees not the good in men. He has poisoned the land." Her lips pressed together, Margery mirrored the outrage she expressed, her color high, her eyes snapping.

"Perhaps you should rest," said Kate. "I will return later."

"No. I will finish." Margery folded and refolded her hands in her lap, as if the activity calmed her. "When the king heard of Thomas's visit to Pontefract and his accusations about Richard's mistreatment, he flew into a rage and called Thomas a traitor, declared that he had meant to poison him." A little sob. "Thomas, Thomas," she whispered, "too late you saw your folly."

Folly indeed.

Hush, Geoff. "He arrived home safely?" Kate asked.

"He came to me in Cirencester, where I had gone to be with my sister, who has not been well. Dear God, I fear for them, Katherine, all my kin. This king—he will murder us all before he is finished." Margery's voice shook.

"Cirencester," Kate whispered. "Kent and Salisbury fled to Cirencester." And they had been beaten to death by a mob. Thomas Kirkby as well?

God help you, Kate, you are harboring a traitor, Geoff hissed in her head.

The shadows beneath Margery's eyes seemed to deepen. "Yes, they did. But Thomas was not in their company. You must believe that."

What did it matter what Kate thought if the king believed otherwise? But Margery searched Kate's face for reassurance. "Believe your husband part of the uprising against the king? No, I cannot believe it of Thomas," said Kate. "But you have said yourself that King Henry turned on Thomas. You say you were followed to York. If his men find you, how will you prove his innocence? *Your* innocence?"

"I should not need to!"

Kate took a deep breath. "So Thomas came to Cirencester and they came soon after?"

"A few days later."

Geoff groaned.

"Do you know anything about how Kent and Salisbury came to be in Cirencester? Did they have kin in the town? One of the priests? An abbot who might give them sanctuary?"

Margery took a sip of the ale, then set the bowl down and composed herself. "Clearly they were fleeing west," she said. "Perhaps to Wales? Followed the Thames to the River Churn and turned north?" She frowned down at the bowl of ale. "The abbot did ride forth attempting to quiet the crowd during the attack. My sister told me that afterward. She said that Abbot John wept for the souls not only of the victims, but of the townspeople. To butcher Christians, their countrymen, men of noble blood."

"How did you learn this?"

"I did not leave at once. My sister risked hiding me that night. She told me then."

Risked indeed. "So Thomas was caught up in the attack?"

"Yes!" More a cry of pain than a word, and Margery bowed her head with a sob.

Kate rose and went round behind Margery, rubbing her back as she did the girls when they were frightened. When Margery seemed calmed, Kate asked, "How did he come to be out in the crowd?"

"He was leaving us, seeking safety. He would not tell us where, only that it was best that he withdraw from the world for a while. An abbey somewhere. I am not sure. Time and again God has abandoned him. That he should be riding through the square just as a harrier saw John Montagu, Earl of Salisbury, ride forth from the inn yard and shouted that it was his man who had set the fire. The groom from my sister's household—he and I had run after Thomas to give him a cordial that my sister had prepared for him. Was it me calling out to him? Is that how he was noticed? Oh God." Margery sobbed, burying her face in her hands.

"You are not to blame," Kate said. "Rest now, my friend."

Margery jerked up. "No. No, the time to mourn will come. He was betrayed, Katherine. By the boy, I believe—" Looking down, Margery seemed to notice her fisted hands and spread her fingers, flexed, stretched. "He told someone that Thomas would be riding through the town and was part of Salisbury's company. I am almost certain. Though my calling out his name might have drawn them down on us, I believe Thomas was already expected. And then the little brute stole his head as a trophy! Ran away with it."

"His head?" Kate whispered.

"I ran him to ground and wrested it from his bloody hands. He lunged for it. Knocked me down in the hay on the barn floor. He was kicking me. I don't know how I summoned the strength, but I hit him so hard I knocked out a tooth. I saw the blood flowing. He stopped, holding a hand to his bloody mouth, just long enough so that I might crawl out from under him. But then he came after me. I took out my dagger, and I stabbed him. Killed him."

"Merciful Mother," Kate whispered.

"My sister promised to do what she could to retrieve Thomas's body and bury it with his head. Then we ran."

"You and Carl."

A nod.

"To York."

A hesitation, then Margery looked away as she said, "I did not know where else to go."

Cirencester to York in midwinter. A difficult, dangerous journey. And though she counted her a friend, Kate knew Margery had far older friends, ones with large homes in which she might have been hidden in comfort.

You doubt her, Geoff whispered.

I don't want to. But something is missing. I don't like it.

What will you do?

What can I do? She is here now, and I have promised to protect her.

"Did you entrust Carl with anything valuable?" Kate asked.

"Valuable?" Margery frowned. "Some clothing, a comb for my hair, little else. Why?"

Kate described the girdle she had seen at the silversmith's. "Considering his disappearance, I wondered whether he thought to sell it so that he might pay for passage somewhere?"

"No. He is loyal. But that girdle—" Margery gave a little laugh and picked at the food before her. "I wondered what had become of it. I'd forgotten that

I'd left it with a silversmith in Stonegate. Last winter. The buckle had come loose."

"Shall I ask whether it is repaired?" Kate asked.

"No!" Margery cried with alarm, then seemed to remember herself. "Of course not," she said in a quiet voice. "No one must know I am here. I am surprised you would ask, Katherine."

Kate merely nodded, more than a little dissatisfied with Margery's tale. But she had what she needed to gauge the danger. "And now, Mary—I must become accustomed to calling you that—you must eat something so that you might assist Griselde with the preparations for this evening's guests. You are a servant here." She smiled to soften her words, but she held Margery's gaze as she warned her that she must listen to Griselde and Seth, do everything they told her to do. "They can protect you only so far. Much is up to you."

Meanwhile, Kate must find Carl.

3

A CELEBRATION

The storm had come on suddenly just before sunset. Outside the guesthouse hall snow swirled in a dizzying dance. The wind was picking up. Water pooled beneath the fur-lined cloak Kate had hung on a peg beside the open door, and she stood near the fire circle drying the hem of her skirt. Would Sir Elric brave the storm for this supper? She had no doubt that his men would come, they were eager to celebrate their fellow's return to duty, and they need just step round the corner to the guesthouse. But their captain would be coming from Sheriff Hutton Castle, which meant riding through the Forest of Galtres in such a wind, and after sunset. An imprudent journey in such weather, and Sir Elric was a man whose every move, every word was measured. The celebration of Kevin's recovery, however welcome, was hardly enough to bring his captain out on such a night. Still, if Elric had set out early, he might have reached the city before the storm. Kate hoped so, for Kevin's sake. And for hers.

That she was concerned for Sir Elric's welfare and looked forward to his presence spoke to the degree to which their partnership was evolving into mutual respect, perhaps even friendship. During Kevin's sojourn in Kate's home his accounts of his life in the Earl of Westmoreland's household had provided much insight into both the earl's and his captain's character. She had learned that the earl, a Neville, cousin to her late husband, was as much an opportunist as she had guessed, but that the knight was a man of conscience and strong loyalties. She liked that in a man. Whether or not she agreed with his policies, she could at least eventually know Elric, predict how he might react to a given circumstance. But she was wary—Kevin worshipped the ground on which Sir Elric walked, which surely colored his impressions.

Still, she could not deny that Elric had kept his end of the bargain she had made with him, keeping a protective eye on her mother and the sisters in her Martha House, and ensuring that her brother-in-law Lionel kept his distance. It had been some time since Lionel Neville attempted to interfere in Kate's concerns. In return, Kate had fulfilled her promise to keep Ralph Neville, Earl of Westmoreland, informed of the temper in York regarding Richard's abdication and the ascension to the throne of Henry of Lancaster, and had returned certain incriminating letters—though not before having a friar copy them, including their seals, in case she needed to defend herself against the powerful earl, now beloved of the new king.

It helped matters that Sir Elric was the very embodiment of knighthood in his physique, his skill at arms, and his courtly manner, as well as being one of the most handsome men she had ever set eyes on. Too bad his arrogant self-regard spoiled it.

But not always . . . When they laughed together she saw a vulnerable, quite likable side to him.

Is that why Berend had left without a word? She'd had good reason not to tell him of her agreement with Sir Elric at first. Helping Kate chase down an assassin the previous summer had brought to the surface memories of darker days, a past for which Berend had done much penance and from which he had hoped he might redeem his soul. When Kate had sought his advice about how such assassins operated she had unwittingly plunged Berend into a darkness, seemingly overwhelmed by his memories of hunting down the enemies of the powerful. By the time Kate realized that it might be a long while before he walked clear of his shadows, she had not known how to tell him about her bargain with Elric. So it was that Berend asked how she could be laughing with the man she swore she could never trust, never befriend.

A forceful knock startled Kate from her thoughts. As her manservant Seth moved past her to admit the guests he whispered that the new servant was spending the evening beneath Griselde and Clement's bed, just in case one of the men chanced to step out to the kitchen. Carl had still not appeared.

"Pray God he does not arrive in the midst of this celebration," Kate whispered.

"If he does, I will loudly berate him for coming too late to help with the evening's event," said Seth.

"Good man."

He grinned and opened the door.

"What a night!" Sir Elric exclaimed as he shook his head and stomped the snow off his boots before stepping up to the threshold. He filled the doorway, face ruddy with cold, eyes bright in the lamplight. His fur-lined cloak was thrown back over one shoulder to allow access to his sword, a leather-gloved hand resting on the carved hilt, his hair, shoulders, and boots dusted with snow.

Armed? Well, of course he was, riding through the Forest of Galtres, and in such an unsettled time.

"It was good of you to come in such a storm," she said. "I would have understood if you chose not to make the journey."

"How could I miss such a celebration?" He stepped aside, gesturing to the five men crowding in behind him and lining up just within the doorway—Kevin, Douglas, Stephen, Wulf, and Elric's squire Harry.

Kate welcomed them and motioned for Seth to assist them with their boots. Douglas waved him away with a laugh. "Many thanks, but we're accustomed to seeing to ourselves."

Elric, however, settled on a bench just inside the door and wagged a booted foot. "Harry." The young man bobbed his head to Kate, then dropped to his knees to unlace his captain's high leather boots. The leg released from the high boots was clad in dark green wool leggings. A fine, strong leg. Kate was glad Elric was too busy to notice her watching him.

Griselde bustled in with a tray laden with hot dishes, which she placed on a brazier set up near the fire to keep the food warm, as she would soon be leaving to see to the supper of Kate's wards. With Berend away and the children now so near, she enjoyed fussing over them with special meals. Indeed, earlier in the day she had chosen treats for the children at the market, an attempt to soften the blow of Kevin's departure. She nodded to everyone and headed back to the kitchen for more items.

"Dame Griselde could use your help," Kate said to Seth.

He nodded and hurried off to the kitchen.

Leaving his men struggling with their own high boots, Elric crossed the chamber and placed his near the fire circle to dry, then peeked at the food. Griselde had prepared for them a variety of dishes—sliced venison in a spicy sauce and eel in cream, two pies stuffed with cheese, nuts, and onions, a salty bread, roasted nuts, and figs.

"You think of everything," said Elric.

"I run a guesthouse." She smiled. "Had I known the weather would turn I would have suggested another date."

"I've ridden through much worse. As have you, I imagine, growing up on the northern border."

"I have, but only when it could not be avoided. Father did not like us risking the horses." She noticed that Elric's men now stood near the doorway in their stockinged feet. "Come, put your boots by the fire and then take a seat. If two of you might put the pies and bread on the table, then Seth will serve the hot dishes."

Elric surprised her by choosing the chair that would put his back to the door. A gesture of trust? As the food was set on the table he rubbed his hands together. "A feast for the eyes. Berend's work?"

"Not tonight, not here." Kate brought several flagons of wine to the table as the men settled. "This is Griselde's domain, and she is quite a good cook."

"I've not seen Berend since my return," said Elric. He had ridden with the earl in the army led by Henry of Lancaster in summer, then accompanied his lord to Westminster for the deliberations about the fate of the deposed king and the crowning. He had not returned to Sheriff Hutton until after Christmas. "Is your cook away?"

"On a brief mission for me." Kate prayed that she was safe in trusting Kevin not to tell his captain that Berend's departure was unplanned, that she did not know where he was. "Wine?"

"Of course. We must toast Kevin's recovery."

As her guest helped himself to a slice of the pie and several pieces of venison, Kate took a few sips of wine to calm herself. She had managed her explanations smoothly, she thought. And the delight on Elric's face as he tasted the pie bode well. She filled her own plate and took a bite of the venison; Berend's tutelage had vastly improved Griselde's skill, particularly in blending spices. And now Kevin and his fellows fell to. For a while the party spoke mostly about the food, the men declaring it better even than the hearty fare at the York Tavern.

"Why is such a splendid cook wasting her talents managing a guesthouse for lovers?" asked Elric. "Griselde and Clement might like spending their elder years away from the bustle of the city."

"My regular guests often request suppers much like this. I presume Sheriff Hutton Castle still needs a cook?"

"We do indeed. Since our former cook's departure we have depended on one of the men who is a tolerable cook in the field, when we are desperate, but he can ruin even the finest venison. And as for something such as this pie—he would not know how to begin."

"A pity," said Kate. "And you've found no one?"

"The castle is remote and the regular occupants soldiers and servants; only occasionally is the cook called upon to prepare a feast for more discerning palates." Elric shrugged. "For a while the wife of one of the earl's tenants took pity on us and assisted with dinner a few days a week. With the purpose of teaching our cook his trade. Things improved for a while, but he did not see the point of all the effort and sank back into his slovenly ways. She refused to return." A pause as he cut another piece of the pie and spooned up more of the creamed eel. "Berend would be a good fit for us. Not many women about, so a man is more appropriate. Griselde could surely cook for your household as well as this one." He glanced up from his food to see her reaction.

She laughed. "I agreed to provide you with information valuable to your earl, not share my household staff."

"I can but try. You said he was away on an errand?"

"Yes. And he is missed. Phillip is a picky eater and Griselde's cooking does not tempt him as Berend's does. Though he is free to eat with us only on Sundays, Phillip had so looked forward to it."

Elric nodded. "Growing lads need fuel. Phillip is Hugh Grantham's apprentice now, the master mason at the minster, is he not? Is it official?"

"He is, and yes, it is official, to his joy."

"A fine lad. How long will Berend be away?"

Kevin cleared his throat loudly, nodding as Kate and Sir Elric looked his way. "You might talk of cooks another time. Is this not my night? Are we not here to drink to my health and welcome me back into the company of my comrades?"

"Your comrades have made some progress in drinking to your health already," Elric noted. But he laughed and raised his cup. "To Kevin."

Silently blessing Kevin for distracting his captain, Kate rose to pour all more wine. After several rounds of toasts, including to Brother Martin's healing hands and Kate, the men broke out in bawdy songs. Douglas's barrel chest produced a deep baritone, Kevin carried the tune with Harry's help, Stephen went high in harmony. Wulf, drunker than his fellows, kept time drumming on his thighs.

As Kate cleared the empty platters and moved the roasted nuts and figs to the center of the table she felt buoyed by the men's wild spirits, familiar from her childhood, with all her brothers and her father's retainers at the long table in the hall, singing, playing fiddles, pipes, drums. She would often twirl and twirl, dancing until she was dizzy and too hot to go on. Her brother Geoff often joined her, and once they were slick with sweat they would dash out into the cold night, running, running, the hounds chasing them.

You do not often remember the good times, Geoff said in her mind.

Is there danger? she silently asked him.

I sense none except for the hidden lady. You are in the company of those who would keep you safe.

Then I conjured you with the memory of joy. She smiled to herself.

"He will eat them all before we've a chance to taste them!" Stephen cried as he dragged the platter of figs and roasted nuts out of Kevin's reach.

Kate laughed. Kevin had eaten quite a few. They were clearly more to his taste than the wine. She had noticed that although he lifted his cup with every toast, his sips were modest. Good. She counted on him to keep a clear head and be discreet.

Elric leaned toward her as she resumed her seat. "I cannot recall when I last saw my men so merry. I will not soon forget your warm hospitality. I hope it has not caused problems."

"Not at all." She touched his hand. "Kevin risked everything to protect Dina that night and we are grateful."

Elric closed his other hand over hers, sending a flush of warmth through her body. There was no denying the attraction, though she would be damned if she was about to let down her guard. Berend and Simon had taught her to tread warily with men.

"How does one ever repay such a selfless act?" she whispered.

"You have already done so with your care. You not only gave Kevin shelter, but purpose, a reason to heal. I am most grateful. He is one of my best men." Elric did not smile as he spoke, but in his gaze was a warmth Kate had rarely seen. "Is it true that he promised Marie and Petra he would return to your home for one more night?"

She laughed. "It is true. Marie begged him, saying she and Petra had a surprise for him, and he agreed." Kate had as well. He had joined her in the kitchen after Petra's tantrum, having heard of it from Marie, and was concerned that it was because of his departure. She had admitted it was the catalyst, but not the entire cause. Still, when he mentioned that Marie demanded he stay one more night, Kate had urged him to do so. "I don't dare to guess what Marie has planned," she said to Elric. "I pray it involves a song they meant to rehearse today, and not a plot to force him to stay indefinitely."

"You have a gift for making people feel at home." Elric lifted her hand with his, and kissed it as he held her gaze.

Confused by her feelings, Kate was relieved when Elric glanced away, startled by Wulf's lurching attempt to rise, almost bringing the table down with him. His fellows steadied the furniture as Wulf weaved toward the door muttering something about the privy.

"You've forgotten your boots," Kevin called out, rising to fetch them.

He'd not quite reached Wulf when the man flung wide the door and staggered back, wind and snow buffeting him and setting the flames dancing in the tapers. "Boots. I forgot my boots."

"Close the door you mutton-headed wastrel," Douglas roared.

Kevin nudged his drunk companion out of the way and shut the door. "Sit on the bench, you sot." When Wulf was safely grounded, Kevin handed him his boots.

Elric apologized to Kate. "I think it is time we departed, while my men can still manage snowy streets." He shifted his long legs and rose. "I almost forgot. In your message inviting me to this celebration you mentioned that you had information?"

"I do. Perhaps you might see the others away, then return for a quiet talk?" He nodded as he turned to see to his men.

Douglas had risen and collared Stephen, who had been reaching for some figs, pulling him up out of his chair. "May God bless you and keep you, Mistress Clifford," said Douglas. "A splendid meal—more than we deserve." He growled at Wulf, who teetered near the door.

Stephen bowed gracefully. "My deepest gratitude for the feast and your gracious presence, my lady."

Elric hid his laughter with a cough as Kevin came back round to thank her.

"Have a care with Marie," she warned.

Kevin laughed. "I promise not to pledge my troth." Leaning close, he whispered, "Your secrets are safe with me, always."

"My dear friend," she smiled her gratitude.

Kate found herself avoiding Elric's eyes as she saw the men out, flustered by their exchange. As soon as the door closed behind the men, Seth came out from the kitchen. He paused at the sideboard with a laugh.

"They ate most of it," said Kate. "Feel free to eat what's left, though it won't fill you."

"Griselde had the foresight to set some aside for me and our guest. She'll be pleased. She enjoys cooking for hearty eaters."

"Sir Elric and his squire will be back," said Kate. "Let our guest know that she cannot yet come out."

Seth nodded. "Brandywine, nuts, figs. Will that suffice?"

"More than enough."

—◦⊚⊙⊚◦—

Elric followed his men as they slipped and slid through the drifting snow while supporting their drunk companion. Wulf would lose his balance and topple into the soft snow, and with much jeering and laughter they would pull him up, steady him, and trudge on, only to repeat it several steps later. At least they had no witnesses. Between Kate's guesthouse and his men's lodging on Stonegate Elric encountered no one else foolish enough to be out in the storm.

At last they arrived at their destination, Harry doing the honors of knocking on the door to rouse the landlord. Stephen and Douglas gave up on Wulf and simply dragged him inside, their landlord shaking his head and muttering about soldiers who could not hold their drink. Sir Elric gave him a few pence for his trouble and a promise that he would keep them far too busy to enjoy another such evening while Wulf sang Dame Katherine's praises.

Back out on the street, Elric, Kevin, and Harry drew their cloaks tight and trudged back down toward Petergate.

"Do you feel well feted, Kevin?" Elric asked.

Kevin laughed. "Oh, it was *my* night? Somehow it seemed Wulf's."

Harry slapped him on the back.

"Dame Katherine is a wonder, is she not?" said Kevin.

"She is," Elric said, with heart. He had never encountered such a woman. Katherine Clifford knew just how to be with the men, putting them at ease, yet not too familiar. They respected and admired her.

As did he, though upon his first glimpse of her several years earlier on the arm of her late husband, Simon Neville, he had imagined that she would prove as tedious as most merchant's wives, more interested in impressing the other guests than in engaging in conversation. It had been Elric's first Christmas at Sheriff Hutton Castle. He'd been named captain of the earl's guard at the castle at Michaelmas. Simon and Katherine had arrived the day before the Christmas feast, she swathed in a fur-lined cloak and accompanied by a brace of war dogs—ridiculous for the wife of a city merchant—he dressed likewise and seemingly concerned that there was snow on the ground and their fine boots would be ruined. When Katherine was relieved of her cloak by a servant, the extravagant silk and velvet gown in a red veering dangerously toward royal purple, her dark hair swept up in a silver crispinette powdered with pearls and emeralds, he found it difficult to look away, and she noticed, studying him with frank interest. A pampered pet tugging at her leash, eager to stray, he had thought. When she watched with unusual intensity his swordplay demonstration, and later surprised him with knowledgeable questions about his technique, he thought it flirtation, or perhaps a ploy to inflame an indifferent spouse. Though how any man could be indifferent to her he could not fathom. Not that she was the most beautiful woman at the feast—her features were too bold for that—but there was a vitality about her that stirred his imagination.

Out on the practice field the following morning he'd looked up with amazement as she approached in the company of her hounds and asked one of the men if there was a target she might use to practice, preferably a straw man. She needed some fresh air and movement after such a rich feast. Practice what? he had wondered, as he and most of the other men crowded round. From her skirts she drew a small battle axe, gave a signal to the hounds to stand behind her at a slight distance, and proceeded to work up a heat throwing her axe, retrieving it, throwing again, until one of the squires began to retrieve it for her. Her technique was flawless, clearly the result of much practice. Time after time she hit all the best points on the straw man to disarm him, disable him, or kill him. The play finished when she beheaded him. Elric's amazement burgeoned.

And then she had asked if she might return in a while for some archery practice.

On that day, watching her prowess, her intense focus, Elric realized she could be either a formidable foe or an equally formidable ally. He had worked hard the past year to turn her from the former to the latter, but he still felt as if he were dancing on the edge of her axe blade. After every encounter he found it necessary to review and revise his strategy. Her hard work toward paying off Simon Neville's debts seemed a part of the discipline that had enabled her skill with weapons. That she was also so compassionate as to take in her late husband's bastard children and love them as her own—he still wondered at that, but sensed that it came from the same place as her fierce protection of her wayward mother and her young niece. But her choice of servants—an assassin and a thief, and he had yet to discover Matt's dark secret, and her invention of the guesthouse, a place of assignation for lovers, as a conduit for the money to buy masses for her late husband's soul—those aspects suggested a dark cunning that unsettled him. Katherine Clifford remained a most challenging enigma. And tonight he must once again try to win her cooperation.

At the corner, Kevin bid him a good evening and trudged off down Low Petergate to Katherine's house where her wards awaited him. Elric put his arm round his squire's shoulders.

"Back into the warm glow of the guesthouse, eh, Harry?"

"Yes! God's blood but it's cold out here."

Elric had much to tell Katherine, including some things she might not like to hear about someone for whom she cared far more than Elric liked. Best get it out and be done with it. He prayed that she would appreciate rather than resent the information.

⸱⊙⊙⸱

"Not a night to be out on the roads," Kate said as she opened the door for the returning knight and his man, and saw the depth of the snow, the continued strength of the storm. "You are welcome to make use of one of the bedchambers tonight, wait for daylight before riding through Galtres." She had chosen an evening for the celebration when there would be no patrons in the upper chambers, so both were available.

Elric gave her a long look. "That is kind of you."

She felt herself blushing. That was all she needed. She hoped in the candlelight it just seemed her natural high color. "Harry as well, of course." She nodded to Elric's squire who was heading out to the kitchen to spend the time with Seth. God be thanked that Griselde had changed the plan and hidden Lady Margery in her own bedchamber.

"I do thank you, but there is no need," said Elric. "I've made arrangements at the York Tavern."

"I doubt Mistress Merchet's chambers are so fine as ours. But as you wish." Kate offered him brandywine.

Elric held out his goblet. "And a good thing it is that I had already planned to stay in the city. On such a night the best horse and rider might lose their way in the forest."

"You have business in York?" Kate asked, interested.

"I will tell you about it. First, what have you for me?"

Sitting back with her goblet, she said, "It concerns Scarborough. They say there are pirates in the coves near the city, Spanish and French pirates, ready to harry our coast."

Elric's frowning concern told her this was news to him. "Spies keen to test the crown's ability to protect the realm?"

"That was my thought," said Kate. "A king deposed, a new king threatened with rebellion."

Elric cleared his throat. "Richard was not deposed, he abdicated." Said as if by rote, insincere.

"The French do not see it that way," she said. "Nor do you, I think." He looked down at his cup. "Nor do the rebels," she added, thinking of the uprising that had been planned for the feast of the Epiphany, the plot to murder King Henry and his sons. "The point is, the French believe Henry might be so distracted by civil strife he would be unable to move quickly should they attack, with his soldiers already spread out in the countryside and towns searching for the rebel leaders. Is it true what they say? The earls of Salisbury, Kent, and Huntington all beheaded?"

Elric nodded and crossed himself, as did Kate.

"You and your fellow merchants are concerned about this because of the French and Spanish pirates threatening trade," said Elric.

"You see the problem. We are discussing how we might protect our ships." •

"Hire your own pirates?" He reached for some nuts and figs.

"It is one possibility. Or we put more armed men on our ships to ensure our defense, though that means less room for cargo. We need someone like Ralph Neville to explain the situation to the king. We would not want His Grace to see our armed men as a threat to him. It is said the Earl of Westmoreland has Henry's ear."

"He does. I will send him news of this as well as your concerns." Elric washed a fig and some nuts down with the last of his brandywine, setting it down with a sigh of contentment. "You set a fine table."

"As I said, you are welcome to stay. Griselde loves men with good appetites."

What game are you playing, Kate? Geoff hissed in her head. *You do not want him here.*

"Old Bess is keen for my coin as well as news of the Lancastrian court," said Elric. "I could use her long knowledge of the city, the families, their alliances, so I count it wise to please her."

Old Bess. She's my reason for inviting Elric to lodge here. Having lived on the other side of the city until a few months ago, Kate's only personal knowledge of Bess Merchet was a comment she made to Griselde, that a woman who flaunted wolfhounds in the city was up to no good. Other than that, Kate knew her only by reputation. Though Old Bess's grandson Colin was the nominal owner of the York Tavern just round the corner and down Stonegate in St. Helen's Square, the elderly widow was said to run the tavern from her parlor off the kitchen, her keen instincts keeping troublemakers away, and she made a point of knowing everyone's business. She likely knew to the day how long Berend had been gone, and that it was long enough for him to have set off to join in the rebellion. That was what worried Kate. If the taverner *had* heard whispers about Berend's absence, she might share them with Elric. It was said she had a fondness for soldiers with a bit of the devil in them, and Kate imagined Elric was just her type, especially his connection to nobility. Kate cursed herself for not having tried to befriend the woman. Perhaps she still could.

"What are you hoping to learn from Old Bess?" she asked as she topped up both of their cups.

"I find it best to listen without expectations." He leaned closer. "I might not need her confidence if you can help me. Which brings me to why I will bide with her a while. On the orders of my lord the earl I am searching the city for Margery, Lady Kirkby."

God help me. "Lady Kirkby is here?" Kate prayed her voice was steady.

Elric did not seem to notice anything amiss. "She is believed to have arrived in York in the past day or two."

"Believed. You have not seen her?"

"No. I am to find her and hold her at Sheriff Hutton until King Henry's men come to take her into custody."

"Into custody?" Thinking of the woman hiding beneath the bed in the next room, Kate felt both dread and anger. If her wards should suffer because of Margery's naïve husband . . .

"What are you thinking?" asked Elric.

She had been silent too long. He watched her so closely she had to remember to breathe. "I fear for my friend," she said. "Of what does she stand accused?"

"So you have not seen her?"

"A year past."

"The rebels you spoke of," said Elric, "those involved in what some are calling the Epiphany Rising—"

"You cannot believe Margery had a part in that?"

"Not her, her husband. The king believes Sir Thomas was part of the plan."

Reminding herself that she must seem to hear this for the first time, she whispered, "Was?" Kate felt as if someone was slowly tightening their fist round her heart as she listened to Elric's account, how much he knew, Thomas's leech, the rising suspicion about his loyalty to Richard, seemingly confirmed by the report of his earlier visit to Pontefract.

"From Windsor he'd gone to Cirencester and was seen in the company of the rebel earls," said Elric. "I must tell you—he was executed by the mob. Lady Margery managed to escape. Apparently with her husband's head."

"His head? Margery witnessed his beheading? God help her." Kate crossed herself. She did not need to pretend distress. She lifted her cup and drank.

Elric was not unsympathetic. "I am sorry to be the one bearing such news" The brandywine helped steady her. "Why would Margery be there?"

"Her sister claims that Lady Margery was visiting her, and that Sir Thomas had arrived unexpectedly a few days before the earls of Kent and Salisbury. But the king believes the earls had meant to join Thomas in the town and ride off together."

"God grant gentle Sir Thomas eternal rest," she whispered. "I find this all—Elric, I cannot believe it of him. He sought peace, not bloodshed."

Elric's blue eyes were steady, neither expressing agreement nor disagreement. "So he claimed. It is not for me to judge him or his lady, merely to find her and hold her. As you have sheltered Lady Margery in the past, I wanted to warn you. Do not take her in."

Too late for that. "Are the king's men also in York?"

"Not yet. I hope to find Lady Margery before they arrive. It will be better for everyone. Especially for you, for you are known to have hosted her fundraising dinners."

"As a favor to my uncle, the dean of York Minster," Kate clarified. "From the first I thought it a rash plot. Naïve."

"I know. But the king and his sons were threatened . . ."

"What of Margery's family?"

"All being questioned. Thomas's head went missing right away, a boy seen racing away with it, Lady Margery in pursuit. Sir Thomas's body was spirited away in the night. Her sister is suspect, though why she would risk her own family—" A shrug. "Someone close to Sir Thomas has at the very least interfered with the king's justice—the bodies and heads were to be displayed as a warning."

"Thomas beheaded," Kate whispered, crossing herself, then reaching for her cup. The king begrudged her the body, including the head, for burial?

Monstrous. "One body out of so many—what can it possibly matter?" she asked. "Her family is being held?"

"No, just watched. For now. But if she is not found . . ."

"What precisely do they want of her?"

"Besides answering for the theft of her husband's body and head, they believe she might know the extent of the rebellion. More names. Additional plots."

So the longer Margery hid, the more danger for her family. Kate did not like this. She did not like this at all. How she wished Carl had appeared *after* this conversation with Elric. Would she have turned Margery away?

"But if Sir Thomas was innocent of this?" she asked.

Elric held up his hands, palms out, quieting Kate's protest. "I merely wish you to know the whole sad tale so that you might make wise decisions should any member of her family appear on your doorstep." He reached for her hand. "I mean to keep you safe."

Did he? Or did he want to feel whether her hand might reveal something, the cold sweat of guilt perhaps? Fortunately, Kate's hand was warm. She let him take it. "Will they execute her as well?"

"Should I find her first, I promise you I will do my best to protect her at Sheriff Hutton Castle until someone with authority—and some modicum of calm—convinces me that she is safe in their hands. Meanwhile, I beg you to have a care. Trust no one as they jostle to gain King Henry's favor. The slightest criticism might be reported."

Such as her sense that they had traded one vicious despot for another. "I understand," she said. God help her family.

Elric poured them both more brandywine. "There is more."

There always was. Kate took a deep breath. "Tell me."

"I know that Berend has been gone a while." Kate flinched. Elric glanced down at her hand in his, then looked her in the eye. "I can understand why you would hope no one noticed."

"Bess Merchet noticed?"

"If she has, she has said nothing to me. I heard it elsewhere. Not from my own men, mind you. It seems you have earned their loyalty."

Bless Kevin. "So Berend is away. What of that?"

"You do know that he was once in the service of Baron Montagu?"

She withdrew her hand, though she was certain he had already sensed her surprise, her fear.

"I see you did not know. Katherine, I am sorry. I want only—"

"To protect me. Yes, you said. You mention his service because Montagu's son, the Earl of Salisbury, was one of the rebels?"

Elric nodded. "In his will, Salisbury's father left Berend a modest property. A house and land to the east of York. The property was deeded to Berend ten years ago, on Montagu's death."

"His son and heir, Salisbury, is he—was he not King Richard's champion?" Kate asked.

Elric nodded.

Kate crossed herself. No wonder he was curious about Berend's absence.

Salisbury had been in Ireland with Richard when word came that Henry of Lancaster had landed in Yorkshire. King Richard had sent Salisbury back to England to secure Chester for him. When Richard was captured, Salisbury stayed by his side in Chester Castle. She remembered Kevin sitting in the kitchen telling them about it. He had just heard it from someone in the city.

And Berend, who had been kneading bread as he listened, said, *An honorable man, Salisbury, to stay with his lord.* Was that where Berend was? Was that the meaning of Petra's dream, that Berend had felt honor bound to obey the summons of his lord's son? Why?

"Richard's champion, and part of the uprising, butchered in Cirencester. I am sorry to be the one to tell you," said Elric.

"Yes." Her voice stuck in her throat.

Berend had referred to himself as an assassin. Kate had presumed he was a mercenary, with no allegiances. But his lord the baron had gifted him with property. If Berend had wealth of his own, what was he playing at, working as a cook in her home?

"How long has Berend been gone?" Elric asked.

Long enough.

"You have remembered something?" he asked. "Something that might help me?"

Had she frowned? She must have a care. He observed her so closely. She shook her head. "You have me questioning how well I know anyone I count a friend," she forced the words past the lump in her throat. She had trusted Berend implicitly.

"Forgive me, but there is more. Berend was seen in Pontefract, met with Salisbury in Oxford, and was seen in Cirencester on the day the mob murdered the earls and Sir Thomas."

Now Kate's hands were cold. She felt the chill in her extremities, flowing toward her heart. "Berend?" she whispered. "But the plot—it is said they meant to kill the king's sons. Berend would never condone that. Never."

"If it is of any comfort, I cannot believe it of him either. But his movements—You can see why he, too, is being sought."

"By Westmoreland?"

"No. Sir Ralph mentioned only Lady Margery."

"So if Berend is caught, you will not protect him, as you have said you will protect Margery?"

"I will not be under *orders* to protect him. But he will come to no harm. I'll do all that I can to keep him safe at Sheriff Hutton, as I will with Lady Kirkby. You have my word." Elric wrapped his hands round hers and leaned close, his breath sweet with the brandywine. "Forgive me for upsetting you. It was such a pleasant evening."

Damn him for saying that. She fought tears. "It was," she whispered. She must remember that just as Simon and Berend had played her, so might Elric.

"Allow me to walk you home," he said.

She nodded. It was time to return to the children so that Griselde could come home, see to her husband and Margery. Margery, damn her.

Elric kissed her hand and released it, pushing his chair from the table. "I will fetch Harry."

"Tell Seth to come along so that he might escort Griselde back here."

"There is no need for Seth to go out. We'll escort her. The York Tavern is not so far from here."

No, not so far. More's the pity. Margery would be imprisoned in this house. For it would be watched, as would all Kate's properties. All whom she loved were in danger. All.

4

THE YORK TAVERN

Kate awoke haunted by questions about Berend, doubting all that she had believed they shared. And Margery Kirkby—the tragedy of her husband's violent death chilled Kate. A man who had risked his life and reputation to broker peace between the warring royal cousins, only to be accused of treason by the victor. How was Margery to prove him innocent? Was he? Was Berend? Kate had so much to lose, so much that she had hoped to build on to secure good lives for her wards.

Her head pounding from last night's wine and her heart bruised, she dressed quickly, throwing on a warm mantle before stepping out onto the landing. There she paused in awe. Snow blanketed the rooftops, softening them, mirroring the pale clouds that vaguely muted the darkness of the predawn sky, the steeples and chimneys reaching out of the ethereal whiteness, calling on heaven to look down at the beauty. Each limb of the great oak rising up from her back garden was outlined in white and lit by the light spilling out from the kitchen window and doorway down below. Even the sounds of the carts on the cobbles were muffled by the snow.

Another time, the quiet scene would bring her great peace, but not today.

She reminded herself of her morning's mission, telling her partner and former neighbor Thomas Holme that she had done it, she was free of Simon's debt. He would be pleased. She was no longer burdened with her brother-in-law as a partner in her husband's former business; now she would trade in her own right, as Katherine Clifford, *femme sole*. With her own property, her dower, and her inheritance from the Clifford estate in Northumbria plus the gift of her uncle Richard's house and horses, she had established her guesthouse—a business her clients protected with silence for the sake of their own reputations. She had also formed a small trading concern with her wealthy friend, the widow Drusilla Seaton, buying materials for silk purses and other small items to be made by Jennet and one of her mother's beguines, both skilled sempsters. Simon's former partner had already expressed interest in partnering with them on a shipment. With those prospects and the rents on her houses, Kate might be quite comfortable. Might be.

A door opened behind her, the girls tumbling out of their bedchamber. They were arm in arm, friends again.

"Ask Dame Katherine for something to help you sleep," Marie was saying. "Oh. Dame Katherine—"

Crouching down to look into Petra's eyes, Kate saw the telltale signs of weeping. She stroked the girl's dark curls, gently lifted her chin. "The nightmares again, my love?"

A solemn nod. "The monster crowned with worms came down the crowded streets wielding a great sword as he cut off people's heads."

"Crowned with worms?" Kevin whispered. "Do you speak of King Henry?"

Kate had heard him climbing the steps, recognizing his gait. She glanced up at him. "What do you mean?"

"At Henry of Lancaster's coronation it is said that when the Archbishop of Canterbury removed the cap the king was wearing those around him gasped, for his head was raw with sores and crawling with lice."

"That was my *first* dream." Petra's voice shook. "Is the king beheading people? Is Berend going to lose his head?"

Kate took a breath to calm herself. "Why do you say Berend?"

"He is in danger. My dreams show him running, hiding."

"No!" Marie whimpered.

Kissing her niece's forehead, then her ward's, Kate tried to calm them. "Berend is an experienced soldier. He knows how to protect himself. Better to pray for his safety than to believe bad dreams, eh?" She looked from Marie's wide blue eyes to Petra's deep-set brown ones, eliciting nods. Another kiss each, smoothing their hair, pressing their hands. "Now go out to the kitchen. Jennet will have risen early to stoke the fire. Warm yourselves."

As Kate rose, she motioned for Kevin to stay. When the girls had clomped down the steps and she saw them crossing the yard, Kate turned to her companion. Kevin exuded solidity with his strong upper body, muscular legs, heavy brows, and abundant dark hair framing his strong-jawed face. He met her eyes with a solemn expression.

"Your captain tells me you've said nothing to him about Berend's disappearance," said Kate. "Nor have your fellows."

A nod. "The four of us have a pact."

"Bless you. I don't know how I deserve such loyalty."

"You have given me back my life, Dame Katherine, and a family. I will not be a stranger to the children. The three of them—" He cleared his throat, gave her a sad smile. "The girls sang for me last night. Two angels."

She touched his cheek. "They love you. Rest assured you are always welcome in my home."

He bowed, blushing. "But Sir Elric knows much."

"Bess Merchet?"

"I don't believe she has yet decided how much to trust him."

"Yet he is lodging there in the hope she will be of use."

"Yes. But he has other sources."

"Has he told you what he learned about Berend? His property?"

"Do you mean that he was one of Baron Montagu's men, Salisbury's father? And that the baron left him some land?"

Kate nodded. "And do you know why your captain is in the city?"

"Lady Margery. We are to search for her."

"On the king's orders. You dare not disobey."

"Sir Elric will see that she comes to no harm."

"So he promised me."

"You can trust him."

"And will he see that Berend comes to no harm?"

"If he said so. He is a man of his word."

She prayed he was right. "What you said about the king, the lice. Did those who witnessed it take it as an omen?"

"The king and his councilors are assuring everyone that it is due to King Henry's stringent penances with which he means to scour out all sin. They twist it to be a sign of his grace. But the folk, they are afeared it is a sign of damnation, that he transgressed in unseating the divinely anointed king, his cousin."

Of course they would believe that, Kate thought. And now Henry would be ever more defensive, overbearing. Hence Elric's warning. "A bad beginning," she said.

"Yes." Kevin shifted his feet. "You should go down to the kitchen, warm yourself. I was just coming to say farewell. For now."

"If I should need you—"

"You have only to send me word."

"Your captain. You are certain I can trust him?"

About to nod, Kevin paused. "He holds you in high regard, Dame Katherine, and I believe he means to keep you safe, no matter his orders. But he is the earl's man, and he will not overtly challenge his orders."

"You are saying that *I* am safe, but perhaps not Berend, or Lady Margery."

"As I said, he will ensure that she comes to no harm under his watch."

Kate nodded. "And if I asked for your help with the other?"

"If you trust Berend, so do I."

His ardent gaze gave her pause. She was taking advantage of his regard for her.

"You would risk antagonizing your captain and the earl?"

"God is my conscience, no earthly lord." He bowed to her, proffered his arm.

She could not deny it was good to have such an ally, but she must have a care not to ask for too much from this gentle man. Lightly touching his forearm, she crossed the landing with him.

As they began to descend the steps, he asked, "Petra's dreams. Does she have the Sight?"

"She believes that she does, but I am unconvinced. In training her in archery I've witnessed her remarkable concentration, and her ability to recall every detail of the instruction even so far as what she sensed I judged most important. And she guesses rightly. I prefer to admire these abilities and think she simply hears and understands far more than she realizes."

"You are very proud of her."

"Of all three children. They have brought me great joy."

"I will miss sharing their lives."

"They will miss you, and we shall all miss your stories." He had a keen eye for people's quirks, turning them into amusing stories lacking all malice. Every evening Marie and Petra would beg him to tell them tales of the folk he had encountered on the street that day. She always knew when he obliged, hearing the peals of laughter even from across the yard.

They parted at the bottom of the steps, Kevin bowing to her, then continuing on toward Kate's manservant Matt who was shoveling a pathway out to the street. As the two men greeted each other, Kate took the already cleared path from the house to the kitchen.

—◦◦◦—

Jennet left a lively argument with the girls to see to Kate as she entered the kitchen.

"Fresh bread and cheese, some ale?"

Kate nodded. "Any news yet?" After the children had gone to bed the previous night, Kate had told Jennet all she had learned from Elric. Jennet was far more than a servant to Kate, she was a friend, confidante, business partner, and a connection to the invisible folk of York, the poor, young, and old, who survived by their wits and little else, her eyes and ears. As a sign of her trust, Kate never asked how Jennet contacted them, who they were, or how they gathered their information.

"So far no word of a bald man," said Jennet. "Or two, one alone, badly scarred. But I extended that to anyone new in the city the past few days. A few had caught sight of a pair who seemed to be traveling together. Flickers, there and gone."

"So they will let you know when they catch glimpses of anyone?"

Jennet grinned. "They will. It is just the sort of tracking we loved best as children on the streets. Ghosting, we called it."

"Sometimes I think you miss it."

"I enjoy being out among them, but I am ever grateful for a true home, safe, dry, warm." A shrug. "They will now also keep an eye out for Berend."

"He was not one of the pair by any chance?"

"You are thinking of Petra's dream, are you?" Jennet asked.

Kate nodded.

"They could not say."

—⁂—

Later, after breakfast, when Marie returned to her bedchamber to change the ribbons in her hair, Kate took the opportunity of asking Petra more about her dreams of Berend. "In the first one, he said he was duty-bound to leave, is that right?" Kate asked.

"That was not the first one," the child said as she rubbed Lille's ears, "but he did say that in the one about leaving." She suddenly dropped her hands to her sides and frowned up at Kate. "You are worried about him. More than you were." A statement, not a question.

But Kate did not want to lose the thread. "In last night's dream you saw him running and hiding. He is in danger?"

Her dark eyes boring into Kate, Petra nodded.

"Is he alone?"

"I saw only him."

"Who is chasing him?"

"The Sight is not like that."

"What do you mean?"

"God does not explain what he shows me. And I cannot look round to see what else is there."

A few months ago Petra had feared she might be cursed by the Sight. But she now framed it as a gift from God. Sister Brigida's doing, perhaps, the girls' tutor in French, Latin, and music, a challenging, but kind, teacher. Whoever had changed the child's mind, Kate was grateful.

"Have you tried praying for guidance?" Kate asked.

"No. Old Mapes said to accept what was given with grace and never ask for more."

Old Mapes was the elderly healer who had raised the child in the Scottish highlands, before her uncle claimed her and brought her to York. Kate stretched out her legs, thinking. "So you had dreamed of Berend before?" Ghent rose and came to settle beside her. She rested a hand on the wolfhound's back.

Petra averted her eyes. "I don't want to talk about this."

"Even if it might help a friend in danger?"

The girl bit her lip, frowning. "I promise I will tell you anything that might help."

Kate leaned over and touched her niece's cheek. "I am grateful. So what is Brigida teaching you today?"

Petra's face brightened. "We are learning new songs in praise of the Virgin Mary for Candlemas." Hence their skipping their usual morning lessons at the school on Petergate for additional time with Sister Brigida. Candlemas was just days away. "Sister Brigida says I have a strong, beautiful voice. Marie is too breathy. I think that means she does not sing, she whispers."

"Did Sister Brigida say that to Marie?"

Petra shook her head. "She said not to fear being heard. Let her voice soar to heaven. She said we must not ask God and his blessed mother to strain to hear our devotions."

They shared a smile at Brigida's discretion.

"Might I hear a little of the song?" Kate asked.

"I would rather wait to sing it when I know all of it."

Kate loved how comfortably the child expressed her preferences. She considered walking with the children and Dame Brigida, as she was heading to the house next to her mother's Martha House. The girls loved walking with the hounds, and she felt in need of their good cheer this morning. But she suddenly had a better idea. She would stop at the chandler's shop near the market that sold wax writing tablets. Petra's was chipped and Marie's cracked. She would have them delivered to them in the classroom. Such a gift might brighten their day, and, in so doing, brighten hers.

"Then I shall look forward to hearing the song anon," she said, kissing Petra's cheek.

-◦◦◦◦-

CANDACE ROBB

The long shelf on which the chandler displayed his goods always caught Kate's attention as she passed into the marketplace, the scent of the more expensive beeswax candles reminding her of the chapel of her youth, the various lengths and shapes, the candles marked for the hours, they spoke to her of evenings in her mother's bedchamber listening to stories, playing with the kittens her mother favored over the hounds. She liked this reminder of the happy moments in her childhood. But this morning she was after items the chandler did not have on display.

"Wax writing tablets?" the shop clerk smiled at Lille and Ghent as he repeated Kate's request. "Oh, yes, the master has a wide selection, and they are easily joined into sets if you wish." The young man whipped out a stack of three connected with leather thongs to open like a book.

"Single tablets will do for my girls," she said. "Do you have any with a nice wood frame?"

A twinkle in the young man's eyes. "I do, mistress." He handled the book-like set with care as he returned it to the shelves behind him, and after a bit of rummaging presented two good-sized waxed tablets framed in a wood with a beautiful grain. "They were prepared for the mayor-elect's daughter, but her mother refused them. Too heavy for her frail daughter."

Poor Hazel. Kate's girls had studied with her cousin's daughter for a time, but of late Hazel had been too weak. Taking one of the tablets in hand, she knew Isabella Frost had been right in rejecting it for her daughter.

"My master might have pointed out that Mistress Frost had never specified the weight, as he would do with any other customer," the clerk continued. "But one does not cross the wife of the mayor-elect. Especially one chosen by royal decree."

"I do not think the king decreed William Frost's election," Kate suggested softly. The young man amused her, but her cousin would bristle at the suggestion that he had not been elected based on his own merits. "Marie and Petra will love these."

He proposed a price higher than she intended to pay. She counter proposed. He argued, then named a sum slightly higher than her counter, and she agreed.

"Could I ask you to deliver them to the little schoolroom on Castlegate, the one run by the beguines?"

"We are happy to deliver, Mistress Clifford. To your niece and the bonny French girl?"

Kate smiled. "Yes, to them." She glanced up for a moment and noticed Jon Horner hurrying into the market square, heading straight toward the booth of a spice seller new in the city. Horner, a scrivener, seemed a bit of a lackwit, with a soft, mincing way about him and a comic delight in bright colors and dramatically draped velvet hats. But those clothes cost more than a scrivener might honestly earn, and it was whispered in the guild that his appearance was a clever façade masking a cunning gamester who preyed on trusting folk who employed him to copy out wills and contracts.

Merek the spice seller was another unsavory character. Together they made a curious pair, their heads bent close now, Merek handing something to Horner, something the peacock began to examine, but the spice seller motioned to him to hide. The peacock seemed uncertain, but Merek waved him on, as if he considered the business concluded. Curious.

Kate had noticed Merek before Christmas, slouching down Petergate as if hoping to avoid notice. Folk said he claimed to sell varieties of pepper never encountered in the city. The guilds were aware of him. He was permitted only to sell in the market one day a week.

The chandler's clerk interrupted her observation with a question about the delivery, and she was just tidying up details when a commotion distracted them.

The spice seller and the peacock had apparently finished their business. Horner stuffed something in the scrip at his waist as he glanced anxiously about, then scurried back in Kate's direction, and Merek was already trotting off at a good clip as a customer shouted at him, "Come back here. I came out of my way—" He cursed as the spice seller disappeared amidst the stalls.

"Passionate about peppers," the clerk quipped.

"One never knows another's heart," Kate said with an exaggerated sigh.

The two of them laughed as they completed their transaction.

—◦◦◦—

Thomas Holme wagged his bushy white brows and congratulated Kate with all the heartiness she might have wished for. He proposed a toast to her success.

But by the time he handed her the goblet of wine he was frowning and shaking his head.

"I need to review my accounts. As you should yours," he said. "You know Lionel, he will demand to see them, ensure there are no outstanding payments or debts."

"Clement has already reviewed mine," she assured him.

"Ah. Clement is a good man. Still fit for the work, is he?"

"His body fails him, but his mind is as sharp as ever."

Clement had been her late husband's business factor, the one who had fixed Simon's books so that his debts were invisible to his partners and the guild. And Kate. He had been well paid for the deception. But his conscience prevailed, albeit belatedly. An old man, bedridden for the most part, fearing eternal damnation should he not repent and make amends upon Simon's death, he had given Kate money toward her late husband's debts. A penance. In turn, Kate had installed Griselde and Clement in her guesthouse. It benefited Kate, as had the money, and she had entrusted Clement with her accounts, satisfied that he had learned his lesson.

"It is good you are wary of Lionel," Thomas said. "A spice seller has been asking rather impertinent questions about him, his properties, and his connection to the powerful Ralph Neville, Earl of Westmoreland. Nor am I the only merchant he's approached with such curiosity about your brother-in-law. Tongues are wagging in the guild."

"I had not heard." That did not bode well for Lionel's future business. "This spice seller. Does he go by the name Merek?" Kate asked.

"The very man." Thomas nodded. "So he has approached you as well?"

"No. I just saw him with Jon Horner—"

"A pair of weasels." Thomas sniffed. "In any case, once my contract with what is now Lionel's business expires I mean to investigate his relationship with Merek before I agree to work with him again."

"You have a reasonable concern," Kate said.

"As for you and I, our ship is expected soon," said Holme, smiling. "As soon as all the fuss of the mayor's feast is past, we will be busy. You will examine the shipment with me?"

"Of course." She took pride in her eye for quality. Her partners appreciated it.

"I do have a proposal." He cleared his throat. "My nephew Leif is a per-sonable young man, has managed my warehouses, and my late brother's, for almost a decade. Honest, hardworking. I believe we would be all the better for employing him as our clerk for sales."

"You no longer need him as a manager?"

"He would continue in that capacity as well. The truth of it is, Leif has a mind to marry."

"I had not considered him," said Kate. Leif Holme was a comely man, in his early thirties, she reckoned, with a good reputation and a pleasant manner. He just might do. "Who is the woman?"

"Cecily Wheeldon." Holme nodded. "I see that frown. He knows he must bide his time, she is so recently widowed. Christmastide, was it not?"

"Forgive me, I should not judge. I do not know her well."

Thomas peered at her. "But?"

With her partner, she could be honest. "There is something sly about her. Too curious, too many questions about the guesthouse." Ever a concern, but more so at present. "I am not at ease in her company."

"Oh?" Thomas and his mistress were regular patrons of Kate's guesthouse. "Hm. I have my concerns as well. And I wondered—You have assured me in the past that you are well acquainted with the financial health of your clients, ensuring that no one has cause to betray a fellow they might encounter at the guesthouse."

Kate, Jennet, and Matt did indeed investigate potential clients. "You wish me to look into the widow Wheeldon? Something in particular?"

"I am concerned that she uses Jon Horner as a sort of factor, representing her in financial matters, but not precisely an accountant. I do not trust the man."

"Did he play that role when her husband was yet alive?"

"I don't believe so. I might be mistaken."

Jon Horner. Kate remembered the incident in the market, Horner and Merek. "I will see what I can learn."

"You are a good friend, Katherine."

"And if you do not like what you hear?"

"I will warn Leif. He might have his choice of young women in the city, being a Holme." A shrug. "I cannot tell whether he is in love with her, or merely keen to make his mark and settle down."

"He sounds an excellent candidate for us. Will he be comfortable coaxing money out of customers? He seems of a generous nature."

"Oh, he has a way with him, Leif does. He will enjoy it. And we want no one too greedy, eh?"

"That we do not." Kate smiled. "I believe we have a new clerk."

They shook on it and parted on that satisfied note.

With a firm hold on the hounds' leads, Kate picked her way down the poorly cleared path from Thomas Holme's house to Castlegate, avoiding the deeper drifts of snow. For a moment she enjoyed a sense of satisfaction. She liked working with Thomas Holme, and he clearly meant to continue the partnership.

"Katherine. What a pleasant surprise!" Her mother, Eleanor.

How did she know her daughter was next door? It was possible she might see Kate from her own kitchen doorway—had it been open. But on the morning after a heavy snowfall, with the wind still brisk?

Wrapped in a costly fur-lined cloak, Eleanor waved to her from across the fence. "Rose and Nan have swept a path for you. Come along!"

A passing whim to wave gaily and hurry on gave way to the practical. Sisters Agnes, Brigida, Clara, and Dina, lay sisters in the tradition of the beguines of Strasbourg who comprised her mother's Martha House, worked among the common folk in the city. In the course of a day they heard all the gossip. If anyone had heard about Lady Margery's presence, or that of her serving man, they would have. Though it was early in the day for them to have been out and returned. Still, her mother expected her now, and so she played the obedient daughter.

A fire blazed in the hearth and lamps lit up the well-proportioned hall, Kate's hall since shortly after she and Simon were wed until Michaelmas, just months ago. How she missed it. She watched Lille and Ghent take up their customary spot by the fire.

"You had business with Thomas Holme so early?" Eleanor asked as they settled on facing benches. "Or are you searching for the woman your knight's men seek? Lady Kirkby?"

A thrust to the heart of her troubles. Her mother had an uncanny aim. But of course Elric's men would inquire at a Martha House, an establishment that might take in a woman in peril. Even more so one founded by the mother of someone known to be Margery's friend.

"He is not my knight."

"As you wish." A little smile. "I see you know something of this," said Eleanor.

"Sir Elric did mention that Lady Kirkby might be in York."

"This is the lady who gave Marie and Petra the brooches?"

"How did you know that?" Delicate gold filigree nests with jets in the shapes of eggs tucked inside.

"Oh, Marie talks of her all the time, Lady Margery said this, wore that, she is beautiful, witty, kind, and loved Marie best of all." Eleanor smiled fondly. "Petra scowls every time, which is just what Marie intends. I am sorry that such a friend is in trouble. Would she seek you out?"

Was it a graver sin than usual to lie to the founder of a house of beguines? "Too dangerous. Too many know we are friends."

"Do you believe she is part of the rebellion?"

"I find it difficult to imagine either Lady Kirkby or her husband plotting to murder the king and his sons."

"But not impossible."

Escaping her mother's close regard, Kate rose and crossed the room as if to admire the statue of the Blessed Mother on the lady altar. "I cannot imagine the circumstances that would so change them from ambassadors of peace to murderers. *Has* a traveler come seeking sanctuary, Mother?"

"No," said Eleanor as she joined Kate, putting an arm round her. "But if she should, would you advise that we take her in?" she asked softly.

Kate met her mother's steady gaze. "If she should appear on your doorstep, get word to me at once."

"And keep her here until you arrive?"

"Yes."

"Would you then give her up to your—Sir Elric?"

"I would hear Margery's story before I decided. But that is not why I came," said Kate. "I hear a little from Sister Brigida, but I wished to see you. It has been too long."

"And so you see me." Eleanor gave her an affectionate shake. "We are comfortable here. I pray we can look forward to a long lease?"

"I am happy with the arrangement," said Kate. Though she wondered whether her mother would still prefer a more central location, such as the house on Low Petergate. Might they swap? She turned and took her mother's hands, smiling into her startlingly green eyes. "I have some news. As I've just informed Thomas Holme, I have paid off the last of Simon's debts."

Her mother's face lit up. "By the saints, you have done it, Katherine. I bow to you."

Kate impulsively embraced her mother.

"Well, well," Eleanor murmured as she patted her daughter's back, then withdrew her arms. "Now what? Will you wed? Now that your cousin William is to be mayor you will have your pick of the eligible men in the city—faith, in the shire."

"I am content as I am at present."

"What of Sir Elric?"

Hoping to hide the flush as she remembered the warmth of his hands around hers the previous evening, Kate moved on to examine a new tapestry hanging on the wall. "He is not quite as irritating as he was, but ours is not that sort of relationship, Mother."

"You may be the only person in York who does not see how he looks on you. But if you do not feel the same, well. What of Berend? Any word of him?"

"None."

"I am sorry." Spoken softly, her expression sincere.

Kate glanced away, fighting tears. "This is French?" she asked, fingering the heavy silk of the tapestry.

"It is. I saw it in a shop on the bridge and I could not resist. The colors are so lively, and the Virgin and Christ child so regal, yet tender."

"And I trust you haggled over the price until the shopkeeper sold it to you for half its worth?"

"Well, there are imperfections. Notice the angel's toes, and that thing that might have been intended to be a tree in the background?"

Kate laughed. "I do see. But is this behavior suitable to a beguine?"

"We work hard for our money."

"You are a wealthy widow, Mother."

"Founding a Martha House is costly. And you charge us a considerable rent."

Kate embraced her mother. "I tease you. I am glad to see the sparkle in your eyes. You seem content in this life."

"It suits me. I feel blessed." Eleanor pecked Kate on the cheek, then held her at arms' length. "So what is next? Will you still have some trade with Thomas Holme?"

"We expect one of our ships any day. Silks and spices. A contract I signed in my own name. Free and clear."

"Will your brother-in-law see it so?"

"I ensured that Lionel would have a separate contract with Thomas, though it is of short duration."

"Sufficient to appease him."

"For now."

"Clever. But what of this woman, Lady Kirkby? Can she harm you? You will not play the fool for her and risk everything, Katherine?"

Yes, yes, Mother, I am doing just that, she thought. Could she read Kate's heart? After all, she had carried in her womb the twin who lived on in Kate so long after his death, why doubt that she had some uncanny powers?

"Katherine?"

"Sir Elric vows to keep Lady Kirkby safe, unharmed, until he delivers her up to the king's men."

"Your voice quieted with those last words. You do not trust what will happen to her then."

"It is said that King Henry knows his reign will not be secure until Richard is dead, and that he sent one of his henchmen to Pontefract to see to it. The French king believes Richard is already dead. If King Henry has so little care for his cousin's life, I cannot think he would blink at ordering Lady Kirkby's death. Her husband was executed without trial."

"What did he do?"

Kate repeated what Elric had told her.

"*Mon Dieu,*" Eleanor exclaimed. "He was executed for committing an act of mercy?"

Kate knew the look in her mother's eyes, the sideways glance, the frown. A test, to prove to herself that her mother did not read her mind. "You *will* tell me if she comes to you, Mother?"

"Do you promise to follow your conscience?"

"In faith, Mother, I find I trip myself up if I attempt to go against what I know is right." Her mother's approving nod seemed a benediction. For a moment she felt good about hiding Margery.

A nod. "I will send you word, Katherine."

Kate thanked her mother and bent to slip the hounds' leads through their collars while she struggled with the urge to confide in Eleanor.

"I must say, I would very much like to meet this Margery."

Kate glanced up in time to catch her mother's sly smile and asked the question before her mother could ask it of her. "She is not already here?"

"No. I am not so cunning as that. I leave that to you."

Kate studied her mother's face, but saw no challenge. God be thanked.

⁂

As Kate walked back out onto Castlegate the sun broke through the clouds, turning the gardens across the way into a dazzling world of diamond-encrusted trees, shimmering in the updrafts from the river below. She was tempted to let the hounds romp in the snow, but she was anxious to talk to Griselde and Jennet, see whether they'd had any news of Carl, or rumors of Lady Margery's presence. And Berend. Where was he?

She was beset with questions and disturbing possibilities. Had Margery somehow drawn Berend into another plot dreamed up by her too-trusting husband? *May he rest in peace.* No, Berend would not be so foolish. Or would he? Even if he felt a debt to his former lord's heir? Whether Petra's insight came from something overheard or was truly a glimpse through the Sight, the "duty bound" was far more likely to have drawn Berend. God help him.

He is a seasoned warrior, her twin Geoff said in her mind. *You have trusted him with your life and those of your children. Why doubt him now?*

I don't doubt him, I fear for him, Geoff.

And?

And I'm angry. She felt her twin's nod. *I feel betrayed. He hid all this from me, his connection with Montagu, the gift of land. That is no small gesture from his former lord. Did he not trust me?*

I will be curious to hear how he explains himself.

If he returns.

Too restless to enjoy the snowy gardens, she headed back toward the center of the city.

On Coney Street, just beyond the Ouse Bridge, Ghent startled her with a bark. Lille followed suit. Their eyes were trained on a man standing at the corner of the church of St. Michael, beneath the eaves, in a shadow so dark Kate might never have noticed him without their warning. Something about him was familiar, and when he carefully raised a three-fingered hand to his mouth, Kate caught her breath. It was Berend, gesturing to the hounds to be quiet. They obeyed, looking away. Her heart raced. Berend, alive and well enough to be standing there, to respond quickly to what must have been an unexpected encounter. But why silence the hounds' greetings? And why was Berend now slowly backing round the corner of the church? Ah, he was not looking at her, but across the street as he disappeared.

Whispering a command to the hounds to continue walking, but slowly, Kate studied the passersby, then looked across the street. Two men in travel-stained clothes tensely watching the crowd, their eyes darting back and forth. She guided Lille and Ghent diagonally so they wound up close to them. She nodded to one as he doffed his hat and bowed to her.

Lancastrian livery. King's men, Geoff whispered in her head.

I noticed.

The second man bobbed his head, but was clearly impatient to be moving on, edgy. King's men tracking Berend and they'd lost the scent?

"Fine hunting dogs," said the more courteous one. "Unusual to see such fine beasts in the city."

Kate nodded. "I take pride in them. I trained them myself."

"But not here, I warrant. I hear the North in your speech."

"This *is* the North," she said. "Good day to you. God speed."

He was bowing when she moved off, Lille and Ghent obediently trotting on either side, though she sensed their confusion, which only echoed her own. Why had Berend been lurking just there? Was he observing the king's men? Or was she wrong about the connection? Perhaps they were simply passing through the city on some business related to the Lancastrian properties. Or searching for Lady Margery, not Berend. As she crossed into St. Helen's Square, Kate paused, considering the York Tavern. The yard was empty at the moment.

The quiet before the bustle of the midday diners. She might catch Sir Elric, find out whether he knew anything about the two men she had encountered. As she skirted round the cemetery in the middle of the square and crossed into the yard, she was busy fabricating a story about why the men made her uneasy without mentioning Berend. But it was simple—he would want to know.

The taverner Colin Merchet welcomed Kate as she stepped through the doorway into the public room, but shook his head at the hounds. "Forgive me, Mistress Clifford, but we permit no dogs on the premises. My granddam will not have them." He was a pleasant-faced man, short, muscular, with the beginnings of a prosperous belly. Fair hair curled round his face, damp beneath a felt cap, a contrast to his dark eyes and ruddy complexion.

"Then would you kindly ask Sir Elric to come out to the yard?" asked Kate. "I will wait there."

"I would, but he is not here," said Colin with an apologetic shrug.

"Ah. Then if you will tell him I wish to speak to him."

Colin was about to answer when he glanced at someone who had just come up behind Kate and said, "And just like that, he appears."

Turning, she found herself face to face with Sir Elric, who smiled as he greeted her with warmth, then crouched to greet the hounds. There was a time not so long in the past when they would have growled at him as they had the king's man, baring their teeth, sensing Kate's distrust. But as she'd grown more trusting of the knight, so had they. They sniffed his face, the hands he rested on his thighs, and then Ghent nudged him with his head.

"Do give their ears a rub. They sense Colin Merchet's disapproval and could use some affection."

"It's not I who disapproves," Colin protested.

Elric glanced up at the taverner. "Disapproval? Merchet, how can you look on this fine pair and not admire them? What problem do you foresee?" He rubbed Ghent's ears, then Lille's.

"They are dogs," Colin said with a shrug.

"They are indeed. Your point?"

"We do not allow dogs in the tavern. Dame Bess's orders."

"No wonder the stable lad is so busy chasing rats," Elric muttered. After one more affectionate rub for each, praising Lille and Ghent as both brave and gentle, Elric rose and turned to Colin. "I vouch for these noble hounds,

A MURDERED PEACE

Merchet. They are better trained, better behaved than most humans, and are worthy guests of your tavern."

"I pray you forgive me, Sir Elric, but my granddam has never permitted dogs in here."

"If you turn them away, you turn me away, for Mistress Clifford is my dear friend."

His dear friend, Geoff repeated in her head with a chuckle.

You may be amused, but his friendship has proven useful, she noted to Geoff.

"My granddam will have my head," said Colin, shaking his head at Elric.

"Then you have little to lose, for she will either way. You might recall that Dame Bess was eager for my patronage. She will not be so sanguine when I ask her to give me the bill. But so be it." Elric shrugged and turned to Kate, his back to Colin, his eyes laughing. "You had suggested an alternative lodging in the city. Is it still available?" Clearly he expected to win this.

"It is indeed," she said, making as if to depart with Lille and Ghent.

"No, I pray you, be not so hasty. I will make this right," said Colin as he stepped aside, motioning them to enter. "Forgive my hesitation, Mistress Clifford."

Kate inclined her head, acknowledging his apology.

"I regret that I returned to the inn only to fetch something from my chamber," said Elric. "I must be away to a meeting."

"A pity," said Kate.

"Indeed." Elric bowed. "I would fain have whiled away an hour in your fair company."

"But it is no matter. I had a question, that is all." She drew him away from the hovering taverner, briefly describing the two men.

Elric thanked her for the news. "If they are the king's men we're expecting, I am glad to be forewarned."

"So you know nothing of them?"

"No. I will find out and send you word." He quickly bowed to her and strode off across the tavern to the corridor beyond.

"I pray you, Mistress Clifford, do have a seat by the fire and dry your skirts. I will bring you a bowl of ale."

It was inviting, now she was here. "And some water for Lille and Ghent?" Kate asked.

"Of course," said Colin, now eager to serve. "In truth I found it hard to part with my own dogs when I inherited the tavern. Granddad had not warned me that Granddam's rule would apply to *my* dogs." He bustled away, returning with the ale, quickly followed by a large bowl of water, and two sizable ham hocks on a platter. Ghent and Lille sat up sharply as they smelled the peace offering.

Kate thanked the taverner for his generosity and nodded at the bowl of ale in her hands, which she found a perfect blend of bitter and sweet, and thick yet not chewy. "Your granddad's recipe?"

Colin nodded with pride. "Best in shire, maybe best in the realm. Granddad was so revered for his ale that folk came from all corners of the North to attend his requiem."

Tom Merchet had died before Kate arrived in York, but she had never heard a cross word about the man, and there was no question this was the best ale she'd ever tasted. The Merchets were respected in York. She had been remiss in not befriending them. She must correct that. Shaking her head at Colin's offer of more ale, Kate was gathering the hounds' leads when Elric returned, nodding with satisfaction to see Lille and Ghent finishing off their treats.

"You're a good man, Merchet," he said, just as the outer door opened and Douglas, Stephen, and Wulf entered the tavern.

Elric greeted them with a puzzled shake of his head. "I thought to meet you later."

"We have something for you," said Douglas. "Thought it should not wait."

As Kate bent to slip the hounds' leads into their collars she overheard a little of Stephen's report to Elric, her ears pricking up at "Lancastrian livery" and "Ouse Bridge."

Elric caught her eye and motioned her over.

"They would state only that they came to York in pursuit of three folk, a woman and two men, perhaps her menservants," Douglas was saying.

Margery, Carl, and—? Kate tried to quiet her mind so she could listen.

"The important thing is the king's men are in York, and need watching," Elric said to his men. "Why is Kevin not with you? Did he follow them?"

"We've not seen him this morning, captain," said Stephen. "We're hoping he's not run off with young Marie Neville. Dame Katherine will have her hounds after him if that's so, eh?" He grinned at her.

"Poor man. He would soon come back of his own accord. The child has sharp teeth," Kate said, and was laughing with them when she noticed a shadowy figure standing quite still in the kitchen doorway. Guessing it to be Old Bess, she thought it wise to take her leave. "Forgive me, but I must be off."

Kate glanced back as she led Lille and Ghent toward the outer door and saw that it was indeed Bess Merchet, now standing in the room, the ribbons on her white cap trembling as she looked aghast at the dogs. She called sharply for Colin.

As the door closed behind Kate she heard Elric using his most silken tone with the elderly taverner. Crossing the yard, she smiled to herself, imagining him charming Old Bess out of her anger.

Old Bess is hearing too much. How much does Elric tell her?

I thought you trusted him, Geoff.

So far as a knight can be trusted. He owes everything to his lord. As does Berend?

As he did, Geoff. I would think Berend owes nothing to his lord's son. Why would he answer his summons?

If he did, Kate. We don't know.

God help her. Berend's disappearance was painful, but Elric's revelations, and seeing Berend this morning, having him flee from her, the possibility that he was running from the king's men . . . She did not know what she felt. Anger? Frustration? Fear?

Dare I trust Elric? With my secret guest?

I suppose you must wait and see. At least you know you can trust Kevin, Geoff assured her. *He might be of help, and I've no doubt he will warn you if his captain does anything that might bring you harm.*

But would he disobey the command to search for Lady Margery?

Ah. That is the question.

Kate thought not. Nor would she ask it of him.

The wind had begun to pick up and she hurried the hounds down Stonegate and round the corner to the guesthouse. She wanted to find out whether anyone in Lancastrian livery had come there with questions about either Berend or Margery.

5

QUESTIONS OF TRUST

Fragrant warmth welcomed Kate as she opened the door to the guesthouse hall. As she crossed the room toward the kitchen she paused, hearing a familiar voice behind her. "Phillip?" She checked her progress and turned back to the door of Clement and Griselde's bedchamber.

"Mistress Clifford, I can explain," said Griselde, hurrying out from the kitchen to intercept.

But Kate was already at the door, pushing it open to reveal her ward Phillip sitting beside Clement in bed, both bent over a portable writing desk. Abacus, tally sticks, ledgers—it was clear her ward was assisting Clement with Kate's accounts. The boy had a skill with numbers and had kept his mother's accounts from an early age. He currently kept the accounts of the master mason to whom he was apprenticed as a stoneworker in the minster yard, but Kate had gently refused his offer to work on hers, for many reasons.

Phillip was intent on completing an entry in the ledger, but Clement glanced up and cleared his throat, nudging the lad.

Quietly, Kate asked, "Phillip, how long have you been assisting Clement?"

Only now did the boy pull his eyes away from the ledger and straighten, his eyes begging her for clemency. "A while. But Master Hugh is pleased with my work in the stoneyard."

"Are you still keeping his accounts as well?"

Phillip nodded. "Just the daily tallies. I do them after Mistress Grantham serves dinner, before I return to the stoneyard to complete my assignments for the day. Please don't be angry with Master Clement."

"I am not your master, dear boy," Clement said gruffly.

Poor Clement. His health continued its steady decline. The only color in the old man's wrinkled face were unhealthy red spots on his cheeks, and the smells of sickness soured the room despite Griselde's efforts to mask them with fragrant wood burning in the brazier and dried herbs hanging near the door and over the bed.

Kate bent to kiss Phillip on the forehead. "I am not angry, but worried. When do you rest? When do you sleep? And why are you not at work in the stoneyard this morning?" She did not need to ask why he had not told her. He knew full well she was already concerned that his accounting work for the master mason added too many hours to his day as an apprentice.

"I completed my morning's work betimes. I am well, Dame Katherine. I am. And Clement needed me. It is not arduous, there are not nearly so many entries as with Master Grantham's accounts."

"The guesthouse and my businesses? I doubt that," said Kate. Though Hugh Grantham was a merchant as well as a master mason, he limited his trading, of necessity.

Phillip bowed his head and gave a little shrug.

Clement patted the boy's hand. "It is my doing, Mistress Clifford. I asked if he might help me. I could not think of anyone else I might trust."

That was the other reason Kate had refused Phillip's offer to keep her books. When she had learned the extent of her late husband's debts, she had received promises from her fellow executors, Thomas Holme and Thomas Graa, that Simon's secret was safe with them; particularly safe from the guild and her brother-in-law, Lionel. Clement had taken on the burden of secrecy as a penance for having kept Simon's situation a secret from her. Such secrecy was a not something she wanted burdening her ward.

"I would have preferred that you consulted me, Clement." She waved him quiet as he began to excuse himself. "The deed is done, but Phillip cannot continue here indefinitely. He has worked hard to become an apprentice at the minster. This is a great opportunity for him to realize his dream."

"Dame Katherine," Phillip pleaded with his eyes.

"It takes you away from the work you love." Kate smoothed his hair.

A reluctant nod.

Behind Kate, Griselde moaned. "Mistress Clifford, I pray—"

"Do not fret, Griselde. Your role in this household is not in jeopardy. I value both of you, and I have long thought Clement needed an assistant. We must put our heads together and find one for him, eh?"

"And until you do?" Phillip asked.

"You may continue to assist until I do." His smile and Clement's tears were Kate's reward. But at what cost to the boy?

She nodded to all of them and withdrew. Clearly it was up to her to find a replacement. Clement had been largely housebound for several years, so any clerks he might have known were either employed or gone. And he would have no idea of their allegiances. She must find someone who could be trusted to be discreet. A challenge.

She found the hall empty, the hounds gone. Out in the kitchen, Lille and Ghent were sharing a plate of cold meats—at this rate they would soon be too fat to run. She stepped over to where the young manservant Seth was demonstrating to Lady Margery how to cut up vegetables. In a plain gown, simple leather shoes, and hair hidden beneath a short veil secured at the nape of her neck while she worked, Margery, or "Mary," looked small and insignificant.

Seth glanced up with a little frown. "I should have told you about Phillip."

"But you did not want to be a tit-tattle," said Kate.

He shrugged. "No excuse."

"What's done is done. Why does Clement have need of Phillip?"

"It is his memory, Mistress Clifford," said Griselde from the doorway. "It slips and slides, upending his tallies, confusing him. And it's not drink. He's had little ale or wine. He wants his wits about him."

Seeing the sagging shoulders and the pain in the housekeeper's eyes, Kate took Griselde's arm and led her to a bench, where she settled beside her.

"You must keep me informed, else how can I help? How often does Clement leave his bed?"

"Not often. His legs are so weak and twisted. I can see it's painful for him to pull himself along on the crutches Seth made for him."

"I'd hoped they'd help," said Seth.

"They do. But he tires so easily." There was a catch in Griselde's voice.

"You did your best, Seth," said Kate. She had a thought. "You are so handy with carpentry. I wonder whether you might be able to replicate Beatrice Paris's chair." She told them about the wheeled chair that had allowed her neighbor's wife to move about the house.

Griselde's face brightened. "A wheeled chair! I do believe he would perk up if he could move about more easily."

"I could make one." Seth loped over to the corner of the kitchen where he slept on a pallet. From a shelf he plucked a wax tablet and stylus, sat down on a bench and began to draw. "The wooden wheels on the old barrow in the garden shed might do. What sort of chair did they use?"

"It was cobbled together from parts of the cart, as I recall."

"We can do better," said Seth, glancing up at Griselde.

"You are thinking of the old chair in our bedchamber?" she nodded. "I used to set it out in the garden so he might have some fresh air. An ugly chair, but serviceable."

"Just the thing," said Seth.

"Is it just the accounting work that challenges Clement?"

Griselde shook her head. "He has been trying to recall something he once learned about Berend, something he has a feeling might suggest where he has gone. Master Simon was concerned that you had hired a criminal out of sympathy for his war wounds. He wanted to know more about Berend. Clement discovered something but failed to write it down, and now he cannot quite grasp it—it stays just out of reach. Something about a place. That he owned, mayhap? But not his parents' tavern?" That was where Berend had learned to cook. "A small farm, he thought."

Her late husband had learned of Berend's gift of land from his former lord? The one she had just learned of? "Did he not share the information with you when he first heard of it?" Kate asked Griselde.

"No. He says he feared I would tell you Simon was interfering. He remembers that part." Griselde sighed. "Maybe once he's able to move about more in the wheeled chair the fog in his head will clear."

"I pray it does," said Kate. She wondered what else he knew about Berend. "But you did not come for all this, I trow."

Kate nodded toward Lady Margery. "Has Phillip met the new maidservant?"

"No. Mary has stayed out of sight," said Griselde.

"I am becoming well acquainted with the storeroom," Margery said, motioning with the cutting knife toward the curtained doorway to one side of the kitchen. "I have a mind to make up my bed in there tonight. But I am grateful."

"No word of Carl?"

Both Margery and Griselde shook their heads.

"Jennet stopped by to ask whether he had arrived, and brought this gown for me." Margery held up the skirts and bowed.

Kate had wondered where she had procured the gown of undyed wool. "I trust she included a linen underdress?" Or it would be scratchy to a woman accustomed to fine clothes.

"Bless her, she did," said Margery.

Without the red hair and bright clothes, the noblewoman was quite transformed. Only those who knew her well might pause before her, wondering what had brought her to mind. Still, Elric knew her well enough. As did all three of her wards.

As Margery turned back to her work, Kate softly instructed Griselde to keep Mary hard at work. The more she inhabited the role of Mary the maidservant, the less likely she would be to move and behave as a noblewoman. And she must earn her keep, she told her quietly. They were risking everything for her.

"Her hands . . ."

"We want them rough," said Kate.

"Of course."

Seth glanced back at them. "You told me to remind you of two things you must tell Mistress Clifford."

Griselde's hands flew to her face and she muttered something about her failing memory. "Oh dear me, forgive me, Mistress Clifford. I meant to tell you something that slipped my mind last night. Come, have a seat. Seth, some ale, if you would."

Kate was about to decline, but, seeing the worry etched in the lines on her housekeeper's face she thought she might need it. "Tell me."

"There is a spice seller with a stall next to Old Cob the eel man in the market. Merek, he is called. Yesterday, when I bought the eel for your celebration, this Merek wanted to know why he's not seen Berend in the market of late."

Kate did want that ale after all. "I've noticed him." Just this morning, in fact. "A sly one, he seemed to me."

"That would be him. Berend had warned me to have nothing to do with either the man or his goods."

"Did he? Why?"

"Said he was the devil, out for souls, not money."

"Berend said that?"

"He did, and with such a scowl that I've heeded his advice without question."

"But yesterday Merek spoke to you?"

"He did. And as Old Cob wrapped the eels I'd purchased the dear man leaned close and said under his breath, 'Begging your pardon, Goodwife Griselde, but most folk at the market have naught to do with yon merchant. Too many questions about our friends. He is cooking up a pot of poison, that one. Just a warning.'"

"So Old Cob knows his reputation." Kate nodded. "Did you say anything to the spice seller, Griselde?"

"I said I could not see as it was his concern where you sent your cook and for how long." Griselde gave an indignant sniff.

"Bless you. That was the best answer."

The wrinkles rearranged themselves in a bright smile. "I hoped it was the right thing to say. Seth thought it was." She nodded to him.

"Come, sit with us a moment," Kate said to the young man, who was hovering over Margery's hesitant gestures with the knife. Jennet was teaching Seth how to listen and watch, skills Kate valued in her servants, so she asked, "What did you notice about this Merek?"

Seth was quick to bring a stool to the table and sit down, leaning toward her, eager to add his observations. "He watched us all the while we were in the market. I noticed him when we arrived, trying to listen in to Goodwife Griselde's chatter with Old Cob—not that there was anything to hear, except that the earl's men would be dining with you at the guesthouse."

Griselde frowned. "Perhaps I should not—"

"No." Kate touched the woman's folded hands. "I am glad he knows the stature of our dinner guests. He might be less likely to meddle." She motioned to Seth to go on.

"Merek watched us even after we moved on," said Seth. "Whenever I glanced back toward him his beady eyes would be just flicking off, pretending I hadn't caught him. He went hurrying away when we were leaving the market."

"With someone?" Kate asked.

"Not that I could see. I slipped round behind a stall to watch him. He was in a hurry, dodging round people."

"Good work," said Kate. She turned back to Griselde. "You had two things to tell me—the second?"

"The visitors, yes. We had visitors, well-spoken men, though not of noble status, two of them, travel-worn, but their clothes were of fine cloth and leather, and beneath their cloaks I noticed badges, livery, but you know I am not good at recognizing the houses."

Kate described the two men she'd encountered by St. Michael's near Ouse Bridge.

"The very men. They said they were stopping at all the inns and guesthouses in the city to warn us of two men and a woman looking for a place to hide. One of the men was probably limping on his left leg. And a woman, not young, but still handsome, well dressed."

Margery had gone quite still.

Lady Margery, Carl, and—Berend? "What did they want with them?" Kate asked.

"They warned me not to give them shelter. That they are wanted by King Henry and it would be treason to help them."

"Was there another man in your company, Mary?" Kate asked.

Without turning to look at Kate, Margery said, "We did walk for a while with a farmer coming to market."

Was Margery lying? Did she come with Berend? "Did they say anything else?" she asked Griselde.

"They warned me to insist on seeing whoever wanted lodging, not agree to make arrangements with a third person." Griselde smiled. "Of course they could not know how careful we are."

"Did you say any more to them?"

"They asked whether we had rooms available. I explained we have no rooms to let at present, so we were in no danger of accepting such lodgers. Then they wanted to know who was lodging here. I told them that we obey all the laws of the city regarding notifying the council of strangers biding here."

Which was rare indeed. "And they accepted that?"

A sniff. "What could they say? They had no standing here."

"Good. You must send Seth to tell me if the men return, or if Carl appears. At once."

Griselde frowned. "Should I keep the men here until you come? What if—"

"No. I just want to know. Seth, watch which way they go as they leave, if you would."

"Do you know who the men were, Mistress Clifford?" asked Seth. Too eagerly.

"Your visitors might have been the king's men as their badges were Lancastrian livery. The king is calling on Lancastrian retainers from all his holdings, so not all wear the royal livery. But now you know, so tell me if you see any others with such badges, or wearing blue and white livery, for that matter."

"God help me," Margery whispered.

Griselde crossed herself. "And Merek the spice seller?"

"Next time, ignore him."

"Gladly," said Griselde. "Cock of the walk, he counts himself."

Seth did not look so sanguine. "He should be watched."

Kate promised him that he would be, by Sir Elric's men. Rising, she thanked all three, then called to Lille and Ghent and began to depart.

"About Phillip," said Griselde, hurrying to escort Kate to the door, "I had not thought how it would rob him of time to rest." She searched Kate's expression, clearly looking for forgiveness.

Kate understood why they had done it, but a woman must always be firmer with her business associates than a man needed to be, else people would take advantage. "I was surprised you risked keeping it from me. I might not be so understanding next time." She was fond of Griselde, and compassionate toward Clement, but disappointed, and wanted them to know that. She put up her hand to quiet another apology. "I will find help for Clement. Until then, Phillip may continue to help him. But you will not send for him. Let him come in his own time."

Chastened, Griselde nodded. "God go with you, Mistress Clifford."

"And you, Griselde." *And with us all.*

⁕◦◦⁕

Back at her own home, Kate led Lille and Ghent round the back of the house to the kitchen, where she found Jennet standing over the fire, her freckled face flushed from the heat and the vigor with which she was stirring. "Marie will have my hide if she discovers I let her fine stew stick to the bottom of the pot." With Berend gone, Marie and Jennet were sharing kitchen duties, Marie assembling something for Jennet to cook before leaving for her lessons. "I don't know how Berend does three things at once. I cannot seem to watch the yard *and* keep dinner from burning." With her forearm she blotted the sweat from her brow, taking a moment to look Kate up and down. "You might want to dry your skirts and boots before you go up to talk to him."

"Him?"

"Berend."

"He's here?" Kate went back to the door, half-expecting to see the king's men. But the yard was empty.

"Up in your chamber, I should think, not in the yard," said Jennet. "He doesn't think I saw him, but I *told* you making the gate at the bottom of the steps open with a creak would stand us in good stead. I caught a glimpse of him as he was climbing up."

Pray God he meant to tell her who he'd been watching, and why he'd left without a word, how he was tied to the uprising.

Jennet tilted her head, studying Kate. "You are not half so surprised as I expected. You knew he was back?"

"I did not expect him to come to the house. But yes, I saw him earlier, near Ouse Bridge." Kate told her of the encounter.

Jennet muttered a curse. "King's men. I don't like the sound of that. Nor his stealing up the steps without even peeking into the kitchen. But he's up there waiting for you. I've had my ears pricked since then. He's not come down."

Kate went to the fire and shook out her skirts, stalling for time to resolve her roiling emotions—joy that he had come to her, fear for him, dread about what he would reveal.

"Well?" said Jennet. "Aren't you going to tell me?"

"We need to listen for Berend," said Kate, taking care to speak softly. "Or for whoever might follow him. Where's Matt? Did you alert him?"

A nod. "He's in the hall. When I went in to warn him we got to talking—well, whispering so Berend could not overhear us from above. That's when this stuck to the bottom of the pot." Jennet muttered a curse and resumed stirring. "I do not want to think what punishment awaits me. That child is cunning." But she was smiling. Both girls loved Jennet and would do anything to be permitted to follow her on her perambulations around York and out the gates, checking in with her eyes and ears. No matter how difficult the lives Jennet described, the girls thought it all exciting. And, in truth, both had lived through difficult times before they had come into Kate's household that hardened them in ways that broke her heart. But Jennet agreed with her that they must now be kept safe and away from danger.

"If a stranger comes asking questions, you know what to do," said Kate. "And don't let the hounds fool you into feeding them—they've just had a feast at the York Tavern, and more at the guesthouse." She returned their leads to their hook by the door.

Jennet whistled. "The York? Old Bess permitted it?"

"I will tell you all about it. And I have a new task for you. Learn what business Cecily Wheeldon has with Jon Horner. Or, rather, what role he plays for her." She met Jennet's curious gaze. "No, not a prospective client. Thomas Holme's nephew is interested in the widow."

"Horner's slippery as an eel. I look forward to it."

Still Kate hesitated. "I don't know what to expect of Berend. He seemed a stranger out on the street."

"Not to the hounds."

"No, not to them." Kate looked over at Lille and Ghent, stretched out near the fire, calm, satisfied after their outing and unexpected treat. She had trained them well. They had seen Berend, known him, obeyed his signal, no hesitation.

"Go on, then," Jennet said softly. "At least he's alive, and moving about on his own two feet."

She was right. Many a night Kate had stared at the ceiling worrying about Berend, what had become of him, fearing that she might never know. No matter what he told her, it was better than forever wondering. She went out into the yard, stepping back close to the wide trunk of the oak, seeing that no one was visible on the second story landing and the doors were shut. Hers was nearest the stairs, then the girls' room, and a spare for Phillip or guests. Each had a small shuttered window looking out onto the landing, and hers had another on the street. None of the shutters were open. Even the snow on the railing was undisturbed. One would never know she had a visitor. Crossing back to the bottom of the steps, she noticed wet prints leading up, but none of them were complete prints, certainly not enough to tell anything about Berend's condition, whether he was limping. She almost wished Matt were not so efficient about clearing the snow from the steps.

You are stalling, Geoff whispered in her mind.

She was. All she need do was go up, see him for herself.

In her old house, the steps up to the solar were inside the hall, an added security; here, the stairs to the second story chambers were outside the house. In warm weather they might keep the door near the foot of the steps open, so that anyone in the hall might see someone approaching, but in winter that was not feasible. So they'd installed a noisy gate at the bottom, not locked, but hung on its hinge so that it gave a loud, harsh squeak when swung open—unless one knew how to lift it and swing it out. Berend knew to do this, but Jennet said she'd heard the squeak; he'd intended to alert whoever was there of his presence. Heartened, she climbed, avoiding the two creaking risers rigged by Matt and Jennet in case an intruder managed to open the gate silently.

She paused on the landing before her own door, taking a deep breath, then drew her dagger from the hidden scabbard in her skirt and kicked the door wide. Just in case.

"It's me. Berend." The familiar voice came from the far corner.

Strange how even now the mere sound of his voice comforted Kate. But she reminded herself to stay alert. As her eyes adjusted to the gloom, she saw that he had the street-side shutters slightly opened and stood where he could watch the busy intersection of Petergate and Stonegate. She stepped into the room and closed the door behind her.

"I expected you sooner," he said. "I watched you arrive a while ago."

Kate told him to step away from the window. "I want some light to see you while we talk."

Berend moved aside as she crossed the room, still holding her dagger at the ready, and opened the shutters.

He eased himself down onto the bench at the foot of Kate's bed with a soft sigh and bent and flexed his left knee a few times, then began to rub it. Limping on his left leg—yes, he would be. So he must be the one seen traveling with a woman and another man. How many trios like that could there be on the road to York?

"An injury?" she asked.

"You know what days on horseback are like."

She crouched down in front of him, lifting his chin. "A new scar beneath your eye."

"It is nothing." The angry flesh twitched as he spoke, belying his casual tone.

Compared to missing toes, fingers, ear, that was true. But the cut had come perilously close to his left eye, and the flesh was still red, angry, likely still painful. He should be applying a comfrey or arnica cream to draw out the heat and keep the skin soft to minimize the scar so that it did not pull. But he did not seem in the mood to welcome advice, no matter how well meant. "Left knee, left eye. Battle wounds?" she asked.

"The knee is stiff from travel, that is all."

His voice was hoarse, and Berend sagged as if he carried a great weight on his shoulders. Sitting back on her heels, Kate studied his shadowed eyes, sunken cheeks, filth caked into lines of weariness. His tunic, shirt, hose, cloak all needed laundering. He stank. As had Margery.

"You left abruptly without a word to me," she said. "Why?"

He fixed his eyes on the floor just past his feet. "So I need not explain."

That he had lost his bearings? That he meant to slaughter the king's sons? She prayed he had not so betrayed his soul. "Why are you here now?"

"The Lancastrians I was watching—they are searching for someone," he said. "Did they question you? Is it Margery Kirkby they seek?"

He had come to find out what the Lancastrians had said to her, nothing more. Her disappointment surprised her. Kate did not know what she had expected—had she thought he would say he'd come because he needed to see her, make sure she was safe, that when he'd seen her on Coney Street his heart had called him to her? Was she so foolish?

Margery Kirkby was uppermost on his mind. She was curious about that, curious about many things. She wanted to learn as much as she could before she told him what she knew of the men, and Margery, not simply spit it out and risk that he would vanish again.

"The spice seller, Merek," she said. "What is he to you?"

Berend glanced up, surprised. "Is he still in York?" He nodded as if that was good news.

So he did know him. "He is. And he seems far too interested in you—where you've been, how long ago you left," she said. "Shall we trade stories? You first." Kate leaned against the wall, too agitated to sit, her arms crossed, holding her breath as she watched Berend, who worked his stiff knee.

In the silence, she could hear a cart clatter by down on the street, a woman shouting, "Stay out in the middle, you blind arse!"

Berend looked up and met Kate's eyes, grinning at the woman's cry. Kate did not mirror his smile.

"Merek," she said.

"I know him," he admitted. "From long ago. He carried messages for the lord I served at the time, but I knew him to be slippery. He would not flinch about betraying anyone for a price. He came here on a mission for the son of my former lord."

So Merek had come here in the service of John Montagu, Earl of Salisbury. Kate had not expected that. "Is he in York because of you?"

Berend winced as he stretched out his left leg. Kate fought her instinct to offer to send for Matt's cousin Bella, a skilled healer.

"Well? Is he?"

"I was his original purpose. Or one of them. Had delivering the message to me been his sole purpose, he would be gone. I fe—I thought he would have been long gone."

Feared he would be long gone, that is what he'd begun to say, what his face expressed, and the relief when she'd said he was still in York. "He frightened Griselde with questions about you," she said.

Berend leaned back and rubbed his eyes. "I will talk to him."

"So he came to find you for the Earl of Salisbury? What was the message?"

He looked stricken. "You already knew of my connection to Salisbury?"

So it was true. "That you were in his father's household. Yes, I just learned of it, and I know that Salisbury was one of the leaders in the plot to assassinate Henry and his sons. Were you part of that?"

A subtle squirm. "I would never agree to the murder of children. His sons are boys—fourteen, thirteen, eleven, eight. It was madness from the beginning. To think they might put Richard back on the throne by committing such a heinous act—madness." Berend sat up straight enough now, his eyes on fire, challenging her and all the world for questioning his honor. But he knew much, that was plain. And the question had discomfited him.

Kate felt she was at last seeing his sincere emotions—outrage, pain, exhaustion. And something else—guilt? For what? He had been among the rebels. She sank down on a bench across from him and leaned back against the wall, closing her eyes. "I could not imagine you harming a child," she admitted. "But when you left without a word I doubted what we had. What was the message?"

"The earl wanted something of me, but when I learned what it was, I refused him. I did not mean to cause you pain."

"Refused to murder the king's sons?' she asked softly.

Her question was met with silence.

"What are we doing, Berend?" When he still did not answer, she opened her eyes and sat up, reaching for his hands, his scarred, strong hands. For the first time in her experience they were cold. He looked away, as if rebuking her gesture of friendship. "You are in danger," she said. "I know that much. I know the king believes you were part of Salisbury's conspiracy."

"Sir Elric told you that?"

"Yes."

Still he did not look her in the eye. "What do you know of the Lancastrians we saw today?" he asked.

She told him what little she knew, including the description the men had given Griselde. "It was you, wasn't it? With Margery and her manservant?"

Berend bowed his head, whispering a curse.

"What has this to do with you?" she asked.

"Nothing but that I chose the worst time to return." His voice was rough with weariness.

"Because you are known to be connected to the Montagu family, now marked as traitors to King Henry? And traveling with Lady Margery Kirkby, whose husband was marked as a traitor?" She did not mention Berend's known itinerary, the most damning piece.

He withdrew his hands—gently, not in anger—and looked her in the eyes. "Salisbury, Montagu, Kirkby. It is dangerous to be associated with any of those names at present. Even you look at me differently."

"I am angry about how you left. And—what I said—I doubted everything, the trust I thought we had. And what I've learned about you since—there is so much I did not know."

"You have been investigating my past as you do potential customers?"

"No! It is not like that. Your disappearance has been noticed. People talk. And I feared for you."

"How much do you know?"

She chose which details to share. "I know that at one time you served John, Baron Montagu. I know that he left you a piece of land in his will. Which made me wonder why you came to work for me. A cook who owns land? Why would you so humble yourself?"

"Land is only so good as the people who work it. I'm a much better cook than a farmer. My property is better off in the hands of my tenant. All revenue goes right back into the land, the crops, the house."

"That is where you go when you leave for a few days?"

"Sometimes. If I intend to stay sober. My tenant is a grim, God-fearing man and his wife finds me frightening on my calmest days. I would not impose on them when I drink until my devils take over."

Kate did not like the ache with which she imagined this life she knew nothing about, these people who knew things about Berend she had never guessed—Montagu, Merek, the tenants. Why had she thought a servant would bare his soul to her?

Because he had been so much more than a servant.

"I always meant to tell you." He leaned his forearms on his thighs, his face close to hers, his hands pressed together as if praying for her to believe him. "But I knew you would find it suspect that a propertied man would wish to work as a cook. *I* would. For once, my courage failed me. Am I correct in guessing that Sir Elric is the source of this information as well?"

"Yes."

Nights of worrying about him, the hollow ache of his absence, the memories like open wounds, burning when touched. Kate reached out and cradled Berend's face in her hands.

"Why did you return to York?"

She felt him flinch.

"I count this city my home. Where else would I go?"

The city, not her household. She tried not to react. "But you said you are not back to stay."

"Not yet."

"So why are you here *now*?"

Berend moved her hands from his face and held them. "I did not expect the king's men to be in the city. Not yet."

"Sir Elric believes Margery Kirkby to be in the city. Why? She has no family here."

"Why do they want her?"

Just ask him if he brought her here, and why, Geoff hissed in her mind. *And why he was in Pontefract, Oxford, Cirencester.*

Be quiet.

"Something to do with her husband's part in the plot," she said.

"I still doubt that Thomas Kirkby was part of it," he said. "He is—was so determined to find a peaceful way forward. But then I hardly believed it when I heard of the plot." Berend turned toward the window, his head tilted toward his missing ear. "Do you know whether anyone has seen her?"

Kate knew that posture. He was thinking. "Not that I know of. Why are you here now, in this room?"

"I told you. To find out what you know about Lady Margery. And whether anyone is asking about me."

Now. Tell him now, Geoff insisted.

"I've already told you about Merek," she said.

"Anyone else?"

"Unfortunately for you, my cousin William's wife considers your absence a personal slight. Isabella Frost is furious that you are not available to cook for William's mayoral feast, and she's made moan to all the wives of the council."

"Overbearing shrew."

"You are not the first person to call her that," said Kate, trying to lighten the blow. For she saw that it had been a blow to him. "And Sir Elric has been asking as well. How can I help you?"

He turned back to her, pressed her hands, then let go to knead his leg. "You cannot. It is too dangerous. You have too much to lose. The children need you. I pray I have not brought attention to you."

Knowing how he cared for Petra, Marie, and Phillip, Kate could not believe that Berend would risk endangering them merely to question her about Lady Margery. And what of Lady Margery seeking sanctuary with her? Is it possible he did not know? "If that concerns you, why did you come? The truth, Berend."

A fleeting smile. "I trusted that once I slipped away you would be forewarned, take precautions to protect the household from king's men, or men pretending to be his. It would be wise."

Kate agreed. "The king's men will hear soon enough that I am Margery's friend. You cannot protect me from that."

"No. At the moment I have all I can do to protect myself."

"And your traveling companions?"

He had averted his eyes again, but she knew that fixed jaw. "The less you know, the better."

"Damn you, Berend. Help me help you."

He bowed his head. "You have. Bless you. Thank you for warning me."

Kate touched his shoulder. "Petra misses you so. She wants everything to be as it was. So do I."

"The royal cousins have murdered peace." He raised his head, rubbing his eyes as if that might revive him. Or had there been tears? No, his eyes were steady as he gazed on her with the saddest countenance. "Wresting the crown from Richard was the worst thing Henry might have done for the realm. With the uprising—He cannot allow Richard to live. So now he not only plucked the crown from the anointed king but he will have his blood."

"God help us."

"We must help ourselves. Look to the children. Keep them safe."

"I will guard them with my life."

Berend rose with a grunt—the leg must be far more painful than he would admit—and limped to the window staying out of sight as best he could while peering out. "Would you check to see if my path is clear to slip away?"

He was leaving so soon, too soon. Kate felt in her bones the danger he faced. Would they ever speak again? She went to him, wanting to embrace him as a friend. But he held her at arm's length, shaking his head.

"Do not make this harder than it already is, Katherine."

"Kevin and his men might help you."

First he looked shocked, then angry. "No. Tell them nothing. Nothing, do you hear me?"

"You've told me nothing that I might share. I merely meant . . ."

"And do not set Jennet on my trail. This is not your battle."

Battle? "I don't even know who they are, or what Salisbury wanted of you."

His expression relaxed. "That was my intention."

He had succeeded. "Will I see you again?" she asked softly.

Now he rested his hands on her shoulders and pressed his forehead to the top of her head. "I pray that you do. And the children, Lille and Ghent, Jennet, Matt. You are my family." He gave her shoulders a squeeze. "I must go."

Kate lifted her face to his and kissed his cheek, then held him tightly for a moment, listening to his strong heartbeat, faster than usual, and no wonder. Injured and on the run. "Come back to us," she whispered.

A deep breath. "If God wills it," he said, his voice husky with emotion.

"Lady Margery is as safe as she can be," she said, despite herself. "But Carl is missing."

She saw how that worried him. Yet he tried so hard to hide that they had traveled together.

"Did you part ways before York?" she asked.

"I will tell you no more, Katherine."

"So be it." She crossed the room to see whether he could safely depart. Checking the shutters, the landing, the stairway. She turned as she felt him behind her. Hood up, cloak belted close, gloves hiding his missing fingers, he might be any traveler.

"God go with you," she whispered as he passed her, beginning his descent. Though a large, muscular man, he moved silently, avoiding the creaking steps, opening the gate with nary a squeak this time. Pausing at the bottom he glanced back, one hand raised, then slipped out into the crowd moving along Petergate.

Kate slumped down on the top step, covered her face, and prayed.

Holy Mother, I pray you, intercede with your son on Berend's behalf, ask him to watch over my friend, see that he comes to no harm. And, if it please your son, send him back to me.

And then she cursed the royal cousins for murdering the peace in her home, the city, the realm. *Arrogant knaves. You use us as if we're merely tokens on a game board.*

It has ever been so, Geoff said in her head. *Look how the French and the Scots ruined our family.*

I know. It was simple of me to think the peace might last. Me, of all people.

What will you do?

She wiped her eyes, forced herself up on her feet. *Prepare.*

6

TRESPASS

A low growl woke Kate. She was stiff and cold, but it was her own fault. She had chosen to remain dressed and ready, perched on a bench in her bedchamber between the door and the window that looked out over the landing and the back garden. Lille sat beside her. The hound had been hesitant to climb the steps, uneasy with this unaccustomed privilege. But it was no privilege—rather the hound was on guard, playing a crucial role in Kate's plan.

It might have been more uncomfortable. Kate would have preferred to stand watch down in the snowy yard. But she did not want to be so obvious that she was waiting for the expected intruders. This way they could not be forewarned. A widow with children, she feared for her safety and took precautions. Effective precautions.

Pressing her back against the wall, Kate slid up until she could see out the open shutter. Lille rose to stand beside her, snout forward, sniffing the air, then pricked her ears and leaned her head out the window, looking in the direction of the steps. She gave another, much softer growl. With a touch on Lille's head Kate signaled *thank you* and, motioning to the hound to *stay*, she stepped out onto the landing and went to the rail to look down into the yard and the entrance to the kitchen. Ghent, who was with Jennet in the kitchen, should have also sounded the alert. There. She could just make out the outline of the open kitchen door, the embers of the hearth fire giving a soft glow.

She need not worry about the girls. She'd sent Matt to Dame Eleanor giving her permission for Petra and Marie to stay the night at the Martha House after their lessons with Sister Brigida, a special treat. Her mother had been more than happy to have them, but, ever on the alert for trouble, Eleanor had made it clear to Matt that she would expect an explanation when she returned with them midday, after their lessons. Kate considered it a small price to pay for ensuring that the girls were not frightened in the night.

In the doorway behind Kate, Lille was restless. Down below, Ghent led Jennet out of the kitchen, stepping with caution toward the corner of the house.

It was time. Kate slipped the lead through Lille's collar, then motioned for the hound to walk beside her. Slowly, silently they went to the stairway where Kate paused, listening. Lille, nearest the railing, gazed down, guiding Kate. In the soft light spilling from her neighbor's shuttered window next door, Kate could see two figures moving with stealth, headed for the side entrance to her hall.

Careful. They will be armed, Geoff warned in her head.

Of course they are. But it's good to have you with me, Geoff.

She and Lille crept down the steps. They were halfway down when the men reached the hall door. She was now close enough to smell the wine on their breath. The one who had spoken to her on the street glanced round as if sensing they were not alone, then shrugged and reached toward the latch. Sawyer was his name, according to one of Jennet's young spies, having gotten close enough to listen to the two for a moment. The other was Parr.

Ghent and Jennet were several strides away from the intruders when Kate saw a glint in the hand of the one nearest her, Parr. Holding her breath, she drew the small axe from her skirt pocket, weighing it, anticipating the pleasure. But Jennet was quicker, coming up fast and yanking the man's arm behind his back before either could respond.

"Bloody—" Parr cried out in pain as he dropped the knife.

The door opened, Matt standing back to avoid Sawyer's wobble as the door pulled him forward. The man managed to grasp the doorframe and avoid falling on his face. The lantern behind Matt illuminated the scene.

"And why, might I ask, are you creeping up to my door past curfew?" Kate demanded from the steps as Jennet started moving Parr past Matt and into the room, Ghent and Lille crowding close to Sawyer. Kate bent down and retrieved the fallen knife. "I want an explanation. Go on. Follow Parr into the hall. Unless you want the night watchman to join us. And some of the neighbors?"

Sawyer glanced at the dogs and warily sidled past Matt.

"I think you can safely let go of his arm now," Kate said to Jennet.

Matt closed the door as soon as Kate and the hounds had cleared it.

"Forgive us, we mistook this house for the one where we're lodging," said Sawyer, slurring his words unconvincingly. They had indeed been drinking, but not that much.

"Well, Sawyer, tell us where you are lodging and we will direct you."

"He lies," said Jennet, dangling a bloody piece of meat she had carried in a small bag. "They tossed this out behind the kitchen to divert the dogs. Poisoned meat."

Lille growled.

"Poisoned meat?" Kate repeated in a quiet voice, working to control her anger. It would not do to kill the king's men in her hall, but oh how she wished she might.

Parr seemed to realize their danger. "Not poisoned. Not so far as we know. The butcher said—"

"Shut up, you bloody fool," Sawyer growled.

Parr bowed his head, but Kate caught his sideways glance at his partner, the subtle smirk. All an act.

"You have no understanding of a well-trained hound, I see," said Kate, pretending to be amused at their bungling.

Pulling himself up to his full height as if thinking to threaten Kate, Sawyer said, "There's nothing for it, then. We are here on King Henry's business. Unaccustomed to the strong ale in the North." Though they reeked of wine. He faked a fierce glower, but there *was* anger beneath it. "How do you know our names?" he demanded drunkenly.

"I asked." She saw by their expressions that they had not shared their names with many. That was no act. Good. The dogs, her readiness, they were forewarned. "If you truly are here on the king's business, he is not well served by you." She called the hounds over to her, and motioned for them to stay at her side, but keep watch on the trespassers.

Neither man could tear his eyes away from them. Kate knew what they saw, wild beasts, untamable, ready to break their training and tear them apart. Never had her hounds disobeyed her. Never. But the men's doubt was useful, rendering the dogs even more effective in protecting her. She took a deep breath. Jennet tucked the meat back in the bag.

"Explain yourselves," Kate demanded.

"Call off your dogs," Parr said with false bravado as he rubbed his shoulder.

"They are not attacking you, which is more than you deserve, creeping up to my home in the dark of the night with a blade drawn, hoping to poison them. I hardly consider it wise to call them off. And you have certainly done nothing to deserve my hospitality."

Matt had busied himself arranging a bench for the two men and two chairs for himself and Jennet. He knew better than to think Kate would sit while the men were in the house.

Kate motioned to the bench placed behind Sawyer and Parr. "Sit."

Sawyer shook his head.

"Perhaps you will permit my hounds to assist you." Kate signaled Lille and Ghent to take a step toward the two men.

They took their seats on the bench without further argument. Jennet and Matt sat as well.

Kate nodded. "Now. What do two men who wear the Lancastrian livery want with me?"

"We wear the duke's livery, but we are the king's men," Sawyer stated.

"Your mission?" she demanded.

"We are rounding up traitors to the king."

"Are you accusing me of treason?" Kate asked. "Me, a hard working merchant's widow bringing up three young wards? When have I had time to commit treason?"

"Not you," Parr growled as he rubbed his shoulder. "A noblewoman and a man lately of your household. Berend, formerly Baron Montagu's man."

No mention of Carl. Because they knew his whereabouts?

"My cook?" Kate frowned. "But I no longer employ him. You say he was Baron Montagu's man? Surely you are mistaken. He did not seem one to have been employed in the kitchens of a nobleman."

"He was no cook then, but an armed retainer. And after that . . ." Parr glanced at his companion.

"You should be more cautious about whom you hire, Mistress Clifford," said Sawyer. "The man left the baron to become a mercenary. An assassin." He punctuated it with a gap-toothed smirk.

Lille growled.

"I don't believe you," Matt cried. "Have you seen the man? Missing an ear, some fingers, some toes. An assassin? Pah."

Jennet snorted. "Now you've had your fun, why don't you tell us the truth?"

"Insolent servants," Sawyer muttered. He'd begun to sag on the bench.

Kate silently thanked her clever servants. Stalling, she noticed that Parr's jacket was puckered as if he had tried to clean the dark stain from it. Was it blood? She looked at his face—dried blood beneath his nose and the beginning of a bruise on his cheek. A bandage peeked from his left sleeve. He, too, slumped slightly, as if wilting in the warmth of the hall. In fact, now she studied their bloodshot eyes, she believed both were more than slightly inebriated. Curious that they had risked their mission. Clearly Parr had been in a fight. With whom? Carl? Had he struggled, fought back? She wished she might speak his name, challenge them, but she could not without revealing that she had at least spoken to Lady Margery. The need for secrecy hampered her.

At least their inebriated states might make it easier to fool them into thinking they had achieved their mission. "My household needs its sleep, so I agree with my maidservant. Tell me what it is you want."

Sawyer straightened as if remembering himself. "Is your former cook here?"

"No."

"Lady Kirkby?"

"No. Is that it?"

"We have the right, as the king's officers, to search your house for the miscreants," he said, beginning to slur his words.

"And then we'll be done with you? Good," she said, not waiting for an answer. "Come. Quickly now." She clapped her hands at them, making Lille and Ghent bark as if eager to proceed. "I want to get back to bed."

Clearly the two had forgotten their fear of the dogs—until the deep-chested barks.

"The dogs—" Sawyer began.

"No bargaining," said Kate, motioning the men to rise. "First, hand over all weapons to Jennet. I will have no incidents in my home. She will return them to you out on the street."

"You already have my dagger," Parr snapped.

"Not the one in your boot." Jennet held out her hand, grinning at his surprise.

"Come now, both of you," said Kate. "I'll grow testy if you keep me up much longer."

Once Jennet was satisfied that the men were unarmed, Kate told Matt to bring a lantern. She ordered Lille and Ghent to accompany Jennet behind the men, and Kate and Matt led the way out of the hall and up the steps, calling to the lagging men to follow them. Her room, the girls' room, Phillip's room.

"Where are the children?"

"Oh, do be serious. They are too young to commit treason, surely," said Kate, shooing them back across the landing and down the steps, round the corner and back to the kitchen, where she invited them to peer down the barrels if they so pleased. Then, quickly, out into the garden and into the garden shed. "And our garderobe. Please, I pray you, peer in. You never know who might be squatting in there."

And then they were out on the street.

"What about the shop front?" asked Sawyer.

"What about it?"

"It is never open."

"It awaits two sempsters." Jennet and Sister Dina—as soon as Kate found a replacement cook. "Shall I inform you when they are open for business? Purse makers—decorated alms purses. Are you in the market for some? When I have some to show you I'll send you word at—where are your lodgings?"

Neither man responded. No matter, Jennet would have one of her helpers track them.

"Well, you might ask your host to recommend a good laundress for that stain on your jacket. If you let blood set it will destroy the brocade." Kate bobbed her head at the pair. "Perhaps I owe you my thanks. I shall not find traitors on my doorstep now you've made a nuisance of yourselves. But if I find you on my property again, I'll not restrain my hounds." She waved them off, greeting the night watchman who was passing, warning him to keep an eye on the drunken knaves she'd found wandering in her garden.

Jennet slipped out into the shadows. So she meant to track them herself.

Back in the kitchen Kate slumped against the wall, catching her breath.

"Berend and Lady Margery. They know they are in the city." She closed her eyes, whispering a prayer.

"They are no match for Berend," said Matt, "or for us. I'm not worried."

"Whether or not to worry depends upon who they really are," said Kate, opening her eyes as Jennet returned.

"You do not look triumphant," said Kate.

Matt gave a low whistle. "They managed to lose you?"

Jennet cursed. "It was clear from the start they aren't as foolish as they pretended."

"Nor are we," said Kate. But she was so on edge that a noise at the door had her holding her breath, half expecting Berend to saunter into the kitchen. But it was only Lille and Ghent returning from a last check of the yard. "I had hoped they might at least lead you to Carl."

"I believe he is dead," Jennet said. "While we awaited the intruders one of my eyes and ears came to tell me of a body found in a ditch outside Mickle-gate Bar the morning after Carl disappeared. A bald man of no distinction. He's been taken to a small chapel out past Ben Coffey's blacksmith shop where the priest buries those found along the road. It might be anyone, but such a coincidence? I will go on the morrow."

"No, I will go," said Kate.

All three bowed their heads.

Kate sat up sharp, still on edge from the night watch despite a few hours of sleep. "What is it? What's happened?"

Jennet sat on the edge of the bed. "Trouble. One of my lads says Merek's been murdered."

Berend's summoner. "When? Where?"

"An alley near the market. Sounds as if it was about the time Parr and Sawyer were here, so if it was them they had a very busy night. The night watch were milling about, so my lad could not get too close. But he says there is a great deal of blood, and the men were saying the spice seller had been stabbed, and his throat slit."

Kate looked toward the window while she thought. Parr was certainly bloodied, but could the pair be so cool as to murder a man, try to wash out the blood, and then come to annoy her? Dangerous enemies, if so. If not them, who? Lionel? Merek had been prying into his affairs. Horner? He had clearly been uneasy about something when he had met with Merek in the market. Berend? No, please no, not him. She saw soft gray light through the chinks in the shutters. Not yet dawn. "Merek seemed a man with no shortage of enemies." She stepped onto the cold floor. "I want to see him. I doubt they will move him before sunrise."

Down in the kitchen, she found Kevin sharing an ale with Matt. The latter was yawning and blinking to wake up, but Elric's man looked as if he had been up a while.

"You've heard about Merek?" Kevin asked.

"Only what a passerby was able to overhear," she said. "I think you might want to find Jon Horner." She told him what she'd witnessed in the market the previous day.

"Jon Horner?" Kevin looked doubtful. "I would not have seen him as a man prone to violence. He seems a timid sort."

She saw pain in his expression. Something he did not want to tell her. "What is it?"

"A witness, a baker who lives near where they found the body, says that he saw Merek and Berend earlier in the evening. They were arguing, and Berend seemed the aggressor. So folk will say it likely follows that he is the murderer."

"No. No, I don't believe it."

"Do you think I do? But the sheriffs' constables are searching for him."

She was thinking about the market and the angry customer. Perhaps he'd overheard something or had seen what the two had exchanged. She wondered whether Merek told Horner to blame anything that happened on Berend.

". . . wanted you to know before he comes," Kevin was saying.

She shook her head at him. "I'm sorry, before who comes?"

"Sir Elric. He will be coming to talk to you. If you would—"

"I will say I heard it from Jennet. He will never know you were here."

"Have you seen him? Berend?" Though Kate said nothing and tried not to change her expression, Kevin shook his head. "Have a care, Dame Katherine. Everyone is frightened, fearing what punishment God will rain down on a realm that discards the holy anointed king. I would not have you risk your life even to protect a friend."

She would have preferred not to, but there was no turning back now. "Did you see Merek's body?" she asked.

"Not closely. Sir Elric did."

"He was about in the night?"

"Dame Bess woke him, said there was trouble, wanted him to find out what it was."

"How did she know?"

Kevin shook his head. "She is as secretive as Jennet about her sources. Maybe Horner?"

"I want to see the body."

"He's already been moved. To prevent the murderer from coming back to snatch the body and hide it." Kevin moved toward the door. "I must go. I will be missed." He turned as Kate touched his arm.

"Thank you, Kevin. I will not forget this."

He lifted Kate's hand and kissed it. "For you, anything." His eyes held hers for a moment, warming her.

"God help us," Jennet muttered when he was gone. "I'll not believe it of Berend. Never."

"Nor I," Matt declared.

"Then we need to prove him innocent," said Kate.

"What of Lionel?" Matt said. "Merek's been asking questions of him. Would Lionel have cause to attack Merek?"

"I thought of that, and I would love to point the finger at him," said Kate, "but who would believe it of that coward? He likes to attack, but whines and runs when his victim turns on him."

"What if Sir Elric was told to take care of someone asking too many questions about Lionel, a Neville?" asked Jennet. "What if *he* murdered Merek? Would he step forward to save Berend?"

Would he? Could she trust him to do the honorable thing?

Matt looked relieved, as if the idea were the answer. "If Sir Elric had been obeying an order from the Earl of Westmoreland, the sheriffs and the council would likely express their irritation but do nothing."

Kate rubbed her eyes. "Pour me some ale."

7

PASSIONS AND POTIONS

Early in the morning, as a wan sunlight lit up the bare crown of the oak, Kate stepped out onto Petergate with Lille and Ghent. Calling out greetings to neighbors as she crossed the intersection with Stonegate, she headed toward the little school in the yard of the church across from the guesthouse. She had decided the girls were safer with her mother for a few more days. The schoolmaster clucked at her as she explained that they were away for the nonce. This was one of the blessings of children in the household, how they pulled her into the ordinary tasks—this morning, dealing with their quarrelsome schoolmaster.

"They missed an important reading yesterday, Dame Katherine. Would it not be better to bring them every day? Let them take their French lessons in the evenings?"

"What if I come to collect the reading at the end of the school day and see that they work with it?" she said.

Master Jonas recoiled. "Let my books leave the schoolroom?"

"My tutor had us copy out our readings." Thankful for the memory. "You might consider that."

"What of the cost of parchment and ink?"

Worried about the cost—not in lives, but in halfpennies. "They could use their wax tablets. They might at least copy out the most important passages."

Jonas shook his head, his oversized felt hat wobbling comically from side to side, along with the wattles hanging from his chin.

How the children must poke fun at him. It would not be easy, teaching impertinent young scholars. But this morning she blessed him for lightening her heart ever so slightly, enough that she bit back a smile. "When the days lengthen I will consider how I might rearrange their schedule. But they are good students, are they not?"

"They are competent when they wish to be." More comical head wagging. "It is not my place to tell you how to order your household, Dame Katherine." He closed his eyes and sighed as a shriek sounded from the classroom. Bobbing his head in farewell, the schoolmaster shuffled into the classroom, shutting the door behind him.

"Are you wild beasts?" He roared so loudly Kate heard it through the heavy door.

As she turned away, she discovered Lille and Ghent eyeing Sir Elric, who stood near her, leaning against the wall of the school. His nearness brought back the memory of his touch the evening of Kevin's celebration, the strong attraction. His blue eyes seemed to shift to a warmer tone when he looked on her and his smile dimpled his chiseled cheeks.

"All schoolmasters are burdened by a belief in the perfect classroom," he said, gracefully pushing from the wall and lowering to a crouch so he might greet the hounds. Strong legs, strong back.

Kate was glad he was so busy with the hounds he did not see her blush at the pleasure she found in observing him. Lille and Ghent had grown fond of him. And she? She was more confused than she cared to admit to herself. Should she trust the hounds' judgment? They'd never led her astray.

"I've no need to ask what brings you here on this frosty morning," she said, pleased to hear the confident ring in her tone.

He straightened, the smile gone. "I should have guessed Jennet would have already told you." He bowed and crooked his arm, inviting her hand. "Might we talk in your kitchen? I would welcome a few moments by the fire."

They walked in quiet companionship until they neared Kate's house, where Elric expressed sympathy for Matt, who was shoveling horse dung from the area near the front door.

"That was my morning and evening chore as a lad. I hated it," he said.

"Not a task anyone could face with enthusiasm," said Kate with a little laugh. She imagined a boy with bright blue eyes, itching to run in the fields or go riding, and in that moment she felt a fierce regret for her deception. "Do you mind if Matt joins our conversation?" she asked. When Elric seemed puzzled, she explained, "Jennet and Matt are more than servants, you know that."

"And you trust them with everything we might say?"

"I do."

A nod. Kate called to Matt to join them when he was finished.

Jennet had the kitchen door opened wide. As she looked up from the three-footed pot sitting in the hearth she called out to them, "Come in, come in. I welcome the company."

"Ale for all of us," said Kate. "Matt will be here in a moment."

"Ah." Jennet wrapped a cloth round the handle of the pot and moved it to the side of the fire, then went to fetch bowls and a pitcher of ale.

Sir Elric gazed around the room as he took the seat nearest the fire. "I've been up and out in the cold for hours." He nodded as Matt came in, bringing a draft of cold air with him.

"About another servant," said Matt as he lowered himself onto the bench beside Kate and stuffed his long legs beneath the table. "Seth says his youngest brother might work mornings."

"We will discuss it later," said Kate. "At the moment I want to hear what more Sir Elric knows about Merek's murder."

They all watched as the knight sat forward, elbows on the table. He was so near that Kate could smell the anise she had noticed both he and Kevin chewed. Calm stomachs, sweet breath.

"As you know, he was murdered sometime during the night. Peter Trimlow was on his way to his bake ovens when he came upon the body near Thursday Market. Maybe an hour before dawn, he said. I examined the body—several wounds on his chest, and a slit throat. The alley where he lay is awash in blood, the melting snow churned—mud, blood, it's impossible to tell whether it was one attacker or many."

"How did you first learn of it?" asked Kate.

"Old Bess had a servant wake me, knowing I would want to hear of it, and wanting to know more. How she heard . . ." He shrugged.

"I understand the sheriffs are searching for Berend," said Kate, watching his expression.

Elric did not look away. "The same baker claims he saw Berend and Merek arguing earlier in the evening."

"It was Trimlow who raised the hue and cry?"

Elric nodded. "And of course he is eager to point the finger at someone else, lest he be suspected. I did speak to his wife, who swears he was abed early. But I don't believe Berend did it. Not such sloppy work. The multiple stab wounds—that is an act of passion, not the work of a former assassin. If it were simply the throat—" He sat back and took a long drink.

"So many wounds," said Kate. "Did you find signs of a struggle?"

"It's clear by the types of wounds and the condition of the alley that he struggled with his attacker. There was a knife in Merek's hand, bloodied. His attacker must be injured." A shrug. "If it is his knife."

Kate told him of Parr's soiled jacket the night before, the bandage peeking from his sleeve. Left sleeve. "Was the bloodied nose part of a ruse to explain the bloodstain? Or suffered during the attack?" she wondered aloud.

"That is a good question," said Elric. "Clever. But not clever enough."

Clever enough to elude Jennet, Kate thought. "Why do you question whether it's his knife?" she asked.

"It's a common ruse for the attacker to leave his knife in the hand of the victim."

"Those two were up to something," said Jennet.

Elric was shaking his head. "If they were king's men they would identify themselves to me, Westmoreland's man. Perhaps not at once, but they would have quickly learned of my presence in York."

"Indeed," said Kate.

"I don't like it," said Elric. "Who are they? You must have a care, Dame Katherine."

"We know that."

"Forgive me. I know you are capable of defending yourself. But we don't know of what they are capable."

A fleeting regret that Kevin was no longer in their household unsettled Kate. Damn Elric for seeding doubt in her mind. But he had no idea how much trouble she harbored. She had made certain of that.

"Do not worry about us," she said.

He looked down at his hands, as if at a loss for what to say.

Matt broke the sudden uneasy silence. "A noisy brawl in the quiet of the evening and no one looked out to see what was happening?"

"Odd, isn't it?" said Jennet. "Only Trimlow has come forward?"

"My man Douglas saw Lionel with Merek outside a tavern on Fossgate, near St. Crux," said Elric. "After sunset—probably after the meeting with Berend. Pity he did not think to follow him until curfew. I have Harry watching Merek's house now."

"Lionel." That interested Kate. She told Elric what Thomas Holme had told her, how Merek was asking round about her brother-in-law.

"Lionel Neville, my earl's bane," Elric muttered. "God help me, if he's involved I'll—" He shook his head. "No, Lionel would not have had the courage or the strength to slit Merek's throat. Which would mean an accomplice."

She sensed no duplicity in his response. So Merek's murder was as much a mystery to him as it was to her.

"A pity you and Lionel are not close," he said to Kate.

For once Kate agreed. "Lionel stabbing wildly, then the accomplice slitting Merek's throat. I can imagine it," she said.

"You said whoever struggled with the spice seller was likely injured—if that was his knife. It should be simple to find out whether Master Lionel has been wounded," said Jennet. "As Dame Katherine said, one of our intruders was. But would he be so bold as to come here after such a deed?"

"My men will track down the Lancastrians," said Elric.

"I wish them luck," Jennet muttered.

Elric glanced at her with surprise, but she merely shrugged. "What about Lionel?" he asked. "Someone should talk to him."

Kate smiled. "I would not mind paying a visit to his wife. I have not been to see Winifrith and baby Simon in weeks. If she won't confide in me, her daughter Maud might."

"That would be helpful." Elric looked round the table. "So Berend *is* in the city? You have seen him?" He turned to Kate. "Spoken to him?" When Kate said nothing, he added, "It would help to know where he has been and why, and his reason for returning to the city when he knows those seeking him will search here. If I'm to defend him I need to understand."

Kate wanted so much to believe Elric was her ally. But to speak of her meeting with Berend felt like a betrayal. "I do not know where he has been, nor do I know why he would endanger himself by coming here."

Elric looked away, clearly disappointed. "I mean to help. If you learn anything, I pray you trust me with it." He sat back and lifted his bowl of ale. "Most welcome." He took a drink.

"What did the baker Trimlow see?" Kate asked.

Elric emptied the bowl, set it aside. "He claims to have seen Berend and Merek near the market square. He said Berend pushed Merek and blocked his hand when he lifted it to strike back. Merek cursed him and turned to walk off, but Berend grabbed him by the shoulder, said something, then shook him and let him go."

Such detail. Kate would like to talk to the baker.

"Once the sheriffs were involved it was impossible to keep it quiet," said Elric. "So Berend will find it difficult to stay hidden, and the sheriffs will be eager to lock him in the castle."

Kate closed her eyes against the image, but that only made it more vivid.

"I pointed out to the sheriffs that Merek seems to have fought, his knife and hand, even his wrist were bloody as if he'd gotten in at least one serious thrust. So if Berend is not wounded . . ." Elric shrugged. "It is all I can argue at the moment."

"What can I do?" asked Jennet.

Kate opened her eyes in time to see Elric consider her freckle-faced maidservant.

"I understand you are as well informed about what goes on in the city as Bess Merchet. Keep all ears pricked for information. Even the smallest detail might help. The sheriffs want to calm the city. They will listen."

Jennet looked doubtful, but she nodded as if agreeing.

Elric glanced round the table. "If Berend is apprehended, leave him to me. I can use the earl's influence to keep him safe until we can prove his innocence." He turned to Kate. "He has spent years seeking absolution for his sins. I do not believe he would suddenly commit such an act."

Nor could she. But others would look at Berend's bulk, the scars that bore witness to his violent past—why would they trust him? And what, in the end, did she really know of him? Kate looked aside to hide her confusion. "Thank you," she said as she fought for composure. As if sensing her distress, Ghent came and rested his head on her shoulder. She stroked his back and took a deep breath. "I will call on my cousin William to put his authority behind you as well."

Elric frowned. "William Frost is hardly the man to defy the king's men. Not when he owes so much to Henry's favor."

She could not deny that. "And you?"

"My lord the earl is also the king's man, it's true. But I know Berend and Lady Margery, and I never had cause to doubt their honor."

"I am in your debt, Sir Elric." She bowed her head to him.

"How times change," he remarked as he rose, thanking her for the hospitality and reminding Jennet where he was lodging.

"About that," said Jennet, as Kate rose to walk out with Elric. "Why the York Tavern? One of the abbeys would gladly accommodate you."

He laughed. "Best ale in the shire, and Bess Merchet—if I can win her friendship, I'll not need my men in the city. I can just ride in once a fortnight, drink some fine ale, and hear all that has transpired. Who has visited, who has left, who has secrets my lord would like to hear."

When Kate and Elric were out in the yard he turned to her, serious once more. "About your cousin William Frost. His election was strongly influenced by the earl and the king himself, letters recommending him as a peacekeeper in the city."

"William a peacekeeper?" Kate shook her head at the concept. In the past, her cousin's strategy in uniting the majority of the citizens of York had been to use the minority who opposed his idea as the enemy. Indeed, the rumor that King Henry had pushed for William's election as mayor had grown out of people's disbelief. He was not a popular man.

"I question it as well," said Elric, "not because of any flaw in him but rather that he is such a part of this community, personally involved—such a man cannot truly keep the peace. But as he has been chosen, I need to know him better. Establish a connection."

A sinking feeling. Here was the truth of Elric's recent warmth—he needed her influence with William. "And that is how I can be of help to you?" Kate asked.

Do not be so quick to jump to that, Kate, Geoff urged.

"I hesitate to ask it of you," said Elric, in a chastened tone.

"We will discuss this further," she said, her tone dismissive.

He flinched.

"Is that true, what you just said?" she asked to change the subject. "Is Bess Merchet so well informed?"

"About the city over all, yes." He lifted one of her hands, then bent to kiss it. "You are more selective. And I am not so confident that you will ever let me so close to you that I could be sure you were telling me all you knew." His eyes teased.

Oh, Heavenly Mother, if he could read her mind . . . Kate forced a smile. "Time will tell." She deemed it wise to offer something. It was not her purpose to alienate him. "You should know that I *have* spoken to Berend. He came here, to the house. But he was careful to tell me nothing."

Elric said nothing for a moment, but the warmth was gone from his eyes. "He loves you. He will never act on it, but he loves you."

Of all the responses she might have imagined, that was the last thing she had expected him to say. "I am his employer."

"Is that all that stops you?"

Damn him. She could feel the warmth in her face. This was all wrong, their duplicity with each other. She delighted in his touch, in the warmth of his regard. She did not believe she'd merely imagined the mutual attraction. Yet she could not let herself trust him with her heart. She tilted her head and smiled up at him. "You forget yourself, Sir Elric." With a little laugh, she wished him a good day. And silently cursed herself for the awkward attempt at flirting.

But it seemed she'd succeeded in confounding him, clear in the questioning look he gave her before bowing and taking his leave.

No more than her own treacherous heart confounded her.

Jennet and Matt had their heads together when Kate finally returned to the table. As she settled back in her chair, they considered her with grave expressions.

"Come, my darlings," Kate whispered to Lille and Ghent. The hounds eagerly joined her, settling at her feet.

"Multiple stab wounds." Jennet shook her head. "Berend would not be so clumsy."

"The slit throat, that could be him," said Matt, "meaning to put a dying man out of his misery. But who is Merek to him?"

Kate had not yet told them of Berend's connection with the spice seller. In truth, she had said little about the exchange, too shaken to speak of it. "I am not certain," was all she said now.

"Shall I find the spot where he was murdered, examine it?" asked Jennet.

Kate should have thought of that herself. "Yes, do. I am going to take the hounds and find out who the customer was who was so irked when Merek hurried away in the market. And then I'm going to call on Jon Horner."

"What about the body that might be Carl?" asked Jennet.

"I said I would see to that," said Kate. "But proving Berend innocent of Merek's murder is our priority now."

⸻⊱◦◦⊰⸻

Griselde and Clement greeted Kate with solemn voices and worried expressions. Already the news of Merek's murder and Berend's danger had reached them. It was all Kate could do to wave off their questions. She needed information so that she might discover the real murderer, and she needed it now.

Clement nodded. "Of course. I pray you, forgive us our questions, but we cannot believe—"

"Talk to Old Cob, the eel man," said Griselde, interrupting her husband. "He has the stall next to Merek's at the market. His little shop is near the river." She described the place, on Skeldergate, close to the Old Baile. "Tell him—No, of course not, you do not want to be bothered with my messages. God go with you, Mistress Clifford. Come tell us the news when you have a moment."

"Mary is proving satisfactory?" she asked.

Griselde and Clement exchanged a wry look.

"She finds it difficult?" Kate guessed.

"We all do. But we are managing. Do not concern yourself with us."

—◦⊙◦—

Lille and Ghent enjoyed the pace Kate set over the bridge, bustling with shoppers and aldermen gathering outside the guildhall before a meeting. Though a chill wind came off the river, reaching out to her in between the clustered buildings as she hurried along, even stronger down along Skeldergate, she was quite warm by the time she saw Old Cob standing outside his shop front chatting with a customer. To interrupt or not? To do so would call attention to her mission, but . . . Her dilemma was made moot by Old Cob's exclamation upon seeing her.

"Mistress Clifford! It is an honor to see you here. Has Sir Elric requested more eels?"

The expression on the face of the woman who had been chatting with him was one of eagerness to hurry away and spread gossip about Katherine Clifford and her knight. For once, Kate was glad of the rumors, she needed the privacy.

Old Cob looked crestfallen when she explained her mission, but quickly cheered. "I *do* recall the incident, and I remember the customer. The blacksmith Ben Coffey, you know him, I am certain."

"His smithy is just outside Micklegate Bar."

Cob nodded.

A convenience. She would ask Coffey whether he had heard of a body. "I did not recognize him."

"He dropped four stone or more while grieving his beloved wife."

That would explain it.

"He's an odd customer for a spice seller," Cob continued, "but Merek, God rest his soul, I mean no disrespect for the dead, but he made quite a profit as a bit of an apothecary, or a healer." He nodded at Kate's frown. "Oh, yes. Why the vintners guild did nothing I cannot say, but he is—was licensed as a spice seller, nothing more. Most of us in the market knew of his extra trade."

"You are speaking of potions?"

He nodded. "Especially for men getting on in years. He promised to revive, stimulate. And attract, that was the big one." He wagged his scruffy brows.

"So Ben Coffey, the blacksmith—"

"Recently widowed, and well, God help me I should not listen to others' conversations, but when the morning is slow . . ."

"Yes?"

"Coffey was there for a love potion. And a bit more. He worried that he had been unmanned by his wife's death and his long mourning."

"So that he might be unable to pleasure a bride?" Kate asked, then apologized for her bluntness as Old Cob turned a dangerous shade of red. "You have been a great help," she added. "Bless you."

"I am glad to be of help. Your Berend did not do it, Mistress Clifford. I would stake my reputation on it."

Kate called softly to the hounds. "If I see him, I will tell him you said so."

—◦⊚◦—

Micklegate was abustle in late morning, and Kate kept the hounds on a short lead as she pushed through the crowd heading toward the river and the city center. She and the dogs were in the minority heading out toward the countryside. At the Bar the gatekeeper fussed over Lille and Ghent, "gray beauties," and wished her well, then grew serious, advising her that he had been commanded to look for Berend and hold him for the sheriffs. Chilled about Berend's deepening danger, she nodded her thanks and continued on out the gate, past the hovels piled up against the walls, cook fires smelling of onions and grease, past a few small but more substantial houses. As she arrived at the wide gate opening onto the blacksmith's yard she took a deep breath and forced her worries to the back of her mind. She needed to be sharp for this conversation, learn all she could. That, and not worry, would help Berend.

Inside the tidy yard she paused to let Lille and Ghent commune with a plow horse waiting to be shoed by one of Ben Coffey's workers, the mare curious about them. Did she imagine they were colts, Kate wondered. Beneath a one-walled shed a man stroked the back of a nervous palfrey and made soothing sounds while lifting a blood-encrusted hind leg to examine the hoof.

A boy left the bellows he'd been working to see to Kate, asking whether the hounds wanted shoeing.

Laughing, she told him she wished to speak with his master.

"Round back. In his workshop." He shook his head at Lille and Ghent. "I'll bet they never feel the cold."

It seemed an odd comment from a lad who worked the bellows. But, remembering the hovels near the wall, she thought perhaps his home was among them.

"There is a benefit to growing your own warm coat, to be sure," she said. Thanking him, she softly called Lille and Ghent to attention and the three moved on.

Behind the more open smithy was a long shed, and beyond that a tidy house with some chickens pecking about. The door of the long shed was open, and she could see Ben Coffey standing within. She called out, but he did not turn. So she stepped inside.

He was alone, running a hand along a panel of intricately patterned ironwork. Feeling for flaws, she imagined.

"Might I have a word?" she said in a voice that he might hear but not so loud he would startle.

Now he glanced up. Soot and sweat streaked his pale face and the front of his linen shirt. Beneath the rim of a leather hat that hid his graying hair, his dark eyes moved to her, then the two hounds.

"Mistress Clifford?" he said with some uncertainty in his voice, lowering the panel and moving in front of it, as if trying to conceal what she had already seen. It was not the accepted work for a blacksmith. He was no doubt concerned that she might report him to the guild.

"Yes. Forgive me for intruding on you, but the lad—" she gestured back toward the smithy.

"Good boy but for his mouth."

"I will tell no one what I saw," she assured him. Brought up in the countryside, she did not understand the fuss about strict guild categories. A skilled craftsman should not be hindered by such rules. "I must say, it shows remarkable skill."

With a crooked smile and a shrug he stepped aside and motioned for her to come closer.

She traced the swirling pattern with a gloved hand. "It flows," she said.

"Yes," he whispered, pleased.

"What is it for?"

"Grillwork for a tomb in the church in Galtres," he said. "I've been working on it since Martinmas. This is the last panel."

"Much more satisfying work than shoeing a horse."

"In some ways, in others—I like knowing I've eased their burdens, the beasts." A flicker of a smile at Lille and Ghent. "They are kinder than people. Closer to God than we can ever hope to be."

Kate reached down to stroke her hounds' ears. "I could not agree more."

"But I am forgetting myself." He tugged at his sleeves, straightened his hat. "You came to see about some work, Mistress Clifford?"

"No. Not today." She explained the purpose of her visit.

The man's genial expression darkened as she spoke. "Ah. Merek, the bloody—" Coffey caught himself, made the sign of the cross. "I can tell you he did not want anyone to see whatever it was he pressed into Horner's hand. It was a small object. I could not see anything but a bit of a glint—gold? No bigger than my thumb, I would say." He held up a sizable digit, blackened by his work. "Maybe as big." He squinted as if peering into his mind's eye, reliving the incident. "Merek sent Horner off, and then he walked away himself. Walked away and left me standing there without the—What he'd promised that day."

"Did you ever get it?"

Coffey shook his head and spat sideways. "Brings up the bile to think of it. I paid good coin for the potion and he died before handing it over. I say God rest his soul, for I am a God-fearing man, but he robbed me."

"Do you happen to know where he lodged?" Kate asked.

A look of distrust. "You don't think I went after him?"

"No. I hoped to see his lodgings. If you described to me what it was you had purchased, I might notify the sheriffs' men."

"Oh, it is no matter. Do not trouble yourself." He directed her to a house near the Thursday Market and excused himself. "I am blessed with more work than I can manage, at present," he muttered. He was a handsome man beneath the grime of days spent in hard labor. And prosperous. Some woman would snatch him up quickly, Kate was certain, and, with any luck, he would have no need of Merek's potion.

"I am glad to hear your business is thriving."

"I would be glad but for the fact that I'm benefitting from folks' fear. In dangerous times they bring a smith all manner of old weapons for repair."

"But the soldiers are long gone."

"That might be more a curse than a blessing. Folk hear of the mobs taking down those who would bring back King Richard. The devil seeds lawlessness across the land. Here we've had the spice man's murder two days after the man found in the ditch across the way, his throat slit . . . Folk are uneasy."

"A man in a ditch with his throat slit?"

A nod. "The lad came across him a few nights ago."

"I wonder—a friend's manservant did not return from an errand outside this gate. Could you describe the man?"

His description fit Carl. "I took the body to Father Michael, in the small chapel just beyond."

⁂

The priest warned her it was not a pretty sight. He was right. Coffey had mentioned only the slit throat, not the shattered hand, the bruised and battered face. Someone had tortured Carl before killing him. The faithful servant had died protecting his lady, Kate guessed. She said a prayer over him, then gave the priest a donation for a separate burial.

"Would that you could do that for all of them," said the long-suffering priest. He asked no questions.

She was glad of that. She wearied of lying.

⁂

Halfway across the Ouse Bridge Kate became aware that Lille and Ghent had gone on alert, looking round, searching the shadows. How, in the press of bodies going about their late morning business they could sense that someone was too interested in her movements, she could not guess, but she was grateful. She had no intention of leading anyone to Horner's house or Merek's lodgings. Once over the bridge she turned down Coney Street, then into St. Helen's Square. Time for a chat with Bess Merchet.

Bess's grandson Colin greeted her warmly, particularly after she carefully secured the hounds' leads just outside the door, but he shook his head at her request, inclining his head toward the kitchen, where a man could be heard declaring that he had never been so ill-used. "Another cook about to walk out,

I fear, and we've dinner to serve. Mid afternoon will be much better. I will tell her to expect you."

At loose ends, Kate stepped back out into the yard and found Kevin and Wulf standing by Lille and Ghent.

"How did they know you were being followed?" Wulf asked.

"So it was you following me? You saw them go on alert?"

"Yes and no," said Kevin. "We were following the men following you. Parr and Sawyer. Well, we were unaware until we caught sight of you that you were their quarry. They hoped you would lead them to Berend, I'd wager."

Not so clever as she had feared. "Have you found where they are lodging?"

"No," said Kevin, "and that is telling, wouldn't you say? King's men would command lodgings at one of the religious houses or the home of the mayor, perhaps one of the aldermen—but we have checked all those."

A busy morning. "So they would," said Kate. "How did you rid yourselves of them?"

"We came up behind them arguing loudly about a man in Salisbury's livery heading into Toft Green," said Wulf with a self-satisfied grin. "They turned and headed back that way."

She bowed to their clever ploy. "Do you have someone following them?"

"No. While we searched we put out the word we're looking for them," said Kevin. "Now we thought it best to see whether anyone comes to us. We thought we might be too obvious following them."

Kate would have sent someone anyway. But Jennet's eyes and ears would find them eventually. "Thank you for setting them astray," she said. "Now I can continue on my errands."

"We will accompany you. At a slight distance," said Kevin. "Best to make certain they are nowhere around."

She was about to argue, but decided against it. "Come on then. Jon Horner's house is just around the corner." If all went well there, they could move on to Merek's lodgings, though the sheriffs' constables might have already searched them.

8

A VICTIM, AN ALLY

"I will not have a mess in here," Horner's housekeeper warned, her beaky nose quivering as she focused her close-set eyes on Lille and Ghent. Goodwife Tibby was a small but solid woman with a fierce frown so habitual it seemed carved into her face. "And I've no time to prepare refreshments. I am just back from market." Indeed, at her feet were two baskets filled with jugs and wrapped parcels.

"If you wish, we will speak with your master where we stand," said Kate. "Let him know that we are here."

"I don't know . . ."

"We will stand here until we speak with him," said Kate.

With a sniff, the woman lifted her baskets and nodded toward the far side of the hall. "He uses his parlor as his office. He has taken to sleeping there as well. The roof above the solar needs mending and he is too cheap—" she caught herself. "You've only to knock. If he's in, he will see you, I'm sure. Always ready to take a client's money, though where it goes . . ." Tibby shook her head as she bustled off to the kitchen.

Kate led with the hounds, Wulf and Kevin right behind her.

"Was a mistress of the house here once, you can see it," said Wulf.

Large cupboards to either side held a few pewter tankards, some plates, and a skilled carving of a hawk on a pedestal. But all was powdered with a thick layer of dust. The housekeeper apparently did not see the cleaning of the cupboards, or, indeed, the hall, as her responsibility. And if Horner ate all his meals at the York Tavern, what precisely did Tibby do?

Kevin had gone over to the door the housekeeper had indicated and knocked. Clucking to Lille and Ghent to accompany her, Kate crossed the room as Kevin knocked again, then shook his head.

"Not here, I suppose," he said. "Surely he would have heard our conversation with his harried housekeeper and come to see who we were. He cannot feel sanguine about her greeting his business associates."

Considering what Jennet had found about his finances, Kate thought such visits might be a rarity. Although there might be more desperate fools who used him as a scribe than she would guess. "Try the latch," she said.

Kevin merely touched the door and it swung open. Revealing chaos. The floor of the small room was littered with clothing, shoes, documents, bowls, feather pens—seemingly most of what had been on the cupboard shelves and the small desk near the one window. But that was not the worst of it.

Jon Horner lay on a small pallet tucked in a corner, his face and upper body caked in the contents of his stomach. The stench of vomit was strong in the enclosed space. Wulf groaned. Kevin crossed himself. Kate lifted a scented cloth to her nose and whispered reassurances to her hounds, though she was the one breathless with dismay.

Wulf reached the bed first, lifting one of Horner's arms. "He's not been dead long. There's still warmth in the pit of his arm. But he's not breathing."

"Choked on his own vomit?" Kevin wondered. "Or poisoned?"

"Or both," said Wulf, crossing himself.

"Stay," Kate ordered Lille and Ghent at the door. "Watch."

She entered the room slowly, shuffling through the debris, toeing things, wondering what someone had been searching for. A contract? The gold item Merek handed Horner at the market the previous day? Beneath a spare pair of boots she noticed something out of place—a woman's glove. Picking it up, she fingered the buttery soft leather, pale, possibly lightened to show off the decorative stitching. An expensive glove, an unlikely item in the home of a man of Jon Horner's means. She toed the debris around it, but did not find its mate. Seeing that Kevin and Wulf were distracted with cleaning the corpse on the bed, Kate tucked the glove into her scrip. Moving along, she looked at what was on the floor, what left on the shelves. Household items seemed untouched, for the most part. It was his business papers and writing utensils that littered the floor. She noticed a small pouch tucked behind a mortar and pestle on a shelf. Curious, she picked it up and opened it. Inside was an object that looked like a stone, hefty, yet the texture and faint herbal scent suggested a dried mass of plant material. She tucked it back in the bag and added it to her scrip.

Kevin finished cleaning Horner's face as Kate joined them. She leaned past him to close Horner's eyelids. "If only I had called on him earlier," she said.

Kevin shook his head at her. "And been caught by the murderer? God be thanked you delayed."

"So you think this is murder, not that he chose to end his life?" asked Wulf.

"Look at the room," said Kevin. "Are you thinking he made this mess and then drank down some poison?"

"A man who drinks poison is not thinking clearly, eh?" Wulf countered. "No telling what he might do."

"He's dressed as if going out, or just returning," said Kate. "Look how his boots soaked the bedclothes." Wulf grunted. "He began to feel ill and headed home?" she suggested.

With the owner of the costly glove? Geoff asked in her head.

Indeed.

Lille barked, a quiet bark, warning of someone approaching, but no one she considered dangerous. Still, Kate stepped back from the bed and fingered the dagger hidden in her skirts as Ghent and Lille parted to allow the house-keeper through.

"Mother in Heaven, what has happened here? Has he gone mad? Does he think I'm—" As Tibby focused on the bed she stopped. "Is he—"

"Dead, Goodwife. Murdered," said Kate. "How long ago did you leave for market?"

A hand over the small mouth, eyes flitting this way and that, not wanting to look. "Early. Very early. My sister's abed. Going to give birth any hour now. I stoked the fire and woke her lazy husband and her little ones. Oh, sweet Master Jon. Who would want to harm him?"

"I hoped you might know," said Kate.

"No," Tibby whispered, backing away. "He was always good to me." She surveyed the messy room. "I will never get this clean again."

"Do nothing just yet," said Kate. "Leave it as it is."

The goodwife put a hand over her mouth as Kevin proffered the sheet he had used to clean the vomit from Horner's mouth. "This you might want to launder," he said.

She tucked her hands behind her and stepped back. "Put it out on the dung heap."

With a warning glance at Kevin, Kate slipped an arm round the woman and walked her out into the hall.

"Men can be such lackwits. You have just discovered your employer dead in his chamber and he—I pray you forgive us, Goodwife Tibby. Might I get you something? Is there brandywine in the house?"

A little shake of the head. "I've too much to do. With my sister—"

"Oh, of course, you said. Forgive me, but might I just ask whether you noticed anything unusual about Master Jon this morning?"

"As I said, I left early."

"Anything last night?"

Tibby's nose and cheeks had reddened with emotion. "No," she whispered. "Nothing."

"A visitor perhaps?"

Swiping at a tear falling down her cheek, the woman shook her head. "I saw no one."

"And you would?"

A teary glare. "Did I not see to you?"

"You did. It is plain you took good care of Master Jon."

"I did that. He was good to me, bless him. A good man, God rest his soul." A sob escaped with the last words.

Kate patted Tibby on the back. "Perhaps it is best you go to your sister's."

A sniff. "I believe I will." She shuffled off.

When Kate returned to the room, Kevin apologized. "Wulf and I will raise the hue and cry after you leave," he added.

"Leave?"

His dark eyes pleaded. "I pray you, we do not want you implicated in any way. You will be of no use to Berend if you are a suspect in a murder."

She agreed, but she did not trust the housekeeper. "What about the good-wife?" Tibby had no loyalty to Kate. Her master was dead, an apparently undemanding master. "She means to seek refuge with her sister. If she mentions me . . ."

"I will escort her, and while we walk I will make it clear to her that if anyone should breathe a word of your presence, the blame falls on her, and she will regret the day she so misspoke."

Kate considered. "While you wait for the sheriffs' men, there is something you could do." She told him what Coffey had told her, describing the small shiny item passed from Merek to Horner, something Merek did not wish Horner to flash about. "I would guess that item is what someone sought—" She gestured round at the mess. "Or a document. He offered his services as a scrivener."

Kevin agreed. "We will search. Now I pray you, Dame Katherine, leave us to it."

Gladly. She had too much to do, and clearly no time to waste.

—◦◉◦—

Considering the fact that Merek's lodgings had likely already been searched and were now being watched by the sheriffs' men, Kate decided to head for her brother-in-law's house across the Foss Bridge. But first she stopped at home to trade discoveries with Jennet and Matt over a hasty dinner. A hasty, tasteless dinner—Jennet was no cook without Marie's help. The meal was not the only disappointment; neither Jennet nor Matt had learned much of use.

As she rose from the table, Kate asked Jennet to put a watch on Coffey and the chapel. A murderer was abroad in the city. She did not want anything to happen to the blacksmith or the priest.

Jennet was happy to oblige, but concerned about Kate. "Would you consider taking Matt with you? All the following and murdering, does it not make sense to be more cautious?"

"Then you will be here alone."

"One of my lads is due here any moment."

"I have the hounds. And Elric's squire is watching Lionel's house."

"You do have the hounds, but these are not ordinary times. As for Harry, he can help you only once you reach your destination. And besides," Jennet wrinkled her nose, "Matt is feeling useless." She winked at Matt, who had perked up at the suggestion.

"We would not want that," said Kate with a laugh. She might make light of it, but she did see the wisdom in Jennet's argument. She nodded to Matt. "Come along with me." She was rewarded by his beautiful smile.

"When will you tell your friend that her servant was murdered?" Jennet asked.

"After I talk to Lionel."

—◦◦◦—

As they crossed the Foss Bridge, Matt asked, "What if it's clear Master Lionel is lying? Will you confront him?"

"We shall see. I need to know whether or not he is injured, whether he might have been involved. I hope to ascertain that without challenging him, or letting him know what I know. Let him stew. Cowards are best left to their imaginations." As they neared Lionel's home she warned Matt to wipe the grin from his face and quietly observe. "I depend on you to hear what I might miss."

Straightening to the full extent of his considerable height, Matt cleared his throat and did his best to present a blank visage, but his eyes belied him, lit as they were with his excitement.

Well, she could but advise him. Kate took a tight hold of the hounds' leads as she led them into the yard.

It was a large house, grand in its sprawl and the stone gateway leading into the yard, but lacking the attention that would make it truly gracious and inviting. The shutters needed painting, the oak standing in the center of the yard was scarred where branches had broken off, the splintered stumps giving a forlorn air to the place, saved by the clutter of abandoned toy swords and daggers and a headless doll lying in the dirt beside the grand door to the hall. Glancing round, she caught sight of Sir Elric's squire Harry doing his best to blend into a small stand of trees by the river from which he was watching the entrance to the house. He had much to learn, as did Matt. Harry nodded, but no more. She did not do even that.

Matt knocked but once and the door swung open to reveal Fitch, Lionel's longtime servant. He bowed to Kate, nodded to Matt, and attempted to hide the shudder that traveled through his body at the sight of Lille and Ghent.

"Is your master at home, Fitch?" Kate asked.

Another brief bob. "He is, Mistress, but he can see no one today."

"Who is that, Fitch?" Winifrith called out from behind him.

As Fitch turned to respond to his mistress, she hastily set aside her embroidery, hurrying to the door to greet her visitors.

"My dear, dear gray giants, what a joy to see you!" As the hounds smelled Winifrith's slender hands she glanced up at Kate. "I fear Fitch is correct. My poor Lionel is abed with an ague."

Was it Kate's imagination, or did Winifrith pause before the last word, as if searching for an appropriate excuse? Matt cleared his throat, a habit he had when he noticed something amiss. Good, it was not her imagination.

"You look well, my friend," said Kate. "I can hardly believe we were so worried for you only months ago." Winifrith's latest pregnancy had nearly killed her. Her body had swelled dangerously and Lionel and the children had almost given up hope. But she was deceptively sturdy.

"Why, I am feeling quite recovered," Winifrith said now, smoothing her skirt. With a little laugh she stood on tiptoe to kiss Kate's cheek, then stepped back and complimented her visitor's obvious health. "There are roses in your cheeks and sparks in your eyes. Is it that handsome knight of yours? Is he good to you?"

Kate made a face. "Not you, too, Winifrith. Of all people I thought you would know not to trust such rumors."

A little shrug. "You are young, and without children of your own . . ." A little wink. "And who is *this* handsome man in your company? I do not believe we have met."

As Kate introduced Matt she searched her mind for a compelling excuse to disturb Lionel on his sick bed. For it was clear that Winifrith was uneasy about something, her behavior was so unlike her. It was more than a possible lie about her husband's being ill. And once Winifrith remembered her duty as a hostess and invited them in for some refreshment before trekking back across the city, Kate found her behavior even more suspicious. A whirlwind of children rushing to greet their Aunt Kate was sternly sent out to the kitchen. Not at all Winifrith's usual behavior.

"Forgive me," Winifrith said when she turned back to her guests. "But they are so loud, and their father's head pounds when they shriek. I do pray you did not come all this way to see him?"

"I had hoped to see him—I have some news about our partnership. But I also hope to spend some time with you and young Simon. I am glad to see you looking so well. And all the children," said Kate. "If I might just have a brief word with Lionel, I believe I will cheer him."

Winifrith shook her head. "I am afraid that is not possible. The fever, you see. I would feel responsible if you took ill. And I could not bear for you to take it to the children."

"Surely but a moment . . ."

"I am sorry." Winifrith commanded Fitch to bring claret for her and her guests and then fetch Maud with baby Simon. "Come let us sit by the fire." She herself settled on a stool near the hearth, encouraging Lille and Ghent to sit beside her. "I am so fond of them," she cooed.

In a few moments footsteps clattered on the stairs outside the house and Winifrith's eldest daughter danced in with tiny Simon in her arms. He had not been so quick to recover the ordeal of his birth and had the translucent skin of a child destined to sit and watch his siblings in their robust play, ever too fragile to join in. But he had a grin that lit his sweet face and a squealing laugh that inspired laughter in all who heard it. Even dour Fitch, sitting on a bench by the door, made a sound that might be a chuckle. Maud, with her mother's delicate features and her father's height, flashed a dazzling smile at Matt and had soon deposited baby Simon on Kate's lap so that she might flit about pouring wine and showing off her charms. Matt was smitten, his own warm, engaging smile beaming brightly.

Simon gurgled and reached out a hand toward Ghent, who was nearest him. His little legs pumping in delight, the baby bounced on her lap. It heartened her to feel his surprising strength. Not so puny after all.

As Kate bounced Simon on her knee and chatted with Winifrith about the mayoral election and Isabella Frost's boasts that the mayoral feast would be the grandest in the city's history, she noticed Matt and Maud slipping away.

Maud was often Kate's quiet supporter in disputes with Lionel. She wished she had anticipated the attraction and primed Matt to ask Maud about her father's illness, how long, details.

Winifrith moved on to the gossip about Margery Kirkby. "I do not know what to think. King Richard was our king for so long, the grandson of King Edward, and now he is imprisoned, or worse . . . And King Henry demands our loyalty, so it is treasonous to support the very man it was treasonous to betray. Were the men committing treason when they captured King Richard? For he was still king when they did. What a muddle." She wagged her head. "So I do not know what to think of Sir Thomas Kirkby's betrayal of King Henry in support of King Richard—or I should say Richard of Bordeaux, as we are now to refer to him. It is difficult to condemn Sir Thomas. And in all the confusion—Well, how does anyone know who is doing what to whom?"

Winifrith's breathless expression of bemused indignation was clearly meant to distract Kate. She hoped it rather distracted Winifrith, and did her best to keep the conversation moving along.

"I find it difficult to believe Sir Thomas would take sides after risking his life and his reputation attempting to reconcile the royal cousins," Kate said. "And to think of Lady Margery being hunted down as she grieves for her beloved husband—I begin to wonder what manner of man wears the crown."

"Have a care, Katherine. Those are treasonous words."

Simon had been nodding in Kate's lap, but as Ghent shifted and meeped in his sleep the baby woke and began to bounce again. Kate turned the conversation to marvel at his strength.

Winifrith's expression softened, and she reached over to tickle her son's feet. "He is a miracle child. My last, I fear. The midwife does not think I can—or should—carry another."

"You have a houseful of beautiful, healthy children to comfort you, eh?" said Kate.

"What about you? You have Simon's, and your brother's child, but what about one of your own, Katherine?"

"One day I should like that. When the time is right."

"These are your best years for it. Carrying them, birthing them, it was all so much easier when I was younger. Sir Elric is so handsome. Do not put business before marriage for too long."

Kate was only half listening to Winifrith, more intent on the sound of feet on the outer stairs to the upper story and a creaking above. Maud and Matt visiting Lionel? She hoped so. She bent to smell the sweetness of Simon's downy hair and tickle him so that he giggled and shrieked, waking Ghent, who barked in response, a noise to disguise the sounds overhead.

"To be frank," Kate said, amidst the ensuing laughter, "I think I shall just steal this adorable child and take him home."

Winifrith was about to say something when the room grew too quiet and voices were suddenly audible up above. Maud's and Matt's . . . and Lionel's. Rising with a gasp, Winifrith was out the door before Kate managed to stand up and resettle the baby in her arms so she might hitch up her skirts to climb the steps.

By the time Kate reached the bedchamber above, Winifrith was berating her daughter for her betrayal.

"It's not right!" Maud exclaimed, her pretty face screwed up in anger. "Your lies could cost Berend his life!"

Simon began to fuss in Kate's arms, and she rocked him gently, giving him a finger to hold. He stuck it in his toothless mouth and was content.

"Cost Berend his life?" Winifrith glanced to Maud, to Kate, then to her husband, who sat propped up against pillows with a bandage round his forehead and his arm in a sling, his eyes wide in uncertainty about what to do. "What has Katherine's cook to do with your—" Winifrith threw up her hands, for it was clear he was not ill, but injured. "Your misadventure?"

"The sheriffs' men are searching for Berend," said Maud. "He was seen arguing with the spice seller the very night he was murdered. Father's story might save him."

Winifrith slumped down on the edge of the bed. "Is this true?" she asked Kate.

"Berend's danger? Yes."

The woman turned to her husband. "Did you know this?"

"I've been abed, weak from loss of blood. How could I hear of it?" He looked at Kate, and sighed. "But now you know, I will have no peace, will I?"

"Peace?" Kate repeated. "How could you ever have peace if you sent an innocent man to the gallows?"

"Amen," whispered Maud.

Winifrith reared up and slapped her daughter. In the ensuing shouting match, Kate sidled over to Matt as she attempted to calm the baby's frightened cries.

"Merek was being attacked and Lionel stepped between them," Matt told Kate. "A brave act, but he was badly wounded. Someone else came along, scared off the attacker, and helped Merek and Lionel." He held out his hands. "I can take the baby out on the steps. That should soothe him."

Blessing him, Kate handed Simon over to Matt. When they were out the door, she went to sit on the bed by Lionel. "Do you recall the feast Berend prepared to celebrate Winifrith's churching after her ordeal with Simon?"

"That was just a few months ago, of course I remember," Lionel snapped, then whispered an apology. "I did not know Berend was blamed. It was not him, I can swear it was not."

Kate's heart raced. At last someone who could help. "I pray you, what *did* you see?"

"It was dark. I'd—God help me, I do not know what happened. We were talking, and suddenly a man came charging at Merek, calling him a thief and a swindler. He stabbed him once, and then again. At least twice. As Merek fell, I—I don't know what I thought I might do, but I stepped between them."

"You tried to save him?" Kate had thought Matt misunderstood. Lionel had always struck her as a coward who would cross the street to avoid an unpleasant encounter.

He sat up a little straighter, though it caused him to flinch from the pain. "I drew my dagger, we circled, and then he attacked. I never had a chance. Don't know what I was thinking." He blinked at the memory, seemingly as surprised as Kate was. Winifrith groaned and crossed herself. "When his dagger sank into my side I could not catch my breath. He reared up as if he was going to finish me off, but someone called out to him to halt. He looked up, then stumbled backward, turned, and ran. I wanted to run as well, but all I could manage was to crawl into the darkness."

"So there was light," Kate noted.

Lionel stared at her a moment, a flicker of something, then looked down, shaking his head slowly. "Yes, there was some light. I could see the attacker's dagger. And Merek lying there. But I cannot think where the light came from. I had no lantern."

"Was Merek dead?"

"No. I saw enough—" He looked at his daughter. "Maud says his throat was slit. Not then. He muttered something. A man makes no sound once his throat is cut."

Was it the second man who finished off Merek? "You saw the man who frightened off the attacker?"

An ill-chosen shrug forced Lionel to bend over, panting with pain.

Kate gently suggested he rest a moment, catch his breath. Winifrith wanted her to leave, but Kate suggested she go take the baby from Matt so that he could come in and listen. To her surprise, Winifrith nodded and stepped out.

Maud took her mother's place at her father's bedside, helping him lie back against the pillows, giving him something to drink. "Forgive me, Father, but I could not let you burden yourself with such a terrible guilt."

He was soaked in sweat, his breathing shallow.

"How extensive are his wounds?" Kate asked.

"The stab wound in his side." Maud indicated a spot just below the heart. "And a deep slice to his upper right arm." Hence the sling to hold it still. "And his head must have hit a cobble or something. The physician wanted to bleed him, but Mother refused. She said he had lost enough blood."

Lionel opened his eyes. "I crawled to a place along the wall with some sort of beam sticking out. I used it to pull myself upright and lean against the doorway. When I caught my breath I saw the man kneel to Merek, help him rise." Lionel coughed weakly. "I do not know how I managed, but I stumbled away and somehow made it home. I don't remember much of the journey."

"It was the middle of the night when he returned," said Maud. "How he made it across the city when he was so weak, losing so much blood, and without alerting a night watchman . . ." She nodded to Kate and cocked her head toward her father as if this was his cue to explain.

Kate leaned close to Lionel. "He carried you home, didn't he?"

Lionel bowed his head.

"Why did you not tell us?" asked Maud. "There is no shame in that."

"I promised," Lionel mumbled.

Maud reached out and lifted his chin. "Father." Spoken as a warning.

"I swore I would not tell. He saved my life. And Merek's. He was alive, Merek was. We left him standing up against a wall, waving us on."

"But if you say nothing, this man would seem guilty of murdering Merek," Maud pointed out.

"I had not thought . . ." Lionel groaned as if it were all too much.

"Berend?" Kate asked.

A nod.

"Was he alone?"

"I do not remember much."

"Father," Maud warned.

He closed his eyes. "I remember no one else. I told you, I recall little of the journey."

"You were in pain, I know," said Maud, touching his cheek.

He leaned into her hand, his face softening into a contentment Kate had never witnessed, never guessed he ever experienced.

"Why were you with Merek?" Kate asked.

"I—He had approached me about our spice shipments," Lionel whispered.

"Thinking to trade with us?" asked Kate. "Is that why he had been asking our partners about you?"

"He had? What sort of questions?" Lionel's voice was little more than a gasp, and Maud touched Kate's hand, as if to stay her, but her father shook his head at her and looked to Kate.

"Holme said he was quite persistent with questions that went beyond trade," said Kate. "He asked about your character, and your relationship with Sir Ralph."

"He hoped I might afford him a tie to my cousin Westmoreland? I did not know—I have been a fool, Katherine."

"Forgive me for assuming you would hear of it," she said, pressing his hand, hoping for a little more before he must rest. "You say Merek was alive when Berend carried you away?"

"Yes."

"So we don't know who murdered Merek," said Kate.

"No," said Lionel. "I cannot swear to the sheriffs that Berend is innocent." A pause for a cough.

Maud helped him to drink something in a cup. It smelled of honey and herbs.

"If I speak up they might accuse me." His eyes reflected his fear, and also his pain and exhaustion.

"Of course they won't accuse you. One need only see your wounds to believe your account," said Maud. She drew back the covers, revealing a bloodstained bandage that wrapped round her father's torso.

"One more thing and then I will leave you to your rest," Kate said. "Where did this happen?"

"We were on our way toward Foss Bridge. We had just come through the Shambles. Near St. Crux, it was."

"Oh," Kate whispered.

Maud looked up. "Is that important?"

It was. "Merek's body was found closer to the market, on the other end of the Shambles."

"See? Not dead yet," Lionel whispered. "Sounds like Merek was headed home."

Kate nodded as she thought what that meant. "Merek's attacker might have returned, found him struggling down along the shuttered shops," she said. "Please, if you have any idea who the attacker was, now is the time to say."

Lionel groaned. "Don't know why I protect the bastard. Jon Horner. Talk to him."

Startled, Kate said nothing for a moment, then, softly, "I cannot, Lionel. He was found dead this morning, possibly poisoned."

"God help us," Maud gasped. "Is father in danger?"

"Sir Elric's squire is watching the house," Kate assured her. Lionel was soaked in sweat, his eyelids flickering. Enough for the moment. "I am grateful for all your help, Lionel."

A weak smile, though his eyes were already closed, his head listing to one side. "Me, a help to you." His attempt to chuckle dissolved into a cough.

As they left him, they found the apothecary Gwenllian Ferriby waiting on the landing. Her eyes keenly studied their faces. Her rich dark hair was caught up in a bronze crispinette, slightly mussed from the fur-lined hood she had just pushed back, but the effect just seemed to emphasize her beauty. Kate had become acquainted with her while Kevin recuperated in her home. She was the foster sister of the infirmarian at St. Mary's, Brother Martin, and had prepared Kevin's tinctures according to her brother's instructions once Kevin left the infirmary. Her apothecary was on St. Helen's Square, next to the York Tavern, a long way to come from her shop in the middle of the day. Curious.

Maud reached out to embrace Gwenllian. "I am so grateful you've come. The drink has calmed Father, and eased his pain, but I fear he is feverish."

"I will go to him, Maud. Rest easy. Between me and the physician, we will put him right." She nodded to Kate. "Dame Katherine," and stepped past them into the room, followed by a servant.

"Personal attention from the apothecary," said Kate with a questioning look.

"She does it as a favor to me," said Maud. "I once saved her daughter from a runaway cart, and we have been friends ever since."

Yet another reason to love and respect the young woman before her.

"Thank you for your help today, Maud."

"Father was of help?"

"He was. I doubt he would have spoken up without your encouragement. I am in your debt."

"Mother was wrong to prevent him from speaking to you," Maud said simply, then started down the steps.

"She means to protect her family."

Maud paused, looking back over her shoulder. "A man who so easily slit another's throat, he is a danger to us all and should not be free to walk the streets of York. If the constables spend all their efforts searching for Berend, the real murderer will go free. My regret is that it is still not proof enough to protect Berend."

Nor, in her right mind, could Kate be certain Berend had not finished the man, except that she could not believe that of Berend. But Parr . . . She said nothing as they continued into the hall.

Winifrith glowered at Kate from her seat by the hounds, Simon asleep in her arms. "You have outstayed your welcome."

"Hush, Mother," Maud hissed. "If Dame Katherine comes to Father's defense, the sheriffs will believe her, for all in the city know they are not friends."

"You risked your father's life before you knew whether she would defend him." Winifrith did not look any more kindly on her daughter than she did on Kate, when she turned back to her. "*Will* you vouch for him, Katherine? Will you do that for him despite your differences?"

"Of course," said Kate. "I seek the truth, always. And, as I told Maud, your house is being watched by one of Sir Elric's men. Now I will leave you in peace." Kate took Maud's hands, pressing them. "Bless you." Calling to Lille and Ghent, she slipped on their leashes, and departed.

Matt, who had stood quietly beside Fitch near the door, opened it for her and followed her out. A wintry sun had turned the snow underfoot to slush, forcing Kate to pay close attention to where she was stepping. As they reached the end of the bridge, she suggested that Matt head toward the Martha House on Castlegate and escort Marie and Petra home. She suddenly wanted them near.

"And you, Dame Katherine?"

"I am going to pass Jon Horner's house, see whether the sheriffs' men are there, and then stop at the guesthouse."

"Ah."

"I will see you at home."

Not far down Davygate she passed Jon Horner's house, unguarded. Damn the sheriffs. But they did not know all that she did.

She hurried on.

—◦◦◦—

Margery pressed a hand to her stomach and moaned. "Oh, my dear man. I pray it was quick, that he did not suffer."

Kate had mentioned only the wound that had killed Carl. A kindness. She impressed upon Griselde, Clement, and Seth that it was more important than ever that they keep "Mary" out of sight. Though, truly, whoever had tortured him would have come to the guesthouse by now if Carl had talked. But the violence inflicted on him was difficult for Kate to put out of her mind.

—◦◦◦—

Marie and Petra rushed into the kitchen, breathless with their news, announced partially by each.

"Berend is in York!" Petra exclaimed. "We must find him."

"We must find him and hide him. The sheriffs' men want him for murder," said Marie, her eyes brimming with tears. "He is no murderer."

"And they call him a traitor," said Petra.

Damn the gossips. Kate opened her arms to the children, hugging them tightly to her. "We will prove them wrong," she said, banishing all doubt from her voice and her heart. She would find a way to prove his innocence.

Marie was the first to pull out of Kate's grasp, sniffing the air. "Jennet, did you burn the stew again?" Stomping over to peer into the pot, she began quizzing the reluctant cook.

"She is a tyrant," Petra whispered in Kate's ear. "But she was so upset when we heard folk talking about Berend, and then when Matt admitted it was the truth she burst into tears."

"And you?" Kate asked, smoothing Petra's hair and kissing her cheek. "How are you?"

Petra bowed her head and shrugged. "I dreamed a woman plucked a rose from a rose bush growing in a little casket. She gave it to Berend, but as he took it, he was pricked by a thorn. A poisoned thorn. He fell, fighting for his breath."

Kate drew her back into her arms, holding her close, kissing the top of her head.

Petra pulled away, her eyes filled with tears. "I don't know what it means, but I do not doubt him. Or you. I know you will save him."

But what if he did not want to be saved? Kate wondered. He had asked her to say nothing of what he had told her. What was Kate's responsibility regarding him? Honor his wish, or help him? What was her responsibility to the community? Surely to do all that she could to find out the root cause of the violence and ensure that it stopped. And what if that meant betraying Berend in order to save him?

"You don't doubt him, do you?" Petra asked.

"No, my sweet. No."

9

CONFEDERATES

Before Kate left for the York Tavern she took Jennet aside. "Any thoughts about where Jon Horner might have spent the night, who he might have been with?"

"Who might be a poisoner?" Jennet shook her head. "What I've learned of him so far, he took advantage of folk down on their luck. That sort has many enemies."

"I would think this would be someone he trusted enough to eat and drink with. How else might he have been poisoned?"

"Someone who sold him a meat pie, or a pint of ale?"

"Anyone in particular?"

"No. None of his victims have been in such trades. I will keep looking."

With a nod, Kate took the hounds' leads firmly in hand and headed off to the tavern, her mind busy considering the players in the game so far—Merek, dead; Jon Horner, dead; Lionel, badly injured; Berend, hiding; Margery and Carl—how were they connected to this? She hoped that Bess Merchet would tell her what she knew about Jon Horner and with whom he dined; indeed, Kate would be grateful for anything the old taverner cared to share. And her visit might come to naught, the woman had no cause to trust Kate. In that case, she might at least leave word that she had information for Elric. She wanted to discuss Lionel's tale with him, Berend's part in it, and, perhaps most important, that Merek had been killed at the other side of the Shambles from where he had been attacked by Horner.

Bess Merchet stood in the middle of the public room, hands on hips, a challenge in her eyes as she watched Kate settle Lille and Ghent just inside the open door, one on each side. Colin Merchet assured Kate he would keep an eye on them, which made her smile wondering why he thought they might obey him.

"They will keep an eye on themselves, Colin. But thank you." She hesitated, remembering the poisoned meat. "Fetch me at once if anyone shows more than a passing interest in them."

He promised to do so.

"You took your time," Bess said loudly, interrupting them. "Come along." She gestured for Kate to follow her to her lair between the public room and the kitchen. Pointing to a chair, she ordered Kate to sit. "You look as if you would welcome a sip of brandywine."

"I would indeed." Kate perched tentatively on an embroidered cushion. "You are kind to offer."

"It has nothing to do with kindness." Kate marveled at the illusion the woman created around her, a large presence, though she was in fact short enough that she stood on a small stool to reach a shelf that would be no stretch for Kate. She brought down a cobalt blue Italian glass bottle, then matching goblets, and lastly a pewter plate with roasted nuts. In steely silence Bess poured a goodly amount in each goblet, setting one in front of Kate, and then took a seat across from her in a high-backed, well-padded chair. Lifting her own goblet, the elderly taverner said, "Let us drink to the health of good friends," and sipped.

An odd toast. But Kate gladly sipped. A fine brandywine.

Bess nodded, as if the drink signaled the beginning of their meeting. "Why did you wish to see me?"

Taking her cue from the woman's blunt question, Kate said, "I need your help." And waited.

Thick white brows drew together over eyes slightly milky with age yet fierce. The taverner's rosy complexion was surprisingly unlined, and strands of copper hair mixed in with the white escaped her snowy, beribboned cap.

"Regarding?" Her tone sharp, as if warning Kate not to waste her time.

"Jon Horner. I understand he took his meals here. I hoped you might tell me what you know of him. If anyone ever joined him, particularly the spice seller found dead last night."

Old Bess sniffed and sipped her wine, her eyes still locked on Kate, who was beginning to wonder whether *she* was wasting precious time.

"Horner." Another sniff. "I paid him little heed." With that, Bess sat awhile studying Kate, so long a while that the brandywine, which she sipped, and the homely sounds from the kitchen and the public room, began to lull Kate. She was startled when the elderly woman said, "Horner ate alone most days, though that shifty-eyed spice seller joined him on occasion." As Kate opened her mouth to ask a question, Bess said, "I do not listen to customers' conversations unbidden."

Unbidden. An interesting qualifier.

"Did he dine with anyone else?" Kate asked.

Bess tapped the table with a broad finger, rough from a life of hard work, the joints swollen with age. She appeared to be a woman of rich complexities, powerful in her own right, with an income sufficient to afford her the luxury of brandywine in old age, yet with no apparent desire to take advantage of her grandson's presence to sit back and take her ease. Kate thought she might like the taverner, given a chance.

"John Paris." Bess spoke the name as if testing it, and on hearing it, nodded. "He is an occasional customer, so I might not have remembered but that he seemed uneasy when he dined with Horner one day, kept glancing round as if expecting trouble. A man of so little significance in the city, what did he fear? It had me wondering. I did not connect it with Horner at the time, but now . . ."

Paris's discomfort while dining with Horner interested Kate. A warehouse he managed for the merchant Thomas Graa stood next to her mother's Martha House, and Paris himself lived close by. He was also a customer of Kate's guesthouse, though he had not been there for a while, and she'd had a mind to refuse him in future for she'd had trouble with him the past summer, though related to her mother, not the guesthouse.

"When was this?" Kate asked.

"Perhaps a week past, a little more." Bess looked at something beyond Kate. A parade of days? "Just about a week ago."

Kate thanked her. She would pay Paris a visit. "Anyone else?"

"Now and then. No one of note. The sort I would turn away if they were on their own, the ones who never seem to have the coin to pay for what they drink."

Possibly useful. "Is there anything else you can tell me about Horner? Or Merek?"

Bess shifted slightly in her chair, as if getting comfortable. Had Kate passed some test?

"I know what you are about, Dame Katherine. You seek information that will convince the sheriffs that Berend did not murder Merek. Or Horner. I commend your loyalty. Berend is no murderer. Not now."

Bess knew that Berend was in the city? Because of Peter Trimlow's accusation? Or was there more? Kate chose her words with care. "I was not aware that you knew Berend."

"No?" The hint of a smile. "He lodged here when he first came to York. In the large room, sharing with the others. He was well-liked, trusted. He told me about his childhood in a tavern, and I was about to fire my indifferent cook and hire Berend when he told me he had found employment. With you."

Berend had never mentioned lodging at the York Tavern. "I did not know." And it hurt.

"No one is ever entirely forthcoming, are they?" Bess gave her a knowing, but not unfriendly smile. "He is a man who seeks redemption. He'd not risk his soul for such petty criminals."

"Then I can count on you as an ally?"

A tilt of the head, the ribbons on her cap touching her broad shoulders, the wise old eyes searching Kate's face with some amusement. "So Berend *is* in the city?"

Caught. Kate wanted Bess on her side; she would be a formidable enemy.

"You say that as if you'd heard, but did not believe," said Kate.

A chuckle. "Once checkmated, it is customary to accept with grace. Do you play chess?"

"I did with my late husband. It has been a while."

"You are Simon Neville's widow, yes. I doubt he was a challenging opponent. A handsome rake with no head for money."

Kate gave a startled laugh. "That sums him up neatly."

"You will do better. I did the second time round."

"You certainly seem far more comfortable than I was on being widowed."

"But you have persevered, and gained the respect of the wealthiest merchants in York." Bess studied Kate over the rim of her cup as she sipped. "I would be your friend, Dame Katherine. But I do not like secrets. Trimlow the baker said he'd seen Berend, but he has been known to see far odder things in his cups."

"He drinks here?"

"He does. Are you choosing what to share and what to keep to yourself? As I said, secrets make a lie of a friendship."

"Even if they were entrusted to me and no one else?"

"Ah." Bess looked down into her goblet. "That is entirely different." She was quiet a moment. "I count on you and Sir Elric to make certain that Berend is cleared of all suspicion. See that you succeed. Come to me in the morning if you have not yet found him, and the murderer. I will keep my ears pricked."

Kate wondered whether Old Bess's ears were similar to Jennet's.

"Is there anyone else?" Bess asked.

"Lionel Neville. Did he ever meet Horner here?"

A roll of the eyes. "That man. He is no stranger to the tavern, but he never sat with Horner. I assure you, I would have made note of that. Why do you ask?" Bess gave her a warning look when Kate hesitated. "I cannot believe you would protect *his* secrets."

Neither could Kate. But his ordeal warranted discretion.

How can Old Bess help you if you keep so much from her? Geoff asked in Kate's head.
Should I trust her with it, Geoff? Do you firmly believe that?
I do.

"Do you have a while?" Kate asked. "I have quite a tale to tell."

A slight grin and a nod. "There is enough brandywine for it." Bess set down her empty cup and began to rise just as Ghent gave a bark from the tavern yard, followed closely by Lille.

Kate jumped to her feet. "Those are warnings."

"I have been selfish," said Bess. "I would not have your hounds come to harm. Sir Elric tells me they sit quietly at your feet, awaiting your command. If that is so, bring them in I pray you."

Kate gave her a cursory bow and hurried out, too anxious to see what was wrong to note Bess's change of heart.

Colin stood at the door watching Lille and Ghent stride back and forth between the door and toward the street to the extent their leads permitted, sniffing the air and growling.

"I don't know what they sense, Mistress Clifford. I've seen nothing awry."

"They often smell or hear what we cannot." Kate bent to untie the hounds' leads, whispering for them to show her. Sniffing the ground beneath the eaves just outside the door, they led her along the tavern building toward the square. The ground close to the house was bare of snow except for quickly melting clumps outlining two pairs of footprints. Parr and Sawyer? Seeing her dogs outside the tavern, had they paused here, hoping to overhear something? And then Lille and Ghent had raised the hue and cry.

"Track," she ordered.

The hounds turned right in the square, leading her past the apothecary and the large Ferriby home, then round the corner onto Davygate. There they were, Parr and Sawyer, trying to push past a cart piled high with barrels. Good. The barking had frightened them off. Keeping hold of the hounds' leads—they were ready to chase the men down—Kate was about to turn back when she noticed a boy calling to the pair. Skulker, a ne'er-do-well who hung around the warehouses near the staithes, working as an errand boy. Once, when Kate had noticed him at Paris's warehouse next door to her former home, she had thought to use him, but Jennet had warned her to avoid him unless she wanted the wrong folk to know her business.

Had the two men hired Skulker? If so, she wanted to see where he was taking them. Down Davygate they hurried, Kate maintaining just enough distance that she did not raise alarms—the hounds did attract attention. For once Kate was grateful for the crowded streets, especially the noisy street barkers calling out their wares, covering the greetings called out to her as she passed. Skulker's path led down alleyways and round the market, gathering speed as he crossed into Castlegate.

Kate felt a sudden twinge of foreboding. Castlegate was home to her mother and her beguines as well as to Thomas Holme, and it led not just to the staithes but also the warehouse John Paris managed, Skulker's favorite haunts. She urged Lille and Ghent to a trot.

John Paris stood on the street in front of the warehouse, shaking his head dejectedly as he caught sight of Skulker and the two men. Parr and Sawyer broke out into a run, shouting something at Paris, who shrugged and gestured toward York Castle.

Hoping one of the beguines might know what had happened at the warehouse to draw Parr and Sawyer, Kate slipped into the little school Sister Brigida had fixed up in the small building that fronted her mother's Martha House. She touched Lille and Ghent to let them know to be quiet and stay at her side. Brigida glanced up from her observation of two girls who were biting their tongues as they struggled to master styluses and wax tablets. As soon as the girls caught sight of Lille and Ghent they jumped up.

"Can we ride them?" a tow-headed girl cried.

"Can we?" echoed her freckled companion.

Lille and Ghent each took a step backward, their ears registering their alarm.

"They are hounds, not ponies," Sister Brigida told the girls. Tall, long-limbed, Brigida was well able to reach out and grasp the girls by their shoulders and draw them back to their bench while quietly but firmly enjoining them to sit down and behave. "This is part of your education, learning not to startle any of God's creatures."

The freckled imp was having none of that, and whispered to Lille, "Come, pup."

Brigida squeezed her shoulders. "Be still and silent, or you will pay with additional copying," she warned.

Kate was glad her girls were at home. They would have posed a larger problem, insisting on following her.

Once the girls settled, Brigida apologized to Kate and asked what she might do for her.

"You have heard no shouting at the warehouse next door?"

The tow-head glanced up. "We did! And we saw the sheriffs' constables rush in."

"And then I ordered them to sit down," said Brigida. "Do you know what's amiss?"

"No. Did you see anyone come out with them?" Kate asked.

"No. I am sorry. But you might ask Sister Dina. She is up above, trying to complete her work on a gown that was promised by this evening."

Ordering Lille and Ghent to sit by the door, Kate lifted her skirts and climbed up the steep ladder-like steps to the small solar above. Sister Dina, her round, sweet face furrowed in frowns as she bent to her needlework, did not even look up. Kate cleared her throat, then walked over to her. One hand came up, signaling that she would greet Kate in a moment. A few more stitches, a satisfied nod, and Dina tucked the needle in the fabric and pushed the work aside.

"Dame Katherine. Welcome."

"Did you perchance glance out the window when the sheriffs' men arrived at John Paris's warehouse just now?"

"Is that who they were?" She nodded. "I did. But I am not certain about what I thought I—" she looked up, searching for the English "—witnessed?"

"Yes, that is the word." Dina had found English difficult at first, but had been rapidly catching up with her companions, Brigida and Clara. "What did you think you witnessed?" Kate asked.

"I saw our friend Berend. He was led away like a—" Dina bit her lip, frowned, brought her hands together as if tied.

"Prisoner?" Kate guessed.

"Yes. Yes. I would worry, but I must be—" Dina shook her head, "in error? He is not in the city, I think?"

Kate silently cursed herself for not realizing the warehouse was somewhere Berend might hide. When they had lived next door to it, he had often taken leftover food to the workers there. They loved him for it and might very well hide him. But they might not think to have a care when Skulker was about.

"Did John Paris witness what happened?"

A nod.

Kate would ruin Paris for giving Berend up to the sheriffs. His infirm wife had died in late autumn, so she would feel no guilt in depriving him of income.

"Berend *was* away," she said, "but he returned recently. I believe that you did see him."

Dina crossed herself, her eyes filling with tears. "Why would they take him? He is a good man."

"They are mistaken." Kate would say no more to Sister Dina, who had endured her own ordeal in the summer, the attack in which Kevin had been injured rescuing her. "Was there anyone else with him?"

Dina frowned up at her. "You ask if he was only prisoner?" She nodded. "Only him."

Kate peered out the window, saw no one outside the Castlegate end of the warehouse, but she did spot John Paris strolling out the back, down Hertergate toward his home. Alone.

Thanking Dina, Kate picked her way back down the steps.

"Was she able to help?" asked Brigida.

"She was. Forgive my interruption. I will leave you to your students."

"You are always welcome, Dame Katherine."

The girls whispered good-byes to Lille and Ghent, their voices sad with lost opportunity.

Signaling the dogs, Kate stepped out and went round the side of the warehouse to the rear, then down the alley into Hertergate. John Paris had not stopped at his house, but was still walking in the direction of the river. Heading to the staithes? She slipped the leads from the hounds' collars and motioned for them to halt Paris, taking her time following. Let his fear of them work to her benefit. For a man as terrified of Lille and Ghent as she knew him to be, it would be an event out of his nightmares to have them appear out of nowhere and crowd close. It should render him eager to tell her anything in exchange for calling them off.

"Foiled, were you?" she said when she reached him. "How much had the liveried men offered you to give Berend over?"

"I—It was not like that! I sent for the *sheriffs*, not those men." Paris was shivering and trying to shrink himself into something so tiny Lille and Ghent might forget about him. "I—It was my duty to Thomas Graa, who owns the warehouse. Berend is wanted for the murder of Merek the spice seller. It matters not a whit whether or not you or I believe him guilty. If the sheriffs discovered that I harbored a murderer in Graa's warehouse, which he entrusts to me, I would be ruined. I sent word to the castle. But Skulker—he brought those other men, the little bastard. I've warned him to stay away, and my workers know to keep him out of the warehouse."

Kate was seething, she'd seen his shoulders slump when he spied Parr and Sawyer, but she needed information. "Where are Skulker and the two men now?"

"Gone. They wanted to go in, search, but I told them the sheriffs' men had taken everything."

"Did they?"

"I did not see them take anything. Just Berend. But the two men looked like trouble. Faith, anyone in Skulker's company is trouble."

"You did not see where they went?"

"I did not watch."

"How did you learn Berend was there?" Berend would have known to stay out of sight of Paris, knowing he was untrustworthy.

"Could you call off your dogs?" Paris whined, the sweat darkening the hair sticking out of his hat.

"I will when I believe you have told me all you know. How did you discover that Berend was in your warehouse?"

"I smelled cooked meat, well spiced, when I went into the warehouse after dinner today. A little thing, but I had heard of the search for Berend, and I remember such a scent coming from the kitchen when you lived near. So I waited. I saw him sneaking in the back, and I sent for the sheriffs' men."

Clever. She would not have believed it of him. "Was Berend injured?"

"By the constables? I do not believe he was."

"Before they came?"

Paris began to shake his head but stopped, as if fearing the dogs would take it as a signal. "I caught only a glimpse of him. Enough to recognize him, that is all."

"So you would not be able to say whether he'd been injured when he returned to the warehouse?"

Another slight shake of his head, eyeing the dogs with terror.

"The men Skulker brought here, had they been here before?"

"I had not seen them before. But my men would be better able to tell you."

"They are well dressed. Why would you think them trouble?"

"I told you, anyone who would arrive with Skulker . . ."

"I don't believe you. I think they've come to you before. Shall I tell the sheriffs you are protecting them?"

"Why would the sheriffs care about them?"

"You thought they were trouble," said Kate. "The sheriffs might agree."

Paris dropped his head. "They might have come to my home, asked me whether I knew him."

"Go home," she said. "I will think what to do about you."

"What? Dame Katherine! I was only—"

She signaled the hounds to herd him back toward his house.

"I had to raise the hue and cry!" he shouted over his shoulder as he stumbled toward his house.

Once he had slammed the door behind him, Kate called Lille and Ghent back to her, commending them as she led them back to the warehouse. There the workers talked over each other, apologizing, assuring her they had done their best to keep Berend's presence a secret. One of them offered to show her where Berend had slept. But Lille and Ghent beat them there, prowling round a quiet spot behind stacked barrels, ears perked, as they sniffed at a pack sitting atop a stack of blankets.

Kate recognized Berend's traveling pack, old, worn leather with bright new buckles Jennet had sewn on for him as a Christmas gift. The girls loved to slip little gifts into it when it sat by the door, awaiting his departure. *Blessed Mother, may they have the chance to do that again.* Calling Lille and Ghent to her side, Kate opened the pack: a shirt, leggings, a leather vest, a pouch of the salve for his scars, especially his ruined ear, a twist of spices, a small cook pot, wooden spoon, and, wrapped in leather, a good skinning knife. Her breath caught in her throat as she touched these pieces of Berend's life. The shirt carried his scent. It had been worn. That it was not bloody gave her hope. She closed up the pack, nodded to the blankets.

"Were these Berend's?" she asked the men, who had followed her.

"No. They're ours. We let him use 'em," said one.

She signaled the hounds to rest while she questioned the men. She wanted no distractions. "Have you seen Berend with anyone?"

They had not. "Quiet, he was. For the first day he just slept," said one. "We kept watch that no one bothered him."

"Did he ask for anything to clean a wound?"

All the men shook their heads. One mentioned his limp, and the cut beneath his eye. "But it was already healing when he arrived."

Nothing new. "Bless you for giving him sanctuary," she said.

"He's a good man," said the one who had offered to show her Berend's spot.

"Skulker is a dead lad," muttered one of the others.

Kate imagined so, either Berend's friends in York or Parr and Sawyer would see to that. The lad would be smart to run away.

"The pair Skulker brought—have they been here before?"

Nods. "A few days past. Claimed they'd come on Merek's behalf to collect what he had stored here. We'd never seen them before so we told them to return with proof Merek had given them the authority."

"I commend you."

A shrug. "There was little left. Merek had sold most of the spices and such. He was moving on, he told us."

Moving on, now Berend had returned? "And you thought it odd they were here to collect his wares?"

"We had a laugh about it. For all their livery and fine speech, they were easy to foil."

Or they like people to think so, catch them off guard.

"Can you show me where Merek stored his wares?"

They led her to a shelf that held a sack, a few jugs. Certainly nothing the two men would have gone out of their way for. "This is it?"

A nod.

"I see why you found it amusing. Did you see the direction they took?"

"Back down Castlegate, toward the city."

She signaled to Lille and Ghent to rise from where they had been resting and gave them a good whiff of Berend's pack, then told them to look about. Just in case.

"We might've done better," said one of the men. "Bloody Paris."

"How did he find Berend?" Kate asked.

"Had a barrel got loose, Berend was helping us get it in hand and Paris saw him. Ran out into the street screeching like he'd seen the dead rise up."

"Why didn't Berend run?"

All the men shrugged. "He seemed to just give up," said one.

"Paris tells a different story about how he discovered Berend." She told them what he'd said.

They exchanged guilty glances. "We did ask for one of his stews." "Course he smelled it. That's why he came in when he did and caught him." "We're as guilty as Skulker."

"No. You did make a mistake, but so did Berend. He was grateful, wanted to repay you, and he forgot that the scent would linger."

They hung their heads. Their friend had been taken, and they realized they were, in part, to blame.

Going in search of the hounds, Kate found them sniffing round a crate tucked in a dark corner. She called for some light. The dogs circled, ears pricked, sniffing, then Lille stood on her hind legs, paws on the top of the crate, licking her lips and glancing back at Kate. Ghent also rose, then leaped up atop it, pawing at it. The men, one of them holding up a lantern, began to argue about what was stored there.

Signaling the hounds to come sit, Kate rubbed their backs as she listened to the men, learning that Berend had borrowed a tool and disappeared in this direction in the early morning, shortly after they had relieved the man on night duty.

When she had heard enough, she asked for a tool that would open the crate, preferring not to reveal the battle axe in her skirt.

One of the men unhooked a long iron bar from his belt and handed it over. She considered its heft, balance. It would do. As she turned back toward the crate, she kicked something that went skittering. "Bring the lantern closer." Several bent nails lay where they must have fallen when someone else opened the crate.

"Two of you, watch the doors," she said. "Call out if anyone approaches." She fell to, prying up a corner.

"The earl's knight approaches," one of the watchers called out. "He is with the one who saved Sister Dina."

Elric and Kevin. Damnable timing.

That is habit, Kate, Geoff whispered in her mind. *You need Elric to help Berend. But will he?*

He said he would. And you seemed to believe him then.

Habit. Of course it was. He seemed sincere about helping. Pray God he did not blame Berend when he learned she'd hidden Margery all this while. "Bring them to me."

She went back to work, prying another corner loose, and had just engaged the one who had stayed with her in lending a hand to pull it open when Elric and Kevin reached them.

"Can we help?" Elric asked.

She motioned to her companion and they both backed away. Elric and Kevin finished the task with ease.

"What do you see?" Kate asked as they peered in.

The man with the lantern stepped closer, shining it inside. "Jars of oil, those are."

"Large jars, standing upright, cushioned by straw," said Elric.

"Looks like one has been removed," said Kevin. "Just a pile of loose straw in that far corner."

Kate poked at the straw with the tool she had borrowed, raking some of it away until she saw what looked to be leather. "Something's hidden beneath the straw."

"If you will permit me." Elric lifted out a pouch. It was small, but clearly heavy. "There is a box of some sort inside." He set it on a barrel near them and stepped back.

Kate untied the leather thong holding the pouch closed and drew out a small carved wood traveling casket secured with leather straps, the sort used to carry valuables.

Elric leaned close and whispered, "I don't know what has happened here, but this might be something the warehouse workers should not see?"

Kate looked round at the men who had been such a help. "I need you to guard the doors. We do not want to be surprised."

As they dispersed, she unbuckled the straps. The casket was secured with a small but strong lock. "I should have brought Jennet."

"I knew her lessons would be of benefit someday," said Kevin. "Might I try?"

He drew a small pick out of his scrip, and, leaning close, one ear to the lock, he worked it. In but a few moments he stepped back with a proud grin.

"Your time in Dame Katherine's household was well spent," Elric said softly. "I pray you, Dame Katherine, do not keep us in suspense."

Hoping against hope that it was nothing incriminating—a bloody dagger, a blood-soaked shirt—she held her breath as she lifted the heavy lid. "Holy Mary, Mother of God," she breathed. "A treasure."

She lifted up a gold ring set with rubies and diamonds, a chain on which hung an exquisite pearl swan with sapphire eyes. The casket was filled with such jewels. She lifted out a small pack, opened it, "Gold and silver coins."

"A hoard," said Elric.

What was Berend doing with this? Geoff whispered in her head.

Or was it Merek's hoard? Kate prayed God it was.

"How did you find this?" asked Elric. "To whom does it belong?"

She told him how the hounds had sniffed it out. "Berend must have been the one to open and then secure the crate," she said. "His scent must have been all over it for Lille and Ghent to lead me to it. He hid this in the crate. But whose hoard it is, and why he had it, why he would hide it here, in this warehouse . . ." She shook her head. It made no sense to her.

"Someone will be back to search for this," said Elric. "We must not linger here."

Closing the casket, Kate wrapped it in the leather pouch. "One of you must carry this, and Berend's pack. I have the hounds."

"Your remarkable hounds," said Elric. "Did the warehousemen know of this?"

"No."

Elric slung Berend's pack over his shoulder and handed the pouch to Kevin, and the five of them made their way to the door opening onto Castlegate. The light was fading. Late afternoon.

"Was it anything of use?" one of the warehousemen asked.

"It might help us discover why Merek was murdered," said Kate. She thanked them once more, promising to send word of Berend, then followed Elric and Kevin out into the gathering shadows.

Once outside, in the cold, Lille and Ghent shook themselves as if shaking off the dust of the warehouse. Blessed, blessed companions, Kate thought.

"How did you happen to come to the warehouse?" she asked Elric.

"I had heard about the sheriffs being called to it," said Elric. "How did *you* happen to be there?"

"I was following Sawyer and Parr—I will tell you the whole tale. Come with me."

"Perhaps Kevin should escort you and I should go straight to the castle. I would rather Berend did not spend the night in their dungeon."

She would as well, but there was much Elric needed to know in order to ask Berend, and the sheriffs, the correct questions. "First come to the York Tavern with me. I prefer to tell the tale to you and Bess at the same time."

"Bess Merchet?" said Kevin. "Why would you share this with her?"

"She believes in Berend's innocence."

"I had heard you were there," said Elric.

"Oh?" Kevin seemed surprised.

"I found her leaning on her cane awaiting your return," Elric told Kate. "I had just sat down with an ale when Kevin came for me."

Kevin nodded. "The men watching Horner's house were called away. They'd been told that the sheriffs' men were headed to Graa's warehouse to apprehend the murderer."

Foolishly confident, Geoff whispered in Kate's mind.

Agreed.

"Kevin, would you mind watching Horner's house?" Kate asked. "I would like to see who takes the opportunity to search it. Do you agree?" she asked Elric.

He nodded. "If someone is anxious to retrieve anything, they will have been awaiting this chance. Do you have anyone in mind?"

"I wish I did," said Kate.

Looking disappointed, Kevin handed Elric the pouch with the casket and took his leave of them, heading up Coppergate toward Davygate.

"Whose jewels?" Elric wondered as he weighed the casket in his hands. "And what is Berend's connection to them?"

"Or Merek's," said Kate. "He might have had the casket hidden in the warehouse. But Lille and Ghent would not have marked it had Berend's scent not been on it."

And the discovery bode ill for his release. A man with Berend's history in possession of such a treasure? Had Salisbury entrusted it to him?

The slush was hardening as the gathering twilight drew in the chill from the river. She had not worn her warmest cloak, not expecting to traipse across the city, and her feet were cold in her boots.

"Where will they put him in the castle?" she asked.

"Accused of murder and of being a traitor to the crown, with no lord to protect him?" Elric shook his head. "I warrant they'll put him in the dungeons. That is why I need to talk to the sheriffs, offer the protection of the earl."

"You would do that for him?"

"Did I not promise I would?"

They were walking through the market and Kate paused for a moment to look into her companion's eyes, check the sincerity. His cheeks flushed with the cold, his blue eyes brighter than ever, and steady as they met her gaze.

"Are you ready to trust me, Katherine?"

She felt a slight lightening of her burden. His cooperation could only be to her benefit. As long as she had a care to protect her heart. "I am," she said. But only so far as she would any man. And not yet with Margery's secret.

He proffered his free arm, but she had a lead in each hand.

"Perhaps one of these days you might train me to hold one of those," he suggested.

She smiled, but thought it unlikely.

—◦◦◦—

Bess sat on a high-backed chair by the door to the public room, hands on the carved wolf's head atop her cane, her eyes snapping. "I do not like the grim looks on both your faces. Who was lurking outside the tavern?" she asked Kate.

"Parr and Sawyer, the men who came to York wearing Lancastrian livery and claiming to be on a mission for the king."

"Ah. I've heard about them. How did the hounds know to warn you?"

"As I said, I have quite a tale to tell."

"And your grim faces?"

Kate told her what she had learned from Sister Dina and at the warehouse, adding Lille and Ghent's part in finding something that might provide a motivation for the crimes, patting the pouch Elric carried.

"Skulker, curse that vermin," Bess growled. "My grandson was foolhardy enough to hire him. Lasted one day. All ears and mouth, no work. The dockworkers will see to him. No place for sneaks. His young bones will wash up with the tide." Bess rose with a grunt, shrugging off Elric's proffered assistance with a shake of her beribboned cap. "I am not yet so old that I cannot rise from a chair on my own two legs."

Bess leaned on her cane and cast an eye on Lille, then Ghent. "They have proved themselves to be beings I would do well to befriend." The old woman took a deep breath, as if to fortify herself. "Come along to my 'parlor'," she said, motioning for Kate and the hounds to enter first. "And Sir Elric is to join us?"

"If it please you," said Kate.

A nod.

Elric settled at the end of the table, and Bess took her usual seat.

"Well then, let us resume," said Bess. "The tavern is about to fill up for the evening."

When Kate and the hounds had settled, Bess called for a kitchen maid to bring Lille and Ghent a bowl of water.

"Begin your tale, I pray you, Dame Katherine," said Bess as she poured brandywine. "I do not wish Berend to spend any more time in that dank, soulless place than necessary."

Kate took a few sips of the wine while she gathered her thoughts, reviewing what she had learned, trying to separate what seemed most likely true from her speculations and those of others regarding all that had happened. She felt the responsibility of it, how much was at stake.

"I do not yet see it as a whole, how it all fits together. I depend on you to help me to sift through it all, find the patterns." Kate settled back in the chair, closing her eyes for a moment, then began.

With but a few interruptions from her companions, she told them all she had gleaned—or most of it. She gave a general description of Berend's visit, including the fact that he knew Merek and did not admit to traveling with Lady Kirkby, nor did he seem to know Parr and Sawyer, or, at least, did not know why they would be in York. She gave a more detailed account of their nighttime intrusion in her home, as well as what she had seen at Jon Horner's house—how they had found him, the evidence of a room turned upside down in search of something—leaving out the glove and the mysterious clump of something possibly herbal—and her conversations with Old Cob and Coffey the smith. Lastly, she recounted in full her visit with Lionel, what Sister Dina had observed of Berend's capture, her conversation with Paris, and what she had learned from the men in the warehouse. She opened Berend's pack, showing them that there was no blood on his clothing.

"Nor did the warehousemen notice any new injuries."

"That is something," Elric muttered.

She omitted Carl's murder lest she slip and suggest she had seen him earlier, or mention Lady Margery.

"If Parr and Sawyer are after the jewels, Berend's capture might propel them to take risks in searching for them," said Bess.

"Which was why I wanted Horner's home watched," said Kate. "And Merek's lodgings. Do you have someone at Merek's?" she asked Elric.

He was not certain. He would see to it.

"I know the woman who keeps his lodgings," said Bess. "Goodwife Mary will cooperate with you. She likes life tidy and lawful. I will send word that she tell you of anyone attempting to trespass."

All three fell silent. Lille and Ghent shifted beneath the table, settling deeper into their slumber. It had been a long day for them.

"Berend was seen with Merek earlier in the evening, then intervened on his behalf when he found Horner attacking him," Elric said softly, as if to himself, as he helped himself to more brandywine. "Why then would he return to slit his throat?" Settling back, he said, "I will send to Sheriff Hutton for more men. We need to scour York for Parr and Sawyer. That Jennet's tribe has been unable to sniff them out makes me uneasy."

"Who killed Merek, that is what we need to know," said Bess. "And Horner. We need to prove Berend's innocence."

"The fact that no one has noticed blood on Berend's clothing is not proof that he is innocent," said Elric. "I need to examine him, see whether he is so well bandaged it does not show."

Kate agreed. Berend might have rid himself of his bloody clothing. And what of the casket of jewels and gold that sat at Elric's elbow?

As if he could hear her thoughts, Elric drew the casket from the leather pouch and set it on the table. "We also need to know what Berend was doing with this."

Bess reached out to touch the casket. "You have opened this?" Elric nodded. "Berend had this?"

"I cannot otherwise explain how the hounds tracked it," said Kate.

As Elric was describing how it had been placed in a large crate tucked back in a corner of the warehouse, out of the way, he lifted the lid, revealing the contents.

"Mary and all the saints," Bess whispered. "I never took him to be a thief."

"What of Merek?" asked Elric. "Is it possible that Berend found it in Merek's belongings and hid it?"

"And the warehousemen had not noticed it?" Bess looked at him askance. "He took a risk with the men. And John Paris."

Kate thought it time they saw exactly what was in the casket. "Is it safe to examine the contents here, with your servants coming past?" They sat in an alcove opened to the passage between the kitchen and the public room.

The old woman lifted her cane and pointed toward a folded wooden screen leaning against the far wall. "I use that to afford myself privacy when I am doing the accounts and do not wish to be disturbed. It is sufficient to hide us from prying eyes. Sir Elric?"

He had already risen, and with Kate's help, they drew it across the opening while Bess used one lamp to light two others.

"Now," she said, her expression one of gleeful anticipation as she plucked a cloth from a nearby shelf and shook it out, laying it on the table, smoothing it. "Let us see what we have."

Kate, still standing, began to lift items from the casket and place them on the cloth. A gold ring, several gold chains, including the one with the swan pendant, a jeweled crispinette—diamonds, a small pouch of pearls, the bag of coins, both gold and silver, from various countries, and a small pouch bearing a crest, a trio of red diamonds quartered with green eagles.

"Salisbury's coat of arms," said Elric, shaking his head. "I am sorry to see this."

So was Kate. She fumbled with the knotted leather tie, finally tipping the contents out onto the cloth. A signet ring with the initials JM, and a delicate gold ring with a ruby in a heart-shaped setting.

"A posey ring?" Kate wondered, lifting the ruby ring and holding it close to the light to read the inscription encircling it. "*C'est mon désir*." She glanced up.

Bess asked if she might see the posey ring, squinting at it as she turned it this way and that, light glinting off its many facets. "A man's ring, and his wife's? Why would Berend have possession of these?"

Elric frowned over the coat of arms and the signet ring. "JM for John Montagu, Earl of Salisbury. He entrusts one of his men to hide a treasure that will support him in exile. It is a common practice. The posey is a love token. Included to remember his beloved while they are apart?"

"And you believe this was Berend's mission?" asked Kate. "To hold this treasure for his lord's son?"

"It would explain part of his travels," said Elric. "Not all. How he managed to protect this . . . Fortune was on his side."

"No longer," Bess whispered. "This looks ill for our friend."

Indeed it did. Kate collected the rings and pouch and put them aside, reaching for a leather bag that lay beneath the hoard. Inside was yet another pouch, this one of silk, holding . . .

"Lady Margery's jewels," she whispered, recognizing the necklaces, a ring, a bracelet, a gold circlet, two crispinettes, one gold with diamonds, one silver with sapphires. All items she remembered her friend wearing. "What are they doing here?"

"You said Berend denied being with Lady Margery?" Elric asked Kate.

"He did not admit to it."

"He did not wish to lie to you." Elric looked Kate in the eye.

As she disliked lying to Elric. Remorse choked her. A casket with jewels belonging to Lady Margery and to the Earl of Salisbury. What could it signify but that she or Lord Kirkby had joined the rebels? And Kate was hiding her. God have mercy. And somehow Merek and Horner discovered it?

"Is it possible that this is what Merek and Horner died for?" she asked. "The wealth in this casket, and what it might reveal?"

"People have been murdered for far less," said Elric. "Or Salisbury might have entrusted Merek with this, to hand over to Berend, and when it came to that, he was reluctant . . ."

All three pairs of eyes met over the sparkling hoard. Mystified. Saddened. Frightened.

"No," said Kate. "No. The Berend I know would not murder Merek and Horner to silence them about this."

"Of course not," Bess said, sounding far more certain than Kate. "We've no time for riddles. Sir Elric will confront Berend, find out how he came to possess this. But first we must hide it. Somewhere safe. I certainly do not want it under my roof."

"Katherine?" Elric looked at her.

She knew of one woman adept at hiding gold—her mother. But would she agree? Even more to the point, would moving it to the Martha House endanger her mother and the beguines?

"What about the house of your cousin, soon to be mayor?" Bess asked quietly, so as not to be overheard. "They say his home is a fortress, guarded night and day, and surely he has a place where he hides the jewels Isabella so loves to flaunt."

"I must think." Kate put Margery's jewels back in the silk pouch, tucked that into the leather pouch, and returned it to the casket, layering the rest on top. She closed the lid and slipped the casket into the leather pouch Elric held open.

"I will escort you home," he said.

"My house is not far from here. And I have Lille and Ghent. You have a more pressing task—you must go to the castle, talk to Berend. He might be able to explain."

"They will permit you to see him, won't they?" asked Bess. "Westmoreland's captain in the city?"

"They would not risk either the king's or my earl's ire by denying me," Elric assured them. "I pray I find some answers. And no open wounds on Berend."

"Amen," Kate whispered.

"Find out who has murdered two men and pointed the finger at Berend," said Bess. "And God help you if you fail, Elric of Bigod," she growled. To Kate, she said, "Trust Sir Elric. You need his help." With a nod, she rose, cautious not to disturb Lille and Ghent. "I would not have believed it had I not witnessed it myself. You trained them well."

Kate bowed to her. "They know a friend when they meet one."

The taverner touched Kate's forearm. "We will save him, the three of us." A sad smile. "I will call on my neighbor, Gwenllian Ferriby. Apothecaries hear much in their shops. The smallest detail might provide the clue we need to connect all these troubles."

"I met Gwenllian at Lionel's," said Kate. "She is seeing to his wounds."

"Good," said Bess. "I will not feel guilty bringing her into this as she is already involved."

"Would you ask her if I might talk to her? If I described Jon Horner—how he looked, smelled—she might have an idea what the poison was, how it might have been given to him. Perhaps she might examine the room, if it's not already cleaned."

Bess looked uncertain. "Her mother would have gladly assisted you, but Gwenllian might be hesitant. I will see what I might do."

Kate thanked her.

"I do it for Berend," said Bess.

"As do I."

As Kate led the hounds through the public room, which was filling up, the patrons made much of them being permitted in the tavern.

"Do not for a moment think you all may bring your dogs in here," Bess bellowed from the doorway. "Lille and Ghent are privileged guests."

Already stepping out into the yard, Elric turned to Kate. "If someone in that tavern recognizes the bag, they will follow you. The wolfhounds or no, I am escorting you home."

Glancing back at the curious faces, Kate could not but agree. "No need to lead anyone into temptation," she laughed at his surprise as she handed him the bag. She quietly thanked him as she separated the hounds' leads, one in each hand.

"I am honored."

Would he be so honored if he knew what she hid from him? She averted her eyes, making a study of the Ferriby house as they passed it. An uncommonly fine home for an apothecary, but then Gwenllian's husband Tom Ferriby was a prominent mercer, like his father, and his maternal grandfather had been a knight. So had Gwenllian's maternal grandfather, though her mother had been an apothecary—a knight's daughter becoming an apothecary, there was a story in that, she'd wager. She had knights on the mind, or one in particular, tall, strong, handsome, with a way of carrying himself that set her thinking about the best chamber in her guesthouse and what they might do there. But it would never happen. Too many lies and half-truths. How she regretted that.

They were a quiet pair as they walked, nodding to folk hurrying home as night closed in over the city and the streets grew treacherous, the shadows deepening beneath the jutting overhangs, the slush refreezing underfoot. Lille barked at a clerk who ventured too close as he swept the area in front of a shop, making him give way.

"Imperious," Elric said with a laugh.

Kate smiled. She liked his laugh. It began in his chest, a deep, rich sound.

Upon reaching the door to her hall Kate stopped, suddenly awkward.

Elric saved the moment. He bowed and kissed her hand. "I will come straight to you with an account of my mission to the castle."

"I will be waiting," she said.

He handed her the casket and Berend's pack. "Keep them safe!"

She held up the pack. "Perhaps he could use the extra clothing?"

"Better that I leave it with you for now, see where they are holding him."

"Of course. Godspeed!"

You are more than a little fond of your knight, Geoff said in Kate's mind as she watched Elric stride off down the street.

He's not—She caught herself evading her own realization. *I am. More's the pity. He is a good man.*

So you keep telling me.

I would give much to travel in his mind for this meeting, Geoff said as Kate made her way round the house to the kitchen.

I would as well, Geoff. But more than that, I wish I could be the one to go to Berend. I need to know whether I've been a fool to hide Margery.

Better that he break his silence with Elric, man to man. And then you will hear all that he told Elric.

Perhaps. If he confides in him. Why should he?

Then it will be your turn.

10

THE KING'S PEACE

Before opening the kitchen door, Kate decided on the simplest explanation for both the pack and the pouch, "Berend's belongings," and then whispered several Hail Marys as she composed herself. Pushing open the door, she found Petra and Marie standing side by side, slicing turnips with an air of gloom. Holy Mother, how she loved them.

"Such sad faces," she said, stepping inside and shutting the door behind her. "You will curdle the cream."

"There is no cream in this dish," Marie snapped, eyeing Jennet with disgust. "Almond milk. Pah. Watery peasant food." She gave a shiver of disgust.

"Peasants cannot afford the almonds for milk. They rely on their goats and cows," said Petra, eliciting a snarl from her companion.

"I don't suppose you thought to ask Bess Merchet whether she knows of someone who might help in the kitchen?" asked Jennet, her voice weary as she stood over the fire, sleeves rolled back, face damp with the heat, stirring the pottage.

"I had much else on my mind," said Kate.

Marie continued to mutter her dissatisfaction.

Petra elbowed her. "You want Berend back, don't you?" she hissed, her eyes brimming with tears.

"You will salt the pottage with your tears," Marie said, sticking her tongue out at Petra. "You think I do not know that he is in danger?"

Time to distract them. "I have a mind to work on the loom for a while before we sup. Do you mind waiting a while?"

"No one is hungry," said Jennet.

Kate understood. "But Mouser spilled my silk threads and they are all atangle." She leveled her gaze at Petra, who had found the cat and insisted on adopting her, and Marie, who had promised they would keep her from underfoot. To their credit, the girls had tried to shut the cat from the hall, but Mouser was a cunning adversary. "So the two of you will take Lille and Ghent to the hall and work on that while I talk to Jennet and Matt." The hounds' presence would ensure Mouser's absence. Though they found her but a nit, not worth fussing over, she clearly feared them.

"But I want to hear," Marie whined, winning herself another jab of Petra's sharp elbows. "Merde."

"That is Berend's pack," said Petra, pointing.

"You are quite right," said Kate.

"What have you in the bag?" Marie demanded.

"More of his belongings. I brought them here for safekeeping." Kate bent to Lille and Ghent, apologizing to them for the assignment. She looked up. "Well? They are waiting. Tell Matt we are waiting."

Wiping their hands on their aprons, the girls went over to the bench by the door and stepped into their wooden pattens, lifted their cloaks from the hooks above, and, ready for the slushy yard, held out their hands for the hounds' leads. Kate drew them both into her arms and held them a moment, whispering assurances that she was doing all that she could to bring Berend safely home. "Now," she released them and handed them the leads. "See to the silks. Sir Elric is on his way to the castle now. I will tell you what he learns as soon as I know."

When the girls had tramped out, Kate left the door ajar, so they might hear the hounds bark, and settled at the table with Jennet, talking idly about the girls while they waited for Matt. As soon as he joined them she recounted the events and discoveries of the day. As she came to the revelations at the warehouse, she opened Berend's pack, showed them the contents, and then heaved up the leather pouch, drawing out the casket. They listened closely, asking few questions until Kate opened the casket.

"Heavenly hosts," whispered Matt.

Jennet usually laughed at his saintly exclamations, but not this time. Her eyes were busy taking it all in. "What is Berend doing with all this?"

"That is what Elric has gone to ask him," said Kate. She showed them the two rings, explained the possible significance.

"The Earl of Salisbury. The traitor." Matt looked so unhappy. "Why would Berend support him?"

"And there is this." Kate lifted out the sack of Lady Margery's jewels, opening it.

Jennet glanced up. "So now Sir Elric knows that she *is* in the city?"

"If you are asking whether I have told him, no," said Kate.

"With Carl's death, now this, might it not be time?" Jennet lifted the posey ring, turning it this way and that, clearly admiring how the ruby caught the light. Was a time when she would have run with it. A remarkable day's catch. Now she treated it as information. "If Lord Kirkby was part of the uprising . . ." She was shaking her head. "The risk . . . Let Lady Margery explain herself to Sir Elric."

"I am of a mind to tell him tonight," Kate admitted. "I believe I can trust him."

"Good. That is good."

Matt tapped the table. "How is this connected to Merek's and Horner's deaths?"

Kate reminded them of the exchange at the market, something small, gold. From this hoard? "Merek was on a mission for Salisbury. It is possible that this casket was entrusted to him, and he betrayed the earl's trust."

"And then it came to Berend," said Matt. "How?"

"Pray Berend enlightens Sir Elric," said Kate. She did not want to think how Berend might have wrested it from Merek.

"Did Kevin find anything in the documents strewn about his office?" asked Jennet.

"If he did, he did not say," said Kate. "We were busy with other things."

Jennet sat back with a sigh. "What a day. And Dame Bess befriending Lille and Ghent." She shook her head.

"Am I right to trust her?" Kate asked. "What do your eyes and ears on the streets think of her?"

"They admire her. She's a cautious woman, it takes much to gain her trust. And somehow you have managed that in one visit."

"I confess I did not expect to like her so well," said Kate. "She has been of help."

"Good," said Jennet. "She is a worthwhile ally in this part of the city."

"Ay, she is that," said Matt. "As is her friend Gwenllian Ferriby, or so says Bella." His cousin the healer. "If Horner *was* poisoned, she might recall who had the means. Though she's not the only source of such a draught. Interesting that Merek was not a simple spice seller, but dabbling in potions. *And* an envoy for the earl of Salisbury. Maybe selling stolen jewelry as well?"

"A possibility," said Kate.

"About Merek being an envoy for Salisbury," said Jennet, "it might have helped to know that sooner."

Jennet's expression chastened Kate. She *should* have told her what Berend had said.

"I am sorry."

A shrug. "I know now."

"You have more information for your eyes and ears."

Jennet nodded. "I will go deliver new instructions to my eyes and ears after supper."

"You are wasted in the kitchen," said Kate. "You both deserve help. Now, let's get this casket safely out of sight. I need to find a place to hide it."

"We all know who proved to be remarkably clever about hiding treasures," said Jennet.

Kate laughed. "I had the same thought about my mother. But for tonight . . ."

"The hearth in the hall has a loose stone," said Matt. "Someone used it for this very purpose. The casket will fit."

Jennet touched Kate's arm, said nothing until she knew she had her attention. "You will confide in him tonight? We can use the additional protection with such a treasure in the house."

"I know. I will, though I dread it."

"You care for him."

"Once he knows, that will not matter."

"If a comrade in arms came to him in such need, do you believe he would turn him away?"

"He will understand my helping her. What he will not forgive is my deceiving him."

Jennet could not deny that.

—◦◎◦—

The colors of the silks soothed Kate—deep blue, vibrant green, bright yellow, warm brown. They were a pleasure to work. It had not been merely a ruse to send the girls away while she conferred with Jennet and Matt, Kate *had* sought solace at the loom, needing to calm her mind in order to see the way forward. And she was grateful—Petra and Marie had created order and even improved on how the colors were arranged. Buoyed by her praise, they had gone back to the kitchen arm in arm, leaving her with the hounds and Matt, who was repairing a shutter.

Weaving forced Kate to draw in her thoughts as she began, remembering where she had left off, what threads to work in next. Then, as she settled into the pattern, she was able to let her mind play over the events of the past few days, exploring possible connections. She was just beginning to relax when someone knocked on the door.

Silently cursing, she called out to Matt to see who it was.

Another knock. She glanced round and saw that the shutter was repaired. She was alone with the hounds, who sat up, ears pricked, awaiting her instructions.

"Stay," she commanded them as she rose, hoping that it was Sir Elric and Berend who interrupted her solitude. "Patience, I pray you!" she called out as the knocking became more insistent. Opening the door, she raised her eyebrows. Her cousin, William Frost, soon to be mayor of York and one of the last people she wished to see at present. But to deny him was to call attention to herself.

"God be with you, cousin," he raised his brows. "Might I come in?"

"Of course." She stepped aside.

"I am relieved to find you at home." Though William's brow was furrowed in a deep frown his voice was soft, affectionate, and he gave her forearm a little squeeze as he passed her.

She did not like that unaccustomed gesture of affection. It meant trouble for her.

As he peeled off his gloves, he said, "I was on my way to the guesthouse when I heard about Berend's trouble. We must talk."

"And leave Drusilla waiting?" He had long been a client with his mistress, the widow Seaton, Kate's good friend and business partner. "She is not a patient woman."

"This is important, Katherine."

Of course he would be one of the first to hear, for soon such events would be his headache as mayor. She motioned him to a chair by the hearth fire and went to the cupboard on the wall beside it where she kept a jug of ale and a flagon of wine.

"A cup of wine?" Kate asked.

Fussing with his rabbit-lined cloak, shaking it out, hanging it with care over two hooks beside the hearth, William rubbed his hands and said, "I would prefer ale if you have it."

"A reformed regimen as you don your mayoral robes?" He had always preferred wine, no matter the time of day. "What next? Are you here to tell me that you will no longer be a patron of my guesthouse?"

"No, nothing like that. My physician believes ale is better than claret for my stiff joints." A shrug.

"Your physician? You are concerned for your health?"

"Isabella is. To keep the peace, I bow to my wife's loving concern."

Loving—that was not a word Kate would ever associate with Isabella Frost. "What inspired her concern?"

"Since my return from Westminster she has noticed a change in my sleep. She finds me walking about our chamber talking nonsense. I have much on my mind, I told her. Participating in a parliament of such significance, a new king come to the throne in such wise—"

"Turning the former king's nobles against him, threatening civil war, yes, there must have been much to discuss in Westminster," said Kate.

"Have a care how you speak of King Henry's accession, cousin. There are spies all about us." He gave her a warning look as he settled down on the high-backed chair, adjusting his brocade jacket, flicking imaginary specks from his rich brown leggings. Elegantly garbed for an evening spent under silken bedclothes.

"Royal spies, yes. I did wonder whether you will continue your trysts with Drusilla," she said, goading him.

He looked at her askance. "Of course I will, cousin. Why would I not? I have needs—"

"Yes, you have often said. But as mayor, and as you owe it to King Henry's favor, you must have a care. It is said His Grace is a pious man."

"He is. But he understands. He himself has a mistress."

"His Grace is, at the moment, a widower. Your wife is very much alive."

William was shaking his head. "You distract me from my purpose. I am here about the murder of the spice seller. And Horner. And Berend being taken into custody."

"Of course." She handed him the cup of ale and settled across from him.

He lifted the cup to her as if to toast. "You will not partake?"

"I am still warm with Bess Merchet's brandywine."

"Old Bess at the York Tavern? I did not know you were friends. But she is a good person to know in this part of the city."

Kate nodded. "About Berend."

"Yes. His situation is grave. He stands accused not only of the recent murders, but of joining the son of his former lord in the plot against the king. He was seen at Pontefract, and in Oxford, meeting with Salisbury. Pontefract, Katherine. Had he attempted to free the deposed king? Would Berend do such a thing?"

"No, he would not."

"So say you. But the king believes otherwise. I have come to warn you, Katherine, for the sake of your name, and your wards, their futures, you must cut off all association with Berend."

He might as well tell you to cut off your right arm, Geoff mumbled in her head.

"Is this not all rumor?" Kate asked.

William sat back with an air of self-satisfaction, taking the time to cross one leg over the other. "I heard it from the king's own men. Two of King Henry's trusted retainers arrived today. I have invited them to bide in my home."

"Sawyer and Parr?"

"Who? No. Sir Peter Angle and Captain Crawford, I've already forgotten the captain's given name. Who are these others?"

Kate waved away the question. "Why are they here?"

"I am not privileged to say . . ."

"Have they come in pursuit of Lady Kirkby?"

A look of surprise. "Why—How did you know?"

"Sir Elric."

"Ah. Westmoreland's man. Yes, of course, he would be privy to such information."

"Is she in the city?"

"They believe so, but they have yet to apprehend her."

God be thanked. But Kate's hands had turned to ice. "And they told you about Berend?"

"They overheard my man Roger informing me that the sheriffs had him in custody. When they heard his name they grew excited. They are convinced that it was Berend who had escorted Lady Kirkby here after their cohorts were caught and executed in Cirencester. Will you promise me to stay out of this? Let the sheriffs and the king's men do their work?"

As if she'd ever had a choice to do so. "The sheriffs have already bungled it, William. Sir Elric is at the castle as we speak, determined to find the real murderer, or murderers, and prevent any more violence in the city."

"Sir Elric? Why?"

"He has been charged by Ralph Neville, Earl of Westmoreland, to keep the peace here."

"That is for the sheriffs and the mayor and council."

Kate almost laughed at William's expression, righteous indignation, insult . . . But she restrained herself. "I thought that as well, but ever since the rift between the royal cousins the earl has kept a close watch on York, with Sir Elric as his lieutenant here. You will want to stay in Elric's good graces."

"In *his* good graces," William sputtered, his feathers now quite ruffled.

She had best smooth them. This was not the time to let her cousin walk away in anger. She needed his cooperation. "I only meant, he is one of the earl's favorites, and a knight, William. Though citizens of York see you as the highest dignitary, come Candlemas—or the day after, one such as the earl sees you as yet a commoner. You have the king's support, but Earl Ralph sits at his right hand at feasts."

A shrug of concession. "It is true." He sipped the ale and stared into the fire. "Back to the matter at hand," he finally said, "I cannot have you rushing to rescue a traitor."

"Berend is no traitor. He condemned the plot against the king and his sons."

"Then what was his—" He looked up sharply. "You have already spoken to him?"

"Briefly. *Before* the deaths of Merek and Horner."

"And you did not give him up?"

"I said, before the deaths."

"Murders. Did you not know he was wanted for treason?"

"Not at that time," she lied.

William leveled his gaze at her. "When I told you the king's men were here you mentioned two names. Who are they?"

"Parr and Sawyer?" Here was information he would find valuable, that she might offer as a concession. She told him what she knew of them, omitting their interest in Merek's goods. She did not want the king's men on a treasure hunt.

He looked suitably concerned. "How dare they invade your home and threaten your guard dogs! I will inform His Grace's men. They sought Berend and Lady Margery?"

"Yes."

"They will be found and apprehended, I promise you."

She did not argue, merely nodded, as if grateful, soothing William's pride.

He murmured more reassurances as he lifted the cup to his lips. Finding it empty, he set it on the arm of the chair. Kate rose to fetch more, but he shook his head.

"So. Will you promise to keep your distance from Berend?"

"In truth, that depends on Sir Elric, what he learns at York Castle."

"Why should it depend on him?"

"We have an agreement. Or rather, I have one with Westmoreland."

"Oh? You never said."

"And now I have. I—keep him informed of the mood in the city, amongst the merchants."

"Ah."

She could see him reviewing in his mind what she might have reported about him.

"You have no need for concern, cousin."

A little tweak at the corners of his mouth. "Perhaps I will take a wee dram more." He handed her his cup.

She filled it, handed it back. "About my agreement with the earl. It would help me if you would keep me informed of what the king's men do, where they go, to whom they speak. Sir Elric will want to know what they know. What they think they know."

"And why would I do that?"

"As I said, Earl Ralph has the king's ear. When you wish a favor for the city . . ."

William uncrossed his legs, adjusted his sleeves. "The day after Candlemas I will be entertaining all of York, Katherine, with a late dinner for the freemen of the city and their families. The following day I hold a feast for the council."

"Two feasts?"

"Isabella's idea. But you see I have much to do in a few days."

"And the king's men. You would not exclude them?"

"Well, no, of course not."

"I should think Sir Elric will also be invited to the first feast."

"I had not thought to invite him, but if he is in the city . . ."

"Perhaps as my escort?"

A hint of a smile as he nodded. "I begin to see the benefit. But how would I get word to you? I myself have not the time . . ."

"I am looking for a groom, a lad to train up as a servant. Can you suggest one?"

"What has this to do with what we're discussing?"

"I need someone to be here when Matt is at your house receiving his morning and afternoon report from your manservant Roger. Or from Tib, if you prefer." A lesser servant in William's household.

"It would needs be Roger. I can trust him not to gossip." He held out his cup once more. "I believe I need what remains in the jug you have on the cupboard."

Kate obliged him, handing him the ornate pewter tankard, though she teased him about too much ale being inadvisable before a night of lovemaking.

He growled.

She laughed. "So do we have an agreement?"

"The Earl of Westmoreland is so concerned?"

Kate leaned forward, making certain she had William's attention. "I tell you this in confidence—Lionel Neville found himself caught up in this trouble. Sir Ralph's kinsman. It seems he was with Merek when the man was attacked. He went to his aid and was wounded for his troubles." She tilted her head, raised an eyebrow.

"Lionel intervened? Astonishing. But, Christ's blood, the man has a penchant for sticking his nose in the wrong feed bags."

"So. Will you do this?"

"I must think." He rested his head back against the chair. "The groom part is simple. Tib has a brother, Cuddy. He's a good lad, clever—as far as Isabella is concerned, too clever. She washed his mouth with soap one too many times and they mutually agreed to part ways. I liked the lad and promised to find a place for him." William opened one eye and smiled at Kate. "He would suit your unusual household."

"Send him by, the sooner the better." She waited, but he closed his eye once more and seemed to nod off. "William, do we have an agreement?"

William grunted. "My cunning cousin." He sat upright, frowning. "How can you be so certain Berend is innocent?"

"We believe in him."

"We?"

"Sir Elric, Bess Merchet, and me."

"You delight in unlikely pairings, cousin. As if all life is a merry jest. I take it Sir Elric will come directly from the castle to report to you?"

"I don't know. Much depends on whether or not the sheriffs will agree to his taking responsibility for Berend." And Berend agreeing to it, she thought.

"You will send word to Griselde about what Sir Elric learned at the castle? I can check with her in the morning as I depart the guesthouse."

"It would be much more efficient for me to send Matt to your house. Mid morning. And then he can return with his new helper, Cuddy. That is, if you are able to arrange that so quickly?"

"Of course. I am glad to find work for the lad. Matt will tell me all?"

"Yes."

William nodded. "Agreed."

⋯⊙⋯

In the kitchen, the contents of the pot Marie and Petra were taking turns stirring now gave off a spicy aroma that made Kate's stomach grumble. It had been a very long day with too little food and too much wine.

"Is Master William going to help Berend?" Marie asked.

"In his own way, yes, he will," said Kate. "As is Sir Elric." She motioned Matt and Jennet to step outside, and told the girls she would be back in a moment.

She told them that the king's men were in the city, staying with William. "We need to warn Sir Elric of all this. It might help him. Which of you will go to York Castle?"

Matt straightened up, excited, but then deferred to Jennet.

Jennet shook her head. "Better for you to go. With your long legs, you will be swifter. But stay a moment. I have something you might need." She disappeared into the kitchen.

"Sir Peter Angle and Captain Crawford—Elric might know these men," said Kate. "He can use their respect for Westmoreland to influence them. And, Matt, you will soon have a lad to help out—Cuddy, from the Frost household."

By the beatific smile she could tell that Matt believed this day to be one of his finest.

"I will be fleet of foot, Dame Katherine."

Jennet rejoined them, holding out a leather traveling pack. "If Elric succeeds in releasing Berend into his custody, our friend might need a disguise."

"A disguise for Berend?" Kate asked.

Jennet shrugged. "Yes. Take it, Matt. But do not leave it behind. It's good cloth."

Matt promised to return it, either on Berend or in the pack.

"You are armed?" Kate asked.

"Both daggers."

"Good. Godspeed."

152

As they watched him lope away, pulling his hastily donned cloak closer round him, they both whispered prayers that Elric would be successful in arguing for Berend's release.

"I never would have believed that haughty knight would use his earl's influence to help us," said Jennet.

"He respects Berend."

Jennet turned and looked Kate in the eyes. "And you, Dame Katherine. This may not work out as he hopes, yet he risks his lord discovering how he used his name. He would not take that risk for Berend alone."

"He might soon regret that."

"Not if he is the man I believe him to be."

"Betrayal undermines the strongest relationship. I would not blame him for shunning me ever after." Kate slumped against the doorframe, weary to the bone. "But at the moment my mind is on the guesthouse. Pray God Griselde has the sense to keep Margery quiet tonight. William and Drusilla know her well. They know her voice, how she moves. May God watch over Margery this night."

"It is not like you to leave it to God," Jennet noted.

Kate bestirred herself. "No, it is not. Stay with the girls. I will leave the hounds as well. If Elric comes, keep him here until I return."

11

A LIE,
HOWEVER WELL MEANT

After the meeting with Katherine and Bess at the York Tavern, Elric welcomed the late afternoon chill. It cleared his head as he turned onto Stonegate. Walking down this street beside Katherine was fresh in his mind, flanked by her noble hounds, her movements graceful, with a rhythmic quality not unlike dance. Beauty and strength in motion. And, considering her keen mind and martial skill, he was glad to be on her side. More than glad. If he succeeded in freeing Berend and proving his innocence, would she . . . ? Might they . . . ? Pah. This was not the time for such dreams. Nor could he shrug off the feeling that she was up to her usual tricks, telling him partial truths.

Shaking his head at himself he turned down Davygate. Not so busy as earlier, the shops closing, people hurrying home to the warmth of their fires. As he approached Jon Horner's house he slowed his pace, seeing in the dusky light that Kevin was in conversation with a handsome woman who seemed vaguely familiar. He did not wish to interrupt, but the cold and his mission made him keen to reach the castle.

Kevin happened to glance his way, raising his hand in greeting, and the woman turned to see who approached.

"Sir Elric, if I might introduce the widow Wheeldon," said Kevin.

Ah, the widow Wheeldon, yes, he remembered now. She was in the company of a maidservant who stood at a slight distance, staring down at her feet, looking far more grief-stricken than did the widow. But then, Wheeldon had not struck him as a woman who would spend much time grieving anyone.

Elric had first met—Cecily, that was her Christian name, yes. He'd met her a few years earlier, at Raby Castle, when her husband, a man of considerable wealth and apparently thwarted ambition, was still alive. Earl Ralph had approached him for the wherewithal for a venture. Eager to oblige, Wheeldon's price was simply an invitation to Christmas at Raby Castle. The earl complied, giving Elric the task of escorting the couple north. The old man and his young wife were annoying travelers, ridiculously surprised by the unpleasantness of a winter journey. But once ensconced at Raby, they enjoyed the festivities, the old man hobnobbing with the nobles and fellow merchants of influence, though he had little of that except for his wealth. No widow then, though she behaved as one, Dame Cecily teased the men with her low-cut gowns, locking her eyes on them, inviting them to her side. Elric danced with her, finding her a graceful partner, but too hungry for gossip about her host. He had not danced with her a second time.

"Sir Elric," she held out her hand, her face sliding from a smile into a mask of grief.

He touched her hand as he bowed to her. "Mistress Wheeldon."

"I was explaining that I cannot permit her inside the house," said Kevin.

"You wished to enter?" Elric asked her. "To what purpose?"

"I was concerned about Goodwife Tibby, Jon Horner's housekeeper," said the widow. "I thought to offer her solace."

"As I explained, she has gone to her sister's house," said Kevin.

"Yes, so you did." Suddenly Cecily Wheeldon seemed not to care for all the attention, averting her eyes, motioning to her maidservant that they should move on, it was near curfew.

Unable to decide whether his hackles were raised for good cause or simply because of his dislike of the woman, Elric proposed to escort her home.

"Oh, no, I pray you, you need not, Sir Elric."

"But your home is on my way. You would not deny me your company?"

She blanched. And it was not simply from the cold, he was certain. Whatever she had intended to do next, it was not heading straight home. And that she did not argue that she had errands confirmed for him his instinct that something was not quite right about her sudden concern for Horner's housekeeper.

As he proffered her his arm, she put a good face on it, resting her hand on his forearm and bidding good day to Kevin. Even on the slushy street, she moved with remarkable grace. So why did he dislike her so?

"Forgive me if I seemed abrupt," he said as they continued down Davygate, the servant quietly following. "You have lost a friend to violence. I pray that you find solace."

"Friend?" the widow said the word as if tasting it. "He was, on occasion, my late husband's trading partner, one of several, and we met a few times in regard to an outstanding contract. I considered him an acquaintance, hardly a friend. My concern was more for Goodwife Tibby, his housekeeper. A housekeeper for a widower is often regarded in an unkindly light. Gossips, you know. An unmarried woman living under the same roof—You see the problem." She paused as they reached St. Sampson Square, looking to see his reaction.

"Ah," is all he said, with a knowing nod, while in truth he wondered why she had chosen to begin such a rumor. What was her purpose in maligning Goodwife Tibby?

Apparently she did not find his reaction satisfying, for she withdrew into silence as they continued down Peasegate, except to greet passersby. No doubt she still enjoyed being on the arm of a knight in the service of the Earl of Westmoreland. He was glad when they reached her home at the foot of Castlegate. Bowing to her, he wished her a quiet evening.

His first matter of business on reaching York Castle was to request that at least two armed men be placed at Jon Horner's home on Davygate and another two at Merek's lodgings.

"But we have the murderer in custody," said the bailiff on duty.

"I very much doubt that you do," said Elric. "Have you examined the prisoner? Is he wounded?"

"The man's head and hands have more scars than I can count."

"Fresh wounds on his arms or torso? So fresh they are still weeping?"

The bailiff wrinkled his nose. "I did not undress him. Such a search is not my responsibility."

"I disagree," said Elric. He reminded him about the bloody knife in Merek's hand. "If Berend does not have any fresh wounds, the murderer is likely still abroad in the city. If you wish to retain your position you will arrange for men to be posted at Horner's house, as well as Merek's, if you have already removed them. Tonight. And, for good measure, at Thomas Graa's warehouse at the corner of Castlegate and Hertergate." He explained why.

"I shall need permission from the sheriffs, sir," the bailiff insisted, but it was clear that Elric had made his point.

"Then get their permission. When I return from my meeting with your prisoner I expect to hear that you have dispatched men around the city."

Though he bristled, the bailiff did not argue, and, as Elric made his way to the stairs that led down beneath the street level, he heard the man loudly ordering someone to watch his station while he went to Sheriff Edmund Cottesbrok's home.

Through the iron-bound door Elric heard a chain rattling.

"Pacing back and forth, back and forth. Has not stopped since I shut the door on him," said the jailer as he put the key to the lock and called out, "Visitor, Master Berend!"

Elric commended him on his courtesy.

"He's a fine man, Berend is. And if he did murder those men, I'll warrant they deserved it." The jailer opened the door and bowed Elric through, handing him an extra lantern and pushing a bench through the door. "Might as well be able to see each other, and to sit."

Attached to a heavy chain secured to an iron ring in the far wall, the iron bands around Berend's ankles were linked together so that he could not stride, but must shuffle. Even so constrained, he had worn a path through the rushes laid on the packed earth floor. Elric could sense his frustration, this magnificent bull forced into a paddock far too small. It was enough to make Elric want to shout for an axe that could cut through the chain. He was glad when Berend paused, shielding his eyes against the light from the lantern he carried, so much brighter than the torch set in the wall just inside the door, out of the prisoner's reach. Apologizing for the sudden glare, Elric set the lantern down where its light would be reflected from the wall, softening it.

The cell was cold, damp, the air not yet fouled, though certainly neither sweet nor copious. Elric noticed the bastards had removed Berend's shoes. Did they fear the chains and the iron-bound door would not hold him? That the snow would better deter him from escaping? Addlepated cowards, all of them. At least Berend showed no signs of rough handling. That was something.

Elric nodded to him. "I hoped we might talk, Berend."

The man shrugged his wide shoulders, as if to relieve a kink in his neck. "Did Dame Katherine send you?"

"I come of my own accord, but I carry words of support from her. And Bess Merchet."

"Merchet? How does she come into it?"

"Katherine sought her out, wanting information about Horner and Merek. In the process, she seems to have made a friend, one who is already *your* friend." Elric moved the bench so that Berend could reach it without straining the chain. "Shall we sit?"

Berend shook one of his feet, rattling the chain. "I am at your mercy, it seems. What is it you want?"

"If you are innocent of the murders of Merek and Horner, I want to find the murderer before he kills again. For that I need your help."

"If I am innocent." A sound that was almost a laugh. "I am hardly that. But I am innocent of their deaths."

"Then you won't mind removing your jacket and shirt?"

"To what end?"

"Merek's attacker was injured. If you have no fresh wounds, I have physical proof to offer the sheriffs."

"And your lord?"

"A fair assessment," Elric admitted. "Before I use the power of the Earl of Westmoreland's name to convince the sheriffs to release you into my custody, I want proof of your innocence."

Berend lifted his bound hands. "This makes it difficult."

"I can remedy that." Elric drew his dagger.

"Why would you trust me?"

"Katherine's entire household trusts you, including the great hounds. Who am I to question their wisdom?"

When Berend extended his arms, Elric noticed that the knot was sloppily done. In time, he might have freed himself. Friends in the castle? Elric sheathed his dagger and untied the rope. "Now if you would remove your jacket and shirt."

Berend's expression relaxed. "Bring the lantern closer." He went one better, rolling up his leggings as well, then turned as best he could, lifting his thick arms, twisting them this way and that, revealing a network of old scars like rivers and tributaries.

Elric saw nothing that could account for the bloody knife. "Enough. I believe you." Thank God for that. The last thing he wanted was to condemn Katherine's good friend. "Dress yourself before you freeze to death," he said. "Who took your shoes?"

Berend rolled down his leggings and put on his shirt. "The bailiff."

"I've met him. Bloody fool, that man."

Berend shrugged on his jacket. "Took my cloak as well. I could use that in here."

"I do not intend for you to stay here tonight."

"No?" Elric felt the man's eyes on him, sizing him up. "It is not your decision to make."

"As I said, I am invoking the power of my lord earl, whose power is at present second only to the king's. Make use of me. Help me leave this place *with* you. I need your help."

"How are you so certain I *can* help?"

Elric settled on one end of the bench, straddling it. "Come, sit down. I will tell you what I know, and you can decide for yourself."

Berend did not move. "I am listening."

"As you wish."

Elric began, doing his best to ignore the rattling chains as Berend resumed his pacing. Eventually, Lionel Neville's account of the night of Merek's murder brought Berend to perch on the opposite end of the bench. He rested his hands on his thighs and bowed his head. Elric told him all he knew, except what

Katherine had told him of her conversation with Berend. He need not know she had shared that.

He ended with a question. "Why did you not run when Paris discovered you? You know how to disappear quickly."

Berend shifted on the bench, the chains rattling. "You believe you can get them to release me?"

Not an answer, but at least it was a sign of interest. "I cannot promise, but if you agree to help I will go to the sheriffs and do my best. It will help if you tell me something I might offer to them as proof you could be of help to me. Then they have every reason to release you into my custody."

Such piercing eyes. "I ask again, why? Why do you care about this? Why are you even in York?"

"The earl charged me to keep the king's peace in the city. Imprisoning an innocent man and concluding that the case is closed while the murderer is still at large is not in my interest, or my lord's. Am I wasting my time? Are we foolish to trust you? You were seen arguing with Merek, and your possession of the casket of jewels—"

Berend glanced up, wary.

"Yes, Katherine found it with the help of her fine hounds. If I did not know you, I would think the sheriffs were right in confining you here. The contents of the chest would seem proof that you at the very least helped Salisbury and Lady Kirkby, both accused of treason."

Berend averted his eyes, but not before Elric saw his confusion. Was it possible he had not been aware of the contents?

"You escorted Lady Kirkby to York," said Elric, "of that I have no doubt."

A mumbled curse. Berend resettled with his back to the light, resting his head in his scarred hands.

"Do you want time to think? Or would this help?" Elric drew a wineskin from beneath his jacket, tapped it against Berend's arm. "Bess Merchet's best brandywine."

Berend took the wineskin, held it for a moment, then drew out the stopper and tilted back his head. Not a long drink, but more than a sip. He closed his eyes and almost smiled as the heat moved down his throat. After a pause, he replaced the stopper and lay the wineskin in his lap, turning round to face Elric. "There are things I would not have you share with Dame Katherine."

"Then we have no agreement." Elric retrieved the wineskin and rose.

Berend caught his arm. By the rood the man was strong. "It is not that I wish to deceive her. But there are things she does not know, and, hearing them now, so late, I fear they will cause her pain."

"As would your execution."

"I might be powerless to prevent that. But I saw how it went to learn from you about the land bequeathed me by my late lord. She might have been glad for me if I had been the one to tell her."

Elric was sorry for that. "If you help me so that I can convince the sheriffs to entrust you to my custody, you will be able to tell her all this yourself. In your own way, however much you judge necessary. But I warn you, Salisbury's crest and his signet ring, and the pouch holding Lady Kirkby's jewels—she means to find out how you came to possess them. Every moment you hesitate causes her suffering."

He watched the man's struggle, the shake of the head, how he clenched his hands, worked his jaw. Who was he protecting? Whatever the reason Montagu lost him, he had been a fool. Elric would give half his men for the one before him. Strength with such a strong sense of honor.

"I'd no time to examine the contents of the chest."

"Well, Katherine has."

A muttered curse.

"Do you think we are looking for one murderer? Or two?" Elric asked, hoping to ease Berend into telling him more. "Can anyone vouch for you after you left Lionel? That you came back to the warehouse for the night?"

"The night watchman at the warehouse seemed asleep when I returned," said Berend. "As to Horner's murder—I would say someone wanted to silence him. But I would have thought that person would be Merek. Horner attacked him—" A perplexed lift of the hands. "Merek killed Horner and *then* was murdered?"

"No." Elric eased back down on the bench, placing the wineskin between them. "Katherine says that Horner had not been long dead when she found him. Merek died the previous night."

"Perhaps Horner was coerced to attack. And then was silenced . . ."

Elric considered that. "By whom?"

Berend shook his head. "I hardly knew the man." He studied the floor. "What if the sheriffs refuse to release me after hearing my tale, they hear my story and still doubt my innocence, and she hears my tale from the city gos-sips?" His eyes were mournful, his posture weary. "It is easier to prove a lie than it is to prove the truth, you know that."

He was right to be cautious. "We can discuss how much I tell them."

Berend was reaching for the wineskin when a commotion outside the door interrupted him. "Here for my hanging already?" he said.

Elric went to the door, listened. The bailiff to whom he had spoken was giving the jailer hurried instructions, too muffled to understand. Another voice interrupted. Familiar . . . A knock.

"Mistress Clifford has sent her man with information for you, Sir Elric," the jailer called out.

Matt. It was Matt's voice Elric had recognized.

"Let him in."

As the door swung open, the bailiff stepped forward and bowed to Sir Elric, this time with due deference. "My lord sheriff sends his greetings, and wishes to know what you have discovered regarding the prisoner's injuries."

"He has no fresh wounds, which tells me that you are holding the wrong man," said Elric. "The murderer is still at large. Tell the lord sheriff that I want Berend released into my charge. I believe he can help me with the search."

The bailiff looked doubtful, but when Elric barked, "Go deliver my request!" the man bowed out of the room and rushed off.

Matt took his place, the jailer bowing to Elric and shutting the door behind the new arrival.

Sweat glistened on the young man's face. "I've come as quickly as I might, Sir Elric." He beamed at Berend. "It is good to see you."

Berend nodded to him.

"Dame Katherine has news from William Frost that she says you need to hear, Sir Elric."

"Come, take a seat." He indicated the bench.

Matt settled down, shaking his head when Berend held out the wineskin. "The lord sheriff took pity on me—I was that out of breath—and he gave me a cup of ale." He quickly delivered his news. "Dame Katherine hopes that this will be of use."

Elric watched Berend as Matt spoke. About the king's men he seemed concerned, asking whether they had proof that Lady Kirkby was in the city, looking relieved when Matt shook his head. Elric knew Sir Peter, and thought the "captain" accompanying him might be his household retainer, given a more impressive title in order to add prestige to the team. That the king had sent an elderly knight more renowned for his piety and his ability to bend with the wind rather than for his military prowess suggested to Elric that King Henry's men were spread so thin he had been reduced to sending someone not up to the task.

When Berend flinched at the mention of Pontefract Castle, Elric interrupted Matt to ask, "You were unaware you had been seen?"

"I must have been careless," said Berend, making a noise in his throat like a growl. "God help me, did I lead the king's men to the gathering in Oxford? Am I to blame for so many deaths?" He bowed his head.

"It was not the king's men who killed most of the rebels but the townsfolk, incensed by the fire the rebels set to draw away the folk surrounding the inn, so they might escape."

"So they say."

"You dispute it?"

"I did not linger to find out."

Berend looked so aggrieved, Elric thought to give him a moment. He asked Matt if he had any more news. But the lad had nothing more.

"Did Dame Katherine wish you to wait for a reply?"

The young man glanced at Berend, back to Elric. "She did not say. Her concern was that you should know what she had learned as soon as might be."

Elric looked to Berend. "Do you mind if Matt stays and hears your tale?"

Berend rubbed his bald pate with both hands, looked sidewise at the messenger. "It is not that I doubt you, Matt. I would trust you with my life. But there are things I must tell Sir Elric that—we must consider how to relate them to Dame Katherine."

To his credit, the young man gave a nod. "I understand. Shall I step outside and wait? Or would you prefer me to go back across the city?" Sitting back, Matt doffed his hat and ran a hand through his hair, still damp from his race here, as he turned to Elric. "And you, what would you have me do, Sir Elric?"

He knew precisely what he wished Matt to do, but looked to Berend, who shrugged and said, "Whether or not Matt awaits you without is not my concern."

Elric nodded. "I would have you stay without, Matt, keeping your ears pricked for any other visitors. I am concerned that the king's men might be too curious about our business. If you hear anything of that nature, rap on the door."

Matt bobbed his head, replaced his hat, and rose. "I am at your service."

"I will rest easier knowing you are on guard, alert for trouble." Elric knocked on the door, and, as the jailer opened it, explained that Matt would be waiting with him.

"Glad of his company," said the jailer as Matt joined him.

When the door had closed again, Elric settled back on the bench. Berend stretched out his legs with a groan. The burden of guilt he now carried was a heavy weight for a man, that he might have led the king's men to the plotters in Oxford. No matter that what they had intended was abhorrent, to die without a chance for confession, absolution, was nothing any Christian wished on another. To ease Berend's burden was not in Elric's nor any man's power. But he might ease his physical circumstances.

"The cold and damp on that injured leg—I hope to get you to a warm space before a new day dawns," said Elric. "Why don't we begin with the casket of jewels?"

"Are they safe?"

"They are."

Berend seemed to consider, examining a spot on the far wall, shaking his head. "To understand you must know what came before."

"I'm listening."

"Merek came to York with a message for me from the Earl of Salisbury. I was to undertake a mission for him, to Pontefract Castle. He called it a debt I owed to his father, for abandoning my post and betraying his trust."

Elric would have told the man he owed no such debt. He guessed Berend did as well. But he asked only, "When precisely did Merek arrive in York?"

Berend shook himself, as if casting out a demon. "Several weeks before Christmas. I was to travel to Oxford, where they were assembling. He assured me I would be back in York by Christmas. The earl presumed I would agree, no questions. Arrogant bastard." Berend muttered a curse.

"You did not go to him at once."

"No. I had no intention of answering such a summons." Berend paused, leaning back, pressing his hands to his face for a moment, then sat up, hands on thighs. "So Merek invoked the name of Rosamund Lacy, Salisbury's mistress."

Ah. She of the posey ring? Something about the way Berend spoke the name, soft, sorrowful, prompted Elric to ask who she was to him.

"We were lovers, once."

"This is what you do not know how to tell Katherine, about Rosamund Lacy?"

"Part of it. God help me, I am not the man she believes me to be."

"You met Rosamund in Montagu's household?"

"Yes."

"Tell me how you came to be in his service."

"There is little to tell. My parents ran a tavern, expected me to continue working for them, but I ran away to war. I knew my way around knives, hunting bows, axes. My strength and speed came to the attention of my captains. Baron Montagu noticed me. One of his men suggested me for his household." He glanced up at Elric. "I was grateful I had landed somewhere. It was a modest household. He came to know me, liked to talk to me."

Much the same as Elric's rise in the earl's household. Westmoreland had found him a good listener. And discrete. "And you met Rosamund?"

Berend took a swig of the brandywine. "She was a servingmaid for Montagu's daughters. Bold, she made a point of being near when I was alone. We talked, kissed, became lovers. It seemed to be her intention, but I—Did I love her? I never stopped to ask myself." He paused, head back, staring up at the ceiling. "I wanted her. Simple as that." He looked at Elric. "I did not have her long. She caught the eye of my lord's son. When Montagu saw how it was between his son and Rosamund, he offered me land so that I might wed her and take her away. It was for me to ask her. I did. With half a heart. She refused me, saying she wanted to stay in the noble household, not be a farmer's wife. Montagu thanked me for trying, assured me there was no honor lost and the land was mine in any case. But—I was disgusted with myself. He had such faith in me and I had failed him. Was relieved to have failed him. I fell into a darkness—drank, fought—and when I saw the disappointment in my lord's eyes, I ran away in the night."

"That was the last contact with the family?"

"No. Years later, when I was at my lowest, Montagu's man found me. He offered me a task. Clean in comparison with what I'd been doing. If I managed this, I would be deeded the land he'd once offered me. He was dying, and he felt he had failed me. Failed *me*. For his repentance, he must give me a chance to right myself, to be the person I might have been had he not sullied my honor with such a request, to wed a woman to save his son. I will never know why he had such faith in me."

"You agreed?"

A nod. "Fulfilled my end of the bargain and the land was mine."

"And now, years later, Merek hoped to persuade you to do something for Rosamund?"

"He told me that her life—and that of her son—was in my hands. If I would not help, she would have no protection from his enemies. If I agreed to help, they would be safe, whether or not Salisbury succeeded in his plan to restore Richard and his good name. When I'd completed my mission to Pontefract I would be free to return to York, I was needed only for the planning."

"Why you?"

"I once succeeded in extracting someone from the castle who'd been held under close guard."

"Your favor to Montagu?"

"Yes. I rescued his—kinsman."

"But you did not love Rosamund, nor do you now, I presume."

"No. I told Merek that Salisbury was mistaken about my feelings for her. And then, as I stormed away, righteously cursing Salisbury for his callous use of another of God's creatures—my own body rebelled. Bile rose in my throat. Callous cur! Who was I to judge Salisbury when I'd so used Rosamund? And after that, my work as an assassin. No mercy. Coldly playing God. I choked on my own sins. What in the name of all that is holy had Montagu seen in me? What had *Katherine* seen in me? What if someone used Petra or Marie as I'd used Rosamund?"

The girls, but not Katherine herself. Of course. She would slit the gut of anyone who attempted to seduce her. "So you agreed to go to Pontefract—why?"

Berend looked him in the eyes. "Knowing a woman and child might die if you refused a summons, what would you do?"

Those eyes, burning into Elric. He knew what he wanted to say, but was it true? "I don't know."

Berend thanked him for his honesty. "I thought it would be easy to say no. And, knowing Merek, he might be using the ghost of Rosamund and the hint that the boy was mine. She might be years in the grave. The boy as well. But I couldn't sleep. The child knew."

"I'm confused. Rosamund's son knew what?"

"Not the boy, Petra, Katherine's niece. *She* sensed something. She kept taking my hand, assuring me that I am a good man." He looked away.

Elric could believe that. The child had a way about her, as if she saw into one's soul. "This boy. He might be your son? Was Rosamund with child when you left? *Your* child?"

"I don't know. It is possible. And how could I refuse to help my son? What would Katherine—" He pressed his hands to his eyes. "Look how she loves and protects children who are not even hers. Marie and Phillip—no one can prove Simon Neville was their father, yet Katherine took them in. Without question. Can I not do as much for a child who might be mine?"

Elric understood. This was what Berend could not bring himself to confess to Katherine, and who could blame him?

"So I went to Pontefract. Not for Rosamund, but for the boy. And to prove to myself once and for all that I was worthy of Montagu's faith in me."

"But this summons had nothing to do with Montagu."

"I did not promise to make sense. Only to recount what I did."

Elric took a swig of the brandywine while he considered his next question. "Did you discover where Richard is kept?"

A nod.

"And then you went to Oxford."

Berend eased his legs in and resettled on the bench. "On the way I had time to think, and I reckoned they were planning far more than the rescue of Richard."

"Tell me how it went in Oxford. Who was there?" This might be information to barter with the sheriffs.

"I knew three of them. Salisbury of course, his manservant, and the Earl of Kent—Thomas Holland, the former king's nephew. He was none too keen to speak with me. Another sign that there was more to the plot."

"Was Ralph Lumley there?"

"I heard his name, but I kept my head down, avoided meeting anyone's eyes. I went straight to my business, showing Salisbury my drawing of the castle.

He wanted me to stay while one of his men reconciled their larger map with what I'd drawn. When I'd told Salisbury and his man all I knew and thought to leave, he said not so hasty. Handed me a map of Windsor Castle and ordered me to draw a route to the royal apartments that would have the fewest guards. I refused. He threatened. I said I had fulfilled my part of the agreement, now I wanted his assurance that Rosamund and the boy were safe."

"Windsor Castle. You knew it well from your days as an assassin?"

A nod.

Elric had not guessed that Berend had done such work for the highest nobles in the land. Did Salisbury understand the danger in antagonizing him?

"You must have many powerful men who would come to your aid rather than have you reveal their secrets. Why have you not called on them?"

"Why would they come to my aid when they would not come to their sovereign's?"

Elric rose to ease a cramp in his leg. "What did Salisbury say to your refusal?"

"Only if I completed the map for Windsor would Rosamund be spared. I demanded to know what they meant to do with it. He said that Duke Henry had sworn that he did not mean harm to King Richard, that he merely wanted the inheritance that was his by right. To Salisbury's mind, when he broke that oath and took the throne he forfeited the honor of his family. Salisbury and his fellows meant to kill King Henry and his sons."

"He did not intend to let you go."

"No. I told him his father would have wept. He told me his father would have understood that with Henry on the throne, or any of his sons, his own family was doomed. As were the men who remained loyal to him. He said it was the same for all those loyal to King Richard." Berend rubbed his injured knee. "For all I know, Rosamund is dead."

"What of the boy?"

"He spoke mostly of Rosamund."

"He might be Salisbury's son."

"Marie and Phillip might not be Simon Neville's children. They look nothing like him. But Katherine did not demand proof."

"No, she did not." What proof could there be? For Berend, the boy's age might expose the lie.

Berend shrugged as if to say no more need be said.

Elric left that line of questioning. "Did they try to hold you?"

"For a day, and then—confusion. Something alarmed them and they fled, leaving me locked up in a windowless room. Warren, an old friend, released me after Salisbury and his companions had ridden off."

"And then?"

"I settled into a corner of the tavern and drank myself into sweet oblivion. Woke on a flea-ridden pallet to the news that the plotters had been routed. Warren meant to seek sanctuary at St. Mary's Abbey in Cirencester. He wanted me to ride with him, guard his back."

"Sanctuary in Cirencester."

Berend nodded. "I disliked the plan, but not for the reason you have in mind. It took me west when I meant to go north and east to York, to Merek. I meant to force him to tell me the truth about Rosamund and the child. But Warren offered me a horse if I would ride with him. I owed him my life."

"He was meeting up with the others?"

"You are asking whether Warren tricked me? I have had long to reflect on that, but I've come to no conclusions."

"Where is he now?"

"Still at St. Mary's, if he is wise."

"Why did he not leave with you?"

"The abbot knows me, knows my sins. He permitted me to stay one night, but then I was to ride on. It suited me." Berend flexed the fingers on his intact hand. "But I rode right into madness, the rabble furious about the fire the Earl of Huntington's man had set as a distraction, and determined to show their loyalty by hunting down the traitors. Or incited to do so. So many townsmen armed so quickly, so adept at slaughter?"

"You believe there were king's men leading them." Elric nodded. "Do you think the abbot knew what you would find in the town? Did Warren?"

"I *have* wondered how I came to the market square just as the crowd attacked the escaping rebels." Berend turned his scarred hands over and over in his lap. "They mobbed Salisbury and his men, shouting curses and 'For King Henry!' while tearing the men off their horses, seething like flies on a corpse, beating them, stabbing them. I fled for my life—down alleyways, through barns—"

"You were chased?"

"A few broke away and came after me, thinking I was one of the rebels. I left my horse in one of the barns and continued on foot. Lost them. For how long, though? I thought to lie low in a barn. God must have guided me. How else did I choose the very barn in which—" He stopped, as if remembering himself.

"In which Lady Kirkby hid?" Elric asked.

A curt nod. "And her manservant. I did not recognize her at first. I saw a woman perched on a milking stool in the corner, staring at nothing, a man whispering to her—'My lady, we must go, we must hasten.' But we were far from the crowd by then, and she was beyond hearing. When he noticed me, he caught up a pitchfork and came at me. By that time I knew her. I shouted my name, and Dame Katherine's. 'Your lady is my mistress's dear friend. I would not harm her. I pray you—' I don't know what convinced him, but he tossed aside the pitchfork before he did me more harm than this eye."

"God in heaven, he came so close?"

"I was certain I was dead. Or blinded."

"But you did not run."

"How did I come to find her? What heavenly agency led me there? I could not run, not seeing how she sat there, holding—it—in her lap, and she had begun to keen." Berend crossed himself, covered his face, his breathing rough.

Are we animals? Is this what happens to a people when we raise up a king who murders his anointed cousin? Elric pushed the wineskin toward Berend. "Drink." He wished he had two wineskins. But his companion was more in need.

Berend picked it up, took a long drink. Coughing, he stoppered the skin, wiped his mouth, faced Elric. "Her man fell to his knees before me. 'My lady has seen such a thing as no wife should ever witness.' He began to weep. I guessed what it was that she held in her lap. I went to her, knelt to her, asked her what we should do with her husband's head." His voice breaking, Berend looked away.

Elric let the silence settle a while, fighting the urge to bombard the man with questions. When Berend's breathing steadied, Elric permitted himself to ask, "How in the name of all the saints did she escape the crowd with the head?"

"A boy took it. A trophy, holding it over his head and crowing. She rushed after him. Her man said she ran swift as a greyhound, holding up her skirts and running like the wind, he had never seen the like. He found her in the barn, holding the head."

"And the boy?"

Berend shook his head. "I saw no sign of him. Of course she was soaked in her husband's blood."

"So she is here in the city?"

A nod.

"Safe?"

"I believe so."

"Why did she come here?"

"I asked her where she wished to go and she said it did not matter. I could not leave her. A sleepwalker she was, until we were close to the city. She seemed to wake then, talking about her husband, talking, talking, like bees buzzing in her head she could not stop talking about him. His love of truth. His belief in basic goodness."

"Did Merek's death have anything to do with the Epiphany Rising?" Elric asked.

"Epiphany Rising? Is that what they call it? An ignoble plot it was, not an uprising." Berend rubbed his head. "It was madness. But to be slaughtered as they were . . . God rest their souls."

Elric tried another approach. "How did you come to possess the casket?"

"Merek gave me the casket on my return. He said I was the only man he could imagine making it across the border with it. The arrival of Parr and Sawyer frightened him, you see. They'd been in Salisbury's household, then Rosamund's, then cast out, accused of theft, abuse of a maidservant, and spying on Salisbury when he visited. Merek believed they might have heard the scheme to return Richard to the throne. He said there could be no other explanation for their arrival in York. And they clearly seemed to know of a casket of great value."

Parr and Sawyer spied on Salisbury? Elric could offer them to Sir Peter as even better informants about the uprising than Berend. "What did he intend to do?"

"Run. Lionel Neville was arranging Merek's passage on a trading ship leaving the following day."

Neville had failed to mention that to Katherine. "Why would Lionel agree to that?"

"I don't know."

"But why would Salisbury entrust the jewels to such a man?"

"Merek Lacy was Rosamund's brother."

It began to make sense. "Hence his determination to convince you the child was yours. So you would protect his sister and nephew. And you believe him? How old is the boy?"

"Old enough to be mine. Or so they say."

"His name?"

"Rosamund named him after Salisbury, hoping he would believe the child his."

"John? Berend, how likely is it—"

"A man with such sins as I carry leaps at any chance for redemption."

Most men justified such a past as little different from battle. Eliminating the enemy. "So you're proposing Parr and Sawyer murdered Merek before they had stolen the casket. Why would they do that?"

"I can't solve this for you. All I can tell you is that evening Merek took me to the church where he'd hidden the casket, and then he went on to meet with Neville about his passage. Have you heard enough to free me?"

Had he? Elric wanted to believe Berend, for Katherine's sake. But could he convince the sheriffs and the king's men?

"I need to find Parr and Sawyer. If I can convince the sheriffs that you are the one to flush them out, they might release you into my custody. But the king's men—I don't know that I can convince them. Perhaps if you handed over Lady Kirkby—"

"No. Even if I knew where she is—which I do not—I would not hand her over."

"You said you knew she was safe. How do you know that?"

Berend looked away. "With all searching for her, would we not hear if she had been found?" he asked.

Elric might have accepted that answer had Berend not averted his eyes. He did not like this. Was it possible that Katherine had been hiding Lady Margery all along?

Berend stirred.

Elric's argument was not with him. "What of the men in the lodging at Oxford? Would you give Sir Peter a list of names?"

"I named the three I knew, and they are all dead."

"What will you do if you are freed?"

"Take the jewels to Rosamund and the boy. I need to know he is safe."

Elric understood. He hoped he would do the same. "And Lady Kirkby?"

"She wishes to go to Rosamund. She says it will give her a purpose, for the nonce." A shrug. "If I am able to find her."

"You spoke of a servant with her. Did he accompany you?"

Berend hesitated. "Yes. He was still with her when we parted."

"You have heard something about him?"

"How could I?"

Elric rose. "I will speak with Dame Katherine." He noted Berend's alarm before he looked away. "I will say nothing of Rosamund and the boy. But you must tell her everything." He described the two rings tucked into the pouch bearing the Montagu arms. "She senses the heart of the tale in that pairing."

"Katherine." Berend groaned.

"We must first devise a plan to get you out of here without the king's men seeing us. They will have a watch on the castle."

"Jennet can help."

"Oh, I've no doubt of that."

❦

This time Elric received a warm greeting from the bailiff, who motioned toward two chairs arranged before a fire, a flagon of wine, and two cups sitting on a small table in between. "Unless the young man will be joining you?"

Elric shook his head. He'd left Matt out in the corridor with orders to warn him at once if the king's men arrived.

He had just settled and the bailiff had offered to pour the wine when Edmund Cottesbrok, one of the sheriffs, strode through the door, preceded by his clerk holding aloft his mace of office as he announced his master's presence. Elric had forgotten the ceremony with which the sheriffs proceeded through the city. Tongues would be wagging. He cursed himself for not thinking of that. Too late now.

"No, I pray you, do not trouble yourself to rise," Cottesbrok said, throwing off his cloak and perching on the other chair, nodding to the bailiff to pour for him as well. He lifted his cup, proposing a toast. "To your health, Sir Elric, and that of Lord Neville."

"You have had some news?"

"I received a message from William Frost, the mayor-elect, who recommends we cooperate in this matter. He believes you are well on your way to discovering the murderer. True?"

Elric wondered how Frost knew of this. Katherine? He found her mark on everything he touched. "What I can tell you is that you have an innocent man in your dungeon, a man who is suffering crippling shackles, no fire, nor cloak, and bare feet in a cold, damp cell."

Cottesbrok made a concerned sound, but a slight shift in posture prepared Elric for the refusal. "There is the matter of the king's men," he sighed. "You understand there is little we can do to deter them. Sir Peter has informed Wrawby and me that he will arrest Berend for treason the moment we release him." John Wrawby was his fellow sheriff this term. "Until you can convince him that Berend took no part in the plot against King Henry and his family, our releasing him only plays into Sir Peter's hands."

Elric glanced back at the pair standing by the door. "Might we speak in private?"

Cottesbrok gestured to his clerk and the bailiff to refresh their cups and then leave. When the door had closed behind the men, the sheriff settled back in his chair, crossing his legs, looking down his long nose. "I can guess what you mean to propose. But before you suggest spiriting him away, Wrawby and I would have you consider the mood of the aldermen and freemen. Everyone has heard how mobs chased down those rumored to be part of the plot against the king and his sons and slaughtered them. Outside the law, without trial. Many here condemn that, it is true, and Berend has friends in the city. He seems to inspire strong loyalty. He *might* be safe, people *might* go far to see that is so. But Sir Peter and Captain Crawford are men determined to prove themselves to the new king. And they may have allies in the city. Are you ready to risk your future?"

His argument gave Elric pause, especially the part about Sir Peter possibly having allies in the city. King Henry might have chosen him for this task for precisely that reason. "What do you propose instead?"

"He stays here until you can clear his name."

"What if I need his help to clear his name?"

"It is not ideal. Nothing is at present. This whole business has the stench of—" Cottesbrok cleared his throat and took a drink. "I merely point out the risk."

Elric took his wine and went to stand by the fire, staring into the flames, considering how quickly word had spread through the city of the shifting fortunes of the warring cousins the past summer while soldiers were massed there prepared to defend it against Henry of Lancaster. Defending the city for King Richard they were, and heaven help the Lancastrian exile. But then, as the word traveled through the ranks of the great army that Henry was collecting as he rode west, and all the nobles and their men defecting to his cause—even York's mayor and aldermen offering Lancaster financial support—the soldiers broke up their camps on Toft Green and quietly slipped out the city gates. They joined the uprising in support of Henry of Lancaster, who promised to be a more generous, wiser, more Godly king. Who could have predicted that sudden turnabout?

And now, how quickly would word of Berend's release spread? How certain was Elric that the people of York would protect Berend? Would he have sufficient supporters with the power to protect him? There was wisdom in keeping him here. Safe.

"Is there another room like this in the castle?" Elric asked.

Cottesbrok frowned. "What do you mean, a room like this?"

"Warmed by a hearth, with a narrow embrasure allowing a little light and air, some comfortable furnishings."

"Ah. For the prisoner."

"For the man being held here for his own safety." Elric marked the man's apologetic wince, but still asked, "Or did I misunderstand your point?"

"No. Of course not. But if Sir Peter hears Berend might walk out at his leisure, that he is not in chains . . ."

"Would you consider yourself fortunate to be locked, barefoot and without a warm cloak, in a cold, damp dungeon with no fire, little air or light, shackled so that you could not take a full stride, and lacking even a bench on which to sit?"

The sheriff bowed his head. "You have made your point."

"Either you prepare comfortable accommodations for Berend, or you assist me in slipping him past the king's men. And swear on your life that no one in your service will reveal that Berend is no longer in the castle."

"You would threaten me?"

Elric inclined his head, but did not speak the words as Cottesbrok glanced toward the door.

"You are not certain of your own men," said Elric. "I understand." A sheriff served from one Michaelmas to the next, one year, insufficient time to form a bond of loyalty he might trust. And the bailiff was likely to be standing right outside the door, doing his best to hear all that passed between them.

Cottesbrok rose. "I will show you the room. It can be locked, a man stationed outside."

"For that I want the present jailer. He will choose a man he trusts to relieve him at night."

The sheriff nodded.

"And you will permit the beguines on Castlegate to bring him his meals and see that he has all he needs."

"God in heaven you test my patience, Sir Elric. Are we to bow to him when we enter?" Cottesbrok snapped.

"I have spent the past hour in a cold, dank dungeon, sitting on a hard bench, listening to a man bare his soul to me. I am in no mood to appease your temper. I simply want him treated as the honorable man I believe him to be."

Raised brows, but a nod. "Of course. It will be as you decree."

12

ORDEALS

When Kate returned, Marie was giving Petra a cooking lesson, with much rolling of the eyes and sighing.

Jennet sat by the door keeping her hands busy with a distaff and spindle, creating a fine wool thread. Without pausing in her work, she invited Kate to sit beside her. "The girls are too busy arguing to overhear if we speak softly."

"I called on Dame Jocasta."

"And?"

"She was sorry Griselde found the maidservant lacking and went to fetch her."

Jennet grinned down at the spindle. "That is a relief."

"Yes and no. I did not mean to involve her."

"She might have refused."

Kate sighed as Lille settled at her feet, warming them.

"I had a visitor," said Jennet with a glint of excitement in her eyes.

"Elric? Berend?"

"No, sorry, one of my eyes and ears, the scrivener I've befriended. He's discovered more about Jon Horner."

A good source, eager to make trouble for a man who gave those in his profession a bad name. Horner had set himself up as a scrivener to prey on the desperate, threatening to reveal their bad debts and illegal trades if they did not pay for his discretion—charging a fee more than double the customary.

"Anything to explain his relationship with Merek?" Kate asked.

"No. I think there is something in this. Maybe Petra's dreams have me heeding my feelings." Jennet paused to attend to a knot in the wool. "There. So. It seems Horner pried into the business dealings of elderly, infirm men with young wives, which included four now dead—Alan Barker, John Atterby, Adam Nottingham, and Ross Wheeldon. He'd also noted Dame Eleanor's evident wealth, and newly widowed with no husband to guide her."

"Mother?" Kate sat back, aghast.

Jennet nodded. "That was disturbing, but I was more interested in the other widows I mentioned. Might whatever Merek handed Horner have been a gift for one of them? Was he seeking a wealthy wife? The lady's glove in his room, the one you have not shown Sir Elric, might it belong to one of these women? Who then poisoned him?" She bent to another snag. "Two of them are betrothed—Alyse Nottingham and Mary Barker. But Philippa Atterby and Cecily Wheeldon are not. I thought it odd, that he was keeping notes on Wheeldon, considering he'd worked for her."

"Was there anything of interest in his business with her?"

"Only that my friend could find no records of it."

"None?"

Jennet shook her head. "Do you think that's why he dressed like a peacock? Thinking women would flock to him, like peahens?"

"Heaven help any woman who pecked at his feet," Kate said, grinning. "What does it mean, that he found no records?"

"Possibly the widow keeps them close. As you do."

Kate searched her memory about Philippa Atterby. Someone had mentioned her recently. An interesting story. Ah, it came back to her. "Not long ago—perhaps a fortnight?—Philippa Atterby spoke to Mother about joining her Martha House. Her family was pushing her into a marriage she did not want and she hoped to escape it by withdrawing into a holy life."

"Do you think her family would have pushed Jon Horner?" asked Jennet.

Kate thought of Philippa's parents. Her grandfather had once been mayor, her father both bailiff and sheriff. "I doubt it."

Jennet leaned closer. "What did Dame Eleanor decide?"

"She explained the sisters' day—all the prayer and work, and asked her whether that was what she truly wanted. When Philippa hesitated, Dame Eleanor offered to speak to her family about her own wishes. Philippa left in some anger." Kate empathized with Philippa as well as with her mother. She knew the lengths a young widow with an overbearing family might go to avoid their interference. "It might be worth speaking to Dame Eleanor about both Philippa Atterby and Jon Horner."

"We seem to go farther from the point with every piece of information," Jennet grumbled.

Kate agreed. If they did not find a pattern that pointed to the murderer . . . "We need a plan for plucking Berend out of the castle and helping him slip away."

"Where would he go?"

"His land?"

They were interrupted by Marie, who flopped down beside Kate with a dramatic sigh. "I despair. She will never be a cook."

Petra remained at the worktable frowning at the watery dough dripping from her hands.

Biting back a smile, Kate turned to Jennet. "I will visit Jocasta and Eleanor in the morning." She pressed Jennet's arm. "Thank you. I do not know what I would do without you."

Jennet ducked her head. "You give me the questions. All I do is pass them on and then wait for some answers. But I will think about the last item."

Berend's escape. Kate nodded.

Marie poked Kate's arm. "Did Sir Elric forget us?"

Kate drew her close and kissed her forehead, smiling up at Petra, who stood perplexed over her failure. "The waiting is difficult, I know." And it was hardest for the girls, it seemed. "We need movement, eh? Come, let's go to the hall." Rising, Kate asked Jennet to see what she might do with the dough.

Out in the hall, where there was space, Kate led Petra and Marie through a set of exercises that strengthened their arms for archery, then made a game out of seeing who could stand still the longest. When at last Elric and Matt arrived, without Berend, the girls were exhausted, their disappointment expressed with long faces and teary eyes, but no melodrama. They each took one of Elric's hands as they led him to a chair by the fire, begging him for information. He looked exhausted, his eyes shadowed, his movements heavy as he settled into the chair. Kate sent Matt to the kitchen to fetch Jennet with some refreshment.

"I saw Berend moved to far more comfortable quarters, and Sisters Clara and Agnes from the Martha House are seeing to the sores from the shackles and ensuring that he has food that will speed his healing," Elric assured Marie and Petra. "Until we have something that will satisfy the king's men, he is safest at the castle."

"Is he? Is he really?" asked Petra.

"I believe that to be so in the circumstances," he said.

She gave him a solemn nod.

"Might we visit him there?" asked Marie.

"No. That would be unwise," said Elric.

The child kicked a stool, but did not whine.

Kate touched his shoulder. "Jennet will bring you food and drink while I see the girls to bed," she told him.

She coaxed Marie and Petra out the door and up the steps, promising that she would tell them all she could in the morning.

"Do you trust that he is safe?" Marie asked when they were settled in bed.

As safe as Elric can make him, Kate thought. But to them she merely said, "I do," then hugged them both before blowing out the lamp near the door. "Now try to sleep. You want to give those muscles a good rest after all that effort, eh?"

She tiptoed out, pausing on the landing with a warm sense of gratitude for the small rituals involving the children. Her touchstones, they steadied her. As she moved down the steps she whispered prayers that she was about to hear nothing that she might not share with the girls in the morning. But the guardedness of Elric's gaze as she entered the hall warned her that those particular prayers would not be answered this night.

—◦◦◦—

As Kate listened to Elric's account, his respect for Berend strengthened her resolve to tell him about her part in Margery's flight. He already knew that she was in the city, Berend had made that plain. But as she, Jennet, and Matt posed questions, particularly regarding Berend's decision to go to Pontefract, her ease dissolved.

"You were satisfied despite his lack of explanation?"

"I left out the parts he prefers you hear from him, not me."

"Because?"

"He saw how it pained you to have learned so much about his past from me." And from Bess, she thought. "I will go to him in the morning."

Jennet was the first to rise, excusing herself to go check the kitchen and the yard even though Lille and Ghent had sat by the door all the while, listening for signs of intruders. Then Matt rose, offering to fetch more ale. Kate thanked him.

Alone but for the hounds, Kate studied Elric, staring into the fire with haunted eyes. She was moved by how deeply he felt Berend's pain, having heard in his tone whispers of Berend himself.

"I am sorry I came away without him," he said.

"No. You accomplished more than I had hoped. I am grateful."

"He curses himself, but I see him as an honorable man. Many of us look back with horror and vow to redeem ourselves. But he has embraced that vow with all his being."

"How did this redeem him? He'd already condemned the plot."

"You will see."

She was quiet a while, retracing Berend's journey, his betrayal by either the abbot or Salisbury's kinsman.

"So much suffering," she said, "and for what? Another king who sees enemies in every corner?"

"How can King Henry be otherwise? A thief knows he has no right to what he's taken. He can never be secure." Elric had begun to tap his thigh with the felt hat he had taken off when he grew warm by the fire, beginning slowly, gradually speeding it up, until he tossed it from him with a curse. "We seem incapable of learning from our mistakes. Think of what happened when Richard's great grandfather was put aside."

"The last King Edward proved a far better king than his father."

"It was not the son who struck down his father, but his mother and her lover," said Elric. "They proved to be tyrants."

This was a change, to speak treason so bluntly to her. Berend's suffering seemed to have pushed back the mask, revealing the man beneath the façade of the great earl's captain of Sheriff Hutton Castle. Not so long ago—could it be but a year?—she had thought him a heartless, self-satisfied instrument of Westmoreland. No longer. About to share what she had learned about Horner, and then steel herself to tell him about Margery—if he could see Berend's pain, surely he could see Margery's—she hesitated as he suddenly rose up and paced over to the fire. When he turned to face her, he had that old expression, cold eyes, stiff, soldierly stance.

"I trust you have told Lady Margery her jewels are safe?"

Startled, Kate said, "Told her?"

"You could not bring yourself to trust me?"

"Who is withholding information from whom?" This was not how she had meant to broach the subject, damn him.

"I promised Berend."

"I promised Lady Margery. It was not my secret to share." Had one of his men seen Jocasta at the guesthouse, arriving alone, departing with Margery? And deduced so much? Had they followed Kate?

Just tell him, tell him everything, Geoff urged.

Now, when he is angry?

"Where is she?" Elric asked so coldly Kate wanted to spit at him.

But she needed his help. *Holy Mary, Mother of God, help me find the words he can hear.*

"Sit down, I pray you," she said. "I have much to tell you. So much I've wanted to tell you."

"But you did not trust me with it?"

"Why would I, when you—" She stopped. This would not serve her purpose. Softening her voice, she said, "I did not know who I might trust. Her manservant came to me for help, and I gave it before I knew the enormity of what I'd undertaken, the danger I had brought to my family."

"When?"

"The night before our celebration. I pray you, Elric, sit. Standing there, looking down on me, *judging* me—I cannot think clearly." He did not move. Mulish man. "I cannot begin to understand her suffering." Kate disliked that his nearness had her whispering. "To witness her husband's attack, to hold his severed head, Elric. And then to have the king condemn her for wanting to bury Thomas. You have heard the tale from Berend, how it sickened him. How can Ralph Neville condone this?"

"I cannot divine my lord's private thoughts. We have communicated through messengers, careful to say as little as possible. But he would *say* it is not for him to judge his lord."

"You do not know his heart?"

"I have prided myself in my honor, my unquestioning obedience to my lord. But of late . . ." A slow shake of the head, as if waking himself. "It is clear I do not know your heart."

Her heart? "Please. Sit beside me and I will tell you all."

At last he came to perch beside her, at the edge of his chair. All the while she spoke, he kept his eyes on the fire, never looking her way.

She told him of Carl's disappearance and murder. Her fear, her doubts about Margery's account. "Berend's tale of how they came to be traveling together—Margery did not tell me. Did he explain how her jewels came to be in the case?"

A part of her enjoyed witnessing Elric's discomfort as he realized he had forgotten to ask about that.

"No matter. I shall ask him in the morning," she said. "Or Margery."

"She is at the guesthouse now?"

"Do you still vow to keep her safe?"

Elric shot Kate an angry look. "I am a man of my word."

"I will hold you to that." Kate explained how she had sent Jocasta Sharp to fetch her. "The Sharp home is always open to those in need. No one will mark a maidservant arriving there."

"Not in ordinary times. But Sir Peter and Captain Crawford, Parr and Sawyer—I have sent for more men from Sheriff Hutton. I will put a guard on her home."

Kate looked at him, surprised. "You will do this for me?"

That did not provoke a look. To the fire, he said, "Not for you. For Lady Margery, and for Berend." He made an exasperated sound. "God's blood, woman, Carl's murder—You curse Lady Margery for her dishonesty? Look to yourself." Now he faced her, shaking his head.

"Had it been you, a friend in need, with the gates about to close and shut them out in the cold for the night, would you have turned them away?"

"No! What do you take me for? In God's name, woman, look at all I have done for you."

He was right. She felt the full weight of her deception. She had betrayed the one person who had done nothing but help her in this crisis.

"I wish I could go back to that night at the guesthouse, when we talked after your men had gone. I wish that the moment you spoke her name I had said, 'She is here. Will you help?'"

"Do you?" He looked doubtful.

"With all my heart."

He grunted and looked away.

"There is more you need to know." She told him what Jennet had discovered about Jon Horner.

"To catch a widow while yet in mourning, while she is most vulnerable. Cur," Elric growled. "Cecily Wheeldon, you said?"

At least he was listening. "Yes. Why?"

"I found her arguing with Kevin outside Horner's house. She said she wanted to comfort the housekeeper, but what if she wanted—" He sat back, raking a hand through his hair. "What?"

"She wanted to find her missing glove?" Kate whispered, determined to tell him all.

"Glove?"

She crossed the hall to fetch the scrip in which she had hidden away the things she had found in Horner's chamber. She handed him the elegant leather item.

He held it out toward the light of the fire, turning it over, back. "It is the sort of thing she would wear."

"The woman who owned the glove might have helped Horner back to his room when he fell ill," said Kate, "dropping the glove as she struggled to get him into bed, then, when she stepped out into the cold morning and realized she had only one, did not care to return. To be there as he struggled to live."

"You think she poisoned him?" He touched the mysterious herbal ball in her hands. "May I see that?" She handed it to him. He sniffed it, felt it, then loosened a small piece of it with his nail and lifted it to his mouth.

"What if it's poison!" Kate cried, plucking the ball from his hands.

"It is a bezoar stone. Used to protect oneself from poison, or lessen the effect."

Interesting. Horner had been protecting himself. "I have heard of them, but I have never seen one."

"Ah." He smirked. "Now you have."

She wanted to slap him. Controlling the impulse, she returned to the point. "So Horner feared he was being poisoned, or might be. He knew he courted danger. But we don't know the glove is Cecily Wheeldon's."

"Nor do we know that it belongs to his poisoner. But it would be worthwhile speaking to her."

"I will think of a way."

He nodded.

"I suppose you won't believe that I had resolved to share all of this with you tonight."

"No, I don't."

They were sitting in uneasy silence when Matt returned with ale, serving them both, then withdrawing.

"Did you tell Berend that Lady Margery was safe?" Elric asked when they were once more alone.

"Yes. Just that. Did he tell you?"

"No. He did not betray you." The words were meant to wound. They did. He put his bowl aside, slapped his thighs. "I need to find Parr and Sawyer."

Kate rose, calling the hounds to her. As she walked out of the hall with Elric and the dogs, a man of the night watch hailed them from the street. "If the sheriffs wish to speak to folk about Berend's honor, I am at your service, Mistress Clifford."

"I will remember that," she said. "Bless you."

Elric nodded to the man, then strode off into the night without a word.

In the kitchen, Kate slumped down onto a stool by the fire, reaching her hands out to the warmth. "Elric knows everything," she said to Jennet.

"Good. He is a good man."

"Is this from your eyes and ears?"

A nod as Jennet handed Kate a cup of something spicy and almost too hot to hold, then bent to plump the pillows on the pallet she had arranged for herself near the fire.

"You will need a man, by and by," said Jennet.

"Hand me the heated stone so I can warm my bed, eh?"

Kate had not the heart to speak of her despair. But apparently it was obvious.

"He did not take it well, coming so late?" Jennet asked.

Kate shook her head and rose, clutching the stone.

—◦◦◦—

Up in the solar Kate wrapped the stone she had brought from the kitchen and placed it beneath the mound of blankets so that it might begin warming the bedclothes while she undressed. Usually she loved the moment when she finally stretched out on her back beneath the bedclothes, the strain of the day draining away. Jennet had found a laundress who scented the bedding with rosewater and lavender blossoms, and the fragrance rose round her as the stone and her body heated the cloth. This was sweetness, the warmth lulling her to sleep.

But not tonight. Her mind raced, and her heart lurched between fear, anger, remorse. There was more to Berend's story, something he felt the need to explain to her. Was everything she had believed about him a lie? And Margery. Why were her jewels nestled with those of the Earl of Salisbury? What was her connection to the uprising?

She cursed herself. As soon as she had learned of Margery's possible complicity in the plot she should have confided in Elric. Stupid stupid woman. No, coward. That is what she was, a coward. Once she had set foot on the path of deception she had been afraid to step off and trust Elric. Now she had lost him. Lost a friend, a comrade in arms, a potential lover. Yes, she admitted to herself that she had hoped to lead him there. Bloody fool. All for the sake of a friend who had not told her the whole truth about how she came to be hunted.

She pushed those thoughts away. Save the anger until she knew all there was to know.

Worry took over. Was Berend warm enough? How were his wounds? Could she trust Cottesbrok and Wrawby to protect him? Elric trusted them.

Damn Elric. She turned on her side, hoping a new position would bring on more relaxation.

But her mind would not still. Had it been only two days ago that she had paid off the last of Simon's debt? Two days ago she had been so—No, she was forgetting Petra's unhappiness. Berend's disappearance. Kevin's return to the earl's service.

She stirred herself to remember how it had felt when she'd realized the extent of Simon's debt. An impossible amount. She'd felt betrayed, robbed, angry—so angry. It had been her anger that had driven her to put all her strength in digging out from under it. She had accomplished it without help, certainly without resorting to something that would put her at the same risk—marriage. Standing on her own two feet, independent, self-sufficient, that had been her goal over these past three years. And she had succeeded.

She waited for the surge of joy, or at least satisfaction. Nothing. Only a yawning emptiness. And a rising fear of what more Berend was about to reveal to her.

—◦◎◦—

Seeing Marie and Petra to school, Kate shrugged at their complaints about the unseasonably warm morning. Yesterday it had been too cold. Tomorrow the sun would be too bright. Mornings were difficult for both girls at the moment. Neither slept well, Petra because of her nightmares, the Sight, whatever it was, and Marie—Kate was not certain why she was wakeful, her queries met with stony silence. Marie's pride might prevent her from admitting that she feared Petra's whimpers and accounts of disturbing or prescient dreams. But when Kate had offered to move Marie to a separate bedchamber, the child would not hear of it. So every morning was a struggle.

Still, Kate disliked how the warmth of the rising sun caused a fog as it touched the moisture-laden chill of the ice- and snow-clad houses and streets. Even more troubling were the clusters of people here and there, their heads together, whispering excitedly. Only something serious would draw them out in such numbers to stand about chilled to the bone by the heavy mist that quickly penetrated all but the finest woolens and furs. She regretted leaving Lille and Ghent in the kitchen. She had not felt comfortable leaving Jennet alone while seeing to the morning chores. Matt had left early for her cousin William's house. If all went well he would return soon with the new servant,

Cuddy, and news of the king's men. But she'd thought it best to leave the hounds with Jennet, worried about the jewels and coins, a treasure.

"Soldiers, they are talking about soldiers." Marie grabbed Kate's hand. "Are we under siege?"

Kate squeezed her ward's hand and assured her that was not the case, that the soldiers were most likely Sir Elric's men. He had sent for them to help search for the murderer.

But Kate was uneasy. She would have expected Elric to do all he could to avoid the trouble such a show of force might stir up. Bedlam, as in Cirencester. Berend's tale should have reminded him of the danger of rumor, how stoking people's fears might spark violence.

She breathed more easily once the girls had been bustled into the classroom by their schoolmaster, relieved that he had shut the door against the fog with naught but a nod to Kate. She was in no mood for a lecture this morning. But as she turned to leave, she heard the door open behind her, then felt a hand on her shoulder.

"Forgive me for my discourtesy," said Master Jonas, "but I did not want my pupils to overhear." With worried eyes the schoolmaster asked if she knew anything about the company of soldiers that had earlier swarmed down Petergate and up Stonegate.

Even he.

"I expect they were the Earl of Westmoreland's men," said Kate. "Come to help restore the peace."

"*Restore* it? They have *disturbed* it."

"They are here to solve the murders of Merek and Horner."

"Sow trouble, reap trouble." He wagged his head as if speaking of unruly children. "I see no need for an armed invasion. In any case, I thought the sheriffs had taken your cook into custody. Did they arrest him in error? Mind you, I do not believe Berend would do such a thing unless he did it for the good of the city. But murder is a crime. Not to mention a grave sin."

Quite a speech from the schoolmaster, and it challenged Kate to listen with equanimity. "Of course Berend did not murder those men. Sir Elric and I agree that they arrested him in haste. As to the armed invasion, I did not witness their arrival. A pity that they inspired fear rather than reassurance."

"Indeed. Well. I wish them success. Benedicite, Mistress Clifford."

"Benedicite," said Kate just in time before Master Jonas opened the door only so wide as to slip inside, as if fearful lest he let a child loose into the streets. He closed it softly behind him, and she waited for his usual loud tirade. But she was distracted by a sense of someone watching her. She felt rather than saw something in the mist, slipping back round the side of the building. Drawing her knife from her skirt, she concealed it beneath her cloak as she stole along the side of the building to Petergate and peered round the corner. No one. But out in the street someone slipped on the cobbles, cursed. Kate hurried forward, but she saw no one until she reached the intersection with Stonegate. There the sun shone down, thinning the mist, illuminating a crowd of folk congregating.

"Soldiers in the yard of the York Tavern," a neighbor said as she joined him. "A great company."

Elric's men had indeed arrived.

⚜

As she passed the shop of Pendleton, the silversmith, she paused, remembering the jeweled girdle she had glimpsed on the shelf in his office, and her sense that Lady Margery did not wish her to know how it came to be there. She knocked on the door.

A young servant answered, the dust in his hair sparkling with traces of silver.

"We are not prepared to receive customers so early, Mistress."

"Would you ask your master if I might speak with him? It is important. Tell him it's Katherine Clifford."

A man shoveled slushy snow away from the front of the shop next door, pausing for a moment to ask if she had seen the soldiers.

"Not as yet."

"I thought we were well rid of them, drunk and rowdy, picking fights with us working folk."

He shivered beneath his much-patched tunic, a skinny man, more bone than flesh. She was searching for a response when the door behind her opened.

"Dame Katherine, to what do I owe the honor of your presence?" Roland Pendleton's hearty voice rang out, turning heads on the street.

"Might we talk inside?"

A glance at the sweeper, and another clerk across the way pretending to be checking one of the storefront's latches, and Pendleton stepped aside, welcoming her in. In the shop the lamps were lit, the lad who had answered the door and another busily assembling materials for the day's work.

"Is it about the soldiers? They're from Sir Elric's garrison, are they not? Sheriff Hutton?"

The lads looked up, eager to hear any news.

"Yes. But that is not why I have come."

"Ah. Well then," he gestured toward his office behind the workshop.

As Kate took a seat, she glanced at the shelf on which she had glimpsed the dymysent. But all she could see were records in a neat stack. "I will not keep you long. I noticed an item on your shelf the other day, a jeweled girdle, that I know to belong to Lady Margery Kirkby." She saw by his expression that he had not known of the connection to Lady Kirkby. So Kate was right, her friend had not brought it here for repair. "Might I ask how you came to have it? A man's life may depend on your answer."

Roland nervously cleared his throat. "A jeweled girdle? Are you certain? I cannot recall—"

"Was it the spice seller Merek who brought it to you?"

"Merek? The man who was murdered?" Roland crossed himself and shook his head. "Lord have mercy." He hesitated. "Why would you think that?"

"Or was it my cook Berend who brought it?"

"Berend?" He blinked, as if caught without an answer. "Is it true what they say? That he has been accused of murdering Merek and Jon Horner? And took part in the rebellion?"

"He *has* been taken to York Castle. I am trying to prove his innocence."

"I swore." A sigh that deepened to a groan. "But this changes everything." A long pause. "Yes, Berend brought it to me to raise some money. For a lady in need, he said. I thought a lady friend in the family way, though I should have wondered. A cook courting a woman who could afford such a piece? But it was Berend—we all trust him. I had no idea it was—Her husband was executed for treason, was he not?"

For a lady in need. Margery? Damn the woman. "When was this?"

"Several days ago. It is a fine piece. I paid him well. I did not know it was the property of a traitor, or that he was so accused. And then the murders—God help me. Dame Katherine, I pray you . . ."

"Berend brought it to you. Did he tell you anything about the lady, where she was, what trouble she faced?"

Roland shook his head. "Nothing. He did advise me to go elsewhere to sell it. I thought a summer fair . . . What should I do with it?"

"Keep it hidden."

"I paid good money—"

"Patience, I pray you. All may yet be well. But say nothing."

"I swear."

"See to it."

"God be thanked I am not always so easily led astray. I was offered another piece and, well . . ."

"Yes?"

"Stolen goods."

"Do you have the piece?"

The man did not meet her eyes as he shook his head. "I expect a client any moment . . ."

She touched his arm. "Master Roland, I pray you. Two people are dead, another badly injured. Sir Elric and I are doing all we can to find the murderer before there is more tragedy. Who showed you a stolen item?"

"Sir Elric, you say? The earl's man?" The silversmith searched her face. "You are asking for him?"

It rankled to play Elric's subservient, but if it put Roland at ease . . . "Yes."

He hesitated a moment, then sighed as he rubbed his forehead. "It was Jon Horner, God rest his soul. He brought in a gold brooch. Fine work, very fine. He wanted to know its worth, whether he had been charged a fair price. He had indeed." He raked a hand through his hair. "But I told him there was nothing fair about his having been offered it for purchase. You see, I recognized the piece. It belongs to my sister-in-law. Stolen weeks ago."

So not from the casket. "What did he do?"

"Plucked it from my hands and rushed out of the shop. My servant tried to stop him, but he moved too fast."

"When was this?"

"The day before yesterday. We were just closing up. I meant to report it to the sheriff in the morning, but then I heard Horner was found dead in his room. Is it true that he took his own life? Surely not over a piece of stolen jewelry? Or was he murdered?"

"I do not know," said Kate. She thanked him. "You can be certain that Sir Elric will appreciate your cooperation. And, for now, your silence."

"I swear, Dame Katherine. But I mean to report the stolen brooch."

"Describe it to me and I will search Horner's house for it."

"Why should I wait—" He breathed out. "Forgive me. I am not accustomed to such troubles. I was not thinking. Of course." He described a golden feather caught in a bare branch. A delicate piece, exquisitely fashioned, with a small piece of coral on the reverse, said to prevent a flux of blood when warmed by her body. "A gift from her aunt for her first lying in. She treasures the piece and has grieved the loss of it, particularly now, as she is again with child."

Kate assured him she would search for it, and they departed with vows of good faith.

Once out the door she let herself feel the full flush of anger. She had given Lady Margery the gift of sanctuary and the woman lied to her face. Why? Why should Kate trust her? What was Berend's task? Gathering a sum of money to arrange for Lady Margery's passage. And his? Damn them. She offered them help and they repaid her with deceit? She thought of the small pouch with the two rings from Salisbury's hoard. She had tucked it in her scrip, thinking to force Berend into addressing its significance. Raising funds for someone dear to Salisbury as well?

Time to confront him, Geoff whispered in her mind.

Yes. But she might need an escort, someone who had permission to visit Berend.

—◦◦◦—

The arrangement of the buildings around the graveyard in St. Helen's Square allowed sufficient morning light for Kate to make out a dozen men in the livery of Ralph Neville, Earl of Westmoreland. They stood in groups of four, one in the tavern yard, two in the square, Douglas, Wulf, and Stephen presiding.

Elric and Kevin stood near the door of the tavern, in heated discussion with an elderly nobleman who had the bearing of a seasoned soldier. A younger man in the king's livery stood to one side, shifting his weight from foot to foot as if impatient to move on. Sir Peter Angle and Captain Crawford, Kate presumed. She took her time walking toward them, straining to hear the matter of their disagreement. Bess Merchet leaned on her cane in the doorway. Noticing Kate, she nodded her head in greeting, but quickly returned her attention to the men. She, too, was listening.

"I should hope you would have already sounded the alarm, Sir Elric," the elderly knight was saying, "encouraged the citizens of York to inform you of any strangers, questionable behavior, treasonous speech."

"They are already uneasy," Elric said, his gloved hands in fists behind his back, his words clipped. "Look how they've congregated at the edge of the square. They have heard what happened in other towns, the mobs taking it upon themselves to execute those rumored to be traitors. None of us want a repeat of that lawless violence."

"It was effective," said the old knight's impatient companion.

"Your captain lacks experience, Sir Peter. I will not entrust my men to him," said Elric.

"Then I must continue my investigations without your assistance." The old knight bowed stiffly.

Kate did not linger, slipping past them, glad she had not brought the hounds and called attention to herself.

Old Bess motioned her into the tavern and waved her through to her quiet space.

"I thought Sir Elric would be discrete about the additional men," Kate said.

"That was Wulf's mistake," said Bess. "Sir Elric's orders had been to have the men arrive a few at a time, without fuss. But they all descended upon the tavern shortly after dawn. Before Sir Elric had returned. We've had all we can do to feed them. Heaven knows where they will all sleep tonight. I've not the rooms to spare."

"Sir Elric was about so early? Before the men arrived?"

"Early? No. Late. He was out all the night."

"Where?"

"He would not say." The elderly woman busied herself folding some bedding. "He trusts me with what he learned from Berend but not that." She shook out a partially folded sheet with a loud snap. Kate judged it best not to offer assistance. "Leaving Berend in the castle." Snap. "Fearful lest Sir Elric and all his men are not enough against the king's men? Have you seen Sir Peter? Rheumatic wheezing, a shoulder that barely moves. Pah."

"He sounded eager to cause a riot."

"So he's a fool as well?" Snap.

"Did Sir Elric seem rested when he appeared this morning?"

"Rested?" A shake of her head, her ribbons bouncing. "No more than you do." Bess looked Kate up and down. "Perhaps not quite so wilted as you. Who kept you awake?"

"*I* did."

A nod. "I trust you were not doubting Berend's innocence?"

"No. But at present we have only his word. We have no proof. To convince the sheriffs and Sir Peter we need more."

An impatient sniff. "Wulf should be the one in chains."

"Sir Elric assures me that Berend is no longer in chains," said Kate.

"Small comfort."

"I agree." Kate settled into a chair. "I need to find out from Berend what Sir Elric left out of his account."

Bess frowned at her. "You do not trust that Elric told you all?"

"I know that he did not, at Berend's request."

"Ah. You will tell me what you learn?"

"Of course." Kate told her about her conversation with Pendleton.

"It is time you speak with Berend."

Kate agreed. "Might Elric have spent the night guarding Berend?"

"Only if Berend is sleeping out in the snow. Sir Elric's leggings were soaked and his cloak heavy with damp."

"It is a long walk from the castle."

The taverner slapped a folded blanket onto the table.

Kate let it be, but she did wonder where Elric had spent the night. Was it possible he had stood watch on Jocasta's house? Or hers?

"He might have warned me so many were coming, but men, they never consider such things." Bess set her work aside and reached for Kate's hand, giving it a squeeze. "Forgive my temper. I see how all this weighs on you. I want to help, but there is little I can do. You must permit Sir Elric to bear the burden of protecting Berend and Lady Kirkby."

"They are my friends."

"Of course. But he meant to prove himself in this. Still does."

"Has he told you . . . ?"

"That you have hidden her all this while?" A nod. "Your distrust cut him deep." Hands on hips, Bess shook her head at Kate. "Do not pretend you were not aware of his feelings for you. That he should choose such a means of wooing might well amuse you—it does me. My Tom would be shaking his head and assuring me that I have it all wrong. What man would woo a woman in such wise, he would ask. But mark me, I have walked this earth a good long while and I know a man in love when I see one. You let Sir Elric help, and I thought you understood. But what you kept from him—you fettered him from the start. And me."

"It was not my secret to share."

"And then it was."

"Because I need his help."

"By the rood, I am wasting time talking to myself." Bess bent to her work, dismissing Kate.

13

SECRETS AND SPIES

Walking slowly through the groups of soldiers, Kate paused just outside the door of the apothecary and glanced back at Elric, still arguing with the elderly knight. Shadows beneath his eyes were the only hint of exhaustion. Back straight, his dress impeccably tailored and tidy as ever—thanks to his squire Harry, no doubt. Had he gone to Jocasta's? If not, she needed to know about the soldiers. The feud between the royal cousins had sown fear in everyone's hearts, and now, with the murders, the soldiers, the king's men, and rumors of a traitor's wife hiding in the city, one stray spark and the crowded tenements would explode in violence.

Noticing some of the soldiers regarding her, she embarked on a meandering course to Jocasta Sharp's house. Crossing into Stonegate, she slipped down the alley that led to Drusilla Seaton's home. The maidservant answered on Kate's knock, shaking her head. Her mistress had returned from a night out and gone straight to bed. It took a little persuading to convince the woman that Kate wished only to pause long enough to catch her breath—the mist was chilling her—before she moved on. Stationing herself in a window, she watched the

alley for a decade of Hail Mary's, and when no one had passed through by
then, she thanked the puzzled maidservant and hurried on through to Grape
Lane, which she traversed only so far as another small alleyway, and so on
until she wound up in Dame Jocasta's back garden. The sun was just breaking
through the mist, creating eerie swirls that dizzied her as she lifted her eyes to
a man crouched on the kitchen roof, replacing tiles. Another man stood near
the rain barrel at the corner of the house, the tool for breaking through the
ice dangling from his hand. She nodded to both of them as if her appearing
there were the most ordinary event, and knocked on the rear door of the house.

A lad opened the door, and Jocasta's terrier, Lady Gray, came rushing out on
her short legs to circle Kate and greet her with happy barks. As Kate scooped
up the dog she heard Dame Jocasta calling to the lad to "step away from that
door! What were you about?"

"Dame Jocasta?" Kate called softly as she stepped into the house, standing
still for a moment with the squirming terrier in her arms, letting her eyes
adjust to the soft candlelight. Every shutter in the house was closed against
the daylight. A wise precaution.

"My dear Katherine." Jocasta stepped out of the darkness to pluck Lady
Gray from her arms and set her on the floor. "Forgive my witless prattle. I
did not anticipate—But why did you come to the garden door? Were you
followed?"

"I noticed no one, but mean to take no risks. I come to warn you of the
temper of the city."

"I have heard," said Jocasta. "Sir Peter Angle is keen to stir up the people so
that he might play the hero. Sir Elric says he will have all he can do to contain
the damage that arrogant fool might wreak."

"Sir Elric? When did you speak with him?"

"Why, last night, of course. He has already suggested ways we might be less
obvious. And he promises that his men will be invisible."

That solved the mystery of where he had spent the night. Kate tried to
hide her surprise with an innocuous comment about being glad Jocasta felt
reassured by his presence.

"I am indeed. He gave instructions to my usual helpers in how to remain
hidden yet with clear sight of the doors or the windows—all the places
someone might try to sneak into the house. And he showed them how to have

the advantage when creeping up on an intruder. They could talk of nothing else when they came in this morning to break their fasts before going to their homes to sleep. He has promised that at least one of his men will be here at all times to assist until the danger is past. Bless you, Katherine."

Was ever a woman more wrong about a man? Kate thought.

Do not taunt yourself, Kate, Geoff whispered in her mind.

Jocasta tilted her head, studying Kate. "You did not know of this, that he had watched through the night."

"No. I had asked him to set some men to watch from today."

Jocasta smiled. "God guided you in this. You opened your heart, and He showed you the way."

Divine providence might guide Jocasta, but it had never figured in Kate's decisions. Her own heart had led her into trusting Elric, and it had not led her astray. She was grateful for that.

"You carried in the chill of the morning, that clinging mist that turns to ice against the skin. Will you come warm yourself?"

"Later, my friend." As she was turning away, Kate remarked, "You have improved on the disguise. For a moment I did not guess who the lad was."

"I thought it wise. But I am worried. She has hardly spoken to me. As long as you are here . . ."

Kate owed it to Jocasta, having thrust this upon her. "Of course."

Jocasta led Kate down the passageway to the hall, where Margery sat primly on a chair near the fire, feet together, posture upright, hands folded, chin up, dark hair escaping the felt hat, falling down over watchful eyes. She made a comely lad, though a close observer might notice a weight about his features, wise beyond his years, the dusting of freckles and the creases that suggested a happy disposition such a contrast to the eyes—grave, unblinking.

"Katherine." In another time, when Margery took her hand Kate would have smiled, anticipating her friend's impish grin and a boast about how well she had disguised herself. *Who would think that Lady Margery, who traveled with cartloads of gorgeous clothing, could be hiding behind such a costume?* But not today. She was solemn as she said, "I would say you look well, but I know you, Katherine, I know those shadows beneath your eyes bespeak nights spent pacing as you worry. I beg your forgiveness for burdening you with my trouble." Her entire being bespoke a spirit drained.

"My complaints are as nothing compared with your suffering," said Kate.

"Would you care for some hot spiced wine, Katherine?" Jocasta offered her a bowl. Kate had never seen her so ill at ease, so uncertain what to do.

Cupping her hands round the bowl, Kate held it to her face and inhaled the steam, appreciating the warmth while she observed the two women, considering how best to proceed. Jocasta, sitting beside Margery, took one of her guest's hands in hers and rubbed it to bring up the blood. Neither woman was in any mood for idle chatter.

"I need to know whether there is anything you have not told me, Margery," Kate said. "If Sir Elric is to argue your case with the king's man, he must understand what happened, and in what order."

"By the king's man you mean Sir Peter Angle," Margery said with heat.

"The king's man who is lodging with your cousin, William Frost," said Jocasta with a knowing look.

They knew much. "You may see that as a compromising position," said Kate, "but it might benefit our cause. I have arranged for a spy in William's household, with my cousin's permission."

"In truth?" Jocasta nodded. "Then it is well done, Katherine." She rose from her seat. "I will bring more wine, and some bread and cheese?"

"I am not hungry," said Margery.

Kate had a long walk ahead of her, to her mother's to fetch one of the beguines to accompany her, then on to the castle. "I would be grateful," she said.

As Jocasta saw to it, Margery surprised Kate by asking after Marie, Phillip, and Petra.

Kate filled the silence with tidbits about the children until the servants had set up the food and wine, and Dame Jocasta had settled, this time choosing a chair that allowed her to see Margery's face.

"You would be wise to have Lille and Ghent with you at all times," Margery warned.

"This morning I felt Jennet needed them more."

Slipping off the hat, Margery ran her hands through her hair. Someone had artfully cut a few locks to fall over her forehead, giving the effect of a lad when she wore the hat. But the color had not been so well applied, coming off on Margery's hands. Lifting her darkened palms she said, "How I wish I might wash this out."

She would look less haggard without the sharp contrast between her pale skin and her hair, but too easily recognized. "Best you keep the disguise for now," said Kate. "At some point we will need to move you again."

"I am preparing a better dye for you," said Jocasta as she passed Margery a rag with which to wipe the dye off her hands. "Oak galls, alum, and urine fix better than the nutshells you have been using."

Margery made a face as the cloth darkened. "I pray that is true."

"Tell me how you came to be traveling with Berend," said Kate.

"Who told you?"

"Berend told Sir Elric. Why did you not tell me?"

"Would you have continued to help me had you known the trouble I brought him? Will you now?"

"You forget yourself," said Jocasta. "One would think you were ungrateful."

Margery pressed her fingers to her eyes. "I would not blame either of you for throwing me to the dogs. I pray you forgive me." She stared down at her hands. "I do not know what I would have done without Berend. I pray he does not pay with his life for his kindness to me."

It is of little comfort that she realizes the danger in which she has placed him, said Geoff.

He was in danger from the moment he answered Salisbury's summons, Geoff.

"I threw myself on Berend, begged him to take me with him," said Margery. "I could not stay there. They would have found me. If they would not believe Thomas had no part in it—why would they accept my innocence?"

As if the king were being reasonable, said Geoff.

"You must find a way to free Berend," said Margery. "He had nothing to do with the plot, I am certain. He condemned Salisbury. He did not come to Cirencester in the company of the rebels. When Thomas saw him, the rebels were already at the inn."

"He came to you?"

"No. Thomas was in the abbey church the night before—" She crossed herself. "The abbot had written a letter of introduction for him, addressed to the abbot of a monastery in Cornwall."

"Previously you'd said you did not know Thomas's plans," Kate noted.

"Did I?" Margery frowned.

Lies were like that, slippery things. "No matter. The abbot had written a letter—"

"Thomas was collecting it when Berend arrived. While the abbot was giving Thomas his blessing, he said the abbot suddenly glanced up with a gasp. 'Berend Osgood? Is it you? But your ear.' Clearly he had known Berend long ago. Thomas stepped away and let them exchange greetings, and then he invited Berend to stay the night with us. But the abbot would not hear of it. 'I must hear about my friend's adventures. Another night, Sir Thomas. Another night.'"

Berend *Osgood.* Another piece of his story Kate had never known. Berend Osgood. Was he from Cirencester? And what was this about his being the abbot's friend? Berend had not described him so.

"So you had no chance to talk to Berend that evening?" Kate asked.

"No. Thomas—" Margery shook her head as tears fell. "No, he came straight back with the letter."

"Do you have it—the abbot's letter?"

"No. Thomas was carrying it when . . ." Margery shook her head.

Pity, Geoff whispered.

"How did you come to be traveling with Berend?" Kate asked again.

"He found me in the barn, with the groom's body. Carl was pacing back and forth, praying and weeping. I was covered in blood—Thomas's and the groom's. God guided Berend to us. He helped my manservant bury the boy. And then—I could not stay in Cirencester, to do so would endanger my family even more than we already had. Berend slipped out after dark with my sister's husband and recovered Thomas's body. My sister promised to bury him as soon as they might do so secretly. This they did for me." A sob. "I hoped that my departure would save them. I told them to denounce me, denounce Thomas, deny any knowledge of his body, say that I had taken it." She stopped, staring at her hands. "I pray they are safe."

Once a family is cursed . . .

It is not the same as our story, Kate.

No, Geoff?

"They recovered Thomas's body, but not the letter?" asked Kate.

"Nothing he was carrying," Margery whispered. "The mob had stripped him of his clothes. Everything."

Why the whisper? Kate wondered. Why now?

You do not believe her?

The story keeps changing. Why?

"Will you rest now?" Jocasta asked.

Margery fixed her too-bright eyes on Kate. "Did you hear that Henry's head was crawling with lice at his crowning?"

Petra's vision.

"I want him to suffer," Margery said flatly. "For all the days left to him may he never feel safe, may he never trust another, may he cower in the sight of God, who will avenge the good men Henry brought down. And then may he rot in hell." She shook her head. "I cannot give myself up to Sir Peter. You and Sir Elric must find a way to free Berend so that he and I can continue to Scotland. We must not fall into the hands of the usurper."

"Scotland?"

Margery studied Kate. "Speak to Berend."

Jocasta made an impatient sound. "My lady, you place yet more friends in danger with your demands."

Margery did not meet her eyes.

"You might be safer to escape separately," said Kate.

"He has my jewels." Margery looked defiant.

"About them. You lied to me about the dymysent I saw in the silversmith's shop."

Margery looked away. "I meant to protect him," she said softly.

Rising, Jocasta declared the conversation over. "Come, my lady, you are overtired. You must rest."

To Kate's surprise, Margery permitted herself to be led away. No, this was not the Lady Kirkby she had known.

--❧❦❧--

After Katherine had departed, Bess could not settle to her tasks. She had a nagging feeling about Trimlow the baker. There had been a cockiness in him when she'd complained this morning about the bread he'd delivered, as if he no longer felt dependent on her custom. The cur. He'd been the one to point the finger at Berend. Now that was interesting. Suddenly in the money, was he? She sent for his wife, said it was urgent she speak to her.

Edda Trimlow's pretty face was marred by a bruise on her cheek and a split lip.

"I had a word with your husband this morning about his delivery. I've never seen the like from your ovens—lumpy and tasteless. Serve that to my customers and they won't return, will they?"

Edda stuttered her apologies for the inferior quality of the bread as her eyes flitted about the public room of the tavern, anything not to look Bess in the eye.

"Come. I do not mean to shame you, my friend." Bess led Edda into her more private space. "Had he told you of our conversation?"

"He said you complained about the bread."

"Did he tell you that he thumbed his nose at me and strutted out as if he could not be bothered? As if he doesn't need my custom of a sudden?"

Edda looked alarmed. "Of course we do, Bess. I will speak with him."

"And suffer more injuries?" Bess laid a comforting hand on the woman's shoulder. "What's he done to you, eh? What's he beaten you for? What's he hiding?"

"He lied, Bess. He lied about seeing Dame Katherine's man with the spice seller. It's those men sleeping in the shed in the back garden. They paid him to say it. He did not go out that night. A baker needs his sleep. I told him he must confess." She touched her bruised cheek.

"Men in the back garden, did you say?" Bess led Edda to a chair, offered her some ale. "I will just go sort this out while you have a little rest. Do not leave until I return."

Out in the yard, Sir Elric was pacing. The king's men were gone, as were most of the soldiers.

"You might want to take a few men and search Peter Trimlow's back garden."

⁂

Stepping out of Jocasta's house, Kate blinked against the glare of sun on surfaces still wet with mist. She closed her eyes and leaned against the wall to wait for her heartbeat to slow. She had been shaken by how Margery's ordeal had transformed her. How had she not noticed it before? At the guesthouse? Had she been too intent on protecting her? Of course. But now, seeing how even when asking about the children she had spoken without her usual warmth, and in those moments when she had exhibited some emotion it did not reach her eyes, it had shaken Kate.

She is much like you when I was carried home, said Geoff.

No. Kate remembered tears, wailing as she threw herself on his body. *Not at all.*

You stood still as death and so pale it was as if the lifeblood had been drained from you as well as me. I could not leave you.

Be quiet. I need to think.

You do not believe her story.

I felt—Something about her time in Cirencester is false. She keeps changing her account. And then there are the coincidences—Thomas and Berend at the abbey. Berend finding her in the barn.

Too many coincidences.

Yes, Geoff.

You do not want to doubt her.

She is my friend. As is Berend. He did not tell me everything either. Scotland?

He meant to tell you as little as possible.

Even Elric was not to tell me all.

But you will help them.

I will.

With Elric's help.

Yes. Apparently his disappointment in me has not changed that. But Margery—In her state, can I trust her not to endanger us all? You say I was like her. Would you have trusted me?

No.

That is why you stayed.

Silence.

And now you do not know how to leave? To go to your rest?

Would you be rid of me?

For myself, no. But for you . . .

You have much to do.

She did. Crossing to the gate that opened into the alley, still in shade, she hesitated, uncertain how to proceed. If she set aside Merek's murder, her focus should be on clearing Berend's name. She must get a message to St. Mary's Abbey in Cirencester as soon as possible. The abbot could testify that Berend had not been in Salisbury's company. Could she get a messenger there and back in time? Would that be enough? As for Margery, Kate could think of no way to prove that Thomas knew nothing of the plot against the king, or that he had not shared information with his wife. As Margery had said, there was no way to prove ignorance. Margery must remain hidden until a plan was in place, and she must know nothing about any such plan until the last moment. God knew what she might say or do.

Kate must find a way to sneak them out of York. Her impression of Sir Peter, albeit brief, was that he would cling to his mission like a terrier its catch. She had no confidence that he could be dissuaded from taking Berend and Margery to the king. So they must slip away.

Would Elric help? Westmoreland had ordered him to find Margery and take her to Sheriff Hutton. It was one thing to defend Berend, quite another to defy his lord.

Bess Merchet might be the one to help her with Margery.

Listen! Geoff whispered.

Someone moved away from her down the alley, trying to do so in silence, but the melting snow and mud betrayed them. There. A shifting shadow along the wall of a house across the alley, beneath a deep overhang. She waited for them to reach the corner where they must step into the light of the back garden—or disappear round the corner. Her patience was rewarded. A skinny lad, tall—Skulker. Still spying for Parr and Sawyer, she presumed. Had he been listening at one of Jocasta's windows? But how had he not been caught? He crouched low, slinking toward the next overhang.

Taking care to stay out of sight, Kate slipped through the gate and followed. He knew his way along the back gardens and alleyways of the city. He was quick, and good at slipping through narrow places, requiring her to wrap her cloak close round her and suck in her breath a few times. Had she any more flesh on her she could not have kept up with him. Once, when she had struggled through a particularly tight spot, she thought she heard someone behind her, and stopped, waiting as long as she dared, holding her breath. It must have been a cat or a rat scuttling across the opening, for she heard it no more.

The pause cost her. She stepped into the Shambles just as a carter shouted to stay clear, his cart rumbling toward her with little clearance on either side. Skulker slipped between two buildings across the way, eluding her. As she stepped back into a doorway to avoid the cart someone brushed her, darting across the street so close to the moving wagon the carter cried out and halted. "Did I hit him?"

"No. Child made it across," a woman shouted back. "Little fool."

As soon as the carter cleared the doorway in which Kate had huddled she crossed the street and considered another narrow, dark alley between two butcher shops, the odor of rotten meat assailing her. She almost abandoned the chase—Skulker would be long gone—but as long as there was a possibility, she would not give up. Lifting her skirts, she plunged into the darkness, placing one booted foot in front of the other, not pausing when she felt the slight weight of something running over it, moving forward, one hand on the wall to steady herself on the slippery ground. The alley opened onto back gardens so small, houses rising all round, that no sun reached them and the snow still crunched underfoot.

A yelp. Human. Kate strained to hear more. Was that a whimper? She hurried across the snow and into another alley, not nearly so narrow as the last one, allowing some light to filter between the buildings.

"I thought you would never come!"

God in heaven, Kate knew that voice. "Petra?" Kate blinked in the dimness, making her way to where her niece appeared to be kneeling on something.

"Bloody bitch," Skulker moaned.

"He's pissed himself, the pig," said Petra.

How did her niece come to be . . . Kate had left the girl in the schoolroom. Safe, she had thought. Master Jonas would hear from her. Drawing her axe from her skirt, Kate placed her booted foot on the lad's neck and told Petra to rise slowly and move away. "Steady now, Skulker," Kate said as he began to reach for her niece. "I have a battle axe in my hand. You do not want to test my skill with it." He went still. "Now I'm going to let you up, but if you try to run, I'll throw the axe. And in this shadowy place I might miss and harm you more than I intend. Do you understand?" How she wished she had Lille and Ghent with her.

"Bloody bitch," he repeated.

She increased the pressure on his neck. "Do you understand?"

"Yes," he cried.

"Now. Do not stir." She removed her foot. Of course he tried to roll away, but she had anticipated that and grabbed him by one arm, pulled him up, and propped him against the wall, holding him there with one arm and a foot on one of his feet. In her other arm she swung the axe. He reached for it and she kneed him.

He moaned and tried to double over, but she held him upright.

"Petra, what's on the other side of this alley?" Kate asked.

"An old shed," she said without hesitation. "I once slept in it." The child spoke of her time on the streets without emotion. It was fact, it had happened. The truth was, the girl took pride in what she had learned in that hard life before Kate even knew of her existence.

"We'll go there to talk."

Yanking Skulker by the shoulder, Kate pushed him ahead of her, Petra staying well ahead. As they stepped out into what seemed an abandoned yard between two dilapidated houses, the blade of a knife glinted in the girl's hand. God help her, the girl carried a dagger to school?

Inside the shed was an old bucket missing a slat. Petra turned it over and Kate shoved Skulker toward it.

"Sit."

The boy rubbed his crotch, then sat down, gingerly, holding a hand to his mouth. As he sucked, a drop of blood rolled down his chin.

"Where are Parr and Sawyer?"

He dropped his hand to his lap. "Don't know 'em."

"You led them to the warehouse on Castlegate yesterday."

"Oh, them." A shrug. "I don't know where they'd be."

"You were spying on me for them."

He spit just to her left. "Not today."

She took hold of his shirt and shook him. Not hard. "The men in that warehouse want you dead, do you know that? They are looking for you."

"Well, they won't catch me, eh?"

"My niece did."

Another spit. "Girls' luck."

Kate glanced at Petra. The child grinned but said nothing.

"You are going to take me to Parr and Sawyer."

"And then hand me over to those what mean to kill me? Hah." He scratched his crotch.

"Is there anything in here we could use to tie him up?" Kate asked Petra.

"I'll look." The child began to search through the debris.

"I don't want tying up," said Skulker, hiding his hands behind him.

"What you want means nothing to me," said Kate. "Unless you're ready to talk."

"Why do you want them?" He sounded sullen, but tired. His tough façade was cracking, and she was keenly aware of the patched clothes and mismatched boots stuffed with hay for warmth.

"I believe they are guilty of murder, and I know the king's men will be interested in them." They were Salisbury's retainers, she would tell Sir Peter, and they might know much about the plot against the king. That should entice him.

"What do you give me?"

"Safe passage out of York?"

"Never been nowhere else."

Of course he had not. He stayed where he knew his way, knew whom to fear, whom to trust. "If you're very helpful, I'll find a place where you can work for your keep."

"Don't know how to do nothing."

"You are cunning. You've kept yourself alive. It takes far less skill to clean out stables, but you would need to be honest and obey orders." She imagined Bess Merchet's laugh.

A shrug. The child's stomach grumbled.

"Hungry?"

"Always."

"Where are Parr and Sawyer?"

"You'll help me?"

"I told you, I will help you if you help me."

He gave an impish laugh. "Your knight, Sir Elric—his men have 'em."

Kate felt a frisson of excitement. Yet another surprise. "How do you know?"

"Saw them being pulled from baker Trimlow's shed back of his house."

"Their hiding place?"

A nod.

"You were with them?"

"They let me sleep there some days, didn't they? So's I would spy round while they slept."

"So why were you sneaking through the alley near Dame Jocasta's?"

Petra returned from her search with several lengths of rope, filthy and frayed but still strong, enough to tie up the skinny lad.

The boy shot up, ready to bolt.

Kate caught him and pushed him down on the overturned bucket.

He whined about she-devils and having rights, but he sat quietly. "I don't want tying up."

"Did Parr and Sawyer have other helpers besides you?"

"Two others. Younger. Squeaks, I call 'em, peepers. Just seeing who's going where."

"Did any of you see what happened to Merek?"

"The spice man?" He shrugged. "Those two you're after, they found him stumbling along the Shambles, roughed him a bit and he fought back, but they ran when they heard someone."

"They did not slit his throat?"

Skulker shook his head.

"Who did?"

"Don't know. I followed *them*."

"Why?"

"I had a bad feeling about what was going to happen."

Jennet said the children who learned to respect such feelings were the ones who survived on the streets.

"Did you see who was approaching Merek?"

A shrug. "Might have."

"Who?"

"Dressed like a lord."

"Jon Horner the scrivener?" Was it that simple?

"Don't know 'im. I only saw a red jacket with shiny buttons when he passed a lit up window."

Kate thought back to Horner lying on his bed in a soiled crimson jacket with the shiny buttons to mark him as a man of means. She turned to Petra. "Go to Jennet. Tell her I need some clothes to disguise him. Then we'll take him—somewhere. I need to think." Where could he stay until one of the sheriffs' men got his statement? Certainly not Jocasta's.

As Petra hurried off, Kate asked, "Why were you sneaking round the Sharp house?"

"Of a sudden I couldn't get close last night, could I? What's she guarding in there? I'm thinking the king's men would like to know."

Had he been watching the guesthouse? Saw Margery moved last night? "Too late. I've decided to take you off the streets."

"You'll feed me?"

"I will." Or someone would. Her mother's Martha House might be too far. "What about a man who was traveling with my cook Berend? Did Parr and Sawyer take him?"

"Bald man?"

"Yes."

"Took him off the street a night or two before the spice man was killed. Searched his pack and it was a woman's things. Clothes. 'Where are the jewels? Where's the lady?' They shook him and punched him and stomped on his hand and he never said a word. So they slit his throat and left him in the ditch right there outside Micklegate Bar."

"What were they doing there?"

"They were hiding there a while. Old plague hut. I didn't tell 'em what it was." A snicker. "Then they found the baker. Didn't want to be around when the dead man was found."

—◦◉◦—

Jennet shook her head. "If I knew where she'd gone I would tell you, but I don't. Last I knew she was headed to the York Tavern."

Elric cursed. "I don't think anyone else can convince him to eat." Kevin had reported that Berend was fasting. Penance. Said God was punishing him through all this and innocents were suffering for it. Not good. If Elric wanted to sneak Berend out of the castle he needed him sharp, limber.

"Dame Jocasta's?"

"I went there. She'd gone." He looked down at Lille and Ghent, napping by the fire. "I don't like that she's out there without them."

"She is armed, sir, you can be sure of that."

He turned round as a whirlwind rushed through the door, pushing him aside, stomping her foot at Jennet.

"Where is she? Where's Petra?"

"At school. Where you should be, Marie. What is this about?"

The girl's pretty face screwed up in what looked more like fear than anger as she stumbled through a story about Petra going to relieve herself and never returning. In her distress Marie's words were a mixture of her native French and her usually impeccable English.

Elric crouched down to her. "Marie, tell me. Did anything happen earlier? Was something said? Something that might draw Petra away?" How better to get to Katherine than through these children so dear to her? But Parr and Sawyer were in his custody. Who, then?

The gray eyes looked here and there as the girl thought back over the morning. She shook her head. "Nothing, sir knight. Dame Katherine saw us to school. We heard people whispering about soldiers, and our schoolmaster stepped out to speak with her after we were inside, but he was not long, and Petra was with me. Do you think the soldiers? She wanted to see them?"

"They were with me in St. Helen's Square. I would have noticed her, as would Dame Katherine."

A great tear coursed down her red cheek. "Something has happened to her!"

"Who?" asked someone from the doorway.

"Petra!" Marie squealed as she ran to her fellow ward and punched her shoulder. Not hard. "Don't you ever do that to me again. I was humiliated."

Petra gave Marie a little punch. "So you missed me?" She crossed to Jennet, nodding to Elric. "Dame Katherine needs some clothes to disguise Skulker. Just long enough to get him to a safe place."

"Skulker?" Elric sat down on a bench and patted the space next to him. "While Jennet is finding what you need, I want to know what's happened."

Petra looked to Jennet, who assured her he was trustworthy.

He was gratified to hear that, listening closely as Petra described seeing the boy following them in the morning.

"You didn't tell me," Marie said.

"I didn't know what to do about it. Dame Katherine would notice him, I told myself. But as I sat in the schoolroom I worried about how long before she noticed, and if he would hear or see too much before she did. So I left. She wasn't at the tavern, so I thought of Dame Jocasta's. This morning she said something about her to Jennet."

The walls had ears, at least where this child was concerned. Elric must remember that. "How did you know him?"

"Before Dame Katherine took me in I was one of the homeless and knew the others in the city, who could be trusted, who couldn't. I'd been warned to stay away from him."

She said he had been circling Jocasta Sharp's house as if trying to find a way in.

"Do you think he heard anything?"

"He could not get near the doors or windows. Dame Jocasta's watchers are not obvious to most folk passing by, but to someone glancing round hoping not to be seen, they find eyes everywhere."

Elric thanked God he had trained the men when he did. Even so, they would soon be noticed. "Where does your aunt mean to take him?"

"She is thinking about that."

"Why is she sheltering him?"

Petra told him what Skulker had witnessed the night of Merek's murder. "I think she means to find a safe place for him so he can tell the sheriffs' men what he saw that night. And keep him from going to the king's men with the news that you've caught Parr and Sawyer."

"He's told her?"

Petra nodded.

"And then, after he's talked to the sheriffs' men?"

A shrug.

The stables at Sheriff Hutton could use a lad. "I will come with you, Petra."

"But you'll be noticed."

"That cannot be helped."

⁘

The boy's whining gave rhythm to Kate's pacing. Her mind was a scramble. Petra's daring was admirable, and had netted just the lad Kate needed. But the child might have been injured, or worse. And she must be disciplined for leaving the classroom. But how to do so when she had been of such help? God help her, Kate had not the heart or the gut to be a parent. She was also of two minds about Skulker. He knew far too much, and she could imagine him going about the city remarking on Jocasta's house being a fortress, calling attention to it. But it was just chance that he was playing eyes and ears for men Kate considered criminals, it should not condemn him. What to do? She alternated curses and prayers, relief and worry. It was only a matter of time before Sir Peter caught on to the watch on Jocasta's home. Lady Margery must be moved again. And Trimlow the baker—it was he who had pointed to Berend, the bastard. Had he truly seen him with Merek, or had he said what Parr and Sawyer told him to say? Was he protecting them? What did he know about Carl? Had he recognized him? He might have seen Carl when Lady Margery had visited the previous winter, but would Trimlow, a baker, have made the connection?

"Bastards, bastards, bas—" she sucked in her breath as footsteps approached. Skulker jerked up. She put a finger to his lips. Two people, a child and an adult from the length of their strides.

Petra appeared at the door, raising the sack of clothing over her head as she saw the axe. "It's just me," she said, "and Sir Elric."

"Elric?"

He bowed through the low doorway. "I came looking for you, Dame Katherine. I need you to come with me to the castle."

"First we must get Skulker to a safe place. Then, yes, the castle."

Elric nodded to the boy who eyed him with curiosity. "Sheriff Hutton Castle up north, in the forest. We could use a lad in the stables."

"First he must give one of the sheriffs' men an account of what he witnessed the night of Merek's death."

"If I go with you, will you feed me?" Skulker demanded of Elric.

"We'll do more than that. Clean you and clothe you and if you prove yourself teachable who knows? You might learn to be a groom, or a manservant to a soldier."

"Learn to fight?"

"I've no doubt you already know something of that. But we will see."

"Let me see to this," Kate hissed at Elric. He shrugged. Insolent know-it-all.

"They're not the king's men, the two you caught," said Skulker. "They killed two men to steal their livery. They did not want folk to remember them as once serving one of the lords taken down at Cirencester."

"What brought them to York?" Kate asked.

"A treasure, held for their earl's cunt and her bastard child."

The posey ring was for his mistress?

"They came here to snatch it. That's what they thought the bald man carried?" Skulker shook his head. "Poor sod."

Had the mere presence of a knight loosened the lad's tongue? Or the promise of a position at Sheriff Hutton? Damn Elric's impertinence, but bless him if this was the result. "That is helpful," she told Skulker. "Anything else to report?"

"Parr's bedded Trimlow's daughter."

God help the young woman.

"How is it you were not there when Sir Elric's men came for them, but you witnessed it?" asked Kate.

"They did not dare move about the city today, with the soldiers milling about and Sir Peter putting on a show. They wouldn't need me till dusk, but they told me to keep guard, warn them about trouble."

"But you didn't."

"Looking out for myself."

Elric touched Kate's arm. "Would Petra be safe with him for a moment while we step outside?"

Kate asked Petra, who said she'd be pleased to keep an eye on Skulker.

"A boot as well, if need be."

Elric led Kate far enough across the small yard that the lad would not hear them. "I could take the boy to the York Tavern and send for one of the sheriffs' men. After they've spoken, Wulf will take him to Sheriff Hutton, his punishment for disobeying my orders and frightening the folk of York. All of my men arriving at once—I could wring his neck."

"A fitting punishment," she agreed. "But I would prefer more men on such a mission. Skulker is slippery. And he's witnessed a murder." She told him what the boy had said about Carl's capture, beating, death.

"Even better to get him out of the city. Two of my men? Wulf and Stephen?"

"That is better. The forest is never a safe place, worse so of late, with all the men who were armed and ready for a battle that never happened. But you know that."

"I am more concerned about the city, with Sir Peter eager to stir up the citizens about Lady Kirkby and Berend."

Berend. She had forgotten his comment. "You said I was needed at the castle. Has Berend asked for me? Has something happened?"

"Berend is fasting. Penance for his sins, for which he fears Lady Kirkby is paying. I cannot have him starving himself. I want him sharp, ready to move as soon as we have a plan."

That was nothing, but Elric did not know. "He fasts often. He says it scours out his bad humors. I've never known him to do it so long that he weakens. He can wait, surely, while we see to Skulker and question Parr and Sawyer. How did you find them?"

"Bess Merchet following a suspicion about Trimlow the baker. Three of my men fresh from Sheriff Hutton found the pair napping, knocked them out, and carted them to a shack in the yard of the York Tavern as if they were sacks of flour."

"Bless Bess Merchet," said Kate. "We need to talk about Lady Margery's account of how she and Berend came to meet in Cirencester."

"You have her permission to trust me with it?"

She ignored that. "But first I want to speak with Berend."

"First Parr and Sawyer," said Elric. "We need to know what they have to say before Sir Peter finds them. He's heard they're Salisbury's men and he means to deliver them up to King Henry along with Lady Margery and Berend."

"Even if we prove Berend's innocence?"

"Should Berend be cleared of the murders, Sir Peter has ordered the sheriffs to hand him over. The king will want to question him about the uprising."

"God help us."

"Are we agreed, then? I'll take Skulker to the York Tavern?"

"Bess Merchet might not be pleased, but yes, do. And one thing." Kate told him about Berend's encounter with John of Leckhampton, the abbot of St. Mary's, Cirencester. "We need the abbot's testimony that Berend had come neither with them nor with Thomas Kirkby."

Elric was shaking his head. "Had we known a few days ago, but now? Even if I had a man to spare, he would never return with the abbot's witness in time to make a difference."

"We can try."

"No, Katherine. I will not spare one of my men on a hopeless mission."

Stubborn man. "I will find a messenger."

He reached out to her, taking hold of her arm. "I am not the enemy, Katherine. I never was."

"Even after my confession?"

"That did not alter my belief in what is right."

"Then help me save him." She saw how he tightened his jaw. He would not send anyone to the abbot. Damnable man.

—◦◦◦—

After the midday meal Kate and the hounds headed down Stonegate for the York Tavern, collecting a small crowd all asking after Berend, offering food, prayers, inquiring whether there was anything they might do. She assured them all that their prayers were appreciated and urged them to give the sheriffs any information about the night Merek was murdered, anything anyone saw on or around the Shambles. Their support lifted Kate's spirits, which had taken a downward turn when she'd heard Matt's news from the Frost residence.

"Sir Peter hopes the city will turn on Berend, the bastard," Matt had said. "He's searching for Parr and Sawyer as well. He's heard that they were likely in the service of the Earl of Salisbury, thinks they might know who else rode in the company of the earl. And he says they came here chasing some treasure Salisbury sent to York for safekeeping, which Sir Peter claims is the king's by right. All the rebels' wealth is forfeit. Master William forbade him to interfere with the city's search for the murderers of Merek and Horner, but the knight and his captain claim the king's safety is the higher good."

Higher good. Pah. And now there he was. Sir Peter stood by the steps to the cemetery in St. Helen's Square, watching her as she moved away from Berend's supporters with a *benedicite*. Arrogant bastard. But better that he serve as a warning. Had she not seen him she might have led him straight to Parr and Sawyer. She turned onto Davygate, heading toward the castle.

She not gone far when Lille growled, alerting her that the knight followed. Glancing over her shoulder, Kate warned the old knight to keep his distance. "She does not know you and considers you a threat to me."

"Might we talk, Dame Katherine? I will not keep you long."

She called the hounds to heel.

Sir Peter bowed and introduced himself. With just that brief walk he was quite out of breath. Frail for such a mission. Did the king not realize?

"Ah, yes," she said. "My cousin's guest."

"I ask for your cooperation, Dame Katherine. I have been told you are trusted by Lady Kirkby, who is said to have come to York. And her escort from Cirencester is late of your household. One Berend Osgood. Formerly of the Earl of Salisbury's household?"

"Berend? No, he did not serve in the earl's household, but that of the late earl's father, Baron Montagu. Years ago."

"That may be true, but he answered the earl's summons."

"About that I know only what Sir Elric has told me." She felt herself trying to breathe for the man.

"If you would simply tell me whether you know who is harboring Lady Kirkby?"

"Then she *is* in York? I thought it a rumor." Kate assured him that she would be listening for any news of Lady Kirkby.

"And you will inform me if you hear anything?"

"I should think you would hear first. But if someone thinks to tell me, I will of course send word to your host, my cousin William Frost."

"I would be most grateful. As to Berend Osgood, you have not spoken to him?"

"I know only what Sir Elric shared about his conversation with Berend at the castle. But I am on my way to speak with him now." *And do, by all means, follow,* she thought. It would keep him away from the York Tavern.

"If you should learn anything . . ." said Sir Peter.

"I would not presume to do your job for you," she said. "I merely wish to deliver greetings from my wards, who are fond of Berend."

The knight reached out a hand to Lille, receiving a bark from Ghent and a threatening growl from Lille.

"I warned you."

"An unusual choice of pet for the city."

"I have not always lived in York, Sir Peter. I brought them with me from the North. Is there anything else you wished to ask me?"

A formal bow. "No. That will be all. For now. I pray that you see your way to assisting me in my search for Lady Kirkby."

"Do you doubt my word?" Kate asked, with a teasing smile.

The pale, drawn face colored. Ah yes, the man was susceptible. That was useful information.

As Kate walked on, she regretted telling Sir Peter where she was headed. She had thought to collect one of the beguines at her mother's Martha House. They had permission to visit Berend. But if Sir Peter's man chose to follow her to Dame Eleanor's house and decided to intrude, it would ruin a special treat for Marie and Petra.

Matt would be escorting the girls to the house on Castlegate in a little while. They were to have their final fittings for the white Candlemas dresses Sister Dina was making for them. Tonight, they would hear from the sisters the story of the Blessed Mother's purification in the temple forty days after giving birth to Jesus. And how all new mothers now went to the church on the fortieth day to give thanks for surviving the ordeal of childbirth. The girls were to stay the night with Eleanor and the beguines, and, in the morning, take part in the candlelit procession to St. Mary's Church across Castlegate. It was meant to be a sweet interlude in a difficult time. The girls had been excited to be invited by Sisters Clara, Dina, Brigida, and Agnes. It was also the day on which households brought candles to be blessed, to be used in the sickroom during the coming year. Dame Eleanor, guessing correctly that Kate had forgotten to set aside a stock of candles for the ceremony, would provide the girls with a dozen for the occasion. Kate did not want the event ruined by Berend's and Margery's troubles. She had even put off disciplining Petra for slipping out of the schoolroom and risking her life. Time for that later.

But surely whatever happened this afternoon would be outshone by the warmth of her mother's beguines and the beauty of the ceremony. They were resilient children. Despite the upset of the morning, they had remembered Berend. In Kate's scrip were gifts for him—two freshly baked pandemain rolls from Marie and a chunk of cheese that Petra particularly loved.

Just as she and the hounds passed the Ouse Bridge and turned up Castlegate, Ghent gave a bark of greeting, and Lille followed. Kate turned to see who approached.

"I commend your quick thinking," said Elric. "Smart to continue on toward the castle when you saw Sir Peter in the square outside the tavern."

"I am not a fool. Nor was I when I asked you to send someone to the abbot in Cirencester."

"It is—"

"Too late. Yes, I know you have decided that."

She hurried on. He kept up. At the castle, he made himself useful by arranging for her admission, then escorted her to Berend's chamber.

"I will stay out here, in the corridor, ensuring you are not interrupted," he said. His kindness confused her.

—◦⊚◦—

Berend was standing by the one window in the tower room when Kate entered. A fire burned in a brazier, a jug of ale and a cup sat on a table, several blankets were folded at the foot of a narrow bed and the pillow was plump and clean. Even from behind she could see that Berend no longer looked as if he had been sleeping along the roads for weeks.

"Have you no welcome for me?" she asked.

Berend turned, his expression quiet, perhaps a little sorrowful. "Dame Katherine, forgive me."

For not welcoming her? Or for leaving, and all that had happened since? She did not ask, but instead released Lille and Ghent from their leads so they might go to him. "You do not look as bad as I feared you would," she said. He looked unhealthy, tired, his eyes sunken, the lines in his face deeper than she remembered. But uninjured, and alert.

He knelt to the hounds, resting his large, scarred hands on their backs, visibly moved by their affectionate greetings. "How is it that of all I have encountered since returning, these two make me feel most human?"

She crossed the room to the window and gave him a moment to collect himself. When she heard his knees creak as he rose, she turned back to him. "Are you eating?" She'd seen no sign of food in the castle chamber.

"I asked the sisters to offer today's meals to the poor. Tomorrow, Candlemas, I will take communion."

He proffered the jug of ale, but she shook her head and settled on a bench beneath the high window. Lille and Ghent padded over to sit at her feet.

"You will be permitted to attend mass?" That was an unexpected courtesy.

"In the castle chapel. Sister Clara has arranged for a priest—one of the friars."

"If she promised, it will be so." Although Kate's mother was the founder of the small group of beguines on Castlegate, Sister Clara was their spiritual guide, and adept at the art of accomplishing her goals by wearing down her naysayers with stubborn persistence. "After communion, you will break your fast?"

He bowed his head.

"Berend, I need you strong and ready to do what must be done. And I've something to tempt you." She opened her scrip and took out the food, wrapped in parchment. "The girls sent gifts. Marie's pandemain rolls, Petra's favorite cheese."

A smile creased his face as he accepted the gift, laying the package on the table beside the ale. "You are right. Already I weaken in my resolve. Marie's bread should be eaten this very day. No later than after mass in the morning."

"They have always known how to coax you from a mood."

He sank down on the bed opposite her. "My greatest regret is disappointing them."

Not me? she thought, and felt foolish. She had never known him to be so ill at ease with her. Even when he had come to her the other day he had seemed more the Berend she knew. He was on alert, guarded. She needed to let him talk for a little while, get to know him now. "Tell me about Pontefract. Did you see the royal prisoner?"

"Pontefract? Why do you ask?"

"I am curious. What did you do there?"

"I went to an old friend who works in the castle gardens. A modest job, he welcomed the money I offered. His grandson, just a lad, is a serving boy in the castle. He enjoyed giving me much detail. Apart from having none of his supporters or friends with him, Richard might have been quite comfortable."

Kate settled back on the bench. "The boy described his lodgings? Just like that?"

"As I said, his grandfather is an old friend."

"A gardener at Pontefract Castle?"

A sad smile. "That is not a tale for today. But, yes, the lad thought nothing of it. Neither the steward nor the captain of the guard seem aware that servants have eyes and ears, and mouths once outside."

"So Richard's prison is comfortable?"

"As much as a prison can be so. The steward gave his own lodgings to him, near the gatehouse, a large apartment over the bread ovens, so it is well heated, with windows facing into the inner ward. Old tapestries on the wall, faded and a bit dirty. There is even a garderobe, a warm one—right next to one of the bread ovens." Berend paused. "Rumor has it that the king is now refusing food."

"Like you."

"Mine is a penance. One day."

"His is not?"

"I do not presume to know his mind." Berend rubbed his injured leg. "But it strikes me as a cruel place to fast, in a chamber directly over the brew house and baking ovens. The aroma." He rubbed harder. "I would find it difficult."

He was sounding more himself. "Is your leg no better?"

"Much better. Just habit now." Straightening, he studied her a moment. "Why do you want to know all this?"

Careful, careful. You are doing well, Geoff warned.

"According to Margery, Thomas Kirkby felt Richard was poorly treated. He railed at the steward and guards about Richard's treatment."

"Lady Margery told me." A shrug. "I can speak only of what I heard from the grandson of a man I trust. A difference in rank? The lad lives with his large family in a small house." He paused, frowning. "Lady Margery. Did she come to you?"

"She did."

He cursed under his breath. "I told her to go to the widow Seaton or Dame Jocasta. I would not so endanger you and the children."

"Bless you for that."

"We had gone our separate ways by then. She must have felt safer with you. Did she come to the house?"

"No, God be thanked." She told him how Carl had waited outside the guesthouse. "I could not in good conscience turn her away, leave her stranded outside the gates on a snowy night. I have done my best to keep her safe."

"And Carl?"

She told him of Carl's fate. "I have seen to his burial."

Berend bowed his head, crossed himself. "She put you at such risk."

"*You* took a risk going to Pontefract," she said.

"I have lost the knack of going unnoticed."

"I did not mean that. Why, Berend, why did you answer Salisbury's summons? Elric left out the heart of the story, what drove you to take such a risk." She joined him on the bed and handed him the pouch.

He took a breath as if to prepare himself. "Elric mentioned this. I'd had no time to examine the contents of the casket."

"Open it."

His thick fingers seemed stiff from the cold, but he managed to open it, dropping the two rings in his left palm.

"I presume JM is the earl himself," said Kate. "And the posey ring belongs to?"

"I remember him giving it to her. Why she is not wearing it—" Berend shook his head.

"Tell me about her."

She watched the emotions play over his scarred face as he told her of Rosamund Lacy. He might have wed her. Fickle woman, or merely wanting the best for her child? Berend's child? Now Merek's part fell into place.

"I understand. I do."

"Thank you, Katherine."

"My dear friend." Gently she took the rings from his warm palm, returned them to the pouch, closed it. "What will you do?"

"Ensure that Rosamund has the means to bring him up in safety and comfort."

"In Scotland."

"Yes. He told you that?"

"Margery did. She seems intent to accompany you."

"She wants a purpose. You say she is safe?"

"For now. Will you stay with them?"

Berend shook his head. "How can I know? Rosamund will not know me. I was whole when we were together."

"She will come to see you are more than you were then."

He looked doubtful.

"And if his age proves he cannot be your son? If it was all a ploy to turn you to their purpose?"

"The point is that he might have been. The way I left—" He crossed himself. "And I owe Salisbury's father a debt. For his unwavering belief in me. He would believe I would protect his grandson."

"His bastard grandson."

"Does that matter? Should I do any less for him than you've done for Simon's children?"

"Oh Berend," Kate whispered, but she could not find the words.

"I will miss the children," he said. "All of you."

"Surely there was another way to help, without being marked a traitor?"

"If there was, I did not think of it. Katherine, I owe it to Rosamund's child, and to the man who helped me climb back out of the darkness."

What could she say to that?

"I took many lives," he said. "My atonement was never going to be easy. I believe God is testing my resolve." With a remarkably steady hand, Berend poured ale, passed the bowl to her.

Taking a small drink, she handed it back to him. "Drink up. And eat the bread and cheese. I need you strong, and ready to move. Margery is safe, but not for long." She told him about Skulker, how he had noticed the guards about the house in which she was hiding. "I will find a way to get the two of you out of York as soon as possible. With the casket."

"You will do that?"

"Of course I will. I have faith in you, and I am certain you did not murder Merek."

"Who did?"

"Do you care? He was no friend to you."

"He was Rosamund's brother. She will want to know. And he did stay in York, even added to what Salisbury had sent, sharing with her what he made on his spices."

"He told you that?"

"Bragged about it. Said the people of York are easily separated from their money."

"Griselde said you'd warned her to avoid him. Were his spices truly unique?"

"Not at all. And folk did not return after trying them. It was his potions that brought in the coin. Valerian powder and whatever else was not selling at present, mixed into watered wine. So. Have you discovered his murderer?"

"Perhaps." She told him what Skulker had told her.

"Jon Horner." Berend ran a hand over his bald pate. "But why?"

Kate told him about the stolen brooch.

"So Merek had tricked him and he felt a fool? I can understand his wanting some revenge, but such a savage assault, and returning to murder him? Then drinking poison? All because he was embarrassed to have purchased a stolen brooch?" Berend looked at Kate askance. "Horner was a coward. He would fear God's wrath if he took his own life."

"But not if he took another's?" asked Kate.

"He would have time to repent."

"Whatever you think of his courage, he did attack Merek and Lionel."

"No one could have been more surprised than I was when I recognized him."

"I agree that something is missing. Or someone," said Kate. "I cannot make sense of it. But the sheriffs were eager to call it solved. And now, they will be even happier to learn that it's mostly likely that Merek's murderer is dead. Everything points to Horner. Tidy."

"You will sort this out," said Berend. "I would like to know who murdered Merek, in case I ever succeed in taking the casket to Rosamund and John."

"*When* you deliver it to them."

He met her confidence with raised eyebrows and a grin. "I would not like to be the sheriffs when they discover me gone." Then he grew serious. "Parr and Sawyer. What will happen to them?"

She told him that she was about to question them at the York Tavern. As she talked, she felt her yearning that he might be there with her at the tavern. This time with him had reminded her how much she trusted his insights. Damn him for making himself so important to her.

"You and Bess Merchet." His old, familiar grin. "A formidable pair. I can believe anything might happen."

She patted his hand and rose. "I should go." She waited as Lille and Ghent padded over to Berend to say their farewells.

He bent to them, stroking their heads. "I will be ready."

"I pray you find the peace you seek," she said. Calling the hounds to her, she began to walk to the door as it sank in that this might be the last time they would speak.

"I pray you do as well, Katherine." Such sadness in his voice.

She waited until she was at the door to ask the most important question, as if it were a mere curiosity on her part. "What really happened in Cirencester?"

Berend had the cup of ale halfway to his mouth. Now he set it down. "What do you mean?"

"Two coincidences—you and Thomas at the abbey, you running for your life and finding the very barn in which Lady Margery was hiding."

"I did not question it. I saw it as God's plan."

"God is not so cooperative."

"You do not believe that he is testing me?"

There was a falseness in his injured expression. God might be testing him, but there was something in the coincidences that was of man's agency.

"Well, we will see when we hear from Abbot John," she said.

He looked dumbfounded. "You have sent a messenger to Cirencester?"

"To John Leckhampton, abbot of St. Mary's Cirencester."

He avoided her eyes. "God in heaven, why?"

So the abbot was the key. "Why not? Lady Margery said you were old friends. Would he not wish to help you?"

Berend tried to shrug it off, but he was troubled.

Quietly, she opened the door, letting Lille and Ghent slip through as she whispered a farewell.

Elric had been leaning against the opposite wall. He must have read something in her posture, or her face, and crossed to her in one long stride, catching her shoulders, looking into her eyes.

"I lied. I told him we'd sent someone to the abbey."

"And?"

"The news worried him a great deal."

"Which you interpret as meaning he was never at the abbey?"

She studied the chiseled face of the man she had once despised and mistrusted. Now, she saw the lines of concern, felt how gently he held her, and how much she appreciated his presence and support. "He was there. But he does not want us to know something about it. The identity of the man with whom he arrived?"

"Whom he escorted," said Elric.

"And still hopes to protect. He is protecting something or someone."

Elric gently pressed her shoulders. "Wulf will escort Skulker to Sheriff Hutton, secure a new mount and a companion, and head to Cirencester."

"Even though we mean to have Berend and Margery away before he can possibly complete the journey and deliver the abbot's report?"

"I want to understand Berend."

"In case he returns to York?"

Elric tilted his head, as if to ask whether he had heard rightly. "In case? Have you any doubt of that?"

"I am no longer certain which Berend I knew. The man behind that door, or a man I conjured."

A little bow. "It will be done. Shall we return to the York Tavern?"

"First I would have a word with my mother. Her Martha House is on the way."

"Of course."

"But I am concerned that Sir Peter might have put someone on our trail," she said. "I do not want the household disturbed. My girls are there."

"I will watch."

She thought better of that. "No, that is not necessary. Lille and Ghent will stay outside. Dame Eleanor might have some useful information. The sisters go about the city. They hear much."

Another little bow. "I will listen with care." His voice was cool, as were his eyes.

That moment of tenderness when she had first stepped into the corridor, had she caught him off guard? He'd smelled of anise, damp wool, ale, and a spicy, tangy scent she associated with him. She'd felt steadied, warmed, supported—understood. Is that what she might have enjoyed had she trusted him from the beginning?

14

THE FEAST OF CANDLEMAS

Candlemas Eve

Lille and Ghent sat up on alert outside the kitchen door of the Martha House while Marie and Petra questioned Kate about Berend. She did not lie to them, but there was little she dare say until Berend and Margery were safely away, and she did not believe it her right to tell them personal tales of his past. That would be up to him, if he should return to the household. When Sister Dina came to fetch the girls for their fittings, they bid farewell with sad faces.

"We will soon cheer them," Sister Brigida reassured Kate as she bundled them out the door. "They will forget the moment they see the dresses."

"They know there is much you have not told them," said Dame Eleanor when the door had closed behind the children. She'd quietly observed Sir Elric while Kate spoke to the children, her silks whispering as she shifted on her seat to turn toward him though he was not the one speaking. Matchmaking, or just curious?

"They understand much of the world," said Kate, "but I do my best to protect them."

"You have done well," said Eleanor. "Petra tells me she wore clothes more suitable for a lad until you took her in, and that she was not happy about wearing a skirt at first. Look at her now, preening in the mirror."

Although Kate might have chosen other changes to celebrate, she thanked her mother for the compliment.

"So now that the children are not with us, will you share more with me?" asked Eleanor.

"I will when it is safe to do so," said Kate.

Eleanor made a face. "You do not trust me."

Not a safe topic. "I do have a question for you, about Philippa Atterby. Do you recall the name of the suitor she was so desperate to avoid?"

Eleanor perked up. "Is this pertinent to the murders?"

"Perhaps." It was best to give her mother something. "I trust you to keep this between us."

"Of course, my dear. But I am afraid she never said, though she did mention a suitor her family had sent away in no uncertain terms."

"Jon Horner?" asked Kate.

"Oh, you knew." Eleanor sighed. "The very man."

"Had she cared for him?"

"I think not. Only in that encouraging him irritated her overbearing father. Surely you do not think *she* poisoned him? Philippa is a gentle, pious young woman."

"Yet not pious enough to join the sisters."

"We did not fault her sincere devotion, only her—" Eleanor frowned down at her hands. "We all believed that she would regret her decision as soon as she knew the suitor she so disliked was safely married to another. Impetuous youth. And now she is betrothed to a man she believes will make her quite content."

"You have spoken to her?"

"She visits often, joining us in morning or evening prayers. In fact she will be with us tomorrow in the Candlemas procession. You will meet her."

Now that was a piece of good fortune. "She need know nothing of this conversation," said Kate.

"Of course!" Eleanor's eyes shone as she asked in a conspiratorial whisper, "So Jon Horner did not poison himself? Do you believe Merek's murderer came after him as well? The girls would tell me nothing."

Kate bristled at the picture of her mother plying the children with questions when she knew they would have been instructed to say nothing. But she was a fool to be surprised. Best to tell her mother what it was safe for her to know and prevent another attempt.

"Might I tell her what we learned today?" she asked Elric, more to warn him than because she felt she needed his permission.

"I think it advisable," he said, bowing to Eleanor. "You and your beguines go about the city seeing to the elderly and the infirm, you might have heard something you did not know to be of importance."

Choosing with care just how much she shared with her mother, Kate repeated Skulker's account of the night of Merek's murder.

Eleanor listened with interest. "And Trimlow the baker? Did this lad see him out and about that night?"

Kate explained why she thought it quite unlikely that Trimlow witnessed anything at all.

"To lie about Berend, such a good man! I hope my nephew sees that Trimlow is run out of the city when he is mayor. But how did you learn of that?"

Kate explained how Bess Merchet had helped them.

Eleanor's eyes had widened with surprise at the name. "Bess Merchet. Now there is a woman I would not wish to cross. Well, if she has seen through Trimlow, she will make certain that he never forgets his transgression." A satisfied sniff. "So Jon Horner murdered Merek and then went home and took poison?" She sat back, frowning. "Do you believe that, either of you? It does not seem likely to me, a man who took great care with his appearance. Would he have taken his life so that he would be discovered in such a disgusting condition, the contents of his stomach soiling his face, his clothes . . ."

"How did you hear such detail?" Kate asked.

"Goodwife Tibby told Sister Clara. She delivered Tibby's sister's baby. You see? You should make it a point to confer with me on such matters. We hear much. But why are you so keen about all this, Katherine? Now that you can clear Berend's name, what is the purpose?"

Well might she ask. It was a sense of unease. Merek and Horner dead, Lionel so badly injured, and someone still on the loose, someone who had silenced Horner. Would he seek to silence Lionel as well? "There is a murderer at large in the city, and the sheriffs are happy to call Horner's death self-inflicted and be done with it."

"Until someone else is poisoned," said Elric.

"Ah." Eleanor straightened. "If I hear anything else I think might be of help, I will send word." She rose to check the pot she had been watching, then saw them to the door, thanking them for their patience, the kitchen being the least comfortable place in the house.

"Not at all," said Elric. "It is warm and fragrant."

"Oh, yes, it is a pleasing scent, the rosemary mash for a cough, though some find it overwhelming."

"I remember you packing my chest with that when I was a child," said Kate. "You said it is your maidservant who is ill?"

"Yes, poor dear."

Now that was something her mother would never have done in the past, take it upon herself to nurse a servant.

—⊙⊙⊙—

Jennet poured bowls of ale for herself and Kate, and sat down beside her near the kitchen fire. "You look weary. Did Parr and Sawyer give you trouble?"

"No." By the time Kate and Elric sat down in the unheated shed to question the prisoners, they were so cold and hungry they were far more docile than she had expected. She had deferred to Elric, guessing that they would be more likely to talk to him.

At first they had tried to lie.

"We chose to leave Salisbury's household," said Sawyer. "When he was caught up in Chester Castle with King Richard we joined up with all the others riding for King Henry." He nodded toward the jacket with the Lancastrian arms.

"Those are, at best, stolen, and, more likely, you murdered a pair of the king's men to steal their clothing," said Elric.

Kate had moved to one side, crouching between the hounds, watching Elric with interest. He stood with ease, speaking in a conversational tone, his expression pleasant. She noticed how Parr and Sawyer kept glancing at him, as if expecting that expression to change.

"We stole them while they were bathing," said Sawyer. "Left them ours." A shrug.

"Why?" asked Elric.

"Like he said. To join up with the others riding for King Henry," said Parr.

Elric was shaking his head. "I will tell you why," he said. "You knew that Salisbury entrusted to Merek Lacy, the spice seller, a casket of valuables, and you followed him here to steal it, slime that you are."

Parr opened his mouth, but thought better of whatever he'd been about to say. Shrugged.

"What do you want from us?" asked Sawyer.

"I want you to answer my questions. Truthfully." Elric smiled, flexing his hands as if itching to punch them.

"And then you'll let us go?"

Douglas, who had been standing in the open doorway, chuckled. Elric kicked shut the door.

"My man has a peculiar sense of humor. Where were we? Ah, yes. Did Merek give you the casket? Is that why you murdered him?"

Interesting, Geoff whispered in Kate's head, *pretending he doesn't know the whereabouts of the treasure.*

But hardly necessary.

"Don't you have—" Parr elbowed Sawyer, shutting him up.

"Here's the truth," said Parr. "We'd been searching for Merek, and there he was, pulling himself along the storefronts in the Shambles, bleeding. We had no reason to harm him before we had what we wanted from him. Someone had attacked him, though. I offered him my arm, but he stabbed it and jerked away. Stumbled backward and fell on his ass." He nodded toward Sawyer. "Will bent to help him up and he got a boot in the groin. So he put a boot on him."

"And then someone was coming and we thought we'd best leave him be or we'd be blamed. We meant to check on him later."

Frustrating that they had not been curious about *who* was approaching.

Kate shook her head at Jennet. "Even Dame Eleanor was helpful." She told her what she had learned. "And the girls were squealing with delight when we walked beneath the window of Sister Dina's sewing room on the way out. All sorrow forgotten for the moment in the thrill of new clothes."

"That they will wear once a year. White." Jennet chuckled.

"No, Sister Dina will dye them afterward."

She closed her eyes and leaned back against the wall, glad to be home, to have nowhere else she must trek until the morning. It had begun to snow as she walked down Stonegate. Blessed be the warm fire and strong ale.

"Was it difficult, with Berend, then?" Jennet asked, pulling up a chair.

"Like Petra, I want things to be as they were."

"As do we all."

He should be standing in the corner in his worn but always clean linen shirt, the sleeves rolled up above his elbows, his muscular forearms flexing as he kneaded the dough, attentive to Kate, sharing his thoughts. God in heaven how it hurt.

And she had lost Elric as well. She shook herself and straightened. "Elric and his men will see to Berend. Bess Merchet has devised a plan for sneaking Lady Margery downriver. Her grandson delivers ale to Bishopthorpe weekly. Rent for his small farm downriver, where he grows the hops. Lady Margery will be the lad helping him the day after tomorrow. The casket will be in the barrel. A special barrel."

"A sound plan. Bess Merchet is a resourceful woman."

"She says she learned much from Gwenllian Ferriby's father, a spy for the archbishop and others."

"The one-eyed Welshman?" A nod. "I've heard much of him on the streets. I thought him a legend until I talked to Brother Martin."

"Yes. His foster father. We could use him now."

"You have Sir Elric. He does not dare disappoint you," said Jennet.

"He does it for Berend now, not me. He has said as much."

"Wounded vanity," Jennet said with a little laugh. "He will recover. So Lady Margery departs the day of your cousin's feast?"

"Early that morning, yes."

"Means of travel?"

"A small boat. Colin Merchet likes to row there. Times it with the tides so that it is not too wearing. Lady Margery won't need to help downriver, they will be moving with the tide. Kevin will already be at Bishopthorpe to meet them, stay with Lady Margery until Berend arrives with Douglas and Harry."

"And how will Berend leave the castle?"

"That is Sir Elric's task. He has taken care to get to know the guards, and has recommended to the sheriffs that on the day of the mayor-elect's feast they post specific ones he deems most trustworthy. Then the sheriffs will be free to enjoy the festivities." Kate yawned.

"Forgive all my questions. Drink your ale and rest. You will be rising early for the Candlemas procession." Jennet rose to assemble her own bed for the night, still the pallet near the fire, close to the door.

But there was so much they still needed to discuss. Kate asked about Cuddy, the new servant from her cousin William Frost's household. The girls had met him before leaving for her mother's house, and declared him most handsome but irritating.

A broad grin. "Eager to be considered a man, though he's not much older than Phillip." Kate's ward was thirteen. "Needs guidance. Matt corrected his use of both shovel and broom. But he's quick to learn, and nary a complaint so far. He has offered to walk the hounds. Seems his family had large dogs, and he's been missing them."

"Trustworthy?"

"Time will tell."

Kate poured herself more ale and returned to brooding. There was a smugness about Parr and Sawyer that troubled her. She had come away from the interview uneasy about what they might know, how they might damage Berend and Margery.

But she had encouraged Elric to hand them over to Sir Peter. "Let Sir Peter think you support his mission. He might relax his vigilance just long enough for our purpose."

Elric had agreed to send word the morning of the mayor-elect's feast.

—◦◦◦◦—

She was drifting off to sleep when she sensed Geoff standing at the foot of her bed.

I choose to be here with you, Kate.

It is not fair to you. You should be at peace. Resting in—Are you in heaven?

I'm here with you.

I have robbed you of that.

She buried her face in the pillow, willing him to go away.

I will when you are ready.

She felt his hand on her shoulder.

You were a boy when you died. How are you now so wise?

She felt his grin in her mind. *Sleep now. I will watch over you.*

⟿⟨⟩⟨⟩⟸

Candlemas

Statues of angels, Kate thought as she stepped into the hall of the Martha House and beheld Marie and Petra in their white gowns, their hair loose about their shoulders, their hands folded before them. And just beneath the neckline on their gowns, each wore the gold and jet brooches Lady Margery had given them. When she touched Marie's, tears started in the girl's eyes. Petra bit her bottom lip. Kate whispered her assurances that all would be well for their friend as she hugged them. How rigidly the girls stood. "You are making the day special for the sisters, do you see how they smile on you?"

For they did. All four sisters stood behind the girls, their faces alight with the sweetness of the vision.

"Poor Sister Brigida combed and combed Petra's hair, trying to untangle it," Marie whispered.

Kate touched her niece's hair, so like hers. "How lovely. Are you pleased, Petra?"

A little smile. "Sister Brigida did not complain."

"Of course not. And, when I speak with her, will she say that Marie sweetly combed her own hair and made no demands?"

Petra giggled, Marie turned away, but not before Kate caught the beginning of a grin.

As Kate rose, she found Brigida, Clara, Dina, and Agnes all laughing.

"Marie is a handful," said Sister Agnes. "But we all enjoy fussing over both of them."

Kate had wondered whether they, too, would wear white on this day, putting aside their simple gray gowns. But they had compromised with white capes over their usual attire. All held candles, ready to be lit as they entered the church.

It was strange for Kate to be in this house that was once her home, a place that held so many memories. The sisters and her wards stood before the lady altar that had taken the place of Kate's loom, where she had turned silken threads into colorful patterns that would remind her of the beauty of the north country of her childhood. Now that loom stood in her house on Low Petergate, the tapestry almost complete. She stood near the spot that had held the blankets on which Lille and Ghent slept. And just to one side was the spot where she had kept Geoff's boots.

I remember, he whispered. *For a time I could reach you only when you wore my boots or the other bits of my clothing you squirreled away.*

What changed?

I don't know. But it was lonely then. It isn't now.

It isn't fair to you. You should rest in peace.

I will when you are here with me.

She shivered at that, and forced her attention to the present, glad to see that Petra and Marie were now whispering and giggling, no longer intimidated by their part in the morning's ceremony.

It was a warm, inviting scene. The candles on the altar were lit, and the scents of incense and beeswax filled the hall, following their early morning prayers and readings. So the sisters began each day, even on such a morning when they would attend a long mass. But there would be little work today, unless Sister Clara was called out to a birthing.

Kate shivered again as the hall door opened and closed.

"Such a snowstorm," Dame Eleanor murmured at Kate's back. "The girls were disappointed to see it."

Kate had wondered where her mother was. "A white world for Candlemas. It seems appropriate," she said. "How is Rose?"

Eleanor's face sagged with weariness. Her veil and the shoulders of her gown were damp with melting snow. "Her fever broke in the night. She is resting now. Bella is with her."

Matt's cousin, a midwife and healer. The fact that Eleanor sent for her . . . "She was that ill?"

"I had not realized, not until after you left yesterday. When I went to sit with her, she was burning up and speaking gibberish."

"You have her in the bedchamber off the kitchen?"

"Yes. Sister Clara thought it was best, we can keep it quite warm there, and it is quiet."

They both turned as the hall door opened, letting in a gust of wind and a flurry of snowflakes.

"Forgive me, I pray I am not too late!" Philippa Atterby said in a breathless voice as she hurried into the hall, the servant Nan closing the door behind her.

"Here is just the person you wish to see," Eleanor whispered to Kate. "I had time in the night to think how to broach the topic after mass." She nodded to Kate, then opened her arms to the newcomer. "Not late at all, my dear Philippa. The church bells have not yet tolled. You have met my daughter, Dame Katherine?"

Kate offered to help her shake the snow from her cloak. Best to befriend her before mentioning Jon Horner. Pray God her mother's plan was discreet. But just as she began, the church bell tolled. A ripple of movement as the sisters waved Eleanor, Philippa, and Kate to their places behind them, and Nan gave them each a candle, then went to open the street-side door. Slowly, in twos, the women processed out into the snow.

At the church they were ushered in by Magistra Matilda, whose sisters had begun to sing the hymn *Nunc Dimittis*. Eleanor's sisters joined their voices as they walked up the nave, Sister Brigida's clear soprano ringing out.

Kate caught her breath as the song transported her to her first Candlemas in York, entering the minster on Simon's arm. The candlelight, the scent of beeswax, the voices of the vicars choral. *Is it not the most beautiful thing you have ever seen?* Simon had whispered, pressing her arm. More beautiful than the windswept hills of the north country? More beautiful than watching the wolfhounds lope across a meadow? More beautiful than her twin's face? *No*, she had thought, *the statues are all staring down on me, judging me. It is just stone upon stone upon stone, a burial chamber of terrifying proportions.* But she had forced herself to smile up at Simon, and he had looked satisfied.

Her betrothed. In time she had grown fond of him, and looked forward to motherhood. She had prayed for a boy to call Geoffrey. As she grew large with child she envisioned the day when she would enter St. Mary's for her churching. But that day never came, and now she knew that while she lay on the floor weeping for her lost child, Simon had lain in Calais with his whore.

"My dear?" Dame Eleanor whispered, putting an arm round her.

Startled, she glanced round, seeing the concern on the sisters' faces. And on Kevin's. He stood to one side, next to Elric, who stared ahead, stone-faced. Elric. He was nothing like Simon. Quite a superior cut of man. In body and soul. How she wished she might spend just one night in his naked embrace. She caught herself. The Candlemas service was not the time to fantasize about a lover who might have been.

—◦◦◦—

Back at the Martha House, Nan welcomed them with hot spiced wine and a roaring fire in the hearth.

Eleanor drew Kate over to the widow Atterby. "Philippa thought to join our household," she said to Kate, "but we knew she was meant to spread her light out in the world, grace one of the prominent families with her calming, inspiring presence."

"Oh, Dame Eleanor, you flatter me," Philippa sighed. Her speech truly was much like sighing, she spoke so softly, with little inflection. "The Graa family honors *me*."

"You are betrothed to one of Thomas Graa's nephews?" Kate asked, thinking his sons all too old for this child.

"His grandson Gregory." Philippa blushed prettily.

Ah, well, no wonder there were roses in her cheeks and stars in her eyes. Gregory Graa was a handsome young man, well-spoken, and would one day inherit a substantial fortune. One day. Interesting that the family would permit him to wed so young. Perhaps grandfather Thomas was unwell.

"So much more appropriate than the man her parents first put forward, or the one who dared put himself forward," said Eleanor, reaching over to pat Philippa's hand. "You will be the most handsome couple in the city."

"Someone dare put himself forward?" said Kate, picking up her mother's prompt.

Philippa set aside her cup of spiced wine in order to make the sign of the cross. "May God grant him rest. Poor Jon."

"Not Jon Horner?" Kate pretended shock.

"Indeed it was. Oh, he was kind to me, but he was such an odd man, and Father said that his business was, well—" She looked away as if embarrassed by what she had almost said. "He was unsuitable."

"And, perhaps I am mistaken, but expected to make an alliance with another," said Kate. "Cecily Wheeldon."

"Oh, no." Philippa shook her head, her pearl and silver crispinette catching the firelight. "The widow Wheeldon was his employer. I cannot think she ever meant to marry him. Indeed, I did at first accuse *Gregory* of having his eye on her. But he swears there has never been anyone for him but me."

The young woman's breathy speech had begun to irritate Kate. Why would she not speak out? But she focused on the information. "She employed him? I had no idea."

"Oh yes, Jon kept her accounts as she took over more and more of her husband's business. He was so frail at the end."

Was he? Ross Wheeldon had walked with a cane and there were days when he conducted his business from his bed, but he had remained quite able to drive a hard bargain. Kate knew. She and Thomas Holme had negotiated a share in a shipment just a month before Ross's death.

"Jon Horner told you this?"

"No, Dame Cecily, when she called on me to encourage me to fight for him." A little frown. "She spoke as if she were giving me permission to wed him. Faith, she seemed offended when I explained that the interest was solely on his side, I had no intention of marrying him."

Kate met her mother's eyes, gave a little shrug. "And all this while Gregory Graa was pining for you."

Another pretty blush. Poor Gregory.

"Aunt Katherine, come, look at the embroidery Sister Dina and Sister Agnes are working on," Petra called from across the room.

Kate rose, congratulating Philippa on her betrothal. It was time to give the girls her attention, letting them extol the wonders of the beguines until she must bundle them off home. For they would have a long day tomorrow at her cousin William's house. The first of the two days of celebration was for the entire city, and began with entertainment for the children.

And Kate had much to do to prepare for all that must happen while the city was so conveniently distracted. She must arrange her part today, for tomorrow she would have a care not to be seen anywhere near either the castle or the Sharp residence. One crucial item sat on the floor beside the sisters' pattens and boots. She slipped over to where Sister Clara was watching her two companions work at their embroidery and quietly explained that it was Berend's traveling pack. She must find a way to leave it with him when she took his meal to him.

Sister Clara looked at her with interest. "It shall be done."

"Did he eat the treats I brought him?"

"He did. But not the meal I took him. I pray that he has done so by now. He will need his strength, I think?"

"He will." Kate thanked Clara for taking such good care of Berend, and received a blessing in return.

"What do you think of the pattern?" Petra asked, having waited patiently for Kate's attention.

Now Kate noticed that the altar cloth was bordered with thistles and gillyflowers, Petra's favorites. "Did you design them?"

A proud nod. "I embroidered the first two." She pointed to a corner in which the needlework was ever so slightly less exact than the rest of the border. But for a child who had sworn she was all thumbs with decorative needlework, it was a revelation.

"They are beautiful. Can you do other flowers?"

"Old Mapes always left the flowers for me to finish. I can do most that she knew."

And as an herbalist Mapes would know quite a few. "We should have some of your work in our house, don't you think?"

"Marie is good with trees and grass. We could do a forest meadow."

Kate hugged her niece.

"You have done well with her," Eleanor said. She stood close to Kate, smiling down on the altar cloth. "It is a joy to watch my granddaughter blossom. You were—" She caught herself and said, "I had my doubts about your capability as a mother, but you have proved me wrong."

Kate knew what she'd been about to say, or at least she guessed. Her needlework had been no better then than it was now. Weaving, now that had always appealed, requiring movement. She glanced back at her niece, so like her, and pictured a boy standing next to her, all elbows and knees, nudging her, whispering that they were missing the snowfall.

Taking Eleanor's arm, she drew her away from the clustered women. "What do you remember of the day they brought Geoff's body home? What did I do?"

"What has that boy told you?"

She had created her own trap, opening a conversation about whether or not Geoff was still with her. Eleanor had dragged her down to York to shake him out of her.

"It is not Geoff. I sat with a friend who has had a loss. She was so unable to let herself mourn for the anger in her heart, she must needs first make things right. She is not the woman I knew. Did I change, after Geoff's death?"

Eleanor looked away, fussing with some imagined imperfection in the drape of her skirt. "You pushed us all away. Only the hounds were permitted to comfort you."

"I remember throwing myself on his body and screaming."

"You lay atop him, but you said nothing. You voiced nothing for weeks. You insisted on wearing his clothes and walking. Walking for hours with the hounds. Of course your father followed you. He was so afraid for you, that you would go after the Cavertons, intent on vengeance. But he said you just walked. When the hounds were tired you would sit and stare."

I remember that. The walks. And the silence.

Kate did not remember the silence. "When did I finally speak? When you brought me to York?"

"Long before that. You sat down to dinner and said, 'Geoff has told me that I must reclaim my voice. Our voice.' I knew at that moment I must forbid you to wear his clothes. And I began to plan our escape."

I don't remember that.

It happened, Kate.

Eleanor touched Kate's cheek. "I cannot begin to understand how hard it was for you. Geoffrey was such a part of you. But I feared I was losing you as well. Now that you have the children, perhaps you see why I removed his things from your bedchamber and took you away from the places that could not but remind you of him?"

"I think I do. And I will always be grateful that you did not make me leave Lille and Ghent."

"I knew better than to try that." She patted Kate's arm. "Are you worried about Lady Margery?" When Kate looked at her askance Eleanor said, "I have guessed you were hiding her. And see? I've told no one. Not a whisper, not even to the sisters."

Kate pressed her mother's hand. "I depend on her not to betray us, especially Berend. And to follow instructions."

"You took no untoward risks on your walks, you saw to the needs of the hounds. Your father found no fault in your actions. But I do not know Lady Margery."

"Thank you, Mother."

Eleanor embraced her, holding her tightly. "I am glad he is still with you, Katherine. I am so glad you are not alone."

Startled, Kate said nothing, though she silently prayed that this was not a momentary truce, but a lasting peace.

"I should go now," said Eleanor, "to sit with Rose. I had intended to go to William's house and help prepare for tomorrow's festivities—to annoy Isabella. Hah! But, alas, God saved me from myself. I do not begrudge Rose. She has been so patient with me over the years."

The beguines had worked a miracle.

"However you are planning to save your friends, Katherine, I pray God watches over you. We are all praying for their safe escape."

※

In the early afternoon, Kate saw Matt off to the York Tavern with the casket of jewels hidden in a crate of spices from her inventory, Jennet off to the Sharp residence where she would give Lady Margery her instructions, and then she and the hounds escorted Marie and Petra to the guesthouse. Griselde had promised to make a feast to celebrate the day, and Phillip would be joining them, as the stoneyard was closed for both Candlemas and the mayor's celebration. He would sleep at home for the next two nights. It would be good to have them all under her roof again. Marie and Petra were particularly excited to show off their new dresses. The snow had stopped for the nonce and they danced down the street, nicely calling attention to the fact that Kate was with her wards.

And then she slipped out the back door of the guesthouse with the hounds. John Wrawby had agreed to meet with her and Sir Elric. She must also stop to speak with her friend Cam at the staithes, ensure that all was ready for the morrow.

―∽◎∾―

Bess looked him up and down, tsking and shaking her head, the ribbons on her white cap fluttering. "As I told Dame Jocasta, the inn is filled with soldiers tonight, so there's nothing for it but to put you on a pallet in my own."

The boy, who kept his head bowed, shrugged to let her know he'd heard.

"Right then, come along." About to send off the man who had delivered the boy, she hesitated, noticing his patched jacket and old boots. Told the cook to give him a bowl of stew and some bread, and motioned him to the bench just inside the door. Dame Jocasta did what she could for them, but the man had done a service, and he looked hungry.

He had also arrived promptly, in time for anyone lingering out in the yard to hear the irritation in her voice. Another good reason to feed the courier—the cold would drive any lurkers off before he finished eating and took his leave. No opportunity for questions.

And just in case someone recalled the lad, not seeing him around after tomorrow, she would shrug and roll her eyes and say Colin returned from a delivery without him. The strays *would* run away, thinking they'd find something better, or still escaping their own private devils. But she was counting on most folk being at William Frost's celebration on the morrow. She herself would abstain, her old hips not liking such a long walk in the cold.

Once in her room she closed the door and took a good look at her guest. "You're a wee bit too pretty for the soldiers."

"I wanted to color my skin, but Dame Jocasta said that would just make me exotic, and some would find that even more appealing."

"Once you're on the road, will you go back to your skirts?"

Lady Margery shook her head. "I do not dare at first. With my shorn hair I thought I might not be a woman until we reach our destination. But Jennet, Dame Katherine's maid, has fashioned a simple gown and wimple I will don when Berend says it is time."

Her speech was fair, of course, being a noblewoman, but there was a toughness to her that explained how she had come so far. And why Berend would accept her as a companion in flight. But Bess felt compelled to warn her. "If you do aught to cause Berend's mission to fail, you will be cursed. I will pray that your maggoty remains dissolve in unhallowed ground and that you burn in hell."

The woman's eyes widened. "How dare you—"

"Must I remind you what I risk in inviting you into my home for the night?"

The woman had the wisdom to doff her cap and bow her head, whispering an apology.

"You are no lady at the moment. You are a waif brought to Dame Jocasta and now delivered up to me as a servant. For your sake and for that of all the good people helping you, you had best remember that."

A knock, Colin's signal. Bess opened the door only so far as she must to allow him in, shut it quickly. "Take a look at her size. Will it work?" Bess put out an arm to stop his bow. "As I was just reminding this little gutter-snipe, such behavior will undo us all. This is a lad off the streets. You are annoyed to have him foist upon you, but I've insisted we give him a chance."

Colin crossed himself. "God help me, I wasn't thinking."

"You had better begin." She called him her grandson, but not a drop of her blood ran in his veins. His father was her Tom's son by his first marriage. Still, her Tom would have been quick to understand the situation and would rise to the occasion. She wished someone else might take the lady downriver, but no one from Katherine Clifford's house must be involved. They might be followed. "In the morning, as soon as Sir Elric leaves to deliver up those two recreants in the shack to the king's men, you hie you to the river. There will be some nice confusion amongst Sir Peter's men, just enough to make them incurious about a cart of ale."

Colin looked crestfallen. "I know my duty, Grandmother. I will not fail you."

He'd best see that he didn't.

15

THE MAYOR-ELECT'S FEAST

Musicians, puppeteers, jugglers, dancers—the yard that separated William Frost's elegant home from his shops and offices on Micklegate had been transformed into a fairground covered by a brightly painted pavilion. And there was more—tables and carts serving savory pies and ale lined the alleyway leading to the back garden where musicians and jongleurs who had not been hired for the main festivities would continue to entertain the throngs of folk who had no invitations for the feast in the hall and beneath the pavilion later in the day. Kate had attended the mayor's feast every year since arriving in York, all lavish affairs, but none could compare with this. Isabella and William had outdone themselves. Even the weather had cooperated, with clear skies and little wind, though it was cold.

Although the festivities had just begun, Kate already found it difficult to maneuver through the crowd. Marie, Petra, and Phillip shouted with glee and tugged her this way and that. Kate almost regretted having brought Lille and Ghent, but if things went wrong, she might need them, and quickly. Instructing Phillip to take charge of his sister and Petra and see to their safety, she was making her way to a relatively quiet spot near the house when Winifrith Neville caught her arm.

"My dear Katherine, I want to apologize for my behavior when you visited." Over her shoulder she commanded her daughter Maud to see to the young children hanging onto Winifrith's skirts. With a laugh, Maud plucked them off and swept them away. "I have some information that might make it up to you," Winifrith said with a conspiratorial nod.

When they had found a bench on which they might sit with the hounds at their feet, Winifrith began.

"While Lionel's been abed I took the opportunity to tidy the small room he uses as an office. And I found, well, he had hidden away—quite clearly meaning for no one to find it—a cache of silver coins and some jewels."

That interested Kate. "Jewels? What did you do?"

"I confronted him, of course. He admitted to having taken payment from Merek the spice seller through Cecily Wheeldon for his passage on a ship."

"For Merek's passage? What had Cecily Wheeldon to do with that?"

Winifrith nodded. "I wondered that as well."

"When? Did he say when Cecily delivered the payment?"

"He said it was the day of his ordeal. He had become impatient and sent his servant Fitch to warn Merek that he must receive payment before their meeting or he would not be sailing the next day. Apparently she appeared at his office shortly after that."

Cecily Wheeldon. Jon Horner and Merek Lacy both had connections with her. She searched the crowd for the woman. "Lionel truly had no idea why she became involved?"

"None. He was taken aback, to put it mildly. He worried that Merek was up to mischief."

"How did he know Merek?"

Winifrith looked down at Lille and Ghent, stroking their heads. "Oh, Katherine, you know how he is. He was so certain that you were cutting him out of his due. So he thought to partner with Merek on a shipment. Approached him with the idea, citing his experience with spice shipments and contacts that Merek would not have, not being from York." A shrug. "My husband can be quite the fool. Even I, who have little time to go about in the city, knew the man was disliked, distrusted. And not merely because of being from the South."

"I will call on him in a few days." If all went well today. Kate had done her best. The rest was up to her co-conspirators. If . . .

Stop it. You need a clear head right here, Geoff hissed in her head.

"Lionel has been changed by this experience, Katherine. And he wanted me to tell you that he has spoken to both sheriffs, Wrawby and Cottesbrok, about how Berend saved his life. He has told them that he cannot believe Berend returned to the Shambles and murdered Merek."

"Both of them?"

"He insisted." Winifrith shook her head. "But it is the king's man who worries me. If there is anything we can do."

"I am grateful." Kate rose as Thomas Holme approached, expecting him to greet her. But his attention was on his nephew, Leif, and a female companion who leaned on his arm and touched his cheek as they watched a group of jugglers.

"Go on, do. I am content to sit here for a while," said Winifrith. "Thomas looks as if he'll have quite a lot to say about his nephew's paramour. Come report back to me."

Her tone was good-humored, with a touch of relief, as if she had not expected to mend her friendship with Kate so easily. It had never been Kate's intention to carry a grudge against her.

Kate promised to find her again later, and signaled to Lille and Ghent to accompany her.

"You look concerned," said Kate as she joined Thomas.

"That Wheeldon woman," he growled. "She is too bold with my nephew in public."

Now, as the couple turned toward another group of entertainers, Kate could see that it was indeed Cecily Wheeldon who hung on Leif's arm, and now patted his chest as she spoke. No question about her intentions. "You were not so against her the other day. Have you heard something to change your mind?"

"I know little except that there is some gossip about the manner of Ross Wheeldon's death. How suddenly he was gone, and how little she seemed to mourn him." He glanced at Kate with a sad smile. "I fear it might be so when I die, they will wonder what my Catherine saw in me, an old, plain man, and she so fresh and beautiful."

Yet he met a mistress at Kate's guesthouse. As did Sheriff John Wrawby, who was just now nodding to Kate as he passed her with his wife on his arm.

—◦◦◦◦◦—

Elric turned his back to Berend to give him some privacy while he struggled into the women's garb that Jennet had provided him. The goodwife who had accompanied Elric would remain behind, surprising the evening guards when they came to check on Berend. She was at present happily dining on the meal the beguines had delivered earlier. She was almost as large as Berend, a precautionary accomplice urged on him by Bess Merchet in case one of Sir Peter's men were watching and had noticed Elric arrive alone and leave with a companion. He'd agreed, having learned to trust Bess's judgment. Pray God his own proved as good. All night he had tossed and turned, questioning his reason. Today he would risk all that he had fought so hard to gain—his place in the earl's household, the land that the earl had granted him for his service. Already he had risked much with Parr and Sawyer, though Sir Peter had expressed only gratitude when he delivered them up.

But what he was about to do—no, this Sir Peter would not forgive. And if he discovered that Lady Margery had been in York, and this evening would be ferried across the Ouse with Berend, then riding north with him—oh, that he would most definitely not forgive. Nor would the earl.

Elric risked much. For Katherine? No. He understood now that he'd never been more to her than a tool to be discarded when she had no more use for him. Had he really believed she might choose him over Berend? He'd seen how her eyes softened when she spoke of the man. He could not fault her taste. Berend was one of the most honorable men he'd encountered. And if even half the stories about his feats as an assassin were true, he was a skilled, fiendishly clever warrior. Elric admired that. So would Earl Ralph, if he were to meet him. If there had been a way . . . But Berend had a mission, a quest. God grant him the grace to complete it. Elric paced, waiting for Berend to tell him he might look.

Wulf and Stephen were guarding the door. Once Elric and Katherine had devised the plan, he'd sent two of his other men with Skulker—Wulf and Stephen were too crucial to the mission, men who were committed to Berend's escape. At the door with them was a lad who could run like the wind and could quickly dispatch any necessary messages to Douglas and Harry, Elric's men awaiting them at the staithes. From there, Berend would be taken downriver to Bishopthorpe, where Kevin waited with Lady Margery. Elric had sent him with a letter to the archbishop's steward, who was a distant cousin of the Earl of Westmoreland. Another mad risk, using his earl's name to beg a favor. But if all went well, the earl might never know. Pray God it was so.

Katherine had made this all possible, with a visit to Sheriff Wrawby and to one of the workers at the staithe yesterday. He had not been invited to the latter meeting, but he had played a role in her meeting with Wrawby, which had been one of the most uncomfortable interviews of his life. Elric knew Katherine was no more comfortable than he, but no one watching her could have guessed, and certainly not Wrawby, who squirmed and complained and then bowed his head and agreed. He was a customer at the guesthouse and feared being exposed not only to his wife, but to his fellow sheriff. God help him. Elric had asked what she would have done had Cottesbrok been the one who would be checking in on the day of the feast and she'd laughed—he was also a patron, though his wife knew of it. A cripple, his wife did not begrudge him his entertainments. She could not predict whether it would be Cottesbrok or Wrawby responsible for choosing who would be on duty today. She needed people who were sympathetic to Berend, or easily moved out of the way.

As Elric paced in the castle chamber the goodwife startled him, bursting into laughter. Looking up, Elric did as well.

"Jennet will pay for this," said Berend, but he was grinning. The dress was made of undyed wool, the girdle woven flax and leather—a bit too nice for a washerwoman, Elric thought, but behind, beneath the darker cloak, it held Berend's sword in a scabbard. The veil—oh dear God the wimple and veil accentuated the scars on his face, though they did cover the missing ear.

"Hell's bells, you're an ugly woman," said Elric.

"No surprise there. I'm an ugly man." Berend grew serious. "How safe is Lady Margery?"

"As safe as we can make her. Colin Merchet took her on an errand to Bishopthorpe this morning, where she now awaits you, in Kevin's company." Elric considered Berend's long skirt. "Walk back and forth in that, become familiar with it."

Berend covered the chamber in four long strides without tripping.

"You would think he had lived in 'em." The goodwife chuckled.

"I once spent two seasons in monk's robes—walking, running, riding, fighting at the end. Much the same," said Berend.

A story in that, Elric thought. "Ready?" he moved toward the door. Berend nodded, as did the midwife.

Elric knocked softly in a rhythm his men recognized. As he opened the door, they framed it, waiting to bring up the back. All pulled scarves up to cover half of their faces. Elric led. Round the corner he came upon a lackey badgering one of the guards about some duty not being fair. The guard had been bought up, but the clerk . . . Elric was moving forward, drawing a knife, when Berend strode past him and startled everyone by grabbing the clerk and knocking his head against the stone wall. He slumped down, unconscious.

"He will live," Berend said.

Pray God he knew what he was doing. "Do nothing to wake him until your fellows signal that we're free," Elric instructed the guard.

With a nod and a shrug, he wished them well. "I'll lose no sleep over him. God speed, Berend."

A round of steps and they were ready to exit into the yard. Stephen and Wulf hurried forward, jostling each other as they walked out into the yard, looking round, then began a loud, curse-strewn, slurred argument about a woman they had both bedded. As they moved toward the gate, Elric did not like the way one of the guards looked at them. Elric chided his men about their language in front of a lady, watching the guard as he did so.

"She's no lady," Wulf protested, saw that his captain was not looking at him, and followed his gaze.

As did Stephen.

They moved closer, Berend whispering to Elric that he knew the guard, he was no friend of his.

As the one they all now watched reached to ring a warning bell, Stephen threw his dagger, pinning the man's arm to the door behind him. His mate covered the man's mouth and hissed at the party to hurry.

As they passed, Berend kneed the would-be betrayer in the groin.

"Stupid," Elric hissed as the man twisted and damaged his pinned wrist.

As Stephen pulled out the dagger, Wulf knocked the man's head, hard, against the door.

"Open the bloody guardroom door," Wulf hissed as the man's fellow looked at a loss.

He quickly did as ordered, and Wulf tossed the man inside.

"My mate's wife wanted to go to the mayor's feast. He vouched for Ben, but . . ."

Elric prayed no others had shared today's plans. God help them, if they made it he could only conclude God truly watched over them.

They pulled down their scarves as they moved out the gate. Now the lad took Berend's hand, as if the large woman were his dam. They walked a little ahead of the other three, who quietly talked amongst themselves. Berend and the lad turned down Hertergate.

"Goodwife Ann, is that you? I—" a woman stopped, stared at Berend and the lad, then hurried on past with a worried frown. Seeing Elric and his men, she stepped up to them. "That woman—she—that is not her child."

"I know," said Elric. "The lad is escorting her home. She fell ill while out on errands. We are following along in case—he does not seem strong enough to assist her should she fall."

"Good lad. I've always said he's a good one. Runs like the wind, he does, and some folk say he learned that from his cousin the cutpurse but I never credited that. God go with you, gentlemen." She bustled off.

"I thought we were done in by a fish wife," said Stephen, breathlessly.

"You smelled it as well?" said Wulf, making a face. "How can they bear it?"

"Where are your heads?" Elric growled. "She was concerned about a lad not her own. Would you do as much?"

"I meant her no ill," said Wulf. "It was good of her. I meant how do they bear standing at their carts all day, as the fish begin to smell, eh?"

They were nearing the King's Staithe. Berend and the lad were already sidling up to Douglas and Harry, the latter sitting on an overturned coracle playing chess with one of the workers.

"That is Cam," said Elric. "He is beholden to Dame Katherine for saving his brother's life."

Elric hurried forward. This was the crucial moment, getting the "old woman" onto the barge that awaited, with barrels arranged so that Berend might doff the apparel as he headed downriver with Harry and Douglas. Harry, young and inexperienced in such things, looked about to burst into laughter. There were few workers on the staithe, most were at the festivities on Micklegate, but there were some men not part of the mission and they must not have cause to examine Berend too closely. From afar he might pass for an uncommonly large woman, but not close up. Surely the goodwife they had encountered had noticed that.

Cam stood up sharp as Berend approached, giving him a little bow and nodding to the lad. "If you would allow me to help your grandam aboard." He proffered Berend his arm, then instructed "her" how to walk up the gangplank. "I have set a bench in a bit of a shelter. It's a nasty wind coming down from the moors today."

Douglas and Harry rose, shaking out their legs, and followed the two onto the barge. The lad waved to them, then turned to Elric for the signal to run to Katherine, and his expression changed.

"Sir," he said softly. "There's two of the sheriffs' men coming toward us."

—◦◉◦—

Looking around, Kate caught sight of Gwenllian Ferriby and was making her way toward her when Sir Peter's companion, Captain Crawford, stepped in her path, smiling and bowing.

God help us, does he know?

He's looking like a suitor, not an accuser, Geoff said.

His smile was quite friendly, and his dark eyes shone with what seemed sincere admiration as he remarked on her fine hounds and the extravagance of her cousin, the new mayor. After she had given him a courteous response he grew solemn, expressing his condolences on the news of her widowhood. "I once met Simon Neville, an amiable man."

"And where were you when you made his acquaintance?"

"In Calais."

"Ah, at the house of his mistress, perchance? Have you met their children? They are just over there by the puppeteer." She bit her lip as she watched his handsome face spasm, uncertain how to respond. "Forgive me, Captain Crawford. My cousin might have warned you to avoid the topic of my former marriage."

"I did not know. I assure you I meant no insult."

She smiled as sweetly as she knew how while glancing round the yard hoping to see Elric, which would be a sign that all was well. "What is your impression of our fair city?"

"The minster is magnificent, and the homes along Micklegate are very fine. But I prefer the countryside, the moors and dales."

"Ah. You are familiar with the North? I thought I detected a bit of it in your speech."

"Durham." He bobbed his head. "Have you been there?"

"No, I have not. Would I like it?"

"I would need to know you better in order to answer that." A dimple had appeared in his left cheek.

How sweet. She had charmed him. Good. He might be less inclined to think ill of her.

"Ah." She spied Gwenllian Ferriby again and was about to excuse herself.

"Your kinsman's knight did us a favor this morning. I believe you will be comforted to hear that the men who so rudely intruded on you a few nights ago have been apprehended. Salisbury's men, Parr and Sawyer."

She had been confused for a moment at the mention of her kinsman's knight—so far removed from Ralph Neville, the earl of Westmoreland, had Elric become to her. But of course this man would think of her in relation to her late husband's family. "Oh indeed? I am relieved to hear of it."

"So you had not heard?"

She dazzled him with her smile. "This morning my three wards woke early, wanting to be here before everything began. I've had little time to hear about more serious issues, Captain Crawford. When you have children, you will understand. Now, forgive me, but I must have a word with the apothecary."

He bowed and expressed his desire to know her better. She waved prettily, as she imagined Philippa Atterby might, and hurried after Gwenllian. Thinking about Cecily Wheeldon and the rumors Thomas Holme reported, Kate was curious. Spying her three wards, she caught them up and introduced them to Gwenllian and the two girls who moved in her wake. A boy suddenly appeared, her son. All six scurried off to watch the puppets.

"Your niece looks so like you," said Gwenllian. "I can see that all three are dear to you."

"They grace my life with joy every day," said Kate.

"How can I help?"

"Forgive me, in the midst of the festivities I should not approach you with serious matters."

"I welcome it."

They had walked over to the edge of the crowd, beyond the pavilion.

"I am interested in what you might know about the death of Ross Wheeldon."

"Ross?" Gwenllian looked startled. "What is your interest in him?"

"My partner's nephew hopes to wed his widow, and I am concerned. Her name arises in all my inquiries about Merek Lacy's murder. She had business dealings with him and used Jon Horner as an accountant."

"Horner? Did she?" A flash of a smile. "Tell me more."

Kate described to her the odd ball she had found in Horner's house, possibly a bezoar stone.

"Ah, yes. Most likely the one his housekeeper purchased for him not long ago."

"Goodwife Tibby?"

"She had quite a fancy for him, doted on him, though I suspect he had no idea. She did not like the arguments she overheard between him and his mistress, and she took it upon herself to protect him."

"His mistress?"

"It was not my place to ask her name, though I was uneasy when I learned he had been poisoned—or poisoned himself. How has Goodwife Tibby taken the loss, do you know?"

Kate cursed herself for not thinking to talk to the housekeeper. "I have not seen her since the morning of his death," she confessed.

"You might want to. She can be difficult to approach. If you say something kind about Jon Horner, she might be talkative. But you were asking about Ross Wheeldon's death. I was stunned when I heard. He was doing well."

As they spoke, Cecily Wheeldon and Leif Holme strolled past.

"We might speak further about Ross. But not here. Too many ears," said Gwenllian.

"Might I come to the apothecary after I take the girls to school in the morning?"

"You will be feasting long into the night. Are you sure?"

"The girls will be up, and so will I."

"Of course you will, as will I. Come to my home. I will have my apprentices see to the opening of the shop. We can talk without interruption."

―⦿―

"Sheriff Wrawby ordered us to search the barge before you depart." The man stood with his forehead jutted out as if he meant to use it to butt Elric's.

Or was it to protect an unusually large nose? Elric, in turn, leaned even closer, close enough to smell the man's sweat. "Search for what?"

The man drew back. "Lady Kirkby, sir. He wants to ensure that she is not on the barge."

Something was wrong about this. Wrawby's fear of Katherine exposing his patronage of her guesthouse had been real yesterday. Elric had no doubt the man meant to keep his word. So who sent these men? Cottesbrok? Should Katherine have threatened him as well? No, Elric could not believe she would be so careless, not where Berend's safety was concerned. Had it been Elric in trouble, she might have . . . No, not even then.

"I am in York on the orders of the Earl of Westmoreland," said Elric, "my mission to find whether Lady Kirkby is hiding in the city and, if she is, to take her to Sheriff Hutton to await the king's pleasure. Are you questioning my honor?" He used his quiet voice. His men usually found it menacing.

"I—I just follow orders, sir."

"And these orders were?" With a strong grip on the man's shoulder Elric prevented him from turning toward his companion. "You will answer me."

"We are the sheriffs' men—"

And they had been steered away from interfering in anything Elric and his men might do. So why were these two following him?

"Wrawby and Cottesbrok know my mission. They would never give such orders. Who has bought you?"

"It's not like that—"

The other man stepped forward. "Sir Peter Angle offered us a sovereign each to follow anyone we thought suspicious during the festivities. When we saw you following a woman, we—"

Wulf started laughing. Elric joined in.

"You fools," he said. "Have you ever seen Lady Kirkby? She is fair, straight-backed, and graceful. You mistook the elderly goodwife for such a woman?"

At that moment Harry led Berend into view on the barge. "Goodwife Sarah wishes to see the men who paid her such a compliment."

"Goodwife Sarah" made a clumsy curtsey, then limped back out of sight.

Elric shook his head at his men, who looked fit to burst. Berend's mime was amusing, but he doubted it would dissuade two men eager for their money. Yet by some miracle, it worked. Red-faced, the two men begged Elric's pardon and headed back up Hertergate.

God led me, Berend had declared. Was it true, then? Did God watch over Lady Kirkby?

Boarding the barge, Elric quietly told Harry and Douglas where they and Kevin would find the horses to ride back to York. But they would not find their fellows in the city. "When those two discover their injured comrades, there will be hell to pay." He would order Wulf and Stephen to round up the others and return to Sheriff Hutton. "Their work is finished. We delivered Parr and Sawyer, and are satisfied that Lady Kirkby is not in York."

"And Dame Katherine?" Berend asked.

"I will offer reparations to the sheriffs, and stand up to Sir Peter," said Elric, "make certain that he does not suspect Dame Katherine had a hand in your escape."

Berend nodded to him.

"Do you all understand what you must do?" Elric asked his men, who assured him he could count on them. "Good. I will leave you then." About to disembark, he thought better about that, and ducked behind the barrels to shake Berend's hand. "I promise you Katherine will be safe."

"Both the king and the earl will condemn what you have done here."

"I do not regret following my conscience."

"And your heart?" Berend's voice was quiet.

"My heart? No. I was mistaken about that."

"Because she hid Lady Kirkby? How could she turn her away?"

Elric had no time to argue. "Would you like me to carry a message to her?"

"I have seen to that." Without warning Berend rose and embraced Elric. "It has been an honor to know you, Sir Elric. I pray that the earl is a better judge of men than the new king."

"And you, Berend. May God watch over you, and may you find the peace you seek."

Stepping away, Elric turned and disembarked, signaling Cam and his mate to depart.

The runner, who had waited patiently all this time, looked to Elric for the signal.

"Go. Tell Dame Katherine it is done." There was still much that could go wrong, but Elric had done what he could. Now it was up to Berend. Or God.

"And you," he said to Stephen and Wulf. "Well done. Now go, find your fellows and leave before the gates close at sunset."

"You are determined we should go?" asked Stephen. "I know I speak for both of us when I say we would prefer to stay."

Their loyalty was gratifying, but Elric did not want them arrested for accosting the men in the castle. "You have your orders. Now go."

Once they departed Elric sat down for a moment, looking round at the staithe. He was alone now, all the other workers having wandered off. Pray God none betrayed them. Cam had assured him they had no cause to do so, but Sir Peter might have a deep purse.

As the chill of the afternoon began to penetrate his padded jacket, Elric rose, dusted off his clothes, and headed up to the Ouse Bridge. Time to join the festivities.

The hounds grew restive and so did Kate. The boy should have been here by now. She had found the hostess, Isabella Frost, presiding over this excessive display from the hall doorway and inquired about her daughter, Hazel, whether she would permit Kate's wards to join the invalid in her chambers. They wished to bring her some gifts from the festivities and keep her company for a while. Tell her all the wonders they had seen in the yard.

The imperious Isabella startled Kate by giving a little sob as she sank onto a bench by the door.

"What is it? Is it Hazel?" Kate asked, bending to her.

"The children—how kind of them. I would be so grateful if they would keep her company. Hazel was so unhappy when the physician objected to our plans—a sedan chair, moving about the festivities. I had not thought her too weak for that, but he was adamant."

Since the birth of Hazel, their only child, William and Isabella had known that she might die any day, ever fearing the next fever would take her from them. Marie and Petra loved Hazel, and Phillip was kind to her, uneasy about the adoration in the girl's eyes when she gazed on him, but knowing that he had a knack for making her laugh.

Kate rose. "I will fetch them."

Isabella reached out to Kate and held her hand for a moment. "Bless you."

For this woman to make such gesture, express such gratitude—Kate felt shaken and heartsick as she stepped out into the yard.

Her mother swooped down on her. "Katherine, you must introduce me to all those you know." When Kate did not answer at once, searching the crowd for the children, Eleanor touched her arm. "What is it?"

She shook her head and promised Eleanor she would return in a moment, after she had completed her mission.

"There is a lad searching for you," said Eleanor as Kate moved into the crowd. "There he is." Kate turned as Eleanor motioned to the lad to approach.

"Mistress Clifford," he bobbed to her, and drew two strands of leather out of his jacket. "What would you offer me for these fine leads for your hounds?"

God be thanked, it was the signal that Berend was off downriver. As she reached for the leather, he slipped a folded parchment into her hands as well.

"A ha'penny," she said.

"For this fine leather?" he feigned dismay.

Laughing with relief, she gave him a penny and shooed him off. Ignoring her mother's gasp of disapproval, Kate moved on, gathering the children and delivering them to their friend.

While the children settled around Hazel in her large bedchamber, Kate withdrew to a seat beneath one of the large windows, the hounds at her feet, and read the parchment. On the outer sheet Berend addressed her, explaining that he could not with clear conscience permit either Kate or Elric to be punished for their selfless acts on his and Lady Kirkby's behalf. When Sir Peter discovered the betrayal he should be given the enclosed document, in which Berend listed all the names he could remember from the Oxford gathering, and swore that he had merely ascertained that the former king was indeed imprisoned in Pontefract. That he had accepted that mission in exchange for information regarding his former mistress and his son. He swore that to his knowledge Lady Kirkby was not in York.

Kate smiled at the last part. Well he might swear, knowing that Lady Margery awaited him at Bishopthorpe. Folding the parchments, she tucked them in her scrip and left the children giggling as the frail Hazel, with her fiery cheeks and too-bright eyes, weakly exclaimed over the baubles and candies the children had brought her.

Down in the yard, her mother paced. "There you are, my dear. Who was that sweaty boy that you felt obliged to buy his shoddy bits of leather?"

"One of Dame Jocasta's rescues, Mother. He is a good lad, carrying messages for her about the city and trying to learn a trade."

Eleanor sniffed. "Well, I suppose. Now, do introduce me to this gentleman coming along."

"John Wrawby, the sheriff? You have not met him?"

"Not in a social setting, my dear."

Wrawby seemed quite uncomfortable as Kate introduced him and his wife. While Eleanor took Mistress Wrawby in hand, he whispered, "When will we know?"

"We do. All went as planned."

"God be thanked."

Indeed.

As Kate moved away from them, she crossed paths with Thomas Holme and his pretty wife. While sitting in Hazel's chamber she'd had an idea.

"Might I borrow your husband for a moment, Catherine?" she asked.

A little nod, a dimpling smile. "Anything for you, cousin." Indeed, she was a Frost, and, like her husband, patronized Kate's guesthouse. Her lover was a cleric of independent means, a man who had won her heart long before she'd wed. "I will be listening to the lute-player," she told Thomas, patting his hand.

"I have a plan that might shake Leif from his obsession," Kate told Thomas when they were alone, "but I need your assistance. If you would make certain he is at your warehouse near the staithes tomorrow at midday. Dressed well. Tell him I wish to get to know him better, to see whether I agree with you about him suiting us as a factor. Dress is important."

"Oh, indeed. But I thought we had already agreed—"

"All part of the plan, Thomas. And how are his accounting skills?"

"Excellent. But what—"

She smiled. "Trust me, you will be happy with the outcome."

"Midday tomorrow." He nodded and hurried off to his wife, who was eyeing Captain Crawford with interest.

~◦◦◦~

Elric bowed to Dame Isabella and proceeded into the large hall, looking up and down the tables for Katherine. He found her, resplendent in red brocade, seated beside her cousin William. No one sat to her left, but Captain Crawford was fighting his way toward that tempting opening. Another time, Elric would concede the floor, let someone else play the fool for Katherine. But this was business. Pushing through the crowd, he watched with dismay as Crawford reached Katherine first. But she shook her head at the captain and, looking directly at Elric, beckoned for him to join her.

"So it is true. You are courting her?" Crawford asked as Elric stepped past him.

He almost denied it, then remembered himself. "Did Dame Katherine not tell you?" He feigned concern.

"I had not the wit to ask," said Crawford, bobbing his head and continuing his search for a seat.

"Sir Elric. As promised," said Katherine, patting the space between her and her mother, Dame Eleanor, who beamed at him.

As Elric straddled the bench, he received a warning growl from Lille, who lay beneath the table with Ghent. He had not anticipated they would attend the feast.

With a hand signal, Katherine ensured that he had sufficient room to place both feet next to them. "I kept them with me in case," she whispered.

A servant appeared across the table, asking Elric whether he preferred wine or ale. He chose the wine. More fortifying.

"All went well, except for two casualties at the castle," he whispered to Katherine, then loudly exclaimed on the magnificence of the affair.

William Frost leaned across his cousin, welcoming Elric and encouraging him to eat and drink hearty.

"I fully intend to," Elric assured him.

When William was distracted by another guest, Katherine asked, "Dead?"

"No. But there will be consequences. We must talk later."

A long while later, after too many courses and almost too much wine, he and Katherine managed to escape for a walk in the garden, which was quiet now, the outside entertainment having given up after sunset as a harsh wind arrived with wet, driving snow.

"Pray God they reached shelter for the night." Katherine held her fur-lined hood close to her face to block the wind. Lille and Ghent trotted at her side.

"It is up to them now. Little we can do." He had given her a detailed account of Berend's departure.

"You have risked everything for my friends."

"I have followed my conscience. If my lord condemns that, then I have learned a hard lesson. But I do not regret my actions. As far as Sir Peter—I saw him slumped over the table, so I've no concerns tonight. But on the morrow . . ."

He was silenced by Katherine's sudden move to stand in front of him, her face close to his. She handed him something.

"You must deliver this to Sir Peter when he comes calling. A thank-you from Berend."

He looked down at the folded parchment, up at her dark eyes. She smelled of wine, nutmeg, cinnamon. Christ, she was so close he might . . . He shook his head, coming to his senses.

"What is it?" he asked.

"A list of all the men he could indentify in Oxford. And a sworn statement that Lady Kirkby was not in York." She smiled. "Sir Peter has little to complain of, with you delivering up Parr and Sawyer as well as this list."

He felt a rush of relief. "But why? He was so adamant."

"He wrote that you had helped them selflessly. He could not but do what he could to protect you from the king's wrath."

Lille gave a warning growl.

Elric drew his dagger.

A man approached, crunching through the freshly fallen snow over the icy remains of yesterday's storm.

Katherine motioned the dogs in front of her.

Arms up, the man called softly, "It's Harry!"

Elric relaxed.

"Forgive me for intruding." Harry stopped well away, eyeing the hounds.

Katherine called them back to her side. "Come closer, so that you need not raise your voice against the wind."

"All went as planned?" Elric asked.

"The crossing was rougher than expected and she was unwell, but he assured us he knew a farmhouse nearby where they would be welcome for the night." Harry turned to Katherine. "Your wards are in your cousin's hall, looking for you. Young Hazel has taken a turn and they were sent away."

Elric assured Katherine that the two of them would escort her and the children home. She did not refuse him.

16

TO CATCH A MURDERER

Moments after Kate lay down, exhausted, Petra's shriek rent the night. Stumbling in her weariness, Kate was opening the door when Marie rushed into her arms.

"She frightened me," the girl sobbed, clinging to her.

Kate crouched down, taking her ward's face in her hands. "You are safe, my love. Come, sleep in my bed and I will go to Petra. She sounds as terrified as you do." She embraced the girl, rubbing her back, then invited her to climb under the covers. Marie needed no more persuasion.

Stepping into her shoes, Kate closed the door behind her.

Phillip stood outside his door wrapped in a blanket, rocking side to side for warmth. "Was that Petra?"

"Yes." The dreams came far more frequently than they had before Phillip began his apprenticeship and moved to his master's house. "We have grown accustomed." Kate touched his cheek. "Go back to sleep. I will see to her."

"She has the Sight, she said."

"I begin to believe that is so."

He retreated to his room, closing the door behind him.

Kate paused, looked out at the night sky, bright with stars, and prayed that this one time it might simply be a bad dream. She regretted that after putting the girls to bed she'd returned to the kitchen to tell Jennet and Matt all she had learned. After the long day and all the wine and ale she wanted only sleep.

Opening the shutter of the small lantern that hung on a hook outside the girls' door, Kate stepped across the threshold and shined the light on the bed. Petra sat with her back against the wall, hugging her knees to her chin, whispering prayers.

"Oh, my poor love." Kate set aside the lantern and climbed onto the bed, taking the child into her arms. "What is it?"

"He hunts them. He has archers with him."

"Sir Peter?"

The child shook her head. "His captain."

"Berend knows how to lose them," Kate assured her. "Come. Let's get under the covers and sleep."

Up too late, and then awakened by Petra's dream vision, the girls lay abed, emotionally and physically exhausted. No school for them this day, though Phillip had been up at dawn clamoring for some food before he returned to the stoneyard. Kate laughingly warned him that she had seen some of the stoneworkers draped over each other in the yard after the feast the previous night.

"Stay far from them when they are wielding tools today."

Curfew had been lifted for the night, and it seemed as if all the city had taken advantage of it, for fun but also for darker deeds. Jennet had greeted her with the news of burglaries in aldermen's homes during the evening. Her eyes and ears had been discomfited by the lawlessness. Drunk revelers daring one another to break into homes.

"And where were the servants?" Kate wondered, nursing her own aching head with some strong ale.

"Out drinking," Matt had answered. "One of my old mates tried to drag me out. As if I would be such a fool."

Cuddy, the new servant, looked less delighted about missing the festivities. "It might have been a lark, just this once." But the walkways around the house had all been shoveled and swept clean before Kate awoke. He might do. If he chose to stay.

Kate walked Matt to the door. He was off to her cousin the mayor's home for his morning report. She was anxious to hear of Sir Peter's frame of mind. "And make certain to ask after Hazel. Remember, *only* if you manage to find a moment alone with my cousin should you tell him that Berend and Lady Kirkby departed as planned." Matt nodded and reached for his cloak. Kate caught his arm. "What do you think about Cuddy?"

"I would not go trusting him just yet."

Perhaps he would not work out. A cook is what they needed. Marie was too young to carry the burden of such duty, Jennet was an indifferent cook, and Griselde had enough to do at the guesthouse and caring for Clement.

Kate thanked Matt and saw him off, then gave Cuddy instructions for the morning, which would entail ensuring that Marie and Petra, once awake, made use of their day off by making a stew. The sharp blue eyes burned beneath the fair curls that kept falling into his eyes. He did not like the prospect of watching the girls. But Jennet had matters to put into motion before Kate's midday meeting with Leif Holme.

Kate brushed the lad's hair back and made a point of holding his gaze. "If my wards stray, I will hold you responsible. You do not want to cross me."

"I will not, Mistress Clifford. But—young Marie seems difficult to guide."

Kate relaxed. "She is. But I ask you only to give my instructions to the girls and then to watch the house, see that no strangers try to enter. Are you able to defend yourself?"

He fisted his hands and took a fighting stance. "I am."

No weapon. Well, if he stayed, Matt could train him.

"Petra is a skilled fighter. If there is trouble, call her to assist you." His eyes had gone wide. "Not that I anticipate such a need. I simply wanted you to know that you are not alone."

Satisfied that Cuddy would make it through the day, Kate reached for the hounds' leads. "I am off on errands," she announced, nodding to Jennet.

Clouds hung low in the sky, threatening more snow. Already the streets were dotted with mounds of filthy, frozen slush that had carters cursing. The relief she had felt last night in the garden had been replaced by a dread of the reckoning ahead. The sheriffs would be more supportive if she found proof that Jon Horner had murdered Merek. And she would not rest until she knew who had poisoned Horner.

A flaxen-haired woman about Kate's age answered her knock at the Ferriby house.

"The mistress is expecting you," she said, eyeing the hounds with poorly concealed alarm.

"If you have some something I might dry them with, they will track in no more damp than I will," Kate assured her. "As for discipline, they spent the entire mayor's feast under the high table with nary a bark."

The woman nodded and hurried away, returning quickly with two large rags—old table coverings, by the look of them. A household with such cloth to spare was rich indeed.

As Kate was rubbing down Ghent, Lille already standing by dry and fluffed, she was greeted by Gwenllian Ferriby with a babe in arms.

"Come through, I pray you." Gwenllian told the maidservant to see to the damp rags.

The hall was bright from a wide window looking out to a large winter garden blanketed in snow. A long table held a jug of ale and two carved bowls. "Merchet ale," said Gwenllian. "Shall I pour?"

After they were settled, Lille and Ghent curling up at Kate's feet, Gwenllian apologized for not speaking out sooner. "I vowed I would never endanger my family as my parents had at times endangered us, so I turned a blind eye on—Well, Ross Wheeldon's death, for instance, and how he did not want his wife to know he was consulting me."

Watching the emotions playing across the woman's face, Kate chose to say nothing, simply nodding as she sipped the ale.

Gwenllian turned her bowl round and round, the carvings of herons becoming a moving study of one heron taking flight. The room grew so quiet that the baby's gurgling sigh and the stealthy approach of a curious cat drew Kate's attention. The cat, a ginger female, stopped a short distance from Lille and Ghent and hissed. Kate quietly commanded the hounds to ignore her.

With a sigh, Ghent lay his head back down on his forelegs. Lille turned her head away from the glaring feline.

"And though I am not in the habit of repeating rumors, I thought you should know that folk have wondered about a grand chapel in a church north of Easingwold being fitted out with grillwork by Coffey the blacksmith—for Ross Wheeldon. He'd been up measuring the space long before Ross's death."

Kate remembered her visit to Coffey's workshop. "I saw a piece of the grillwork. Quite elaborate."

"I would think nothing of it but for the fact that Ross was *better*. But why would Cecily risk so much? He left her wealthy. Could she not wait?"

"Why indeed? A troubling tale."

They talked a while longer, sharing stories of their children, until one of the apprentices appeared at the garden door, begging a question. Kate thought it best to move on before the ale made her drowsy.

She rose, thanking Gwenllian for the information. "I will use it only to find out the truth. I will not share it. Nor will anyone know the source."

"I trust you." As Kate moved away, Gwenllian called out, "My girls are eager to see yours again soon."

A welcome bonding.

—◦◦◦◦◦—

Bess Merchet received Kate in a chamber that was clearly the elderly woman's living quarters. Harry and Elric sat at a table making short work of a savory stew and hot bread. Hearty meal for first thing in the morning.

"We can talk while they eat," said the taverner, smiling at the men's appetites. "Here we're safe from prying eyes and curious ears."

Kate reported what she suspected of Cecily Wheeldon. "We need to find something to connect her to Jon Horner's poisoning."

"That would most likely be in her home," said Elric. "No doubt you have a plan."

He managed to make the comment sting.

"Rest easy, it does not involve you. Thomas Holme and Jennet are my conspirators. What is crucial is that we resolve this quickly, to appease the sheriffs. We need their support."

They all turned at the sounds of an argument in the public room. Bess rose, opening the door just wide enough to hear Sir Peter loudly demanding to see Sir Elric.

Kate began to reach for his hand, stopping herself just in the nick of time. "Show him the list. He cannot scoff at such information. Swear to him that you saw Lady Kirkby neither arrive nor leave the city. You've sent your men home because Parr and Sawyer have been delivered, Lady Kirkby is nowhere to be found, and Berend provided the information the king wanted."

Elric rose. "Go. Leave this to me." With a tug on his jacket, he strode out to face the king's man.

"Come." Bess gestured to Kate. "I will take you out through the kitchen. Move quickly. I will put up a fuss so that you can go wherever you need to be."

Kate said a silent prayer for Elric's safety.

⁓⊙⊙⁓

Coffey knelt to Lille and Ghent, praising them, clearly a play for time to think how he should respond.

"As a merchant yourself, you understand the need for customer trust, Mistress Clifford. I cannot be sharing such information without good cause."

"What if I were to say folk are talking about this elegant tomb being prepared long before Ross Wheeldon gave anyone cause to believe he would soon be dead?" Kate knew it a risk, that it might make put him even more on the defensive, but she did not have time to dance about with him.

His large hands, every crease lined in soot, paused on Lille's and Ghent's backs. Ghent put his muzzle to Ben's hand, wanting more. They had taken a liking to him. It spoke well of the man.

"I mean to make no trouble for you," she said. "But it is important that I know if the grillwork is for Ross Wheeldon's tomb, and who commissioned it."

"You will not mention me?"

"Only to the sheriffs, if necessary. They can be trusted."

He grasped the side of his worktable and eased himself up. "I suppose, as he's passed on . . . It *is* for Ross's tomb, but he is the one approached me in the autumn. Said he wanted it rightly done, for his wife would not be so keen. He paid me up front, a goodly sum."

Kate was disappointed. All the fuss was about an elderly man's mistrust of his wife's willingness to honor his memory. She saw enough of that. "Has his widow consulted you?"

"She has. A fine woman, the widow Wheeldon. A fine woman."

"Your work is so skilled, she must be pleased."

The smith scratched his cheek and seemed about to shake his head, then shrugged. "She did worry it was too grand, might offend those with more call to be so remembered in the church. But I told her that I contracted with her late husband, and I would break such an agreement at the peril of my own soul."

So Cecily hoped to recover some of the money Ross had invested in his memorial. "You are a man of conscience," said Kate. "I should think she found that reassuring. A man who honors his contracts is a man who can be trusted."

Coffey was shaking his head as he fiddled with a tool on his workbench. "You are kind to say that, Mistress Clifford. But I do not believe the widow would agree. She accused me of taking advantage of a dying man's vanity."

"No!"

He shrugged. "As far as that, I never guessed he would die so soon. He rode with me to the church on several occasions and met with me weekly as I began the work."

"Rode through the Forest of Galtres to Easingwold with you?"

"He did. Our last journey was in early December—Feast of St. Nicholas, it was. Cold, a sharp rain, but he would not turn back. And we sat in the tavern just outside the gates there having several tankards afterward. I saw him once more after that. I felt the news of his death like a blow, I did. I had become that fond."

"He was fortunate to make such a steadfast friend," said Kate. She let Ghent comfort the man, butting his head against his hands, begging to have his ears rubbed. When the strain of Coffey's emotions softened in response to the dog's sweetness, she felt she might ask her last question. "Did Jon Horner prepare the contract for the tomb?"

"Ah, no, that would—" Coffey shook his head with vigor. "Master Ross would have nothing to do with that man." The look on the smith's face suggested he had more to say about that.

"I thought he saw to his accounts."

"That knave Merek thought that as well."

"Merek?"

"He came sniffing round here about the work I was doing for Master Ross as well. Fool I was, giving him my good coin for nothing."

"Merek knew about the memorial?"

"Claimed Horner told him about it."

"When was this?"

"After Master Ross was dead, to be sure. So I thought, well, the widow must be using Horner to sort through her late husband's papers. But I did not like Merek coming round asking about that. What business was it of his?"

What indeed? Kate thanked him, her initial sense of defeat quite turned around. Here was evidence of Ross Wheeldon's good health. No wonder his death had caused gossip.

⁕

A dark mood closed in around Kate as she passed the Frost residence on her way from the smithy to Thomas's warehouse. In the yard, Sir Peter paced in front of Elric, who stood between two men wearing the king's livery. Would Elric have gone to Berend's aid if not for her? Would he have Lady Margery safely lodged at Sheriff Hutton awaiting the earl's pleasure? Would the earl have believed Lady Margery's innocence?

How would she bear it if Elric lost his standing, perhaps even his land, and then they found Berend and Margery had been part of the Epiphany plot? God help her, what was her responsibility to Elric? What had she done?

Everything you have done, you have done with the best intentions, Geoff assured her.

Small comfort if I have ruined a man for nothing. I've lost his love, his respect, and *ruined him?*

Busy rebuking herself, she was halfway down Micklegate before she realized she had not seen Captain Crawford in her cousin's yard. She must pay more attention to the crowds, especially as she crossed Ouse Bridge. To her surprise, folk were talking about Berend's escape—so it was common knowledge now. Many waved to her and expressing their delight. Some were more cautious, no doubt fearful of king's spies. She pushed herself along, keeping the hounds on a short leash.

Once across the bridge, Lille gave a soft bark as the warehouse came into view. Jennet stood across the way, in the company of a woman in a thin cloak over a simple, oft-mended gown. One of Jennet's eyes and ears, perhaps? As Kate drew closer, Jennet came forward to greet her and the hounds, who were ready for some affection, made skittish by their mistress's agitation.

"Leif arrived a little while ago. Dressed as if attending the more private feast at Master William's home today." The second day was for the aldermen and other powerful men of the city.

Kate was relieved. "And the woman with you?"

"My new friend Henna, currently the widow Wheeldon's cook, but eager to work for you—until Berend returns."

"You are a wonder, Jennet." Kate glanced at Henna, wondering at the old clothes—she hardly looked the part of a cook in the household of a prosperous York merchant. "How did you meet her?"

"Asking round the market, I learned that she has been keen to leave since the master died."

"Loyal to Ross Wheeldon, not his widow?"

"Much to say about that, I think."

"She will help us tonight?"

"If you agree to test her skill on her day off tomorrow. Will you speak with her?"

"I will. But briefly. I must not miss Leif."

Jennet motioned to Henna to join them. As the woman approached she held her skirts close and leaned away from Lille and Ghent.

"You have nothing to worry about," Kate said, "they are well trained."

"Do they—Would they be in the kitchen?" Her face was chubby, but pinched, as if wary of the world, expecting the worst of it.

"They would be, yes. Are you willing to try to trust them?"

An honest hesitation, then Henna nodded. "Yours must be a grand kitchen to have room for them."

She might be disappointed in that. It was large, but not at all grand. Kate considered her. Good teeth, apparently robust health, that spoke well of her own cooking. Time would tell. "Come tomorrow, mid morning. Jennet will tell you what you will need, how many dine most days, the girls' preferences."

She excused herself, whispered some instructions to Jennet, and crossed over to the warehouse.

—◦⊚◦—

Her breath smoked in the cold, damp building. It was the first staging area for their goods before being moved to various storerooms around the city, drier, warmer, better for spices and the rolls of cloth being counted by an elderly clerk who stood near the entrance. Seeing Kate and the hounds, he made a face.

"Velvets, Mistress Clifford. Their fur. If they shed on—"

"*My* merchandise. You would be wise to remember that." As the man hurried to apologize she waved him silent. "I am meeting Leif Holme. Fetch him for me." She was sorry to snap at old Arn, about whom her late husband had once joked that he had been born in the warehouse. But the clerks had been slow to accept her as their superior, and she would not tolerate chiding from the man.

My oh my, she thought, her mood brightening as Leif approached. A dark blue padded jacket in the latest style over deep red leggings and knee-high leather boots with pointed toes, a dark red hat with a hawk's tail feather swooping from it and down along his cheek. He had not been so impressive at yesterday's feast. He would do as a factor based on his looks alone, that was certain. Pity that so few were women, but she knew several cloth and spice merchants who might find him appealing. And the wives would think of him when they were entertaining. He would have access to the best houses.

"Mistress Clifford," he bowed to her. "My uncle said you wanted a word?"

Well spoken. "Shall we walk? I have a few matters I would like to discuss with you."

As they stepped out into the snow, he gave not a thought about his clothing, intent on declaring his eagerness to prove himself as a factor. She asked whether he had traveled to Calais or the Low Countries, knowing full well that he had made several trips with his uncle to the former, but had never been elsewhere, except London. He did not try to claim experience he did not have, though he did express his interest in traveling far and wide, and prided himself in having never been seasick. He admitted to a tendency to be truthful. "Some might find that a flaw in a factor, for sales." She liked his crooked grin.

"We do not trade in inferior quality goods, Leif. You have no need for concern about that. But you cannot be shy about encouraging customers to buy as much as they can afford, nor should you permit them to go away and consider. They rarely return."

"I have no qualms about that."

"And what about keeping the accounts? Have you any experience there?"

"In truth, that is my strongest skill."

"So you would not mind taking on some additional duties in that regard? For me. My guesthouse accounts."

"I would be happy to do so."

"I understand you are thinking of marriage. A wealthy widow would suit you?"

His silence caught her attention.

"Forgive me, I did not mean to embarrass you."

"I—Mistress Clifford—I would not presume to think—You will be my employer . . ."

"Oh. No, I did not mean me, Leif. I noticed you with Cecily Wheeldon yesterday."

An enthusiastic nod. "Dame Cecily has my heart. She is beautiful and clever, and she puts me at ease like no other woman. At first I thought she saw me as a sweet boy and was being kind. But then she kissed me."

Bold woman. Was she kissing Jon Horner and Leif Holme at the same time? Merek? Was that possible? Patience, Kate schooled herself. All might be revealed if this interview went well, and the widow cooperated. Her heart raced a little—so much depended on her being right in her impressions of Leif and Cecily. "A kiss! When will you pledge your troth?" She asked it teasingly.

He answered sincerely. "She will observe a year of mourning. She said she would be pilloried if she wed betimes."

"Being a widow as well, I agree, she must have a care if she wishes to protect her good name. That did not prevent my husband's brother from trying to match me up with a husband within the year, but he had his reasons. Do you know, he went so far as to suggest I visit my mother in Strasbourg, let my intended follow me as if for trade, and we might wed there, then I might return to York in a few years, no one the wiser about how long we'd been wed."

Leif gave little laugh. "So that is not so uncommon."

"You thought of that?"

"It was Dame Cecily. She asked me what I thought of such an arrangement."

"What did you say?"

"I disappointed her. Or, no, I am not certain she was serious."

Kate put a hand on his forearm. "Do not doubt your worth."

A grateful smile. "I told her I need to establish myself here." He sighed. "I might be a fool. I believe she is willing—*very* willing to—I did not know a woman could—We have—In the garden—But I stopped, fearing someone might see us. She laughed at me." He turned a deep red. "Forgive me for saying such things. You are so kind, I forgot myself."

"No need to apologize. I have encouraged you. I hoped to understand you, what would make you content in your work, your life. I do have an idea . . . But you must be careful, for your sake and for hers, and as quiet as possible." She smiled at the irony of what she asked, and how impossible that was. "I would not want Griselde, who runs my guesthouse, to think I'd become a bawd. Or expected that of her." It was important for him to believe Griselde would not know he had a companion in the room.

Leif's handsome face registered both shock and hope. "You do not mean—Dame Cecily and I spending the night there?"

"Would you dare?"

"Is this a test? If I say yes—"

"No test. A sincere offer."

His brows knit together in a suspicious frown. "Why would you do this for us?"

"Our trade is nothing if our factor is disloyal. If you are happy, that should not be a problem." He still looked doubtful. "But tonight is the night," she said. "Tell her that you are staying at my guesthouse because something is amiss at your lodging and I have kindly offered a room, and you thought, 'might this be our chance?' Paint yourself as the bold one."

"Oh, if she would—"

She had him. "You will not know unless you try. But I should think that a woman of her . . . experience, well, she might wish to sample the goods." She gave a little laugh and patted his hand, telling him to send word if he decided to take her up on the offer, and if Dame Cecily seemed willing. If so, Kate would have her servant Seth there at the bottom of the steps at the designated time. "But you must be quiet."

"And the job as factor? And accountant?"

Once he had reaped the rewards of the guesthouse, he might just be her solution to the problem of Clement's decline.

"Suppose this proposition *is* a test—of your determination and your skill in persuasion." God in heaven, she was playing the bawd. She would do penance for this.

⌐◦⊛◦⌐

It took little time to sort out duties at the guesthouse, though Griselde expressed some surprise. Kate assured her she was seeing to the safety of York.

Back at the house, Marie and Petra were squabbling about the proper way to cut a carrot for stew. Cuddy, his back to them, played sentinel by the partly opened door. The poor lad looked weary.

"Has anyone been about?"

"I thought I heard someone in the yard not long after you left. I searched. Nothing. No one."

"But you believe you did hear something? Where?"

"By the steps up to the first story."

"But no creak of the gate."

An eager nod. "That is it! Yes. That is what I heard. And then it stopped. Like it scared them and they moved off."

Working as planned.

"Matt is in the hall," Cuddy added.

Kate left Lille and Ghent resting by the fire with some water as she went to hear Matt's report.

"I was there when Sir Peter returned to the mayor's house with Sir Elric," said Matt. "But your cousin's man Roger said he'd already looked to burst earlier, when Sheriff Cottesbrok admitted that Berend was gone. Sir Peter had heard folk talking."

"All the city seemed to know this morning," said Kate. Who had spread the word? The goodwife who had taken Berend's place? One of the injured guards? "Did they know of injuries amongst the castle guards?"

"Cottesbrok said nothing about that. Roger says the sheriffs distrust the king's men."

"What about Captain Crawford? What was his response?"

"Roger said he had gone out early, before dawn, returned at some point and rounded up men, then hurried away."

"Before Cottesbrok arrived?"

Matt nodded. "As you said, folk were talking about it all over the city. Berend's a hero."

Kate laughed. "Because he did not murder Merek Lacy? I've heard no mention of Lady Kirkby on the street."

"Nor have I."

"And Hazel Frost?"

Matt crossed himself. "The child is dying. The household—The feasting tables are being disassembled, no preparations for the second feast. Roger took me outside to give me the news, and told me that Dame Isabella told Sir Peter he must find lodging at Micklegate Priory, he and his men must leave, the household must be quiet, peaceful."

"Oh my dear child." Kate slumped down on a bench and let the tears come. Sweet sweet Hazel.

⚬

A late afternoon nap with the girls revived Kate and seemed a comfort to them. They had felt responsible for endangering Hazel's health, fearing they had caused her too much excitement.

Kate assured them that was not true. "Remember how she laughed, how she enjoyed every moment, sending you out to see more, bring back more stories. Your visit yesterday brought her joy."

Marie woke from her nap with a plan—to persuade Phillip to carve a likeness of Hazel as an angel for her tomb.

Petra crossed herself and warned Marie against planning a tomb *before* a death. "She will return to haunt you. Old Mapes said so."

What about if the person planned their own memorial? Kate wondered, thinking of Ross Wheeldon.

Now, at twilight, Sister Brigida sat with the girls in the kitchen, helping them compose a letter to their friend. Her companion, Sister Agnes, busied herself making a calming tisane for the girls and preparing a stew for the next day.

Matt and Cuddy had gone on errands. All was well in the household. Leaving Petra and Marie in the beguines' loving care, Kate collected Lille and Ghent and went to the hall to work at her loom while she waited for Jennet. If all went as planned, she would soon be searching the Wheeldon home.

Trying to still her mind, she remembered her mother saying that the beguines approached all that they did as prayer, offering up all effort to God for the benefit of others. Kate gathered the fine colors and sat for a while staring at the pattern emerging on the loom, choosing which colors would be prayers for Berend, which for Margery, which for Hazel. When she had settled that, she took a deep breath and began. Her hands steadied as she worked. Sensing her deepening quiet, Lille and Ghent moved from the fire to settle nearby, out of her way as she worked the shuttles, but close. The work warmed her, and the prayers absorbed her.

Later, when Lille and Ghent rose to greet Jennet, Kate felt as if she were waking from a trance. Her body ached a little, but a glance at the loom confirmed that was reasonable—she had worked a long while. Hours.

"Well?" She poured ale for both of them and settled on one of the chairs by the fire, handing a bowl to Jennet. She stood with her back to the fire, letting her skirts dry, while she took a long drink of ale. Her face was red from the cold, but her eyes shone.

"Look in my scrip," she said.

Kate lifted the bag sitting on the other high-backed chair, and opened it. A gold brooch—"Jennet, this is the one Pendleton described."

A satisfied grin. "Seems Horner gave her the brooch despite knowing it was stolen."

Kate was excited. Also in the scrip was the mate to the glove she had found in the room where Horner died. "I might have left it lie there," she whispered to herself.

"But you didn't," said Jennet. "Most importantly, you'll find by the door a box of tally sticks and accounts going back several years, showing how Dame Cecily had been siphoning off money Master Ross believed he was investing in property, through Horner, by way of Master Ross's clerk. Evidently Horner had information about the clerk, wanted for theft in Lincoln. And, in that sack by the door that the hounds find so menacing, a gown stained by blood—a lot of it, and vomit."

"All that? Were you seen?"

Jennet made a face. "Henna has a heavy tread, and a maidservant came up to see who was in her mistress's chamber. But when she saw Henna—I was behind the door—she just asked her not to do anything she would be blamed for by 'the whore' and left."

"Beloved by all." Kate rose. "How late is it?"

"Matt is walking Sister Brigida back to the Martha House and the girls look ready for bed. I took it upon myself to have him call at Sheriff Wrawby's home to ask that he meet you here shortly after dawn, to catch a murderer."

About to protest such certainty, Kate smiled at herself. The dress did seem damning. "You are a marvel, Jennet. I cannot think what else we might do to prepare before dawn, so I'll to bed. An early night would be welcome."

—⚬⚬⚬—

The morning dawned with a hard frost and the scent of snow, though none yet fell. As Kate stepped into the kitchen she paused, her heart quickening. Elric sat with Jennet and Matt, listening to their accounts of the previous day's discoveries. His jacket was not as clean as was his wont, and there were dark circles beneath his eyes, but he was here.

He glanced up, nodded to her.

"How do you come to be here? Did you escape?" Kate asked.

"I would like to hear that as well," said Sheriff Wrawby, joining Kate in the doorway. "Did that fool Sir Peter finally see reason?"

"Not as such," said Elric. "Mayor Frost has a backbone. He said he might not be able to help his child, but he would be damned if he would let an incompetent jeopardize the city's relationship with the Earl of Westmoreland. He released me and said he would deal with Sir Peter. Who is no longer biding in their home, by the way. Dame Isabella sent them to Micklegate Priory. Sawyer and Parr as well. She permitted me to spend the night, locked in the shed in which Crawford had stuffed me."

"She might have done better for you," Wrawby growled. "But I am much relieved to hear that about Frost. I feared he would prove the king's toady."

Elric rose. "Are we ready? Harry and Douglas are at the guesthouse, ready to detain Dame Cecily if she leaves before we arrive."

"Cecily Wheeldon?" Wrawby gave a little whistle. "Are we also going to find that she hurried my friend Ross's death?"

"One accusation at a time," Kate warned. "I must make a stop in Stonegate before I join you."

Elric and Wrawby chose to go straight to the guesthouse.

At the silversmith's Kate was rewarded with an excited nod.

"That is it, my sister's brooch," said Pendleton. "Might I have it?"

"Soon. Very soon."

Satisfied, Kate continued on with Lille and Ghent, joining the sheriff and Elric at the table in the guesthouse hall, the door ajar so they could watch the steps. Seth was in the kitchen with Griselde and Clement, and Harry and Douglas were out in the alleyway beneath the stairs. All ready for Leif and Cecily to appear on the landing.

At last the footsteps. Cautious, light. It would be Cecily. Leif would have no cause to depart quite so early, and certainly not before Cecily. He would wait to make certain she encountered no trouble from Griselde. Lille and Ghent sat up, sensing the interest in the hall. Wrawby rose and quietly moved to the door. As Cecily reached the bottom step, the sheriff called out to her.

"Dame Cecily, if you would be so kind as to step inside."

"What? Sheriff Wrawby? Oh, my dear man, it is not what you think." With a little laugh she stepped to the door, but retreated as soon as she saw Kate and Elric. She turned to hurry away, but found Douglas and Harry blocking her escape. Face flushed, she demanded they let her pass.

Sheriff Wrawby repeated his request, his tone sharper than before.

With a dramatic sigh Cecily marched up to Wrawby, forcing him to take a step backward. "Explain yourself," she demanded.

Quickly regaining his composure, he gestured toward the items displayed on the table—the soiled gown, the opened box of accounts, the brooch. "It is you who must explain, Dame Cecily."

Someone clattered down the stairs. Leif burst into the room.

Kate did feel for him as his eyes widened in horror.

"What is happening? Cecily, I am so sorry."

"You. You set this up so that they might search my house, you—" She slapped him. Hard.

Holding his cheek, he protested that he knew nothing.

"Sit down and be quiet, Leif," the sheriff commanded.

Kate motioned to him to sit down beside her.

"What have you done?" Leif hissed.

"Saved you, and your family. Now hush."

Sir Elric had risen, and approached Cecily. "What sort of person stands by and allows an innocent man to be imprisoned for a murder she knows he did not commit? The sort of person who would then poison the murderer? So that no suspicion would fall on her? The sort of person who would steal money from her own husband? Perhaps hasten his death?"

Cecily had gone quite still. She stood with hands at sides, staring at Elric. But Kate could imagine how her mind was working to come up with an explanation.

Wrawby cleared his throat, said, "Dame Cecily, do you care to respond?"

"The gown—I thought the laundress had ruined it. I've not seen it for months. Why in heaven's name would I know who murdered Merek Lacy? I presume that is the murder of which you speak." She glanced at Kate, her eyes burning. "You are so desperate to clear the name of your lover. Open your eyes, woman, he is an assassin. To think you welcomed him into your home, with those innocent children."

"And these accounts that tell the tale of your deception?" Elric asked, lifting a parchment roll from the box. "How do you explain them?"

"I have no idea what you are talking about. I trusted Jon Horner. I saw no need to inspect his work. I am but a woman, sir. I have no head for numbers."

"So it was all Jon Horner?"

"He—He loved me, you see. He gave me that brooch as a token."

"A stolen token, did you know?" asked Kate.

"Is that what this is about? I wondered why he asked me not to show it to anyone. He said he wanted to wait until the bans. Poor fool. He thought I would marry the likes of him?"

"You spent much time with him. You were with him the night he murdered Merek Lacy," Kate said as she tossed the glove onto the table. "I found its mate on the floor of his room that morning."

"That is proof I was with him? Hah! You think yourself so clever. Had I been wearing those gloves that night they would be soaked . . ." Cecily stopped.

Kate felt weak with relief. The moment she had challenged Cecily she had wished she might take it back. Berend, Elric, Margery, perhaps even Lionel depended on her keeping her head. Yet she had lashed out in anger. Her heedlessness might have made Cecily more cautious. God be thanked it had not. But only a fool depended on God's help to correct her missteps.

"If you would come with me." Sheriff Wrawby touched Cecily's arm.

She backed away from him, pointing at Kate. "You, of all people, you should stand with me. For years I tolerated that old man's hands on my body, for years he refused me money of my own, doling out every penny with those palsied hands. I earned the money Horner set aside for me. I earned it. And just when I was free at last, Merek intended to ruin me. I rejected his advances and then he meant to ruin me. *What happens when your late husband's family discovers you poisoned him?* he crooned in my ear. The man stank of spices. And who fueled his suspicions? Ross, the old wretch, arranging for his own tomb. Merek thought *I* had planned that. As if I would waste the money on such a memorial to that hateful old man."

Leif made a little noise.

Cecily glanced at him. "I might have made you rich. But you proved a craven coward."

"And when you tired of me?" Leif asked.

"Are you confessing to the murder of Merek the spice seller, Dame Cecily?" asked Wrawby.

"I dragged Jon to the Shambles to finish what he had begun. But he could not do it. Sniveling coward. Merek accused me. He lunged for me. I finished him. You are all so weak. So weak. I am finished with you. With all of you." She pulled something from her scrip.

At Kate's signal Lille and Ghent knocked Cecily into the table. A small metal vial fell to the floor and Elric retrieved it.

"Come now, Dame Cecily." Wrawby helped her up, but did not release her once she was standing.

Leif jerked to his feet as Douglas grasped Cecily's free arm and the two led her toward the door. "Don't hurt her!" he cried.

Cecily turned and spat at him. "Craven coward."

17

A VIGIL, A HANGING, AND TOO MANY QUESTIONS

Elric insisted on escorting Kate home. Drained of all emotion, she did not argue, though heaven knew he still looked at her as if she were anathema. They walked in silence. Cuddy met them on the pathway to the kitchen, his arms loaded with wood.

"Dame Eleanor and Sister Brigida came for Marie and Petra," he said. "The mayor—his daughter asked for them."

Kate crossed herself. "Thank you, Cuddy. How were they when they left?"

"Brave, they were, doing their best not to cry."

Elric touched her arm. "You will want to be there." For the first time in what felt a long while he spoke gently, in kindness.

She left Lille and Ghent in Jennet's care.

"What should I do about Henna?" Jennet asked.

Kate had forgotten her appointment with the cook. She asked that Jennet observe how the woman comported herself, think how she might fit into the household, and keep the food warm for the household to sample when they all returned.

As she and Elric made their way along the frozen ruts on the streets, they said little, nodding to those who greeted them. Much later Kate realized why so many smiled at them, she leaning on his arm—another kindness. Did people not know the mayor's only child was dying? How could they smile so? But of course few knew about the family's sorrow. What they saw was a knight and his lady proving the gossips right. No matter. His presence was a comfort, how he respected her need to be quiet with her memories of Hazel, prepare herself for a sorrowful vigil.

-◦◎◦-

In the weeks after Hazel Frost's death, Phillip worked on the angel statue, guided by master mason Hugh Grantham. Sister Brigida came each day to teach Marie and Petra at home, seeing them through their sorrow.

The Earl of Westmoreland summoned Elric to Raby to answer for his actions, but allowed him to delay the journey until the child's funeral, deeming it important for his relationship with the mayor of York.

Kate arranged for the beguines to take meals to Cecily at the castle, and she herself went to see her. Now the widow was eager to talk about Merek, how he had threatened to expose her if she did not pay him hefty sums, including his passage on a ship that would take him across the North Sea. Cecily had guessed why Merek insisted she deliver the payment. Lionel Neville would start asking questions—*he is a sly one, that Neville, always poking his long nose in others' affairs*—and she would be ruined anyway. *Merek had to die. I convinced Jon of that. Pity he proved such a weakling.*

Thomas Holme praised Kate's solution to the problem of Cecily Wheeldon. "You saved my nephew from ruination. What if he had wed her and then she had been hanged for three murders?"

For hanged she was, a week after Hazel's burial.

"I owe Leif an apology, but what can I say to defend myself? I used him." Kate was not proud of it.

But Thomas scoffed. "Young fool should be grateful. I have told him to stand up and be a man. He will come round. He has met with Clement to go over your accounts?"

"He has, but Clement is wary of showing him too much. Will Leif try to retaliate?"

"I have made it clear to him that if he does not put this behind him I will change my will. He has assured me that he holds no grudge."

"That is his head speaking. But what of his heart?"

"He's an ambitious young man. Already he's looking round at the daughters of the aldermen."

Elric had been gone a week when Kevin rode into the city bearing the abbot of Cirencester's response. That evening William Frost called on her. "I have received a letter from John Leckhampton, the abbot of St. Mary's in Cirencester."

"I have as well. Or, rather, Kevin has shown me the one sent to Sheriff Hutton Castle." Kate invited William in.

The abbot of Cirencester Abbey offered his condolences to Berend, "should you see him," on the death of his old friend Warren, the bastard son of Baron Montagu. He claimed Warren had chosen his fate, venturing into the town and right into the hands of King Henry's men.

"What do you think?" Kate asked William as she poured wine. "Is the abbot honest?"

"I doubt it. I think he was fearful lest King Henry not support him against the townsfolk who have petitioned to be free of the abbey's control, so he handed him over, violating the rules of sanctuary."

"The abbey's control?"

"The citizens of Cirencester have long contested the charter the abbey holds, giving it the rule of the city and much of the surrounding countryside. They claim an earlier charter granted them the right to rule, much as the one King Richard granted York. When the earls of Salisbury and Kent fled to Ciren-cester, the townsfolk saw their opportunity to ingratiate themselves with King Henry by slaughtering the rebels. No doubt the abbot thought that by giving up Salisbury's half-brother he would show the king that he, too, rejected the rebels, but in a lawful manner." He coughed. "Though one could argue that violating sanctuary is not lawful."

Kate stared into the fire. Berend had saved Montagu's bastard twice. Once from Pontefract, as the abbot had recounted to Kevin, once from King Henry's wrath. He would mourn him. Would he blame himself?

Who had chosen the abbey? She might never know. There was so much she might never know. "Have you any news of Captain Crawford's hunt for Lady Kirkby?" she asked.

"No. Have you?"

"Why would I?"

"Berend?" William held her gaze. "I know what you did, you and Sir Elric. Cottesbrok and Wrawby confided in me."

"They did? I hope they waited until after—"

"They did. Once they could see that I had taken up my duties."

"I have heard nothing."

"Had you known that Berend escorted Montagu's bastard to sanctuary?" William asked.

"No." But of course she had guessed that he was hiding something. Margery as well. In his letter, the abbot denied any meeting with Thomas Kirkby, any letter of safe passage. But that, too, might be for the benefit of his relationship with the crown.

"Do you doubt the wisdom of helping Berend?" William asked.

"No. He condemned the plot against the king and his sons. I do not doubt that. He answered the call of his lord's son, honoring the memory of the man who helped him in his darkest time, who believed in him."

"And Lady Kirkby?"

"No. Not at all. I am sick of women being punished for their husbands' foolishness."

William raised his eyebrows in surprise, but said only, "Sir Elric said much the same about both Berend and Lady Kirkby. Have you word from him?"

"Not yet."

"Are you? Might I ask—Sir Elric loves you, you know, though he seems hesitant to surrender to his heart."

She did know. On Elric's last night in York she had invited him to dine at the guesthouse, intending to speak to him of her regret, to apologize, ask how she might make amends. That he'd accepted the invitation gave her hope that he was willing to listen. But the evening almost ended before it began. It seemed he had expected to dine in the hall, and when she had taken his hand to lead him up the stairs to the large chamber on the first floor, he had backed away from her, his eyes flinty.

She knew that look, and softened her voice as she would with the children when they needed reassurance. "I do not mean to seduce you, Elric. I merely want time with you without interruption, to enjoy a conversation before your departure, to speak of our friends near and far . . ." She stopped as she sensed her voice about to catch, already missing him, fearing for him, sick with remorse for her part in causing his lord's anger.

It worked. He had followed her then, albeit grudgingly, not relaxing until he beheld the elegantly set table. Griselde and Marie had outdone themselves, with help from Henna.

While they ate they spoke of her cousin William's courage, Hazel's funeral, what Elric expected of his meeting with Westmoreland, the small shop about to open in the storefront on her home on Low Petergate, the promising cook Henna had recommended for Sheriff Hutton, anything but the two of them. They avoided the heart of their differences—trust. Until she poured the brandywine and set out the spiced nuts.

"I am grateful for this chance to explain how I came to shelter Lady Margery. Carl came to me just as the gates—"

Elric interrupted her. "I know. I understand why you helped your friend, Katherine. I would have done the same."

"Then why have you been punishing me ever since I confessed all I knew?"

"Punishing you? I had been behaving as if—" He seemed to search for words. "My heart had misled me." He met her eyes, and she caught her breath at the tenderness of his regard. *His heart.* "You are a remarkable woman, Katherine. Faith, you would make a fine captain of men." He laughed, but his eyes did not. "I wanted—It does not matter. Forgive me if I have seemed to be punishing you."

His awkward speech disarmed her. She, too, was at a loss about what to say. Arguments were easier than declarations of love. Or lust, if she was honest.

Time for me to leave, Geoff whispered. *Speak to him. You both deserve joy.*

"You thought I might love you?" Kate asked.

"I am not the first man to play the fool in love, and I will not be the last. At least I did not act on it."

"A pity," Kate murmured as she refilled their cups.

"What?"

"We might at least toast our success in freeing Berend and Lady Margery."

"Indeed." He tapped her cup and drank his down. "You are a master strategist."

"I'd wondered whether you'd noticed."

"Have I not celebrated how well it went?"

"Celebrated? Not with me. I had expected some expression of gratitude."

"Is that why you poured such a stingy amount? I am grateful, Katherine. For all you did."

"Now who is being stingy?"

He threw up his hands. "I am at a loss."

"Are you? What if your heart did not mislead you?" She rose, stepping behind him, placing her hands on his shoulders. When he twisted round to see what she was about, she leaned down and kissed him on the lips. "I have yearned to do that," she whispered, crouching down beside him, looking up into his widening eyes.

He touched her cheek. "Katherine?"

She learned toward him for another kiss, but he drew back, studying her face as if seeking a clue as to her sincerity.

"I feared I had lost any chance of being with you," she said. "That night, celebrating Kevin's recovery—I woke up to what I feel for you."

"Yet you continued to lie to me."

"I was trapped in Margery's secret. It was not mine to share. I've told you—"

"Do not toy with me, Katherine." He rose with an abruptness that almost knocked her over, strode to the door. In a moment, she was alone.

She sat down on the floor, stunned. How had it gone so wrong? Her face grew hot. *Damn him, insufferable man. Unbending. His heart is ice. He—*

Footsteps on the landing. He was still there, pacing back and forth outside the door.

All might not be lost. Pray God he just needed coaxing. Rising, she fortified herself with brandywine, brushed herself off, and opened the door. "I fear my boldness offended you. But we have so little time."

Elric halted before her, shaking his head as if at a loss to understand. "Katherine—"

"I want to be with you, Elric."

"What of Berend?"

"He is my friend, my brother, not my lover."

Crossing his arms, Elric bowed his head, paced away, returned, his expression still cautious, questioning. "I cannot promise—"

She put a finger to his lips. "I don't ask for promises. Only a night with you."

She'd held her breath, and, as the minutes passed, felt a bitter defeat. But then . . .

"Are you armed?" A teasing smile.

She guided his hands to the front of her skirt. "You are free to examine me."

He moved his hands out to cup her hips and methodically worked back to center, watching her face, witnessing what that did to her.

"Hah!" He drew out her dagger and tossed it into the room behind her, then pulled her into his arms, kissing her.

She was not shy in her response.

"Do you mean it?" he whispered. "That you want to be with me?"

"Can you doubt it? Must I take it into my own hands to drag you to the bed?"

"No need." He lifted her up and carried her back into the room, kicking the door shut behind him, tossing her onto the bed.

She pulled him down to her. When they came up for air she rolled away, so that she could unbutton the bodice of her gown.

Gently brushing her hands aside, Elric took over. When it was her turn, she knelt on the bed, dodging his exploring hands to undress him. He was everything she had imagined he might be when she had watched him demonstrating his martial prowess at Sheriff Hutton on that Christmas Day long ago.

He moaned as he pulled her to him and rolled so that she was atop him.

They slept little that night. Just before daybreak, Elric drew her into his arms and asked whether she would consider marriage.

"To you?" She kissed his belly, his chest, then his mouth. "I might."

"But . . . ?"

"I do not trust myself to make a wise decision after such a night."

His laugh was low in his throat.

She smiled now at the memory of that last lovemaking before parting.

"Katherine?" William was watching her with a bemused expression. "I believe you have answered my question."

Feeling herself blush, she smiled at him. A knight and a woman in trade—with such a guesthouse as hers—she did not think it a likely match. But if it stopped William's matchmaking . . .

Her cousin looked well pleased.

—◦◦◦—

Her presence at Cecily's hanging had been requested, as an "honor," but Kate had excused herself. The truth was, Cecily haunted her. *You, of all people, you should stand with me. . . . I earned the money . . . I earned it. And just when I was free at last, Merek intended to ruin me.* Were they so different? Her anger stemmed from the opposite of Cecily's, Simon's extravagance—he had denied her nothing, but had she not plotted and schemed, and found part of the solution in a morally questionable guesthouse?

You never considered murder, Geoff said.

No? I'm not sure of that. But he was already dead.

Her dreams were as wild as Petra's, though not the Sight, clearly her heart questioning, questioning everything. How childish she had been with Berend, seeing him as her anchor, her support, believing him when he had promised that she could depend on him. And now Elric—was she making the same mistake, seeing in him what she had believed she had with Berend, only more? Was he Simon Neville all over again?

You are robbing yourself of happiness, Geoff warned.

Am I? Or am I taking responsibility? The children depend on me. I must be clearheaded for them. They deserve all my love.

—◦◦◦—

They sat in the hall of the Martha House, the altar cloth on their laps, Eleanor working a chalice in gold thread, Kate following Sister Dina's faint sketch of the Virgin's gown in shades of blue. Wind howled without, the fire crackled within, warming the two embroiderers and the hounds sleeping by the hearth. Such peace.

A cramp in her fingers forced Kate to pause and relax her hand.

"You hold the needle too tight, that has ever been your problem," Eleanor murmured without glancing up. She hummed softly as she stitched.

"I know," said Kate, smiling at her mother. "I admire you. You have created a sanctuary here, something precious."

Now Eleanor looked up. "Bless you, daughter." Her eyes glistened. "*You* are the one being fêted by the city, catching a murderer."

"But I have no peace. You lost your sons, your husbands. You suffered such betrayal. Yet you have found peace in this house."

"I am healing, yes."

"How? How might I do the same? And please do not say I should ask for guidance."

Eleanor laughed. "I am the last one to advise you to seek someone else's advice on how to move forward. No one knowing me in the past would have advised me to found a house of poor sisters. You yourself thought I had gone quite mad."

"I confess it seemed an unlikely match."

Eleanor reached over to squeeze Kate's hand. "You must be patient with yourself. You had a happy home, and now there is a yawning emptiness where Berend steadied it, always there, dependable, safe. And the girls lost him as well as their dear friend Hazel. It is a difficult time. You feel helpless, and that makes you angry."

Did it? Was it that she felt helpless? "One night I dreamt I was hunting Lady Margery. I meant to kill her."

"Perhaps you blame her for Berend's absence? I do. Though it was not she who summoned him in the beginning, her presence now endangers him."

"Her story was so riddled with coincidences," said Kate, "I cannot trust it. The abbot denies having seen Sir Thomas. I thought, there it is, her lie. But William believes it is the abbot who lied, that he meant to ingratiate himself with King Henry."

"Do you believe him?"

"Would such a small thing matter enough for him to lie about it? That he had seen Sir Thomas?" Kate did not see it. "Even more, Margery said the abbot tried to stop the violence, and that he prayed for the victims as well as for the souls of the townspeople who had so brutally taken the lives of their countrymen. She painted a man with no thought to pandering to the king."

"Do you doubt Sir Thomas's innocence?" Eleanor asked.

"I wonder. When Henry turned on him, and on Richard, was he able to remain neutral? Yet if I question that, everything is in question. It's all ashes. Even Berend. He told me what he wanted me to believe."

"And it seems a betrayal to you."

"Perhaps I betrayed myself, depending on him. I knew better."

Eleanor pressed Kate's hand. "You are strong, Katherine. It is you who caught Cecily Wheeldon. You who devised the scheme to free Berend and Lady Kirkby. You who earned Sir Elric's respect, and his love. You have a rich life. You will find your way, and your purpose."

Kate threaded a blue the color of sky in early May.

"Do you love him, your knight?" Eleanor bent back to her embroidery as she asked the question, as if she were merely making conversation.

But it was no small question to Kate. "He is not my knight."

"Do I hear a note of regret in that denial?"

"I care for him," said Kate. "But I don't know whether it is love."

"Ah. Time enough for that."

"He said I would make a fine captain of men."

Eleanor smiled into her embroidery. "And a fine mother of sons."

To Kate's relief, Eleanor left it at that, humming as she completed the chalice. When she straightened to consider her work, she said, again as if simply making conversation, "Richard, he who was king, is dead. Have you heard? On the Feast of St. Valentine. They say he chose to starve rather than to live so confined and solitary. The same day as dear Hazel's requiem."

Her mother's mind was a complex mosaic.

"Yes, I had heard," said Kate.

But "chose"? That is not how Petra had seen it. Starving to death in the large chamber with its faded tapestries, waking each morning to the scent of bread baking in the ovens that warmed his floor, pounding on that floor, demanding service, until too weak to rise from his bed. But it was a murder Kate had no stomach to solve.

"May God grant him peace," Kate said.

"Amen," Eleanor murmured. "Shall we see whether the girls have finished their lesson?"

AUTHOR'S NOTE

The history of Henry IV's reign did not captivate me until I read Terry Jones's *Who Murdered Chaucer?* His depiction of the deep paranoia of Henry's court intrigued me. "The opening months of Henry IV's reign—the last of Chaucer's life—were not placid times. They were chaotic and dangerous. Those who had been fearful of what the future might hold were right to be fearful."(140) Shakespeare put the words in Henry's mouth: "Uneasy lies the head that wears a crown." (*Henry IV* part 2, III, 1, 31) The line has become a cliché much misquoted, but he was spot on.

Shortly after Henry ascended the throne a plot was hatched by Richard's supporters. This plot, known as the Epiphany Rising, provides the background for *A Murdered Peace*. Jones writes, "A plot to assassinate Henry shortly after Christmas was apparently hatched around the dinner table of the Abbot of Westminster. . . . By a *remarkable* stroke of good fortune for the usurper, the non-clerical ringleaders were lynched by furious mobs in various cities, leaving Henry able to carry on with the appearance of clemency.

"Whether the convenient dispatch of his enemies was orchestrated by Henry's agents, we'll never know, but certainly Archbishop Arundel seems to have been uncharacteristically supportive of this particular instance of mob rule. In a letter he sent back to the convent in Canterbury he turns *lynch mob* into 'the virtuous common people'."(140)

Clemency. Yes, well, as for that . . . The uprising, failed or no, sealed the fate of the former king; as long as Richard lived, Henry and all his family were in danger.

As I have noted in other Author's Notes, historians are not always agreed on the fine points of history; the Epiphany Rising is no exception. I've used Michael Bennett's brief account as my outline (*Richard II and the Revolution of 1399*, Sutton 1999). I preferred it to other accounts because of a longstanding conflict between the citizens of Cirencester and the abbey regarding the claim that the citizens were tenants of the abbot.

In Bennett's version, when the townsfolk surrounded the rebel nobles and their men at an inn, the Earl of Kent's chaplain started a fire to distract those standing guard and enable the rebels to escape. But the townsfolk set up a hue and cry that the rebels were endangering the town, dragged the nobles and their men out into the square, and killed them (Bennett 189–91). The alternate story is that the townsfolk entrusted the rebels to the abbot of St. Mary's Abbey, Cirencester, and only when the captives started a fire in the abbey to make their escape did the townsfolk round them up and execute them. Why would the citizens of Cirencester give up an opportunity to gain favor with the king by disposing of those who had dared to threaten his life and the lives of his sons? And, especially, why would they hand this honor to the abbot?

"In 1385 some of the townsfolk attacked the abbey. Richard II issued a commission to the keepers of the peace in Gloucestershire upon information that divers of the king's lieges of Cirencester had assembled and gone to the abbey and done unheard-of things to the abbot and convent and threatened to do all the damage they could. The townsfolk were kept in check for a few years, but in 1400, when they rendered Henry IV a signal service by crushing the rebellion of the earls of Salisbury and Kent, whom they beheaded in the market-place, they seized the opportunity to put forward their complaints against the abbot and his predecessors. At the king's command an inquisition was held by the sheriff. Five juries from the town and the neighbourhood testified against the abbot, and it was claimed that the town of Cirencester had not been parcel of the manor until 1208, when the abbot compelled the townsmen to perform villein service. The king's decision was postponed, and there is no record of it" (*A History of the County of Gloucester*, fn. 51–54).

Oh, the ambiguity!

WORKS CITED

Who Murdered Chaucer?: A Medieval Mystery, Terry Jones, Robert Yeager, Terry Dolan, Alan Fletcher, and Juliette Dor (Thomas Dunne Books, 2003)

Richard II and the Revolution of 1399, Michael Bennett (Sutton, 1999)

A History of the County of Gloucester, vol. 2, (originally published by Boydell & Brewer Ltd., 1907): http://www.british-history.ac.uk/vch/glos/vol2/ pp. 79–84

ACKNOWLEDGMENTS

It's difficult to pare down my gratitude list. It has been my good fortune to find the community of scholars studying late medieval history and culture welcoming and generous with information, support, and enthusiasm. Thank you, thank you.

Regarding *A Murdered Peace*, special thanks . . .

To Louise Hampson, my go-to guide for York history. Thank you for reading the manuscript and making suggestions, for answering my emails despite an insane schedule juggling a doctoral thesis and a more-than-full-time career in the Center for Christianity and Culture, and for organizing our event at the York Festival of Ideas in June as well as taking me around the city to show me what's been learned about medieval York since my last visit. You're the best!

To Ian Downes, Senior Heritage Officer, thank you for spending a very soggy Saturday morning taking me around Pontefract Castle and sharing the latest theories about Richard II's last days in the castle. And for ongoing help at a distance.

Lille and Ghent wish to thank Molly Gibb, a remarkable canine advocate, for her advice on all things canine in the books. The hounds love you! Any mistakes that have slipped in are all my fault (or my cat's).

ACKNOWLEDGMENTS

To my dear friend Laura Hodges, thank you for your careful edit, as well as advice and suggestions regarding clothing, jewelry, and more. Your books on Chaucer's symbolic use of clothing are my bibles.

To Joyce Gibb, thank you for being my early warning system when I'm veering off the clear path of the story.

To Mary Morse, thank you for a clearheaded edit despite being busy with your own research sabbatical in Paris.

To Jennifer Weltz, thank you for being my literary agent, a fierce advocate for my characters, a reader with a gift for calling out missed opportunities in a story, and the one who has been an enthusiastic supporter of Kate from the moment she strode into my life.

I count myself most fortunate in my partner, Charlie Robb, who supports my work in countless ways. I thank you particularly for creating the beautiful maps for my books. You are a wonder, my love.